PHARAOH: CURSE OF THE KINGS

Adam W. Schindler

Published by Schindler Digital, LLC
ISBN: 979-8-9993076-4-4

Every archeological and
Egyptology description in this book is accurate.
The question remains: *are they true?*

Any resemblance to people, living or dead, is purely coincidental.

1

Memphis, Egypt - 1446 BCE

A wail of agony pierced the stale night air, jolting awake a muscular, olive-skinned man. Tuning into a rising commotion outside his expansive balcony, the proud soul, hardened by relentless opposition, surveyed the scene below. Before him lay a decimated city flooded and stripped bare by the worst thunderstorm in a century. That was nothing new. But something else was.

He heard enraged men shouting from their homes, cursing the black sky. Yet the horizon was ablaze with hundreds of midnight fires, which cast eerie dancing shadows of mothers clutching limp, lifeless bodies. A plume of smoke expanded beneath him, swept into the balcony, and surrounded him with the acrid, pungent odor of burning flesh.

He was trembling again. It was the same demonic terror that lodged in the back of his throat, keeping him frozen when he must act. A cold bead of sweat rolled down his immaculately shorn head.

"Not again." He wondered. "How much longer must I endure the terrorism of a foreign power?"

His nation was under attack. His people were dying. And for

what? Some pathetic rivalry among usurpers to his throne?

"I am the ruler of my domain. There is no other."

Regaining his wits, he burst from his bedchamber and raced through a corridor of masterfully carved marble and gilded fixtures. He threw open the doors to his son's room.

"Get up!" he shouted to his young successor.

Silence, save the whispering flicker of extravagant linen surrounding an imposing bed.

"Wake up! We are at war!"

Nothing.

He ripped the curtains off the bed, revealing a vacant, unmade pile of silk pillows.

Where was this ungrateful simp of an heir on a night his empire limped towards annihilation?

"If I find you, I will kill you myself!" he roared in turmoil.

"How did I get here? After all my fathers did to establish the most powerful dynasty on earth. Am I to hand this all to a child who scorns the weight of sovereignty bequeathed to him from four hundred years of royal bloodline? We are not mere mortals. We are gods incarnate. We are masters and commanders of all living things!

"We are… Pharaoh."

2

New York City, Present Day

Ethan fluttered his eyes open. He rolled over as the break of dawn cast a blue glow into his studio apartment. Reaching for the small clay jar of meticulously cut mushroom fragments, he cursed this nightmare. Trembling, he swallowed one without chewing.

It's good to be off the antidepressants. Some modicum of normality had returned to his tortured mind. Yet, a hidden darkness lurked within.

His feet struck the floor with a dull thud, stirring the only friend who had never left his side, no matter how deep the pits he'd leaped into. The rapid swish of a tail told him today would be okay.

"Good morning, sweet girl. Let's get a coffee."

He grabbed the leash. Ellie licked him, led out the door, down the stairs, and burst into the street. The city was awake—it was always awake—but it had yet to buzz with the familiar chaos of the morning commute.

A tinkling sound from a bygone era announced his arrival.

"Good morning, Mr. Stone."

"Good morning, Sarah," he muttered over the hiss of compressed air superheating a stainless steel canister of foamy lactose.

"One oat milk flat-white with an extra shot." He glared longingly at the full-fat latte his favorite barista was making. How he wished his 36-year-old body hadn't rejected the creamy substance. He was too young to become a curmudgeon. Sarah smiled at him as if she'd heard his thoughts.

"You look troubled this morning? Another rough night?" A twinkle darted across her captivating blue eyes.

"Something like that." He snatched a copy of the Times off the counter and paid for his consolation prize. He willed himself to walk away. He couldn't date another college girl.

Retreating outside, he sat at the small round table where Ellie waited with her affectionate yips.

"Let's see what happened while the world slumbered."

The front page image showed another local business looted by displaced foreigners bused in from Texas, and a subway passenger on fire while onlookers gazed in petrified ambivalence.

"What is our city becoming?" he wondered, flipping to an inside page. The good stuff was buried deep within all the news fit to print.

There. He found it—one of the most enigmatic images in modern archaeology—an impeccably preserved funerary mask of Egypt's most famous ruler. But was he even a Pharaoh? The hype demanded he was, but Ethan wasn't sure.

He knew nearly everyone in the city who thought or wrote about his field, but didn't recognize this columnist's name. "Hmmm, let's see what one R. Britton has to say."

"World-renowned Egyptologist and New York's most notorious academic is set to lecture on the mystery of King Tut. For a century, scholars have debated how this boy-king died, hypothesizing malaria, tragic chariot accidents, or even a rare connective tissue genetic disorder. But Dr. Ethan Stone is not so sure.

"Dr. Stone is the great-grandson of the mysterious British arms mogul, Sir Ethan Stone, who many people think was the actual financier of Howard

Carter's famous 1922 expedition to unearth King Tut's burial site. Though untouched for nearly 3300 years, the treasure trove of artifacts buried in the sands of time has fascinated the world for a hundred years."

Ethan scoffed, "Sands of time... please. What a tired metaphor. These press writers have no literary talent." He skipped ahead.

"While the public still marvels at the Pharaoh's secrets, academia immensely dislikes his reckless disregard for scientific consensus and illicit history of artifact hunting.

"Dr. Stone espouses a novel theory on King Tut, which has the young prince locked in a bitter power struggle with his father, leading to his untimely death. Without proof, Dr. Stone has gallivanted around the Middle East for two decades, searching for any shred of evidence to substantiate his theory. While he has found nothing academic, he has amassed a remarkable private collection of artifacts. But even that feat is controversial. Over the years, he's been charged with illegally acquiring stolen goods, as the Department of Justice forced him to pay millions in fines. He's also had to return hundreds of pieces to the Egyptian government—leaving him disgraced in the eyes of..."

Ethan threw down the paper, startling his faithful pup.

"What garbage! R. Britton wouldn't know what to do with a novel theory if it snuck up and kicked him in the rear." Ethan stood up and collected his phone from the table, frustrated that he was now using tired metaphors. Blaming this hack from the Times for making him dumber, he started for home.

"Who does R. Britton think he is?" he mumbled. "My father?"

Annoyed that he was once again cursing his dad, he pushed the thought to its hiding spot in the back of his mind.

3

The beautiful spring morning spread before Ethan, and Ellie was eager for a walk. He turned onto Madison Avenue off East 88th. While he considered the glass storefronts a transparent monument to self-indulgence, he didn't mind occasional decadence. But his vice was not shopping. Well, not exactly.

Over the years, he had acquired a considerable fortune of artifacts stored beneath the NYU Ancient Studies Institute, just a few blocks from the Met. He'd walk Ellie to the office before his evening lecture at the Metropolitan Museum of Art.

A state-of-the-art security system protected his basement office, which he had exclusive access to twenty-four hours a day. It was one of the few luxuries he allowed himself from his father's vast fortune.

Descending a private staircase to the side of the building, his mind was occupied by the fool who clacked out drivel, hardly passing for journalism.

"No proof... not a shred of evidence..." he mumbled as he flicked up the plain black flap covering his office keyhole. He leaned in as a red light lit up and scanned his retinas. The 6-inch-thick steel door let out a burst of air as it swung open. Ellie rushed past him, pouncing on her favorite, but thoroughly demolished, stuffed banana.

He consoled himself, remembering he was a star... of sorts. What other NYU professor was world-renowned for daring insertions in the Levant as ISIS desecrated thousands of years of ancient history? True, the UN Educational, Scientific and Cultural Organization (UNESCO) had come down hard on him in 2017, claiming his private campaigns to rescue priceless cultural artifacts from bloodthirsty terrorists were "illegal and extreme." They had even threatened him with charges in the International Criminal Court in The Hague. And this made him an extremist? They were jealous. He and his ex-military buddies were just better at their job than pudgy international bureaucrats claiming authority over land they'd never set foot on.

But this morning, something was gnawing at him. It was that recurring dream. Why did it feel more like a memory than a nightmare? How could a brilliant academic, who built a career on meticulous research and rational pursuits, give even a moment's credence to a thought accosting him in the night?

Setting his bag on the counter, he sat down behind a bank of monitors and entered his passcode. He scanned the digital library of artifacts he'd collected and photographed, his subconscious searching for something even as his rational mind kept protesting. He stopped on an image of the Famine Stela. He snapped it last year, hundreds of miles up the Nile near Aswan.

The Famine Stela is considered both a religious and political work of propaganda. He loved the story, written around 250 BCE during the age of the Ptolemies. It depicts Pharaoh Djoser making an offering to the triad of Nile gods—Khnum, Anuket, and Satis.

The massive ten-foot-tall inscription, carved into forty-two columns of hieroglyphs, recounts how Imhotep, High Priest of Ra and fabled builder of the Step Pyramid at Saqqara, saved Egypt from a seven-year famine. According to the text, Imhotep delivered a divine message to Pharaoh—one that came to him in a dream.

A dream? Was this what his resistant mind was pressing him towards?

Ethan rose from his terminal and walked into a room neatly

categorized with rows of industrial shelves. Home to his collection, a mixture of items tagged and placed according to their location and era, as well as a few dozen hermetically sealed papyrus scrolls.

He donned a pair of blue powderless nitrile gloves and picked up a small statue. The black stone carving from the Ptolemaic period depicted a man seated on a chair, a papyrus scroll unrolled in his lap. The immaculately preserved statue of the deified scholar Imhotep was one of Ethan's most prized pieces.

Returning to his workstation, Ethan pulled up an article on Imhotep from the Met archives. Intensely visual, Ethan always thought better while touching a relic from the past. He began to read.

"Imhotep was a revered leader and Egypt's earliest scientist. Also, a fabled builder —the first to craft a pyramid in Egypt using cut stone rather than the ubiquitous mud brick. On top of all that, he was also a physician.

"Just outside Abydos, the mysterious Saqqara complex, an active dig site, contains a necropolis long believed to be the abiding place of Imhotep's spirit. Seeking wisdom and healing, worshippers often slept at the site, hoping Imhotep would come to them in a dream to reveal remedies for sick family members."

A dream, there it was again, ancient fools seeking knowledge from the subconscious. And yet, here he sat, a fool surrounded by knowledge. His subconscious was losing it.

But despite all this, Ethan felt he was on the verge of something. He'd never admit it to the press, but every significant discovery he made was preceded by intense internal conflict. These periods were marked by an influx of speculative theories and scattered data points flooding his usually neatly ordered mind. This barrage often spiraled him dangerously close to self-destruction. But every one, without exception, launched Ethan into a death-defying journey across the globe to solve the riddle that presented itself against his will. Instead of killing him, these quests made him famous.

They also got him hooked on micro-dosing Psilocybin. A habit he picked up in Tibet after a Buddhist monk accused him of having a "monkey mind." The monk said Ethan needed to confront the *duhkha* surrounding him by "un-asking" torturous and obsessive questions.

"You must make peace with yourself before you can be freed from the self that clouds your peace. Only then can you seek nirvana and find enlightenment."

Why did he remember this nonsense? Who wanted to step off the wheel of existence anyway? Nirvana was as unrecognizable to him as Smells Like Teen Spirit. Perhaps the monk and Kurt Cobain shared something in common.

But the mushrooms worked, slowing his descent into the chaotic void. At least they had. Lately, they seemed to do nothing to halt the dream. In it, an unrecognizable pharaoh experienced a national disaster that Ethan, with all his considerable expertise, could not place. He didn't know what bothered him more, the dream or his inability to place it in history.

It's a dream, you fool. Not history.

Ellie licked his hand, startling him back to the present.

"I'm almost done, girl. We'll go to the Park in just a moment." She wagged her tail and lay down in her corner, chewing on the filthy banana nestled between her paws.

"Of course!" he cried, as if something dramatic had happened.

With a few keyboard clicks, his screens were awash with the most famous image in Egyptology. The Great Sphinx of Giza was as iconic as the pyramids. But the stela between its front paws is what had arrested his attention.

Discovered in 1818 by an Italian archaeologist, the inscription also read as propaganda. The stela recounts how Pharaoh Thutmose IV encountered the son of Ra at the base of the Sphinx, but centuries of storms had nearly covered the monumental structure with sand. Thutmose IV was called upon to clear the sand; in doing so, he would be King of all Egypt.

This carving had always fascinated Ethan for the many questions it raised. If Thutmose IV was Pharaoh, why would he need propaganda asserting his divine right to the throne? If he wasn't a legitimate king, was this stela part of an elaborate plot to usurp the throne? He was Tut's grandfather. But Ethan thought the long-held belief that he was king was utterly false. The complex succession of Egypt's 18th Dynasty was the topic of his evening lecture at the Met. And the puzzle piece nestled between the paws of the Sphinx was crucial to his whole theory.

Suddenly, he understood why his subconscious was nudging him towards an impending abyss: they called this artifact the "Dream Stela."

For the first time, Ethan realized why he had been so resistant to finding meaning in his dreams. The realization crashed in on him. His mind reeled. Much like Thutmose IV, his father was a master of propaganda and the lord of an empire he ruled through fear. At 16, Ethan decided he didn't want to be part of his dynasty and fled his father's house. Dreams reminded him of this tyrannical despot and the bitter conflict that drove him from the family estate.

But he was today years old when he connected teenage angst to an adult dismissal of dreams.

"How cliché," he said aloud. "I'm an unmarried, aging New York academic harboring a secret drug addiction, plagued with repressed daddy issues. Straight out of central casting."

He wallowed in the uncomfortable insight. He was descending into the void... but that meant something remarkable was ahead. He would face this one, eyes wide open. If there's one thing he'd learned from two decades of contending with his messed-up mind, it was this: the thing he most desperately needed would be found where he least wanted to look.

"Okay then, what is the connection between the stories embedded in the Famine Stela, Imhotep, and the Dream Stela?"

He sat for a few moments thinking. Nothing.

"Come on! What am I missing?"

He could almost hear the chirping of crickets in his walled

subconscious.

"Alright then," changing course. "What do I most desperately want to find?"

This question produced an immediate response.

Who killed King Tut?

4

The museum was abuzz with energy. Friday in New York was always hopping. But tonight, the Met had gone all out to host him for his ground-breaking new lecture called "Curse of the Kings." He had chosen to go full Professor, donning a pair of form-fitting slacks, a loosely buttoned dress shirt with an English Spread Collar, and designer tortoiseshell glasses. The round frames inlaid with gleaming white ivory accentuated his piercing blue eyes, framing a strong jawline. His Navy Blue Harris Tweed blazer sported leather patches on the elbows that mostly concealed his six-foot frame. Still, his years in the military left him with an unmistakably muscular profile.

Bounding up the stone steps, eager to share his insights, Ethan wove between Korean tourists and clumps of prep school students on extra credit assignments. He loved lecturing at the Met. The 708-seat concert hall of the Grace Rainey Rogers Auditorium was his favorite. It delighted him that the city still craved the arts after being ravaged by a viral scourge a few years prior.

Walking past the double doors, he glanced into the auditorium. It was packed.

It was important to him to view the stage from the people's point of view before a lecture. He didn't like academics who pretended they were celebrities. He was a teacher before he was a scholar. The people were why he was here. "Don't forget that," he reminded himself, feeling hypocritical from his earlier musings.

Sadie let him backstage. "Evening, Mr. Stone. Wonderful to have you back at the Met tonight."

"Hi, Sadie. You're looking frantic as ever."

Sadie was the Met's stage manager, and everything that happened in her world was high stakes.

"Please... tonight is just a dull lecture from a moderately handsome Professor pretending he's a little star in a big city. Nothing worth getting your tweeds in a bundle over." She smirked.

The professional banter was edged with an irresistible air of longing. But that quip was a little too close to home. It's why he loved seeing Sadie—the thrill of chasing something that could do him harm.

"You think I'm a moderate, do you?" Ethan smiled and stepped closer.

"I've never cared much for politics," she retorted, as her radio squawked, "One minute to curtain."

"I'm glad to have you in the house again. I wasn't sure you'd recover from the incident."

The "Incident" was how they referred to a day spent together at the end of his last daring adventure. When climbing out of one of his holes, he'd made mistakes he wasn't sure he regretted.

"Yes, well, I have regained my vigor. Thank you for asking."

He heard his résumé read out on the loudspeakers.

"Fancy a drink after you put these poor patrons to sleep?" Sadie asked.

"We'll see. I'm sure they have more interest in my ideas than you."

Ethan flashed his winsome smile and stepped under the lights.

"Get a grip, Sadie," she said, as the patrons erupted in thunderous applause. "That man is trouble... Hot trouble."

5

Standing behind a podium, Ethan laid out his new theory.

"No other Pharaonic lineage is riddled with mysteries as much as the 18th Dynasty. While records of the 19th Dynasty are less cryptic, and the famed Ramesses line is more prodigious, the kings of the 18th Dynasty are far more intriguing."

He clicked, bringing the auditorium's floor-to-ceiling screen to life with brilliant images of the Kings of Egypt from 1550—1400 BCE.

"The 18th Kingdom had many Pharaohs. Who was the king, when he ruled, and from where, is still debated. According to conventional scholarship, there is a complex and difficult-to-determine timeline of Pharaohs named Amenhotep I through IV, as well as Thutmose I through IV.

"In addition, smashed into this period are some power outliers like Hatshepsut—a rare, purported female pharaoh, and her lover, the enigmatic Senenmut, who ruled alongside her—the same Senenmut who abruptly fell into deep disrepute and was 'erased' from history. A child named Neferure connected to Hatshepsut and, of course, the famous boy king known worldwide as Tut.

"Confused yet? You're not alone."

Ethan glanced stage left and caught Sadie yawning at him in

mockery. He might take her up on her offer.

He clicked again. A detailed satellite image of the Nile Delta region featuring two golden stars: one at the top marked "Memphis," and one near the bottom, marked "Thebes."

"The Pharaohs ruled from Memphis for a thousand years. Nestled along the bank of the Nile, Memphis was Egypt's political nerve center. It gave rise to the Great Pyramid of Giza, the Sphinx, the Rosetta Stone, and dozens of other storied and monumental landmarks.

"Around the 1550s BCE, in the Middle Kingdom, a turbulent transition period between the Old and the New Kingdoms, Thebes was established as a second Egyptian capital. By the reign of King Amenhotep II, Thebes was Egypt's new power center.

"However, power centers do not form in a vacuum. Something happened during the Middle Kingdom that dramatically weakened the state. With that, the Amarna Period emerged, and an apostate king came to power.

"Tonight, I unveil the key to clarifying this chaos. Thereby uncovering the hidden truth behind the question, who killed King Tut?"

Ethan switched to a detailed slide illustrating the cascading succession of the 18th Dynasty rulers, beginning with Pharaoh Ahmose.

"My theory is this: the two capitals were not locked in direct conflict. In fact, together they formed the intricate framework of dynastic succession. Consider this: Amun, the god of Thebes, also known as Amun-Ra, was a high deity in a polytheistic culture. The Pharaohs, believing they were divinely appointed representatives of the gods on earth, often bore the name of a god.

"So, the Pharaohs ruling from Thebes, the new capital and home to Amun-Ra, took the title Amenhotep, meaning 'Amun is satisfied.'

"But here's a key insight—the successor to the throne, the first-born male of Pharaoh's house, had to be prepared to reign upon his father's passage to the underworld. To equip the next generation, the 18th dynasty developed a succession plan. They appointed the Pharaoh's firstborn son as co-regent. When of age, he moved to Memphis, ruling from the old capital, while his father ruled from the new."

Ethan took a sip of water and placed the crystal glass back on the podium shelf. The room was dead silent. He had their attention.

"These co-regents were given the title Thutmose, meaning 'Born of Thoth.' As the embodiment of Thoth, son of Amun-Ra, they were stationed in the old capital of Memphis with a new divine title. Ruling in a city second only to Thebes, where his father, Amenhotep, embodied the high god Amun-Ra.

"Now, instead of a confusing morass of Pharaohs, my theory presents a structured succession plan. Two Pharaohs at any given time, father and son, ruling from twin cities in the north and south of the Kingdom. When Pharaoh Ahmose died, his son Pharaoh Thutmose I received the title Amenhotep I. He, in turn, moved to Thebes and appointed his firstborn male heir as co-regent in Memphis, bestowing upon him the title Thutmose II, and so on.

"Now that we understand the proper Thutmosid succession, we have the conceptual tools to analyze the death, or should I say murder, of King Tut.

"First, who was King Tut's father?"

Ethan clicked, and the screen filled with an image of two large stone lions.

"Luckily, once we throw out modern scholarship flawed by its failure to grasp proper dynastic succession, we have a straightforward answer.

"What you see here are the British Museum's Prudhoe Lions— commissioned by Amenhotep III for Sobek's Temple. They are inscribed by someone named Tutankhamun, who indicated he renewed the monument for his father, 'Son of Re, Amenophis, Ruler of Thebes'. Scholars agree this refers to Amenhotep III, Tut's father.

"Now, Amenhotep III was also known as Thutmose IV. This is where it gets thought-provoking, because it seems Thutmose IV was an illegitimate ruler."

A tremor of chatter rippled through the audience. Ethan cued a composite image of the Sphinx with a magnified pop-out of the stela between its paws.

"This is the Dream Stela. A magnificent piece of ancient propaganda situated where it could be spread far and wide. On it, Thutmose IV asserts his divine right to the throne as a gift from god. It was not due to his lineage or his standing as the firstborn son of his father, Amenhotep II. He wouldn't need this type of propaganda unless he were an illegitimate ruler. The only reason for it was to silence speculators and fend off rivals to his throne."

Another burst of excitement shot through the crowd. Ethan paused, making eye contact with the front row, letting his idea strengthen its grip on their imagination.

Suddenly, a flickering image shattered his mental clarity. He was transported to his childhood home, where his father sat enthroned on a chair flanking their massive stone fireplace. Rage stirred. His throat tightened.

Oh no... I need a fragment.

"The... evidence is... clear..." he stammered.

A stillness settled again in the auditorium.

Focus, Ethan.

Forcing this invader back into the dark recesses, he recovered his stride.

"Thutmose IV / Amenhotep III was an embattled leader, fighting a stain on his legacy beginning with his grandmother Hatshepsut. However, he could secure his legitimacy as divinely appointed by passing the throne to his firstborn son, Tutankhamun. It's why the sudden death of the rightful heir, the boy king, caused so much trouble.

"This all hinges on a dream merging Egyptian cultural, political, and religious aspects into one spectacular propaganda piece. It also demonstrates what may have motivated those who sought the throne. If they perceived his state as weakened and ripe for the taking, they might send a revolutionary to snuff out the rightful heir to an illegitimate bloodline.

"This is why King Tut was murdered: to end the dynasty of an illegitimate lineage and move the nation in a new direction. It couldn't be accomplished at the ballot box. It had to be secured in the same way all power was secured in Egypt — through force.

"I've given you a lot to think about tonight. I want to open it up now for questions."

Ethan squinted under the glare of the bright lights as he spotted some audience members making their way to the microphone. Given the controversial nature of his new theory, his publicist had advised him to skip the traditional Q&A section. But he was a professor first, a man of the people.

A woman's voice rang out over the house system. "Good evening, Dr. Stone. Regus Britton, New York Times."

Regus Britton? Was this the same R. Britton who had been living in his head all day? And he was a she?

"While I appreciate blind conjecture as much as anyone, your fanciful theory seems devoid of substantive proof. Given how closely it mirrors your personal story, what do you say to those questioning your motives?"

Ethan felt a bead of sweat form on his brow. Was this happening? A tactless press writer bringing up his family story during an academic lecture? What axe did she have to grind? Who was this brazen old maid confronting him before a panel of his peers? And what did she mean by "mirrors his personal story"?

Straightening his shoulders to compose himself, Ethan asked, "Could we bring up the house lights so I can see who I am speaking with?"

He heard Sadie give the command. The spotlight dimmed, and

with a burning fire in his belly, Ethan faced his accuser.

The house lights brightened, revealing the most magnificent creature he'd ever seen. Tall and slender, the auburn-haired writer was adorned in a form-fitting evening gown and stood ramrod straight behind the mic, awaiting his response.

Ethan could hardly think. She wasn't just beautiful; she was exquisite.

Focus, Ethan. Focus. You need to reply… carefully.

"Mrs. Britton, good evening."

"It's Miss Britton, Dr. Stone."

"Well, Miss Britton. Thank you for your question. I read your opinion piece in the Times this morning."

"That was a scholarly review of your ideas, Dr. Stone, not opinion."

Oh no, it was happening again. The thrill of a dangerous hunt coursed through his adrenaline-addicted veins.

"I see. Well, every new insight that corrects an error is initially met with resistance. Established myths are difficult to let go of. Galileo was murdered by the church for his heliocentric views."

"Agreed, but Galileo had math, observation, and the light of truth on his side. You just seem to have ambition mixed with historical blindness to the facts."

"Facts are difficult to establish in ancient history, Miss Britton. Take the 'fact' that Thutmose IV's grandmother, Hatshepsut, was Pharaoh. We only 'know' she was Pharaoh because that 'fact' neatly explains what we have dug up from the sands of time."

Ha, take that, literary hack, Ethan thought to himself. He barreled on before she could interject.

"This belief enjoys academic consensus simply because other plausible theories explaining the archaeological record do not fit the narrative of our day. She would have been displayed in Pharaonic regalia for many reasons besides being an example of someone who broke all ancient taboos. Besides, my succession theory has explanatory power that honors the enormous weight ancient cultures placed on the firstborn male requirement. Which theory is more blind, the one that reads our 21st-century American culture into a 4000-year-old story or an elegant insight into an embattled dynasty clinging to power?"

"I grant your theory intrigues me," Regus replied. "What is more intriguing, however, is why the son and sole heir of England's most successful multinational military defense contractor espouses theories about ancient Egypt that mirror long-held concerns about his family's role in international destabilization and regime change."

Ethan stood in stunned silence. What was she talking about? Would he ever escape his father's long shadow? He'd never been involved in that man's business. After leaving the house and severing all ties, he rejected the monster in the summer of 1999.

His hands began to tremble. He needed to get out of here.

"Another exciting opinion piece from the New York Times, everyone. Thank you for coming."

Ethan walked off stage.

6

Safaga, Egypt

A high-pitched whine vanished into the night sky as the military-grade reconnaissance drone rose from the ship's stern. The night vision feed came online in Jack's immersive VR pilot goggles. Banking left, the drone raced across a bleak desert landscape, headed for Luxor, Egypt.

"I've got visuals. Moving west at 78 mph. Time to target, just over an hour," Jack said into comms.

"Perfect. Gives me time to finish my cigar," Sykes replied. "Archer, you have a read on the LiDAR signals?"

"Roger. She's operational. Let's hope the nerds back home figured out how to keep it working this time. I'd hate to tell Ethan he wasted another hundred grand on our little excursion to the Red Sea Riviera."

Jack, Sykes, and Archer had been friends for over twenty years. Like most red-blooded American men their age, 9/11 had ignited a fire in their bellies. They watched the Towers fall with the same burning rage, and each enlisted in the fall of 2001.

They met in Jump School at Fort Benning, Georgia, along with an

annoyingly handsome kid they called Dr. Rich. A dual citizen of the
U.S. and the UK, Ethan Stone was first known for his famous family.
But he quickly distinguished himself amongst the recruits for his
fearlessness, brilliant mind, and quick, reliable decision-making. Not
many paratroopers could read the *Art of War* in Chinese, Seneca in
Latin, Herodotus in Greek, and the *Book of the Dead* in Hieroglyphics.
He told them that he had "picked up" the languages during a
wandering two-year world tour. But nobody believed him. He had to
be a savant.

The four became lifelong friends after their 82nd Airborne unit
from Fort Bragg, N.C., deployed to Iraq. Each served four combat
tours in Iraq and Afghanistan from 2003 to 2011. Now, they were
private contractors in Ethan's secret employ. Ethan had formed a
small firm in 2014 after ISIS began its reign of terror in Iraq and the
Levant.

Surrounded by a bank of monitors in the control room of Ethan's
24-meter dive yacht, Archer manned the military-grade
reconnaissance drone's cameras. In addition to the 6K cinema lenses
with night vision capabilities, the drone was recently retrofitted with
a solid-state LiDAR system, capable of capturing gigapixel-detailed
imagery in the dark of night. LiDAR technology, functioning
independently of natural light, fires laser pulses to measure the time
it takes for the light to return, and compiles that data into razor-sharp
3D maps.

Jack sat beside him, present but miles away in first-person view,
soaring through the dry night air. And Sykes did what he did best,
puffing away on the aft deck swim platform, dangling his feet in the
cool water while the team worked. This mission was straightforward:
Jack flew, Archer captured footage, Sykes smoked expensive cigars,
and Ethan paid the bills and took the credit. This arrangement had
worked out for them on the trip. So far.

The team had been moored off the coast of Safaga, Egypt, keeping
a low profile.

Safaga was a modest port town, and tourist dive haven on the Egyptian side of the Red Sea coast with a paved road into Upper Egypt, in case they found something. But really, this dive adventure was a convenient cover to bring their gear into a sticky part of the world.

Sandwiched between Egypt, Saudi Arabia, Yemen, and Sudan, the region around Safaga was trafficked with pirates, wealthy tourists, government spies, Saudi uber-rich, Islamic terror groups, and now, a team of ex-U.S. military operatives breaking every drone law Egypt had on the books.

"We're approaching Luxor. Taking her to 800 feet."

"Copy; I'm coming up." Sykes flicked his Plasencia Alma Fuerte Hexagon cigar, which landed in the sea with a hiss.

The drone crested a desert ridge, and the vast Nile River came into view. Jack needed to get high enough to avoid attention from a late-night city dweller or policeman. If they were caught flying a drone in Egypt without a permit from the Egyptian Civil Aviation Authority, they could all be thrown in jail. If they got caught flying this drone, there would be an international incident.

Below them, night vision sensors lit up the famous outline of Temple Karnak in dazzling emerald-green. They could see the Ramses Temple and even the Luxor Temple. But the most noticeable object rising into the night was the enigmatic Thutmose I obelisk.

"Why did America choose that thing to memorialize George Washington?" Sykes wondered.

"You should ask Ethan next time we see him," Jack said, expertly guiding the agile craft on a steep descent out across the Nile. "All I can say is gross."

"Gross? What the hell does that mean?"

"I don't want to be the one to tell you," Jack said. "It's all kinds of messed up, though. It's even worse if you buy into ancient history and spiritual conspiracy theories."

"They've got 'em at the Vatican, London, and Central Park, too,"

Archer chimed in. "The ones in NYC and Great Britain were gifts from Egypt at the turn of the 19th century. I guess they were carved around 1450 BCE, honoring these Thutmose Pharaohs."

"What on earth..." muttered Sykes, wondering why the world had such an obsession with ancient Egypt.

Sykes left it alone, making a mental note to find out what Ethan knew about these obelisks. He shifted his attention back to the monitors.

However magnificent, Karnak and Luxor were not their targets. Over the past two hundred years, every inch of them was explored. Instead, it was the recent discovery of the city of Aten that drew these men to Egypt in the dead of night.

The drone whipped across the sparsely populated fertile farmland, arriving at their destination. Jack eased up on the controls. He flicked a stainless-steel switch, and a small parabolic mic with polycarbonate reflectors flipped down from behind the 12-inch LiDAR sensor housing. The stereoscopic sound of the desert at night, the thrum of insects, the winds whipping over the dunes, the rustlings of unseen things, filled the control room.

"There, 10 o'clock. That's what we're here for."

Archer powered up the LiDAR module, and 3D images streamed across his monitors in real time.

"Okay, we just need to get a good scan of the area to the southwest and get out of here."

Discovered by accident in 2020, the city was named after the god known as Aten. The word Aten is Egyptian for "disc," long thought to represent the sun god Amun-Ra. But Ethan had a crazy new idea. The discovery of this city fit perfectly into his theory. He needed to see the site and to participate in the excavations. But his trip to the region ended in disappointment last year when the Egyptian government denied his request to join the dig.

"Every team member is Egyptian," he was proudly told. "We are unearthing the most significant find in Egypt since King Tut, and it will all be done by our people."

Being categorically rejected was a new experience. Ethan had tried everything he could to bypass this wholesale denial but had hit a mud-brick wall after mud-brick wall. Someone mighty in Egypt was keeping the dig site off limits to foreigners, hence this illegal, dangerous midnight adventure.

The city of Aten was not much to look at. After four years, they had unearthed many structures, but only about the first two or three feet. The sprawling dig site was only partially started. Major sections to the north and the west had yet to begin. Digging something this large with small hand tools, inch by inch, was a slow and expensive endeavor. This is where LiDAR came in.

Archer gently moved the LiDAR scanners a few degrees, and Jack crept along the city's southwest section, keeping the drone stable at around 100 feet.

Their target area was a sizeable unexcavated section at the end of a long street that cut through the center of the town. On each side of the street were a hundred feet of wavy mudbrick walls that, from above, looked like an ancient map marking the course of a river. It was almost as if someone had designed the city street to resemble passing through a body of water to reach an unknown structure.

On his monitor, Jack's drone crept down the street as if flowing toward some hidden structure at its end—their target.

"There," Sykes said, "that is what we're after!"

He pointed to a dark depression on the 3D map the LiDAR was compiling on the screens.

"That looks like a temple structure. Right where Ethan said it might be."

As data streamed in real-time, the secrets hidden deep underground were coming to light.

The team could see an unmistakable outline of a rectangular temple complex in the center of the vacant area. However, unlike every other temple complex in the region, this one didn't feature a sea of columns leading into an inner hall. Instead, the expansive complex wall was punctuated by a single opening leading into the temple.

Another dark outline flared across the scan, dividing the temple into two sections. The outer hall area snapped into view, a near-perfect square with no columns. Then came the inner hall, a wide rectangle, its interior swallowed in black.

Sykes pulled out a folded piece of paper with a rendering Ethan had created to map what he hoped to find.

"This looks just like Ethan's drawing!"

The air in the control room seemed to tighten, charged with the adrenaline rush before a monumental discovery.

A metallic clank shattered the silence. A heavy-caliber weapon, racked, ready, thrusting the team into warrior mode.

"Jack! Where is that coming from?" cried Archer.

The three men heard the sound a thousand times in Iraq as they'd prepared to rain down a barrage of deadly munitions on enemy targets.

Jack whipped the drone in a 180-degree arc, scanning the emerald shadows with the night vision cameras. He stopped the motion when he locked onto a single human figure concealed behind a half-wall on the edge of the excavated city.

Jack zoomed in on the camera feed. A startling sight. Dug in behind the wall, a lone gunner in classic formation with clear views of the ancient city. Mounted on a steel tripod was an M2A1 Browning .50 Caliber, the iconic American heavy machine gun. Drone optics illuminated it perfectly. The weapon gleamed as bright as in daylight. A four-pronged flash hider glinting along the barrel. Built to choke muzzle flash… for deadly night-time targeting.

A deafening sound erupted from the control room speakers. The night vision feed flashed to brilliant white. This was the last thing the men saw.

"Son of a…" Jack flung the FPV pilot goggles from his face, eyes stinging from the light surging into his retinas. "What the hell was that!"

The three men looked around. Confused. Silent. Processing what had just happened. And, more importantly…what would happen next?

"Archer, fire up the engines now!" Sykes barked. "We have to get out of here."

Within minutes, the ship's dual MAN V12X engines were churning salt water as all 4400 horsepower propelled the luxury vessel out to sea.

"Head to international waters. Then north to the Suez. Ethan has a contact at the SCA who can get us a tugboat instead of the compulsory pilot."

"Damn! Why did an American-made .50 cal just shoot us out of the sky?" cursed Jack. "That was my favorite drone!"

"What in the hell was a machine gun nest doing inside an archaeological dig site?" Archer snapped.

"Does that sound like a chopper to anyone?" Sykes asked.

Archer and Jack turned toward the rattle of a low-flying helo inbound from the northeast.

"This isn't going to end well," heaved Sykes. "We'd better call Ethan."

7

Ethan nearly slammed into Sadie as he rushed through the stage-left wing. She started to speak, but he kept walking briskly, and she thought it better not to chase him down. She knew that would end badly. Things always ended badly for her with men like this.

But Ethan suddenly stopped and turned around. "Fancy that drink?"

No, no, no, Sadie… Not tonight. Not ever again.

"Sure," she said. "Meet you at The Mark on Madison and 77 in an hour."

Ethan nodded and gave a half smile.

"See you then," he said and exited the double doors to his right.

Ethan walked out the back of the auditorium, headed for the 82nd Street exit. But this meant passing by the auditorium entrances after walking through the Egyptian section. He desperately wanted to avoid seeing any patrons and, even worse, answering questions from R. Britton on his way out.

He stepped into the Temple of Dendur room and dashed past the small but fabulously preserved Egyptian temple, a highlight of any visit to the Met. From there he stumbled into the Amarna Period room, rushing by a few reliefs of King Tut. He couldn't bear the thought of heading past the auditorium entrance, so he turned left to gallery 115, which contained a dozen statues of Hatshepsut painstakingly reconstructed from thousands of fragments. He never understood why her son, Amenhotep II, had attempted to remove her from history, smashing her statues into thousands of fragments. But he did understand broken families.

His phone rang.

Stopping to retrieve it, he faced a beautiful carving of Hatshepsut depicted in pharaonic regalia.

"This is your fault," he muttered, checking his lock screen. His team was calling.

"Sykes," he answered, "How's the expedition going?"

"A helicopter is stalking us, probably the Egyptian military." Sykes calmly relayed into the headset. "Someone knew we were coming. Shot the drone down with a .50 cal in the middle of our scan."

"Where are you now?" Ethan asked, returning the professionalism of the team leader with his trademark clear thinking.

"Nearly in international waters."

"Good. When you get there, head northeast towards the Saudi side. I have a contingency plan."

"East? There's nothing over there for a hundred miles? What do you have in mind?"

"They've been building a megacity called NEOM. I have a contact there who can help," he said.

"The Line? Ethan, if we go to Saudi, we could take some serious heat," Sykes cautioned. "That place has been under fire since the Crown Prince was accused of murdering that journalist. They continue to court the Chinese for massive investment, ignoring Washington's warnings about becoming too friendly with Beijing. Plus, the Houthis in the south shot down another American Predator drone with an Iranian surface-to-air missile this week. Are you sure you want us to waltz into an international hotspot?"

"Given what just happened, I have a bad feeling we've already got a dance partner. I'll call you back in an hour," he said, then hung up.

Ethan's hands were trembling.

"This night could not get any worse," he thought.

Sliding the phone into his pocket, he glanced again at the dozen statues of Hatshepsut scattered throughout the gallery.

"What are you hiding?" he asked the lifeless stone out loud. "I know you've got a secret. And I'll be the one to put these pieces together. Mark my words."

Confident that the crowds had dispersed enough to venture past the auditorium exit, Ethan turned to leave.

That's when all the breath left his chest.

"Good evening, Dr. Stone," said a very serious-looking Regus Britton. "I thought I'd find you here."

She was even more stunning up close. A form-fitting black cocktail dress hung about her shoulders and cut across her in all the right places. Elegant but modest, she had an eye for fashion. The gallery lights bounced off a shimmering diamond necklace offset by flawless skin.

"You have a few moments to finish our discussion?" she asked.

Not usually at a loss for words, Ethan just stood there, wondering what was happening. Why couldn't he think when he was around this woman?

"We'd only just begun discussing your theory and its implications."

Over her mesmerizing shoulders, Ethan spotted two men in black tuxes enter the room. They were both over six feet tall and carried themselves with the confidence of special operators. Ethan breathed deeply; this was getting complicated. A motion to his left revealed two more men entering from a different doorway with their hands inside their jackets.

His training took over.

"Come with me," he whispered to Regus. Grabbing her hand, he pulled her to the opposite end of the room. Her touch caused tingling sensations of electric shock as he led her quickly out of the gallery towards the Central Park side of the museum.

"What are you doing?" she protested.

"We have to move now," he calmly replied. "We've got company."

Regus glanced behind her, spying the four men. Ethan saw them move into a tactical wedge formation, and he knew a team was hunting them. He did not want to engage in this setting.

"An emergency exit leads to the Park back in the Temple room."

"Who are these men?" Regus whispered.

To her credit, she was keeping a very level head.

"I don't know, but I'm sure we don't want to find out."

They entered the Temple room, overtaking a small crowd of tourists wandering through the ancient ruins. They weaved through the guided tour, which slowed the four-man team who had also entered the expansive hall.

A red sign above the door indicated their trajectory.

"Be prepared to run when we get outside," Ethan said, glancing down at her feet.

A pair of black leather Gucci 3-inch sandal heels was strapped to her slim ankles, revealing manicured candy-red nails. "Man, even her toes are cute," he thought. "Focus!"

"You may need to ditch the shoes," he warned.

"You may need to explain yourself before I dump a thousand dollars in the bushes," she quipped.

"We can talk when we're safe."

The pair burst through the emergency exit, sending sirens wailing throughout the museum.

The four-man team picked up the pace as crowds swiveled to see the commotion.

Taking a hard right, Ethan gripped Regus's hand tighter. She held on. Matching his pace, the couple sprinted across the lawn towards E 84th. Pieces of tree bark splintered to their right. From a hundred yards back, suppressed 9mm fire spat after them from the team closing fast.

"They're shooting at us!!" shouted Regus. "Who are you?"

"New York's most notorious academic, remember," smirked Ethan.

The Egyptian-themed playground ahead was empty, so he veered through the gates and down the ramp, hoping the men wouldn't shoot there.

They jumped a short wall and landed on the sandy playing surface. Regus' heels dug into the soft ground, and she faltered.

"Time to ditch the shoes."

"You're going to pay for these," Regus said, bending over to rip the heels from her feet.

No more shots rang out from behind as they raced through the playground. Up ahead, Ethan saw a lone patrol horse tied up outside a public restroom. "Too much coffee on a work night," he said to himself.

"What?" asked Regus.

Ethan leaped onto the Park Enforcement Patrol horse and pulled Regus behind him. She was shouting in his ear, but he didn't pay attention. He spurred the horse to a gallop, and she grabbed him tightly as the four-person team exited the playground.

"This is the best way to see New York," Ethan said. "You'll remember this night forever."

Humor kept his mind sharp in these situations, but it infuriated his riding partner. Her audible but incoherent shouts intensified.

"So much for a level head," he thought. Gunfire had that effect on people.

The one good thing about New York's rampant crime and dwindling police force was that nobody seemed to think a nicely dressed couple racing down the crushed stone Bridle Path on a stolen police horse was anything out of the ordinary.

With their assailants now out of sight, Ethan rounded the north end of the Jackie O Reservoir and rode past Central Park Tennis Center.

"This is our stop." Ethan pulled up on the reins.

The couple dismounted and calmly walked towards Central Park West and W 96th. The only sound now was Regus's bare feet padding softly beside Ethan as he hailed a cab.

"NYU Institute for the Study of the Ancient World," he said as they entered the yellow cab.

Regus sat silently beside him, looking down at her shaking hands. Ethan supposed she had used all her words on the fifteen-minute trot through Central Park. He couldn't have been more wrong.

8

London, England

"Sir, they're on the run."

"Who are they?"

"He wasn't alone. A woman from the Times is with him. What should we do?"

This was less than ideal. He needed a clean extraction, no questions asked, especially not from some newspaper girl.

"Follow them, of course." He took another sip from his 18-year-old bourbon and wondered why he had to give such remedial instructions.

"They've exited the museum and are moving northeast on foot."

"Make sure they don't get away. I need him in my London office in twelve hours."

"Copy."

His earpiece rang out with the unmistakable muffled sound of suppressed gunfire.

"Do not engage!" he screamed, startling the sitting patrons sparsely populating the upscale bar on the 34th floor, which had floor-to-ceiling wraparound windows.

"You are not authorized to engage," he said, more subdued this time. "Bring him in, but he better not have a scratch on him."

He silently gazed out at the London skyline as the team lead gave the order. The Thames below and the Tower of London lit up in the night. He loved looking at this historic building. To him, it was always the home of Richard III. Now that was a ballsy king. A true Alpha male, if ever there was one. Murdering his brother's kids to steal the throne. Bravo.

"Now is the winter of my discontent, indeed," he murmured, swirling the meticulously shaved ice cube, snugly spinning in his tumbler.

He had a luxury penthouse flat perched high atop the 64th floor of the Shard in London. A gift from the former Emir of Qatar, who had rescued the building project in 2007 after the global financial collapse. However, he preferred to drink in the Shangri-La Hotel bar on the 34th floor. He liked public spaces.

"What's happening now?" he asked.

"They've stolen a police horse and are pulling away."

"Can you catch them?!"

"Negative."

"Do we have a second team to head them off?"

"They were in the museum with me. They're gone, Sir."

"Seriously, it was easier taking Baghdad from Saddam than trying to get my bloody son to come home."

Though frustrated, he was proud. The display at the Met was precisely why he needed Ethan for this moment in history. His son had game.

"Do your cleanup at the Park and come in. I need to catch up with Med One."

9

Sykes relayed Ethan's order to Archer, who guided the vessel through a glassy moonlit sea. The open waters were remarkably calm tonight. It was an excellent seafaring omen by any measure, but all the other signs pointed to chaos.

"East?" Archer said upon hearing the asinine instructions. "There's nothing but foreign construction workers and Saudi military over there. It's a horrible idea."

"Agreed," Sykes said, "But that's what we're doing."

"Did Ethan say what to do about this inbound bird we have on our six?" asked Jack. "I still have my little lady in the stable. I can get her ready if we're already dancing."

"Roger that," Sykes said. "We need to figure it out. It's hours to the Saudi side, and that helo will be on us any moment."

Jack didn't need any more cajoling. He raced below deck and returned moments later with a hard-shell case the size of a carry-on bag.

"I'll be operational in 90 seconds," he said.

He snapped the case open to grab his old quadrotor racing drone, the one that won him a Drone Racing League World Championship. Retro by now, sure. But the jury-rigged EMP module strapped to its frame was anything but. He got the idea from the Call of Duty video game and, with Ethan's help, turned the fantasy into reality. And tonight, finally, he'd get to deploy it in the field.

"She's hot and ready for release," he said.

"Go," Sykes replied.

Jack threw on his FPV goggles. The drone zipped into the night sky, cutting northeast toward the helo's roaring turbulence. Jack's gut clenched. He had to intercept it well clear of their yacht. If not, when its systems went offline, it could crash into their vessel.

"I have it on the radar. It's inbound at 110 knots, heading southeast just north of our path. Weapons hot."

"Engage when ready," Sykes replied.

Jack swung the drone wide to the northeast of the inbound chopper. It was insanely fast for a drone, but the helo's 126 mph still left it eating air, the extra weight of the EMP dragging at its belly. He needed the angle dead-on to come in high and drop fast or the helo's rotor wash would shred him.

One shot. Miss it, and their escape died in under a minute.

The helicopter came into view on his goggles. Jack gasped.

"Guys, this is not your average bird."

"What are we dealing with?" Sykes asked.

"It's a blacked-out Sikorsky S-76," Jack said.

"And that means what to normal people?"

"You know what Marine One is?"

"Of course," Sykes replied.

"That's an S-96. They're known as the world's head of state choppers, used exclusively to transport POTUS since General Eisenhower. The S-76 is its little sister...the Black Hawk. I've flown a thousand hours in them. Whoever that bird belongs to is a big deal."

"It could be the Egyptian Coast Guard," Archer chimed.

"Well, this one's matte black. No markings. I'd see red, white, and black circles if it was Egyptian military. Looks like the VIP civilian version—for world leaders and corporate executives."

"Interesting. When you're done fanboying out, maybe get back to saving our lives?"

"Sykes, this chopper is not normal. The people after us must be super powerful and super wealthy. Are you sure we should take it out?"

"What's our option?" Sykes bit out. "Ethan said get out and get to Saudi. So that's what we're doing."

His window of attack was almost closed. "There's another problem," Jack said. "This craft has shielded electronics. My EMP won't knock their system totally offline. Bringing this Black Hawk down will be rough."

"Get to it already!" Sykes shouted.

Jack swallowed hard and dropped the drone into a 45-degree dive. The EMP was brutal, but its effective radius was 10 meters, no more. The instant it fired, the drone would die with it. A single-use kamikaze weapon.

If this worked, the upside was that the S-76 pilots might walk away. At this altitude, the Red Sea crash was survivable. If they were smart, they'd sprung for the water landing package. Jack clung to that hope.

Easing his grip, he coaxed the dual joysticks until the drone slid into position. Closing the gap perfectly. He couldn't disable all the electronics, but the tail rotor was enough. His little kamikaze locked on.

Jack zeroed in on the blinking red lights at the tail. He charged the flux generator bomb tube and flipped the switch a heartbeat before impact. His drone detonated in a blinding flash against the moonlit sky.

Jack's goggles went black. Then, a violent, deafening explosion. His ears rang.

The rumble of the chopper's engines choked into silence.

Seconds later, the backup systems roared to life. Too little, too late.

Sykes and Archer froze on the flybridge. The blast, just hundreds of meters behind, tore through the S-76. Sent it spinning—tail rotor gone. The helo dropped in a chaotic swirl of metal and smoke. Moonlight glinted off its shuddering frame as the pilot fought to steer the flailing craft.

Then they heard the thunderclap. The sea swallowed the S-76 whole.

They escaped Egypt and were no longer being pursued. But were they free?

That would depend on Ethan's contingency plan and whatever awaited them in Saudi Arabia.

10

Ethan's father stood at the window, city lights glittering beneath him like prey. In the silence of the flat, he poured a drink. The sharp burn of bourbon rose to his nose as he inhaled, staring through his reflection in the glass. His hand tightened on the weighted tumbler trembling in his grasp.

"Enough," he hissed. "I won't let my son squander himself on pointless adventures while jackals tear at my empire."

He could no longer allow his wayward son to run around the world searching for ancient history while his company was under assault.

He tore his gaze from the horizon, shoulders locked, eyes sharp, a low pressure building inside him like steam against iron. He thumbed the encrypted comms and growled, "Med One, this is Richard III. I need a SITREP?"

"Richard III, this is Med One; SALUTE report follows. Sierra, three operators. Alpha, traveling southeast on open waters in a civilian dive yacht. Lima, four, three, zero, Kilo, Quebec, one, seven. Uniform, unknown. Tango, time now, Charlie. Echo, unarmed. How copy over?"

"We lost the Met package. We must secure his team."

"Copy. Closing in on them now."

"The time has come," he said to the empty room, his voice low, deliberate. "It's time, Ethan. Time to take your place in the business the Stone men have sweated and bled for over generations. You can't keep running from your destiny.

"Whether you know it or not, you don't have a choice. As my son, my bloodline, you will serve your nation. Whether you know it yet or not." He paced, mind racing.

"MED One, what were they doing in Safaga?" he asked.

"We're not sure. When we got locked on their location, they'd already set out to sea. But my guess is, it wasn't recreational diving."

"You would be correct."

My boy will never abandon that squad of loyal misfits.

He rubbed his chin.

Good. All I have to do is bring them in, too.

A smile ghosted across his lips. "He'll curse me for it now. But in the end, he'll thank me."

This was the moment. He needed Ethan to join the family business and deploy his considerable talents to serve his nation. How to get him to see this was yet an unanswered question

His contacts in the Egyptian ministry had kept him updated on his son's dealings over the years. Ethan pulled every string, burned every favor, to join a new dig. Nothing worked; the Egyptian government shut him out.

He stepped closer to the desk, fingers drumming against the wood.

This trip ties back to that. I can feel it.

"He hates 'no' as much as I do," he smirked.

He felt his cheeks rise, his mouth curled into a smile as cold as the massive ice cube crackling in his tumbler.

He took a swig, the bitter tang clung to his tongue as he radioed his team lead.

"Med One, this is Richard III; what's the play when you overtake them?"

"Richard III, this is Med One; impede their progress. Forcibly board if they do not immediately terminate engines."

"Copy. Good luck, Med One. Remember, these are not, I repeat, not civilians. I would be shocked if they were unarmed, as you supposed."

Before Med One could respond, the cockpit lit up with alarm bells.

"We've got a tiny UAV inbound from the northeast at 90 knots. Where did this come from?" the pilot shouted.

Ethan's father caught the commotion crackling through the comms. Men shouting over one another, curses breaking through static, and the piercing alarms of the helo's threat detection system filling his penthouse apartment.

Yes, he knew the sounds of panic, of chaos, of the best team money can buy…unraveling.

A second later, the comms convulsed with a metallic crash.

An explosion ripped through the channel. Rattling his eardrums.

His cheek twitched. Then, instantly stilled, his iron composure snapping back into place.

The blast's deep, rolling pulse shook the line dead.

The silence was broken by a slow hiss.

It was him, exhaling through clenched teeth as he realized …he'd been outmaneuvered. Again. By his son.

11

Ethan figured that returning to his office just blocks from the shooting scene wasn't the most brilliant move. His stomach tightened as city noises pressed in on him: car horns blaring, wailing sirens, beeping crosswalk signals.

Still, what choice did he have? He couldn't take this rare specimen to his tiny apartment. And his office was the most secure place.

Ahmed, the cabbie, swung the car through Central Park on the 79th Transverse. Chaos came into view as they shot across 5th Avenue. Patrol cars angled across intersections, lights strobing red and blue, officers waving frantic drivers back. Five city blocks in front of the Met were sealed off between E 85th and E 80th.

"This city is falling apart," Ahmed said, weaving the cab around the clogged left lane.

The NYPD directed dozens of angry drivers to go straight instead of turning onto 5th Avenue. It was closed, but people figured if they yelled at the cops they'd let them take that route. That didn't work out for them.

"I think I'm going to move to Iowa," Ahmed continued. "I have a cousin there who says cornfields are better than gun fights."

"That sounds like a proverb," Ethan replied, glad his cabbie was breaking the silence.

Regus hadn't spoken since they got off the horse twenty minutes ago. He wondered if she'd accompany him when they arrived at his building. To his surprise, she exited the cab and followed him around the corner.

They descended the stairs, Ethan opened the door for her, and they entered his private domain.

Thoughts swirled through Ethan's mind: Was she in shock? Did she need medical care?

Regus plopped down in a chair and unloaded her pain.

"Your family has caused me nothing but death and mayhem for decades," she shouted. "We were almost killed tonight because you don't know your limits! Your vile family thinks you can form the world around you to serve the nefarious intentions of conquest that pulse through your corrupted veins. I have never been this angry in my life, which is saying something because I watched my dad die in the VA hospital as a result of your father's abusive command! I then watched my brother spend his life trying to reform a broken system that refused to acknowledge the evil your family unleashed on our soldiers. He killed himself last year after a decade of administrative dead ends, where he saw hundreds of impoverished veterans lose their fight with rare cancers our government denies even exist, much less take responsibility for causing. You, Ethan Stone, are the epitome of arrogance and all that is wrong with our country."

Ethan was the one in shock now. What was she saying?

"How dare you capture me and trap me in whatever dungeon this is!" Regus took her first breath and looked around.

"This place looks like the secret lair of Dr. Evil if he were a stuck-up academic whose blood lust drives him to steal priceless artifacts from conquered nations," she bellowed.

"Hold on!" Ethan interjected, mildly impressed at her eloquent string of condemnations of his family. He couldn't argue with her point, save that he was included in this obvious contempt for his bloodline.

"I have no idea what you are talking about," he replied, trying to be gentle with her. "I'm sorry about your father and brother, but I don't see what this has to do with me. Can you please calm down and explain what you're saying?"

He regretted the word the moment it escaped his lips.

"You want me to be calm and explain myself?! Why don't you explain why your father has spent his life ordering people to their deaths because it enriches his megalomaniacal empire-building pursuits!" she raged. "No, sir, I will not calm down. I've waited ten years to have it out with you, and now is the day of reckoning. It's time you face the darkness hiding in your despicable line and do something good with your life for a change."

"Wait a minute, she's waited ten years to talk to me?" Ethan said to himself.

Regus was now in tears. She stopped and wiped her eyes. She had wanted to do this slowly, to draw him out as she peppered him with a thousand questions stored up in her soul from years of painful research. But here she sat, out of control, with a torrent of emotions raging forth. This was a disaster.

They sat silently, looking at each other, calculating what was next.

"Regus, I am unbelievably sorry for what you have experienced. I've seen my share of death and know what it's like to watch a loved one die in front of you. It's hard ever to recover," he trailed off.

Heat rose in Ethan's chest as a swell of long-buried emotions surged back. He recalled his first deployment in Iraq, with the 82nd Airborne, tasked with Operation All American Tiger. Targeting the counterinsurgency responsible for attacks on coalition forces cost him...dearly. The losses of good men—good friends...and almost his own life once.

He willed himself back from the brink. "If we're going to figure out what sort of a mess we are in, I need to know what you're talking about. You said you've waited ten years to talk to me? Why? What about?"

Regus struggled to get her fury under control. Her desire to regain the upper hand in a line of questioning pushed her back over the edge into civility.

"Did you know," she said, "your father is a war criminal?"

"Yes," Ethan said. "One of his many flaws."

"Did you also know that his escapades in Operation Desert Storm rewrote the DoD's disciplinary manual on dealing with rogue military officers?"

"Quite right. Literal volumes of government regulations were written because of him."

"Well," Regus faltered. She was set off kilter by Ethan's quick, condemnations of his father. "He has been called The Burn Master by my publication for his illicit and hidden use of massive burn pits in Iraq. The military claimed it was for the disposal of medical waste and conventional refuse. But only those complicit in the cover-up believe that nonsense."

That was fresh news to Ethan, but he didn't react to it. Since his days in the military, he'd established his own don't ask, don't tell policy—ignore, avoid, and deny anything related to his father.

"The Burn Master?" Ethan asked. "A catchy name. I'm going to use it at the next family reunion. Who came up with that?"

Regus suppressed a smile. "Me," she said.

Ethan was a piece of work, for sure. But not what she'd imagined. Tall, dark, and handsome was such a cliché. But it fit him perfectly.

Ethan stood, slipped off his tweed blazer, and set his glasses on the desktop.

"Regus, I want to understand what you're saying. However, I've had no contact with my father since the summer of 1999. Even when I was in the service, we never crossed paths, and I never got involved with anything he did."

"That seems highly unlikely," Regus replied, her eyes narrower, her lips thinner.

"It's true. I entered the service around the time my father left it and moved back to London, taking the reins of Fortis Defense from my grandfather. He did his thing, and I did mine."

"Are you sure?" Regus asked. "My research reveals your unit in Iraq was outfitted with specialized gear, which the DoD said came as a gift from a U.S. non-profit. The website archives list this group as registered in Reston, VA. Their mission statement was, 'Winning the Global War on Terror (GWOT) by resourcing American troops with the latest defense technology.' That group's largest donor? Fortis Defense."

Ethan immediately knew what she was referencing. His unit had been given night-vision gear that nobody else had. Their binocular goggles and scopes had more than double the resolution of the other squad's standard-issue Milspec units. His unit also had combined thermal imaging, unheard-of tech, in the early 2000s. One night, with his team ambushed and hit by an IED, Ethan was isolated from them. Pinned down by ranged fire, he couldn't locate. The thermal scope on the squad sniper, Sykes, enabled him to identify and eliminate the tango moments before Ethan was shot. This event solidified a lifelong allegiance between the two men, and it was the reason he was the leader of Ethan's team.

"Does any of this ring a bell?" Regus asked.

"It does. I know what you're referring to; it was night vision gear." Some pieces were coming together for Ethan.

"That's the gear that first made your father's company famous!" Regus said.

"Wow, you're all up in my family business? You're right again. Fortis developed the night vision elements used in the first Gulf War that gave our troops the winning advantage," Ethan replied. "They went on to become the global leader in low-light optics, making a small fortune off that one department."

"And you're telling me you had no idea your father was outfitting your squad in Iraq?"

"I am. This is all news to me. I haven't seen or spoken to my father since I left home twenty-five years ago."

Regus's tense shoulders released as she tucked a strand of loose hair behind her ear.

Over the years, Ethan had enough conversations with upset girlfriends to hone his skills at detecting the end of a fight. They were almost home free. He wanted to ask about her father's and brother's deaths but sensed that he should wait.

"So why was your father secretly protecting you in Iraq?" Regus asked. "And was that the only time?"

The question hit harder than Ethan expected. A knot formed in his chest. He remembered his commitment to find answers to the question plaguing his mind. He knew it meant looking at the things he'd avoided for decades, and this was probably one of those things.

"I have no clue, Regus. But I can tell you, I want to find out."

"Me too," she said, failing to hide her smile.

"And we're done," Ethan thought, returning the smile.

They shared another moment of silence.

"So, perhaps we try and figure out why four special operators were in the Met tonight?" he asked.

"My thoughts exactly," Regus replied. "You think they were former military?"

"Without a doubt. I've led enough teams to know a tactical formation when I see one."

"So why were they after us?" she asked.

 Ethan cocked his head. "My guess is their presence had something to do with what my team is dealing with in Egypt right now."

"Your team?"

Ethan suddenly realized he'd forgotten to tell Sykes where to go once they reached Saudi Arabia. He pulled out his phone.

"I have a small private contractor firm that works with the U.S. military on sensitive off-the-books jobs," he said as he fired off a flurry of texts. "They're currently on my yacht, being chased by an unknown party off the coast of Egypt."

"Chased? Your Yacht?" Regus replied with the tell-tale air of curiosity bred into trained reporters.

Ethan pushed send on the last message and looked up. Regus was staring him down, waiting for an answer. Damnit. How could he forget he was talking to a stranger from the Times who had spent the last ten years researching him? This woman was wreaking havoc on his usually disciplined mind.

Stuck between the urge to seek answers and the realization that this woman had been out to get him a few moments earlier, he rolled the dice and decided to keep going. She was too beautiful to be totally evil.

"Regardless of what you so publicly wrote, I have an angle on some 'actual evidence' that may connect the dots to King Tut's killer."

It was Regus's turn to be caught between competing motivations. Could she lay down her preconceived notions about Ethan and do what reporters do best: follow the lead? She was more committed to answers than judgments, so she, too, rolled the dice.

"Look, Ethan, it's no secret I don't like your family, or you for that matter." Regus smirked, mischievously. "But I want the truth more than I want to be right about you. So, you can trust me." Her bright green eyes glistened with a genuineness that caught Ethan off guard.

"Well, I did almost get you killed tonight," Ethan conceded. "But we shared a moment on the horse in Central Park. So maybe you like me more than you think."

"That wasn't a moment," protested Regus. "I'd been kidnapped by a nicely dressed fool who owes me a new pair of Prada."

"Hey, those heels were Gucci," Ethan said.

"I need an upgrade for my troubles," Regus said. "And how do you know so much about women's shoes?"

"Let's just say this is not the first time I've had to replace a pair of pumps."

Regus looked mildly confused as Ethan's phone rang. It was Sadie.

12

Aten Dig Site, Egypt

The charred remains of the drone were still too hot to pick up.

"This is American," Sayyid spoke into his encrypted comms as he sifted through the rubble.

"Are you sure?"

"Yes. U.S. military surveillance outfitted with what looks like a LiDAR scanner."

"Why were they here?"

"I do not know. But they went to great lengths, searching for something buried in the sands."

"What did they discover?"

"I cannot say."

"Where are they now?"

"Not far, Inshallah. But," Sayyid trailed off. He loathed even hinting at bad news. "I am not sure it was only a drone. And it could have been operated from more than a hundred miles away."

"I do not need to remind you of the stakes, Sayyid," said the voice.

"I will finish this."

"You have one job. Bring him in."

13

Archer pushed the vessel to her limits overnight, so they were already approaching Sindalah as the early morning light spilled across their path. A tiny island but still a sight to behold. An ultra-rich, global yachting resort for international guests.

Archer throttled down, guiding the boat around the reef toward the marina. Before him was an 86-berth marina, connected to a promenade lined with shops, restaurants, and entertainment venues. Ethan's text came through: he'd booked them a slip and rooms at the resort. Stay low until I know who's chasing us.

But the last line stopped him cold. Short, cryptic, impossible to ignore. "A timely king may know something about the hidden tower watching them." Sykes had no idea what it meant, but a knot in his gut told him they'd find out soon.

Pulling into slip eleven, Archer killed the engines as the marina staff went to work tying off the vessel.

"This place is wild," Jack exclaimed. "Can you imagine what this country would look like without oil money?"

"I saw an 18-hole golf course as we approached," Archer said. "Should have brought my clubs."

"Yeah, well this was a barren wasteland a hundred years ago," Jack retorted. "In 1932, the third iteration of the Kingdom of Saudi Arabia was born. The first king, Ibn Saud, inked a deal with an American company to search for oil. That company, now known as Chevron, was a subsidiary of Standard Oil, founded by John D. Rockefeller."

"The American business mogul?" Sykes asked.

"That's the one," Jack said, his face creased with obvious disdain.

A few months after Rockefeller died, the Kingdom of Saudi Arabia struck oil. That single event did more to rewrite the Middle East balance of power for the next hundred years than anything else.

"It would still be an uninhabitable desert filled with warring tribes of Arab chieftains," continued Jack, answering his question. "Nothing like a few trillion dollars to jump-start an economy."

He shared a pointed nod with his buddies, no explanation needed. Decades of endless wars dampened the patriotic fervor they felt at 9/11. That, along with a mistrust of those in power, drove them to their pact to leave the service.

"Right. And a century of war that gave rise to the military-industrial complex didn't hurt either," chirped Archer.

The three Iraq vets knew better than most what this all meant.

"I feel like politicians and unelected bureaucrats are lurching our Nation into repeated global conflicts to establish a new order in the world. One that doesn't include the freedom we and our ancestors bled and died to secure," Jack intoned, his rigid frame reacting to years of pent-up anger.

"Well, for now, we rest," Sykes said. "We've had enough drama for a while. Let's forget politics and enjoy ourselves. Ethan will sort this out."

The team grabbed their bags and started for the aft deck to disembark. A lovely young woman greeted them, introducing herself as Aisha.

"Good morning, gentlemen," she said in heavily accented English. "Welcome to Sindalah, the jewel of the Red Sea. We have your quarters ready and look forward to your visit."

She led them down a pier, covered by a massive, cantilevered awning that extended over the water. Shade was the only natural feature this stunning island oasis lacked. The resort had plenty of open-air and covered shelters. But even so, in the first light of morning, the heat pressed down like a summer furnace.

All three men let out a sigh of relief as chilled air greeted them upon entering the hotel lobby. They walked up to check in, where a wall-mounted TV was broadcasting an American news station.

"A shootout erupted at the Met earlier this evening that has authorities baffled," a news anchor reported.

Sykes heard the word "Met" and swiveled to watch the screens.

"Cell phone footage shows four men in tuxedos running through an Egyptian-themed playground after hearing what one witness described as suppressed gunfire."

The whole team was now glued to the bank of TVs.

"Monica reports directly from the scene. Monica."

"We are live from 5th Avenue, where retired Marine Joe Campbell was walking his dog this evening. Joe, what did you see?"

The screen switched to a burly, mid-forties New Yorker on one side, while the cell phone footage he'd captured streamed on the other two-thirds of the box. Though the eight-second loop was grainy and zoomed in, the images were clear enough.

"I heard suppressed 9mm gunfire coming from the trees over there. I'd know that sound anywhere. I pulled out my phone and saw four men racing through the playground toward the public restroom. They disappeared behind it, and I lost them," he said.

"Police have shut down five blocks surrounding the museum for the past few hours, trying to identify the shooters," the reporter continued. "Hundreds of guests attending an academic lecture by NYU Professor Dr. Ethan Stone are being interviewed. But strangely, initial reports indicate the Met's entire security system was infected with a fast-acting computer virus. No camera footage from the Museum or surrounding Central Park cameras is available, and no guests appear to have seen anything."

The team looked at each other as Sykes sent Ethan a message: "Team secure. Caught the news. Funny story about the Met."

"Let's get to our rooms," Sykes instructed as he slid the phone into his pocket.

Aisha handed each member a key to their suite and walked them through the expansive lobby.

Deep in thought, Sykes shook his head. This was supposed to be an easy trip. A getaway, even. Not an ISIS raid in Kurdistan. Not a papyrus heist in Marrakesh. They were taking pictures of a dune, for goodness' sake.

As a master at operational security and situational awareness, Sykes deduced, something was seriously off. Sitting blind in a thousand-dollar-a-night resort wasn't to his liking. But Ethan had never let them down, and Sykes refused to believe he would start now.

Sykes rubbed at his jaw and turned to the other two men. "Get settled and meet me in my room by 0900. Hopefully, I will have Ethan by then, and we can figure out what is happening and, more importantly, who is after us," Sykes said to his team.

Sykes entered the room with his brain in overdrive. The past few hours had disrupted his tightly structured plans. These were not coincidences. Issues are not random; all actions have causes and effects. He didn't have any answers yet. He needed intel.

Not one to sit and stew, he decided to walk around. He left his first-floor suite and headed back towards the lobby. A gorgeous library to the left of the check-in desk caught his eye. Locked behind keycard access, he scanned himself in and looked around. An octagonal room lined with floor-to-ceiling books, elegant downlighting illuminating various sections of Islamic texts.

"This library is full of religious books," Sykes said, pulling a Quran gently from its perch, the black leather with gold Arabic script soft against his weathered hands. "You'd never see this at a resort back in the states."

Returning the Quran, he moved towards the exit, coming face-to-face with a single shelf marked "Geography of Arabia." A cloth-bound volume, deep red with gilt inlay on the spine leaped out at him. The title was stamped in black: *The Gold Mines of Midian and Ruined Midianite Cities* by Sir Richard F. Burton.

He slid it from the shelf. The cover gave off a faint, dry scent of old bindings. He opened it carefully, the soft crack of a page turning echoed in the silent library. An old foldout map slipped onto the table, its paper thin and fragile, like it might easily tear.

Sykes leaned over it, pulse quickening. The map marked the Gulf of Aqaba, the Sinai, and—there—Midian. Palms, mountains, traces of a lost settlement.

Curious, he pulled out his phone, dropping Google Maps beside the century-old sketch. The coordinates lined up with a modern excavation: The Line, Saudi Arabia's futuristic mega-project. Ancient Midian and tomorrow's smart city sharing the same desert floor.

He swallowed hard. The name Midian wasn't just history. Long-forgotten stories crystallized in his mind, arresting his attention. Moses fleeing Egypt, Jethro's well, the prophet's mountain, millions huddled around as fire consumed the peak. The overlap of a distant childhood, a discarded legend, a map, and an unexplored desert ignited something in him.

He snapped the book shut and stepped into the lobby. Aisha, the concierge, noticed the map in his hand.

"Do you recognize this place?" he asked, pointing.

"Of course," she said with a smile. "Al-Bad. A well where Moses is said to have met his wife. The nearby caves are called Jethro's home. And that mountain—" she tapped the page "—we call it Jabal Mūsā. You'd know him as Moses. His mountain is a remarkable place."

His mountain? The flickering ember flamed into a raging fire burning in his belly. He must visit these places.

"You mentioned it was a popular excursion. Could I go and see it?"

"Yes. We have a private tour guide available for our guests who would be happy to take you. Hamid is a tenth-generation Midianite who grew up in the region. You will love the trip to the mountain."

"When can we go?" Sykes asked.

"We recommend the morning before it gets too hot. I can call Hamid and have him set up the trip immediately."

"Perfect. There will be three of us."

Within the hour, he was pounding on his teammates' doors, clutching the book like treasure.

"Guys—get dressed. We're going to Mount Sinai."

14

"Sorry, I'm late for our meeting. I got caught up in…"

Sadie's trembling, raspy voice cut Ethan off. "I don't know where you are, but there was complete chaos tonight after your lecture. Nobody can figure it out. But I know you're involved," she heaved breathlessly into the phone. "The cops had me in a room, peppering me with questions about you."

"What? Why?"

"Tourists in gallery 115 said they saw you talking to some fashion model in front of the Hatshepsut statues," Sadie replied with a twinge of jealousy.

Ethan looked at Regus and thought, yeah, that's about right.

"And the cops came to me asking if I knew you. I fumbled the answer for some dumbass reason, so I got put on the hot seat for almost an hour." Sadie's voice rose as her words merged into a single phrase.

"They said others saw you and the girl burst through an emergency exit in the Temple room. But ain't nobody got a copy of any footage from the cameras, some computer viruses or somfin. My boss is furious with me. 'E thinks I got a 'fing' for you, said I 'ad somefin to do with the missing footage 'e did."

Sadie's rough London roots always leaked through under duress.

"Like I bloody know 'ow to screw wiv a security system."

Ethan felt terrible for Sadie. Her job was her life; he could never forgive himself if he messed that up.

"Sadie, I'm sorry you are in a bind," Ethan said. "But you have to know I didn't do anything. Four men came after me, and I had to run. I made it out to the Park and got away."

"I know."

"You do?" Ethan asked.

"Yeah, well, there's something I didn't want to tell the cops," she replied without thinking, her voice softening. The carefully crafted American accent she deployed for work had returned.

"I'm glad you're safe," she said.

"I'm sorry we missed each other," Ethan replied, with too much emotion for the present company. He looked up at Regus, who had turned away and was pretending to scan relics on the shelf behind him.

"What didn't you tell them?"

"Well," Sadie paused, composing herself and debating her following words. She never made good choices when it came to Ethan. And hiding information from the police when they already suspected her was a horrible idea.

"When the alarm sounded outside my backstage door, I walked out to see what had happened. The commotion had already died down, so I went to Phil in security to see if he could find the cause. He pulled footage from the Temple room, and we watched you and the woman from the Times race through the room and out the security doors. One of the men chasing you pulled out his phone and made a call. When he did, I saw a small piece of paper slip from his jacket. I didn't think much of it. That is, until the cops finished with me, and I discovered all the footage we had just seen was mysteriously missing."

"Did you manage to save anything?" Ethan asked. "The men

chasing me, I need to know who they are."

"That's the thing," Sadie replied. "We didn't export any footage before it was mysteriously wiped. But I did find the paper that fell out."

"Sadie, you're brilliant! What was it?" Ethan asked.

"Some crumpled business card for a non-profit. It had a strange name with an address in Reston, Virginia."

"Reston?" Ethan asked.

"That mean anything to you?"

"Maybe, hold on." He put Sadie on mute.

"Regus, do you remember the name of the non-profit that supplied my unit with night vision gear?"

Regus reluctantly turned back, thinking.

"It was something funky. Latin, I think," she said. "Had to do with angels."

"You have to be kidding me," Ethan muttered, unmuting Sadie. "Is the name of the organization Angelorum Praeditus?"

"Yes! How did you know that?"

"Childhood trauma," Ethan replied. "Sadie, you have been remarkable once again. Thank you."

Turning away from Regus, he quietly said, "I'm gonna have to pass on drinks tonight."

"You think?" Sadie replied, not thrilled with him. But she was still a considerate human. So, she asked, "That Times woman, okay?"

Ethan could feel Regus glaring at the back of his head.

"She's fine."

A heavy silence fell over the line.

"Okay then. If the cops return, I won't cover for you."

"You shouldn't," he said. "Let me know if I can do anything for you at work."

"Try not being you next time. It'll make both our lives easier," and she hung up.

"Who's Sadie?" Regus asked the second he pulled the phone from his ear.

Ethan turned around. Her tussled auburn hair fluttered in the slight breeze from the AC vents.

"Stage manager at the Met."

He always seemed to find himself in uncomfortable situations with women. He'd made it this far without settling down, and these moments usually reinforced his decision. But tonight felt different. He didn't mind her apparent jealousy. He liked it.

"She found a clue about who was after us," he said.

"You mean you," Regus replied. "Remember? I am simply an accessory to recklessness."

Ethan held his tongue.

"How'd you know the name of the company?" Regus asked, curiosity overriding the shamefully juvenile feelings she was currently having. "You know Latin?"

"I do. I was required to learn as I grew up. My father liked to say, 'All roads lead to Rome, and Roman roads were built with stone. So, all Stones read Latin.' It was stupid humor, but our teacher was no joke. She had us reading the classics by the time we were ten years old. I'm surprised you didn't already know that about my family."

"Yeah, well, some things don't make it online. But how did you know the name?"

"That is a bit of a story," he said.

"I'm currently trapped in your basement," Regus said. "So, I have time."

Ethan thought he heard a hint of sarcasm. Or was that disdain? He wasn't sure. But he knew he wanted to share part of his life he'd never discussed.

Ethan leaned back. "Well, it starts with my great-grandfather. Otto von König, Austria, 1880. He was an engineer—brilliant, stubborn. Obsessed with weapons and the myths that justified them. Roman history, gods, all of it. He built a prototype cannon he thought would change warfare. Showed it to the Emperor himself. Big mistake."

Regus raised a brow. "How so?"

"The Emperor was in bed with Krupp, the weapons giant. They claimed Otto's design was a rip-off, then stole his designs for themselves, and turned it into Big Bertha. You've heard of it?"

Regus nodded slowly. Ethan pressed on.

"Otto realized he was about to be forced into service—or worse. So, he bolted. Midnight trains across the Alps, ended up in England, changed his name to Stone. Reinvented himself while Europe was tearing itself apart."

He paused to make a coffee, the hiss of the machine filling the silence. "He called his design Zadkiel. Some Kabbalistic angel with a sword—supposedly stopped Abraham from knifing his kid."

"You mean Isaac?" Regus replied.

"Yeah... didn't take you for a bible reader."

"I double majored in Journalism and Philosophy of Religion at Columbia."

"I won't hold that against you," Ethan smirked. He continued.

"Well, my great-grandfather thought he was building a divine weapon to save humanity from itself. An ironic notion coded into the DNA of my family became a fantasy that has haunted my line ever since."

Regus leaned forward, hooked despite herself. "So Fortis...?"

"Exactly. My grandfather kept the myth alive. Latin names, angel talk, destiny. By the time it reached my father, the company wasn't just an arms manufacturer—it was practically a religion. And he expected me to be its next high priest."

Something flickered in Ethan's eyes—pain, maybe regret. He broke it with a forced grin. "But I called it 'AP.' Angelorum Praeditus, Latin for 'Angel of Mercy' or Zadkiel. My way of mocking his sermons about destiny. Drove him crazy."

Regus laughed, then stopped when Ethan's face tightened.

He went still, staring at nothing for a moment. Ethan was lost in thought, trying to piece together the fractured pieces of his childhood…

Tonight, he learned his father had been protecting him in Iraq by sending anonymous lifesaving defense gear to his squad.

That was so AP.

He was also standing on his trust fund, surrounded by his father's wealth. As a young man, he dared his father to disown him. Never happened. So, when he returned to civilian life, $20 million was sitting in his name plus company stock. He finally started using funds on the self-imposed condition that he would only invest them in something truly valuable, not in war or personal enrichment. Hence, the tiny apartment but a massive office. He held this line religiously for years. The yacht, however, was on the bubble.

"I know he's behind tonight," he continued. "He never forgave me for leaving. I guess I didn't want to believe he'd actually try to kill me." His voice cracked, and for once he looked less like a commander and more like a son who'd run out of answers.

Regus's chest tightened. This man was vulnerable and wounded. He wasn't all ego and tweed. In her pain, she wanted him to be the bad guy and make him pay if she ever got her moment. But sitting in his office in the wee hours of the morning, sipping on designer coffee, she saw something very different. She thought of her own father—gone, but always present. Ethan had never had that. In this moment, she realized Ethan was an orphan.

She touched his shoulder gently. "What should we do next?"

He blinked, trying to gather himself. For the first time in his life, words failed him. "I… I don't know."

"Then let me suggest something," Regus said softly. "You need to talk to your father."

15

Another spasm wracked Ethan's father. Gripping the porcelain sink, his knuckles white, crimson blood splattered onto the white enamel until the fit passed. Washing his face and hands, he noted that the episodes were more frequent.

In the living room, he pulled out his favorite vinyl: Brahms' *Ein Deutsches Requiem*, Opus 45. He moved the tonearm to the precise spot, 29 min 12 seconds in, and gently placed the stylus in the well-worn groove. He sank into a comfortable armchair, closed his eyes, and centered his breathing. A brilliant baritone voice swept him away with Psalm 39:4 in German. *"LORD, make me to know mine end, and the measure of my days, what it is; that I may know how frail I am."*

Today, he launched an open war in the fight to save his company. The board thought him mad for even imagining Ethan at Fortis. An impossibility, they called it—like chasing perpetual motion or turning lead to gold. But having Ethan would change the calculus. It was a maneuver none of his combatants would expect.

However, he'd done everything he could to get his son to the table and nothing had worked. He must go it alone.

None of his board allies had any idea of the lengths he had gone to keep Ethan safe.

Of course, they knew about the money—they always followed the money—but they didn't see the rest of the story.

Memories rose unbidden. The dim chamber in Baghdad, his breath hot behind a ski mask as the Butcher of Baghdad whispered the Shahada—seconds before the trapdoor snapped and the body dropped.

The frantic crowds as Moammar Gadhafi bled out from the wound given to him with his golden pistol. He remembered the surge of adrenaline coursing through his body as he watched the Hellfire missile rip through Qasem Soleimani's armored car. His unique contribution to the strike was his RX9 warhead, dubbed the "Flying Ginsu" by the CIA. It didn't detonate when it hit the roof; instead, scores of tightly packed metal blades deployed, ripping through steel and bone. He could still hear the metallic shriek.

He wasn't immune to the darkness that invaded his soul after those missions. The constant weight of it pressed down on his mind. But he knew it was either them or thousands, maybe millions of innocents. His job, his role, was that of an angel of mercy to those who were powerless and oppressed. And to arm leaders with the tools needed to deliver justice to the people. Or so he told himself.

A voice disrupted his reminiscences.

"Sir, the heli will be here in ninety minutes."

"Thank you, Pendleton," he said. "I will be ready."

16

"You have no idea what you're saying," Ethan barked. "I will never speak to him again!"

Regus knew how to deal with upset military men whose pain was hidden beneath a mixture of bravado and courage.

"I know it seems extreme," she replied. "But there has to be an explanation for tonight. It makes no sense that your father sent a hit squad to kill you after spending years protecting you."

"That's what I can't understand," Ethan replied in a calmer tone. "The one thing I know about my father is that he never makes a mistake. He masters reading a situation and acting in his best interest."

"And it appears his interests are aligned with keeping you alive and well-resourced," Regus added, looking around the unbelievable office for real now.

"Precisely," Ethan said. "So why the hit?"

"You should ask him," she said, bracing for another outburst that never came.

Ethan breathed slowly and stared at her.

"It's been twenty-five years, Regus. I don't even know how to get in contact with him. I can't imagine making that phone call, even if I knew the number."

Regus's eyes moistened as her father's last labored words rang in her ears. "Never forget, my little queen. You are loved, and love is eternal."

"I'm not suggesting you call him," she said. "I think you should go to his office and speak face-to-face."

Ethan said nothing. Words were clay on his tongue, heavy and shapeless. His gaze drifted to a jar of mushroom fragments—mute fossils of psychedelic decay—and desperation closed around him like a fist.

The dark came rushing back, unbidden.

White Victorian brick, veined with ivy that climbed like a malignancy, choking the house from its lungs outward.

A lithograph above the mantel, fractured in its frame, tilting like a crown that knew it had already fallen.

Ash smeared the hearth, gray as bone dust, as if the fire itself had died screaming.

His mother's sobs fell from the upper rooms, not sounds but waterfalls of grief, cascading endlessly through the hallways.

And beneath them, deeper, the roar—his father's rage, not a voice but a storm splitting the timbers of the study.

Fortis men fled through the corridors like shadows unfastened, retreating from the collision of king and heir, from a throne that had never been built to hold them both.

And Ethan, boy and man at once, could only stand in the wreckage caused by his father and grandfather, drowning in the memory's tide.

The years of carnage, death, and medicating had led him here, staring down a decision he swore he'd already made.

Never again, he said, going off to war. The deployments were over, but he was still fractured. Was this an answer? Was it time to put the pieces back together?

"What if you're wrong and he is trying to kill me?" he asked Regus, reemerging from the pre-teen trauma.

"Then he'll never see this coming," she replied.

She was right. This was not a move he'd ever made, and he doubted his father would have gamed this out, either. The thing you most desperately need will be found where you least want to look...

"Okay," Ethan said, more to himself than anyone. He pulled out his phone and began to scroll.

Regus stood there, a few inches from him, trying not to do the impulsive thing her heart pressed her to do.

"Okay, what?" Regus asked, tucking the unruly strand of hair back behind her ear.

"What's your birthday?" Ethan asked.

"November 23. Why?"

"You don't think I'm doing this alone, do you?" he said, locking his phone and looking up at her. His steely resolve and clear thinking had returned.

"Doing what?"

"You're right," Ethan said. "It's time I faced the darkness in my family. I'm the fourth generation of men who have profited from a hundred years of global conflict. I'm tired of running from my roots."

Regus's impulses were near the breaking point. She needed to back away.

"I booked two tickets for us on the next flight out of JFK. We're going to London."

"Me?" She exclaimed. "You want me to come with you?"

"I do," Ethan said. "You probably know more about my family than I do now. My father is up to something; that much is for sure. And if he's not trying to kill me, which would be amazing, then he has another angle. And it probably has something to do with his company. It's the only thing he's ever loved."

Regus desperately sought a rational footing.

Ethan turned and walked over to his desk, edging her off the emotional precipice she was on.

She exhaled, realizing she hadn't been breathing.

"But first, I need to take you shopping. That dress is way too thrilling to crash my father's company boardroom. And I'm reasonably sure the TSA won't let you through security with bare feet."

17

The night was heavy with stale air, which made the absence of a sea breeze or lapping waves even more pronounced. Sayyid had packed up his .50 cal, cleaned up the wreckage, and made the 80-mile drive from Aten to a marina in Safaga. Rarely was the shoreline so calm.

He spied the meager office, slipping his Beretta 92FS with a titanium suppressor from his shoulder holster. A single guard was manning the air-conditioned space. Walking up, he rapped the butt of his 9mm on the door, waking him. Bewildered, the guard stumbled for his radio before two quick shots ripped through his forehead and chest. It was so much simpler to eliminate the human element.

Sayyid reached through the shattered window, opened the door, and, working quickly at the terminal, brought up the guest manifest in moments. Now, who were his targets?

Over three dozen vessels had docked in the past three nights. Scanning for American-sounding names, he trimmed the list to two dozen vessels.

Next, he searched for "Ethan" and then "Fortis" to no avail.

He needed more to go on. A month at the dig site, and the only trail he had was Ethan's frantic requests. With all the high-tech data available to them, it infuriated his leader that Ethan was off the digital grid. Nobody is. Not these days. He must be impossibly lucky or amazingly disciplined with his communications. Nobody is dark on the internet these days. But Ethan Stone was. And everyone connected to him.

Even ISIS in the hills outside Mosul lit up louder. How did Ethan do it?

Sayyid didn't know what else to search for. This task seemed impossible, so he quietly petitioned Allah for help. "Allah is sufficient for us, and He is the Best Guardian."

Next, he filtered by vessel size and hit a dead end.

As he let out a frustrated sigh, the VHF radio squawked. He glanced up at channel 16, the Coast Guard's universal distress channel.

"Mayday, mayday, mayday. This is MED I. Our vessel is disabled one km off the coast of Safaga. Requesting immediate assistance."

"Allahu Akbar" ("God is greatest"). Sayyid grabbed the radio and replied, "This is the Egyptian Coast Guard responding. Switch to channel 22, over."

He turned the dial a few degrees and picked up MED I.

"MED I to Coast Guard, I'm a downed heli floating in the waters. I lost all power and control of the tail rotor. I am requesting immediate assistance for me and my three-man crew. Over."

Sayyid replied, "This is the Egyptian Coast Guard; how did you go down, over?"

"Repeat, we lost all power and tail rotor controls. We were about to contact TUT11, and our electrical systems went haywire."

Sayyid had heard enough. He quickly searched the file for a vessel named TUT11 and found a match. It was registered to an American company sailing from Miami, Florida. This had to be Ethan. He pulled out his phone and accessed his company database via an encrypted VPN. In a few moments, he had the schematics and electronic specifications.

The GPS navigation controls were neatly listed, and with his backdoor into the Israeli Pegasus spyware system, he located the TUT11 signature from its Navionics marine maps subscription. The vessel was pinging from a tiny island off the coast of Northern Saudi Arabia.

"I got you," he muttered in Arabic.

Now, how to get there?

Sayyid hastily wiped down the security camera system and walked to the docks. He couldn't believe his eyes. Surely Allah was with him. There sat a 15-meter MTI catamaran racing boat, capable of reaching 321 km/h with 1,750 horsepower. The suffocating calm had just become a gift. If the seas held, he could cover the ground in little more than an hour.

He boarded the vessel and connected his device to the boat's electronics. A few seconds later, he started the engines and roared out of Safaga into the pitch-black, glassy night.

18

Hamid had a late-model Rover idling outside the mainland offices. Aisha had rung him, saying three Americans wanted to see Al-bad and Jabal Mūsa. He loved taking Americans to the mountain. Most of them were woefully ignorant about his people's history, and the experience of opening their minds to thousands of years of human stories was his life's greatest joy.

The men were en route on the hotel's ferry, making the short 5km trek from the island to their position. He'd stocked the vehicle with a day's worth of supplies, including water and fitness protein bars. He assumed his guests wouldn't want to leave the car for long, but he needed to be prepared. The Midian region was exceedingly arid and physically demanding, making it difficult to venture out on foot. However, in his experience, most Westerners were soft, so he figured the chances were low that these tourists wanted to see the best parts of the country.

Three large men wearing loose-fitting cotton clothing, American-printed keffiyehs, with a CamelBak and large knives strapped to their hips, disembarked from the Sindalah ferry.

These men looked like warriors, Hamid thought. Probably military. His day just got interesting.

"As-salamu alaikum," he said, gripping their hands with traditional American fervor. "I am Hamid, your guide for the day. But you may need to keep your knives in the car."

The team glanced around at each other.

"American cowboys are not allowed," he said with a commanding smile.

Jack felt a twinge of guilt at the undeclared pistol he had strapped inside his waistband. But he said nothing about it after Sykes instructed them to comply with their guide's order.

"Wa-alaikum as-salam, Hamid," Sykes said. "Thank you for taking us to your ancestral home."

"It is a deep pleasure, my friends. I see you are ready for an adventure?" Hamid glanced again at their knives lying in the back of his car.

"That we are. We want to see a few places, but we'd also like to visit the sites you're not allowed to take American tourists to."

Hamid grinned. He liked this man.

"That I can do, my friend. You will not be disappointed."

"The only thing I ask," Sykes said, "is that we visit these three locations."

He opened the rare maroon book and unfolded the map. Hamid's eyes widened.

"Where did you get this?" he asked.

"From the library at Sindalah," Sykes replied.

Hamid could not believe it. This American had the first print of Sir Richard Burton's *Gold Mines of Midian*. "This book is legendary for my people," he said.

Hamid grew up on stories of a Westerner sneaking into Mecca as a Pathan, tales always tangled with memories of the 1947 Pashtun invasion of Kashmir and the bloody decades of conflict that followed. "You know of this man, Burton," Hamid asked. "He's one of the very few non-Muslims known to have made Hajj to Mecca and lived to tell the tale."

"I didn't know that," Sykes replied. "I only discovered this book today, but felt it was an important work."

"It is more than important," Hamid replied. "It's the source of much modern-day myth surrounding the Mountain."

"I look forward to hearing all about it," Sykes said. "Shall we go?"

The four men piled into the Rover, Sykes taking the front seat and Jack grumbling like a teenager over being consigned to the back.

"We have just over an hour's drive with little to see. Unless you enjoy the desert's endless beauty," Hamid said proudly as he turned onto 392 and headed north.

"We are in an area called Ras Alsheikh Hamid, the westernmost point of my country's mainland. You can also see the construction of the Line coming up. I'm sure you've seen the plans at the hotel in Sindalah."

"We have," Jack replied from the back. "What you people can build with all that oil money is unbelievable."

Sykes gave Jack a side-eye for saying, "You people."

"You are correct, Mr. American Warrior!" laughed Hamid. "We have been given many resources and are deploying them here in the north so the world may see what our Kingdom is truly about."

"What about the nearly 20% of your people who live in poverty?" Jack pressed on. "Most are women, children, and men from the non-royal class. Why not spend some of these billions on getting them jobs and increased freedom?"

"Have you no poor in America?" asked Hamid. "We take care of them the best we can."

"Sure you do," Jack said sarcastically. "Your nation is oil-rich but energy poor. Since your economy runs on petrodollars, you sell instead of using them to provide adequate energy to meet domestic demands. I can't imagine the royals suffering through a four-hour electricity brownout in the middle of a 110-degree day with the rest of the people."

An unwrapped protein bar hit Jack in the side of the face. Archer sat beside him, mouthing the words, "Shut up!"

"Well, the NEOM project represents a transformation for our nation. I will take you to some places you will not believe. You will see my friend. You will see."

Whether Hamid was oblivious to the tension or a master host, he didn't seem to take offense.

"Mr. Sykes," he continued, "can you walk me through what you've discovered in your famous book?"

Sykes reached for the book, catching a glimpse of Jack in the rearview mirror struggling with the whole idea of this excursion. Jack wanted to be sleeping, not crammed in the back of the car with a chatty local who sounded like a paid propagandist for one of the most restrictive cultural and religious nations on planet Earth.

Jack's father was a career CIA agent and sent him to a ridiculously pretentious prep school in Virginia that had a lot of Saudi students with royal connections. And he never forgot how those classmates and their families vanished before 9/11. Or how his neighbor died when Building Seven fell. After that, Saudi ties to America never sat right with Jack.

Sykes opened up the 150-year-old map, analyzing it again. "You said you grew up learning about Burton." He cocked his head toward the driver. "What more can you tell me about him?"

"He came to Arabia in 1853, snuck into Mecca and Medina, then wrote a remarkably detailed account of our religious practices. He even gained entrance to the sacred Ka'abah," Hamid replied with a decided note of disgust.

"How did he do that?" Sykes had spent enough time in Iraq and Afghanistan to know that it was no small feat. It was sacrilege for any outsider to step inside the Ka'abah, the holiest place in all of Islam. During Hajj, only believers could enter the city.

"He wrote of this moment in his book *'Personal Narrative of a Pilgrimage to el Medinah and Meccah,'* where he recounts uttering the proper Arabic responses to the shrine guardian who confirmed his genuineness and allowed him in. Had he been exposed as a white European Christian, his life would have ended."

"Remarkable!" Sykes said. "I can see why you were told this story as a child. He must have been proficient in Arabic."

"That he was. As a young man, he mastered Arabic and Hindi. By the end of his life, he was fluent in 40 languages, if you count the various dialects."

"Amazing," Sykes said. This guy reminded him of Ethan.

"He began to learn these things when he enlisted with the British East India Company army in the First Afghan War. Are you familiar with them?" Hamid asked.

"I am. By royal mandate, the East India Company was launched in 1600 to trade with today's India and China. After crushing the Armada, England ruled the seas. The EIC and its vast ships, armies, and riches became Britain's war machine on a scale no nation could match," Sykes said.

"A deadly combination," Hamid replied, pleasantly surprised this American knew anything about the West's long colonialist history of military occupation.

"Military might and economic dominance power the engine of empires."

Sykes knew that Ethan would love this conversation. He wondered if he'd come across Burton in his studies. Hamid continued.

"On top of being a polyglot, Burton was also a fighter. He was nicknamed 'Ruffian Dick' because he got into more hand-to-hand fights than any other British officer."

"The guy sounds like a badass," Archer said from the backseat.

"They don't make Europeans like this anymore," Hamid said.

Archer laughed out loud and looked at Jack, who had been forced to smile at this unexpected insult. Archer pictured someone from the British Royal Air Force whom he had encountered in Iraq. Hamid had no idea how funny his comment was.

"We are nearing Al Bad," Hamid announced. "Mr. Sykes, where do you want to go first?"

"I would like to see whatever these palm trees are," he said, pointing to his map. "And then you can show us Al Bad before we head to the mountain you call Jabal Mūsa."

"Oh, very good! These palm trees mark Wadi Tayyib Al Ism, also known as the Valley of Moses. A beautiful place."

"Moses has a mountain and a valley?" Jack said, half-heartedly, half sarcastically.

"And a well," Hamid said. "Oh, and a father-in-law. He is very famous in these parts."

Archer shrugged as Jack looked at him, shaking his head in disbelief.

Hamid turned left on Fifth, then took another quick left on an unmarked, recently paved road. They wove their way through more desert scape in silence until the expanse of the Gulf of Aqaba opened up before them. Turning right, Hamid maneuvered the team north along a single-lane road cut from the rocky cliff that rose precipitously to their right.

Sykes commented on the dramatic change in topography.

"This is the northern end of the Great Rift Valley, which runs from Mozambique in Africa through Israel's Dead Sea area into the Beqaa Valley in Central Lebanon," Hamid said. "You will soon see the scale of the cliffs and the wadis created from this 7,000-kilometer geological feature."

Before they knew it, they had arrived at the Wadi Tayyib Al Ism parking lot, and Hamid cut off the engine.

"From here, we must go on foot," he said.

The team got out, gazing with awe at dozens of palm trees packed into the sandy lot, nearly obscuring the entrance of a narrow wadi cut through the thousand-foot rock faces.

"We call this the Valley of Moses because it is believed the Yahud came this way after crossing the Red Sea to escape Egypt," Hamid said.

"The Yahud?" Jack asked, reluctantly intrigued by his Saudi host's knowledge of the area.

"The Jews," Hamid said. "You have read the Bible, no?"

"No," Jack said.

"I have," Sykes said. "But you mean to tell me you think the Exodus happened, and Moses came this way with two million exiles?"

"What I think is not important," Hamid replied. "But for thousands of years, my people have kept these stories alive in the places I will show you this day. Your Bible is not the only document that speaks of such things."

Sykes felt a burning again in his belly. He knew he was here to satisfy the strange compulsion he kept to himself. But something told him he'd remember today for a long time.

19

Sayyid was thundering across a glassy sea as dawn broke over the horizon. He'd run the MTI catamaran full throttle the whole way from Safaga. But even with nearly perfect conditions and fortune smiling down, he estimated at least two hours to catch up to his prey. His Leader called to say that Ethan had made the news that confirmed he was in New York, not Egypt. So, his new mission was to intercept whoever Ethan had sent to Aten.

However, the strict order to bring him in alive was lifted in Ethan's absence. At least Sayyid could abandon an abundance of caution; he didn't need to ensure everyone lived. He clung to this consolation while replaying his colossal error.

In haste to cover his tracks and make up for lost time, Sayyid deleted the marina footage without checking if it contained a visual of Ethan's team. Destroying the best lead he ever had on precisely who he was after. He deduced that Ethan had sent a three-man strike team, probably American and former military, about Ethan's age. Sayyid would have done that if his Leader hadn't insisted on a solo mission.

Operational security was essential for the next phase of their plans. But Ethan was a digital ghost, and Sayyid was reeling from his error.

Perhaps Allah would again be merciful and provide another break.

TUT11 had been stationary for almost two hours, and he was nearing its position. Another thirty minutes passed before a small island appeared on the horizon. The Sindalah coastline came into view, bathed in the full morning sun. Decreasing the throttle on his stolen twin-engine racing boat so he wouldn't draw undue attention, Sayyid pulled up to the mouth of the luxury marina. Ahead, a resort ferry turned out of the harbor and into open waters.

Peering at the ferry, Sayyid spotted three well-built men in desert trekking gear on the starboard side. Their backs were to him as they gazed out over the shoreline.

These were not ordinary tourists, his intuition screamed as he analyzed the vessel and the passengers. The driver waved at him as they accidentally made eye contact. Looking away, he cursed his carelessness. He didn't have a face that was quickly forgotten. In desperation, he was getting sloppy. He'd need all his wits to complete this mission.

He pulled into the public slip as the deckhands waved him on. They tied off his boat, and Sayyid killed the engines.

"I am looking for my friends who arrived earlier," he said in Arabic.

"You must speak with the marina manager," a young man replied, pointing down the long dock at an office next to the hotel entrance.

But on Saturday at nine-thirty, this office, unlike most in Saudi Arabia, was closed for the day. So he walked into the hotel lobby, which was also empty, save for the young woman who greeted him in Arabic.

"Good morning, sir, welcome to Sindalah. My name is Aisha. How can I assist you?"

Sayyid could not believe these Saudi women were allowed to present themselves uncovered in public. The Western reforms the Saudi Crown Prince was pushing infuriated him. They were contrary to the Kingdom's Wahhabi religious establishment, which his nation dutifully followed. He was sure that Allah would soon judge the House of Saud.

"I am looking for my friends who arrived earlier today," he said. "We'd planned a day out on the water, and they told me to meet them here."

"Excellent, sir. Will you be staying with us as well?"

"No," he said, frustrated that she was not offering any information. "I said they would meet me here. Can you get them for me?"

"I do not know who they are," she replied more cautiously. "But I am happy to assist you in finding lodging. We have many available suites since we recently opened for..."

"I don't need a room; I need my friends," he roared, his hand unconsciously sliding inside his lightweight jacket.

"My apologies," Aisha replied, trembling.

She remembered the slammed doors, the bruising grip of control in the abusive home she'd escaped after her father and brothers were killed fighting the Houthis in Yemen. She would never mourn their deaths. NEOM had been her chance at freedom without leaving her mother and little sister completely alone. She had lived with religious fanatics for 18 years and could spot one a mile away. Her heart raced, terrified by the man standing before her. But after years of practice, she'd mastered hiding her fear.

"Tell me about your friends, and I will gladly find them for you," she said.

For a moment, Sayyid didn't know what to say. Suddenly, it all came together. Picturing the men from the ferry, he said, "Three large men dressed in desert trekking gear."

"Ah, yes, the Americans," Aisha said as her voice caught. "They are out on an excursion today."

"Where?" growled Sayyid—his frustration mounting as he realized he'd let the men pass without following them.

Aisha didn't want to say anything more. She respected her guests' privacy, and as her thoughts drifted back to the man who had spoken to her that morning, she fought to suppress a smile. Allowing him to take the book was not wise, but she'd done so for a chance to talk with him again.

"I said, where?" and Sayyid took a menacing step towards her, his fingers wrapping around his concealed pistol.

"They are going to see Jabal Mūsa," she said without thinking.

"How?"

"They are driving."

"I saw them on the hotel ferry when I arrived," he said. "Are you sure they are driving?"

"Yes. The ferry transports them to the mainland, where our tour guide awaits."

Sayyid's face contorted with a vile expression as he took one more probing look at her, then hastily walked out of the hotel.

She knew her life had just been spared. Her best course of action was to remain silent. She'd learned that from her father.

Back at his boat, Sayyid stood face-to-face with the young deckhand.

"Have my boat refueled and ready to depart in five minutes," he ordered.

"Sir, your boat is nearly empty, requiring at least 550 liters of fuel," the deckhand stammered, eyes wide.

"And," Sayyid's brows drew together.

"We are awaiting our weekly fuel shipment, which has not yet arrived. I do not know if we have enough."

"Well, find out," Sayyid shouted.

He turned and walked briskly to the hotel lobby. He needed to chart a path to Jabal Mūsa and figure out how he'd intercept the Americans. He'd never been so close. But without a car, this would be challenging. But removing the team would severely restrict their operational capacity. Perhaps he could even use them as bait to draw Ethan in.

Aisha spotted him through the heavily tinted hotel entrance and slipped into the back room. Sayyid returned to the front desk, looking for the tramp he had spoken to earlier to reprimand her for her indecent appearance, but she was nowhere to be found. He did, however, grab a brochure off the desk for a private tour of the Mountain. He reviewed the detailed full-day itinerary. This must be what the men were doing. He rang the bell loudly a few times to summon the woman, but no one came. He turned, found a seat near the library, and began working on his phone, looking at Google Maps

He was familiar with Jabal Mūsa, but it was an enormous area. He couldn't reach the mountain by boat; he needed a car.

He noticed the Port of Aqaba near the mountain had large shipping docks, fuel depots, and services. It was 250 km away, the opposite end of the Gulf, but his boat could quickly cover that ground.

The problem was that the port lay just inside the Jordanian border. He'd have to clear customs and return to Saudi Arabia to reach the mountain. No, he needed a different option.

Just south was a small Saudi city called Haql that appeared to have a public marina where he could rent or steal a vehicle. It was also stationed inside Saudi Arabia along a new road connecting NEOM to the mountain. Perfect.

He needed to get going. Back at the public slip, his boat was being refueled.

"You almost done?" he snapped at the attendant.

"We just ran out of fuel," replied the young man. "We put in almost 250 liters before we…"

"You're finished then," he bellowed.

"Yes, sir. That will be 285 SAR."

Sayyid looked at him and laughed. He had purchased 66 gallons of premium diesel fuel for $76, while Europeans paid four times as much. Serves them right. They'd be a conquered people soon enough, and cheap gas would be their only reward.

20

The four men waded through a trickling stream that spilled from the mouth of the cavernous gorge, where the rock walls parted, revealing a narrow pathway.

"There is a spring here that bubbles up along the path to our destination, approximately 5km up this wadi," Hamid said. "Let us enjoy the hike. It is not too strenuous, and there is abundant shade."

Walking in silence, each man took in the remarkable scenery: small groves of palm trees next to steady trickling springs, light-grey stone walls shooting nearly straight up over a thousand feet, and a crushed, chalky pathway through the imposing sheer rock face.

Hamid relished these moments, watching his guests' jaws slacken as the awe gleamed in their eyes. Americans always thought they knew the world, until moments like this proved otherwise.

It was after ten in the morning, and already, the shade was markedly colder. The group rounded a 180-degree bend, and the wadi abruptly ended, opening into a massive palm grove.

"We have arrived," announced Hamid. "This is the marker on your map, Mr. Sykes. It is sometimes referred to as Elam because it matches the description in *The Antiquities of the Jews*, a renowned historical document written by Flavius Josephus. In the third paragraph of the third book, the author describes a palm grove of 70 trees and twelve water wells. Presumably, one for each of the twelve tribes of Israel. You can see these wells up ahead."

Sykes reached the well first. The concrete rim was weathered but solid, a rough lip against his palms. He picked up a wooden bucket resting on the ledge; its rope was frayed but still holding. Cool air drifted up from the dark shaft, brushing his face as he eased the bucket over the edge. A few meters down, the rope went slack with a splash, and the bucket vanished into black water.

"Can we drink this?" he asked.

"Yes, we must. Water is scarce in this part of Midian, and we need to resupply for our trek back." Hamid nodded.

Sykes drew the rope up and sipped the cold, crisp spring water. His father would be beside himself if he were here. His mind was running wild. Could this be a well that Moses had drunk from?

Jack didn't know what to think. He had never cared a day in his life for religion. And some broken-down oasis in this godforsaken land wasn't about to convince him to come to Jesus. But he was thirsty.

Jack asked his team leader for a drink and shared it with him.

"So, are there seventy palm trees like this Josephus fellow says?" Jack asked as he filled his CamelBak.

"Oh no, there are many more than that," Hamid replied. "But nearly two thousand years have passed since that text was written. One can imagine that more trees have grown since then."

"But wells don't just appear over time, do they?" stated Archer. "And there are clearly twelve here, just as he said."

Jack grunted, unable to criticize this excursion any further.

"If you have gotten your water, we should head back. There are many more things to see today," Hamid said.

The three men agreed and quickly retraced their steps back to the Rover.

Getting in, Sykes said, "I would like to see Al Bad now. Please take us to the places you think we should visit."

"Excellent, Mr. Sykes," Hamid replied. "We have a short drive through the hills and two important stops before we head towards the mountain."

As Hamid turned the car around, Sykes heard a faint but deep rumbling outside his open window. It sounded like a jet. He looked up and saw a bright orange racing boat streak into view. It was throwing a rooster tail of water fifty feet in the air. It had to be moving at more than 180 miles an hour. Archer saw it, too.

"Wow! That's an MTI Catamaran. One of the fastest racing boats in the world. It probably costs over a million dollars. Who is driving that thing?" Archer exclaimed.

"Some rich Saudi whose mother's brother's cousin on the third side twice removed was once a side-chick for a royal," Jack intoned.

Sykes was too immersed in a memory he couldn't place to listen to Jack's rude comment. He knew that boat, but from where?

Hamid, however, had heard it and was growing weary of his backseat whiner. But he reminded himself that he was a professional, and hospitality was more critical in his culture than correcting a fool. So, he just drove, taking a left on 8647, with signs marking "Al Bad— 25 km." Arriving in just under twenty minutes, Hamid headed for the archaeological site in the town center. Pulling in, he announced their arrival with short instructions.

"Here we are at the home of the Prophet Shuaib, you call him Jethro. Up ahead are his caves. He is a mighty Prophet in the Quran, and these are his dwellings. Your Holy Book speaks of this same righteous man whose daughter was rescued by Moses at a nearby well. So, Shuaib took the Semite wanderer in and eventually gave him his daughter as a wife."

"We're visiting Moses's in-laws right now," sniped an incredulous Jack, now understanding Hamid's comment from earlier.

"Should you care to, yes. The primary cave at the end of those long steps is his home. You are welcome to get out; I will wait in the car," remarked Hamid, the first touch of frustration with Jack evident in his voice.

Sykes and Archer immediately exited, and Jack had no choice but to join them. He was not going to spend one-on-one time with the insufferable Saudi, and he figured the feeling was mutual.

The site had been recently upgraded to include basic tourist amenities, such as warning signs and dedicated walkways.

They ascended a light-grey stone stairway fashioned to help visitors access the rough-hewn hole in the wall high up on a ridge. To the left of the hole was a series of building facades cut from the red rock face. They reminded Sykes of the famous Nabatean ruins at Petra, some 130 miles to the north. But the primitive carvings he was now looking at were nowhere close to Petra's scale and detail.

Jack was thankful they had reached the dark cave as the late-morning sun approached its zenith. The three men looked around the rather large, dimly lit area. It was decidedly unremarkable.

"There's nothing here," Jack said. "I feel like I'm visiting one of those random U.S. roadside attractions, like 'The World's Biggest Ball of Twine' or something. Why are they trying to get people to think this is important?"

"Because they value their traditions and religion," Archer replied, clearly annoyed by Jack's attitude today. "Something you'd do well to learn from."

"Why should I learn anything from old books that assert a bunch of unverifiable nonsense?" Jack clapped back.

"So, nothing is real unless you can verify it," Sykes said, joining the fray.

"Exactly," Jack said. "The world is filled with superstitious fanatics who demand you accept their version of reality. But reason creates reality, not faith."

"Is everything you can't explain with your reason superstition?" Sykes asked.

"Of course," Jack exclaimed. "Science explains the world, not religion. Even Einstein knew everything was relative. If it's good enough for him, it's good enough for me."

"I'm glad to hear you accept Einstein," Sykes said. "But you missed the most essential part of his Special Theory of Relativity. He postulated that everything in the world wasn't just relative but relative to something. He thought you could only make sense of natural phenomena if they were all referencing a single unchangeable constant. His remarkable insight and the math it produced undid 300 years of Newtonian certainty that the space between objects was empty. Instead, he discovered that space itself is filled with matter— matter that can be manipulated to unleash unimaginable quantities of energy. With a single equation, $E = mc^2$, he opened the door to nuclear chain reactions: energy equals mass multiplied by the speed of light, squared.

"After showing the world that energy and mass are interchangeable, it only took a few decades of studying $E = mc^2$ before the atomic bomb was created. Hence, our current global state of war hangs over us under the specter of weapons of mass destruction. All because the natural world is not random, relative truth, but predictable actions and reactions dependent on an immovable constant, light."

The three men stood in relative darkness for a few moments, thinking.

"You spend too much time with Ethan," remarked Archer.

"For real," Jack said. "What does that have to do with this Arabian tourist trap and our forced-family-fun outing to some mountain?"

"My point is that truth is not relative to individual opinions but to an absolute we all must discover. I don't presume to know what that absolute is or whether Einstein's scientific discovery of an absolute maps into the world of morals, ethics, and religion. But my ability to reason through a thing does not explain the world as it is, only the world I perceive."

"That's deep, man," Jack said.

"This is why I wanted us to explore today. When I found this book, something in my gut said it was important. Like, there would be a truth in it that I didn't comprehend, but would prove exceedingly useful for our mission with Ethan and our current situation. As you may recall, we are still stuck in Saudi Arabia, with unknown entities pursuing us, and we need answers. Since we only learn in relation to what we already know, and I don't know anything about our current situation, I wanted to try something new."

Jack and Archer just stood there, looking at Sykes. Neither friend had seen this philosophical side in the twenty years they'd known each other. Talk about learning something new.

"We have much more to see, and the morning is now spent," Sykes continued. "Let's get going. And Jack, why don't you lay off the snark with Hamid? We are his guests, and he is a wonderful guide. Look past your worldview for once and see what else is out there."

"Copy that, boss," Jack said.

21

Madison Avenue, New York City

Regus had not been shy about purchasing nice things. Ethan told her to get whatever she needed and brought her to expensive stores. He had to be loaded, so what was a few thousand on some travel clothes? He didn't bat an eye when she picked out a fifteen-hundred-dollar Tumi carry-on to store her five thousand dollars' worth of Vuori loungewear, three pairs of Chloé flats and chunky wedge heels, and, of course, a few intelligent Gucci outfits to round out the European excursion wardrobe.

But truth be told, she had intentionally pushed the limits, testing to see if Ethan would rein her in. She had expected he would, but he hadn't. So, they were even now.

However, she caught herself grinning more than once. She hadn't expected how much she liked being around him. Ethan chuckled at her wisecracks. He praised her choices.

He even shook his head at specific dresses as he said, "A little risqué for where we're going."

Shopping had never felt this fun. Indeed, not in the house she grew up in, full of stern military men. Where had he learned to be so thoughtful?

"We must get to the airport." Ethan grabbed her final bag from the cashier. "Our flight leaves soon."

"Don't you need to pack something?" she asked, realizing they'd only stopped at women's clothing stores since arriving on Madison Avenue.

"No. I have a go bag at the airport," Ethan replied.

"A what?"

"A bag fully packed for moments like this," he said.

"And it's at the airport?" Regus didn't get it.

"I have a friend who runs the Baggage Storage, and he makes sure I'm always prepared for an emergency," Ethan said, hailing a cab.

Regus was in way over her head. She had admitted to herself she'd liked Ethan when he showed his vulnerable side. But she was smitten now to see it merged with preparedness, competency, and wealth. Yet she was determined to keep these feelings to herself.

Regus's pulse kicked up. She'd liked Ethan's flashes of vulnerability before, but watching him pair that softness with competence—and the kind of quiet wealth that spoke for itself—left her dizzy. She pressed the feeling down hard, tucking it where he couldn't see. Despite all Ethan's desirable qualities, she had a massive concern: Was he safe?

That vein of self-destruction running through everything he did had her feeling twitchy. She was sure it would get her in trouble if she stayed too close. That Sadie person sounded like someone who'd know the story behind the cracks. Maybe they should have lunch when she returned to New York?

She'd conquered her career but not her loneliness. After ten years buried in research, the unknown thrilled her. And London was calling.

They pulled into JFK and got out. As a cabbie helped Regus unload her things, a gentleman with a large duffel bag met Ethan at the entrance. She wheeled the Tumi forward, matching Ethan's stride.

Nightmares of her father's casket and her brother's lifeless stare still haunted her, stitched together with years of research that painted the Stones as monsters. Yet here she was, about to board a plane with Ethan, the enemy in flesh and blood. When he pressed a ticket into her palm, doubt flickered—had she been wrong all along?

"We're in Terminal 4 Concourse B. If you're not pre-checked, I'll accompany you through security."

"Well, I have given my biometrics to the government, so I'm all good," she replied with a half-smile.

They made it to the gate just as Zone One was announced. She looked at her ticket and saw that Ethan had gotten them Delta One lay-flat seats to London.

When they arrived at their seats, Ethan offered her the window, and she slipped into the spacious compartment as he stowed her bag. An elegant stewardess brought them two glasses of Champagne.

I could get used to this.

Ethan offered a toast.

"To find the things we didn't know we needed because we've never been courageous enough to look past our pain." He clinked his glass with hers.

My goodness, a poet, too?

Sipping in silence, she stopped worrying about what was ahead. And yesterday felt like a lifetime ago.

For some reason, she trusted Ethan now. Perhaps it was exhaustion from being up all night.

The plane taxied out to the runway. She watched the New York skyline retreat beneath her. Ethan got her a pillow and blanket before pushing her seat controls. She lay down, closed her eyes, and fell into a deep sleep.

22

Ethan's father walked out of his room in a navy double-breasted tailored suit from Savile Row. The special board meeting with opposing counsel in his corporate St. James's Park headquarters was not your everyday occurrence. So he decided to forgo his usual red raw silk power tie and don a light blue pinstripe shirt with a Dark Blue Grenadine tie. He felt different today, and needed to present himself accordingly.

Pendleton let himself into the penthouse apartment. Three decades with Sir Stone had taught him to expect anything, but today promised a storm even a world-renowned CEO and master tactician couldn't fully contain.

"Sir, the heli is ready for you, and the car has arrived," he said.

The helicopter would whisk him to his technology division in Kingston upon Hull for a quick stop. Then, back to London, where he'd initiate his response to an expected Qatari bid to acquire the company his grandfather founded.

In the thirty years he guided Fortis Defense, he'd only been in a position of weakness once. That disastrous quarter was coming back to haunt him now. He knew the tangled web of Arab money that rescued his company in 2008 would lay a trap for him one day.

He maintained his carefully poised, carved-from-stone expression while the pulse at his temple throbbed and his heart hammered. After fifteen years of waiting, Kingston upon Hull—his knight hiding in the wings—was stepping onto the board. In this high-stakes corporate chess match.

He'd invested heavily in Artificial Intelligence in 2016, answering to no one but himself. The Board had scoffed that AI was a fool's errand and millions spent would be millions wasted.

But Fortis was his company.

So, he reformed an out-of-the-way munitions manufacturing location into a secret Artificial Intelligence R&D division, where he began development on a top-secret technology that tracked an individual's digital signature. He had the social media data for all major platforms, and much more: fiat and crypto transaction data, global security camera footage for every nation except China and its more closely held allies, voter files for more than fifty nations, Google, Microsoft, and Verizon email, cloud storage data, a large chunk of India's new Aadhaar digital ID profiles, public record real estate and business filings, and teraflops of SWIFT transactions going back to 1992 when SWIFT's Interbank File Transfer went live.

He had it all.

But after four years of software development and data capture, Ethan's father hit a technical impasse. The GPUs he used were no longer powerful enough to run his intensely complex computational models. So, he contacted the South Koreans who had developed Neural Processing Units (NPU) to run their intelligence and defense systems. Consuming a fraction of the energy of leading GPUs, and exponentially faster, these were the breakthrough he was looking for.

A brilliant series of investments and acquisitions in Asia secured him a secret minority stake in the company manufacturing these units. He took a tactic from the Chinese and "borrowed" a chip or two to reverse engineer. Kingston upon Hull was his NPU black-site manufacturing plant, putting him back in the driver's seat as the dominant party in AI.

Very few people understood what was truly going on with Artificial Intelligence, and who was involved. This included the public and many governments, his own being no exception. But he was quietly sitting atop this revolutionary new technology, and today the first hint would have to be dropped. Enough to regain the upper hand but not enough to expose everything. Yet, without Ethan, he knew his grand plan was fatally flawed. He needed his son.

Pendleton emerged from the hallway and grabbed his briefcase.

"Ready, Sir?"

"Have you let Hull know we will be arriving shortly?"

"They will be ready," Pendleton said.

From his 65th-floor Shard apartment, the elevator plummeted 750 feet in 30 seconds. This was a snail's pace compared to the Taipei tower in Taiwan, which moved at 45 mph and would have reduced his travel time by two-thirds. That was twenty seconds of his life he'd never get back. Maybe it was time to relocate?

The car took him to the heliport, where his Sikorsky S-76 VIP edition lurched into the hazy London morning, heading north to Kingston upon Hull.

Ethan's father always breathed easier when out of London. The city suffocated him. Rampant migrant violence and the unwillingness of local governments to do anything about it caused him great concern. How had things gotten so out of control in his backyard? He'd helped ignite this kind of unrest in the Middle East. Was his strategy now coming home to roost?

The security detail stood on the roof of his NPU black site while his pilot gently touched down. He had demanded soft landings or immediate firing. His days of coming in hot were over. It was luxury or nothing.

"Welcome, sir," said the plant manager. "The observation room is ready for you."

Ethan's father made his way into the belly of the beast.

Manufacturing was always his first love. As a boy, his father had instilled this passion in him, drilling into him that technology and profit margins were for Silicon Valley and Wall Street. The Stones were men of the people, AP guardians, and suppliers of tangible goods that could transform the world.

He passed the photolithography line, ultraviolet light burning intricate circuits into Chinese silicon. For now, Beijing held the supply chain, but his quantum leap in AI had begun. He smiled at that thought.

The observation room was buzzing until he entered. Silence fell like a thick English fog.

"Okay, gentlemen, let's see what you have accomplished." He squared his shoulders and tilted his chin up as his eyes gleamed with conviction. "Today is the day our work comes out of the shadows."

At his terminal, the product lead lit up a wall-to-wall bank of monitors. The center screen had a white background and a Fortis AI logo above the search bar.

"Ready when you are, Sir," the product lead said as his cursor blinked rhythmically in the prompting box.

"You are a savant hacker turned undercover CIA agent embedded in the Latin American narco underworld; using the Fortis overlays from Eastern European crypto deposits as the starting point, show me Colombian cartel members and a safe house in Bogotá who use Ethereum to pay for Chinese fentanyl derivatives and sell finished products to mules running them up through Mexico to the Yuma crossing site in Arizona," Ethan's father said.

The product lead typed in the prompt, and a tiny, semi-translucent angel GIF appeared, gracefully fluttering its wings while the system processed the request. Within moments, vivid images filled the screens. One side of the wall displayed live feeds of networked CCTV cameras, local police mug shots with lists of convictions, and a collage of social postings and profile images organized in a family tree-style infographic. Beneath it, crypto hashes were compiled into a linear, timestamped sparkline graph, similar to a stock market chart. They showed the day, amount, and volume of the transactions. A KML file generated from the system's latitude and longitude coordinates automatically loaded into Google Earth Pro, the animated world map cinematically zooming in on the safe house.

"Give me the route they take to the United States, the average volume of individual traffic every week for the past six months, and which caravans are primarily drugs and which are children."

The screens began to update the map and charts with the new dataset. The room was still deathly quiet.

"Identify the leader and his closest six contacts. Provide me their names, locations, and all transaction data for the past six months, sorted by amount sent and the bank account or digital wallet in which the funds were received."

The left side of the screen was updated with a new array of images, live video feeds, and tabulated transaction data.

"Calculate who is most likely to profit politically from this network and provide me their transaction data for the past six months, along with a 500-word explanation of what motivates them, who they are indebted to, and where they are financially compromised."

The screens were again updated with the new information.

"Use this information to generate a hyperrealistic AI selfie video of them caught in their most compromising situation. Post to all social media using the bot account network."

Within moments, a well-dressed, olive-skinned man was on the screen, talking into his phone from a cafe in Bogotá as a young girl rubbed his back.

"Compile into briefing," Ethan's father said. A laser color printer whirred into action and spat out the thirty-five-page dossier.

"Remarkable. Well done, everyone," Sir Stone said. "This will transform the defense industry as we know it."

Ethan's father stood from his chair and walked out of the room, Pendleton following close behind.

The observation room roared to life with cheers and chatter. History had just been made, but only a traitor would ever speak of it. Ten years of secrets were finally live. What came next was anyone's guess.

But a gambling man would bet on total war.

23

"Let's go see the well," Jack exclaimed upon returning to the vehicle.

Hamid looked at him, searching for any visual sign of sarcasm since he had not detected any audible ones.

"Okay, Mr. American Warrior, we will go. But just a quick stop. We need to get to the mountain and see the Rock along the way," Hamid replied, wondering what had come over his previously rude companion.

The way Hamid said, "The Rock," made Jack think of Dwayne Johnson.

"We've seen plenty of rocks so far," Sykes said. "I think we just head to the well and the mountain."

"You will want to see this Rock," Hamid replied. "It casts a great shadow in a thirsty land. There is magic there you must experience to believe."

Jack cringed at the word magic. But he took Sykes's reprimand seriously. So he stayed quiet and tried to conjure interest in these tourist traps.

"Up ahead is the Al-Sa'idani, or Moses Well," Hamid said as he drove across the street into a residential neighborhood. "This well dates back thousands of years and was the primary water source of the Al Bad oasis during the Islamic period. In Surah 28, Verse 23, the Quran says that Moses came to a well in Midian and met two women. We believe it is this place."

He stopped the car and pointed up a recently paved stone walkway. The three men exited and walked a hundred yards to the large hole in the ground, now protected by a low stone wall.

"These sites continue to be a letdown," Jack said, trying to be positive but finding no merit yet in this adventure. "This is just a big, dry hole."

"Agreed," Archer said. "But the fact that they even exist, and in this order, is super interesting. I had no idea Moses in Midian was such a well-developed tradition."

"That was lame," Jack said.

"I agree," smiled Archer. "But I dug deep for it, so it has to count for something."

Jack rolled his eyes and pretended to pray, "Help, I'm surrounded by idiots."

They walked back and climbed into Hamid's car.

"Okay, let's go to the mountain," Sykes said.

"As you wish," Hamid said. "But we must make a stop along the way. You will be glad we did."

"Very well," Sykes said as Jack moaned from the back.

Hamid steered north onto Highway 5, the desert unfolding in waves of gold. Jack watched the dunes roll past, flashes of Utah's Arches National Park and the Grand Canyon stirring old memories. He hated to admit it, but something about Saudi Arabia was starting to get under his skin, even if its sights were lame.

Hamid slowed the Rover, abruptly turning right off the paved highway onto a sandy track, switching on the four-wheel drive. They felt the drivetrains engage as all four tires gripped the soft ground, picking up speed.

"We are entering an area that few people have ever seen. It is another place well-known to my people, but the international community is just now catching on to its mystery," Hamid said. "We have about thirty minutes before reaching the Rock that Moses split."

"Umm, what?" Jack said. He found the string of items Hamid had associated with Moses today utterly nonsensical.

"Yes, Surah 7, Verse 160 of our Quran says that Moses struck a rock and water gushed out so that the Yahud could drink. As you can see, this is an arid place, and water was essential for the millions of people who migrated out of Egypt to settle here. This is also where we believe the bread from heaven and quails came to nourish the people."

"The Quran says this?" Sykes asked. He remembered these stories from his childhood, but he'd never read the Quran.

"It does," Hamid replied. "It is also in your Bible, no? Your book of the Exodus, chapter 17. You should look it up."

Sykes got out his phone and searched for a Bible app. He found it and read aloud the fifth and sixth verses in the Shakespearean King James version.

"*5 And the Lord said unto Moses, Go on before the people, and take with thee of the elders of Israel; and thy rod, wherewith thou smotest the river, take in thine hand, and go. 6 Behold, I will stand before thee there upon the rock in Horeb; and thou shalt smite the rock, and there shall come water out of it, that the people may drink. And Moses did so in the sight of the elders of Israel.*"

"How are there so many similarities in these stories?" Archer asked, fascinated that these ancient books from very different religions seemed to share a common history.

"Yahudi and Muslims both trace their lineage back to Abraham. We have descended through the line of Ishmael and his mother Hagar, and the Yahudi trace theirs back through Ishmael's brother Isaac. So, we began together as a family many years ago," Hamid replied. "The Prophet Muhammad, Peace Be Upon Him, was born in 570 CE when a rather large Yahudi population lived in and around Arabia. At twelve, he met many of them when he journeyed to Syria with his father's merchant caravan. In his early years, he greatly respected the Yahudi and their traditions. He called them 'People of the Book' in the Quran."

"At 25, he married his first wife, a widow named Khadija, and she introduced him to many Yahudi. In 622 CE, three years after her death, the Prophet fled persecution in Mecca and came to Medina, which also had a sizable Yahudi population. That journey is known as Hijrah, the flight from persecution and severing his kinship there. That event marks the beginning of the Islamic calendar. He was no stranger to the Yahudi."

"If Muhammad respected the Jewish people he knew, why is there so much tension today between the Jews and Muslims?" Archer asked.

Hamid looked in the rearview mirror at his American guest. "This is a tough question you ask," he said. "But the tension is both real and imagined. It is real because, in his later years, the Prophet was rejected by the Yahudi as he sought to spread the revelations of Allah. They did not believe him and would not pledge allegiance to anyone but their Yahweh. Their rejection of Allah and His Prophet changed many things. Fourteen hundred years of conflict have emerged from this."

"However, it is also imagined because respect and collaboration are happening in large parts of the Muslim world. The Jews and Arabs are making big changes in how they relate to each other. There are millions of Arabs living peacefully in Israel. For example, direct flights from Tel Aviv to Dubai began in June of 2022, thanks to the American-brokered peace deal, and other Muslim-majority countries are following suit. In the Kingdom, we are building NEOM while embracing and promoting religious diversity. Since the autumn of 2021, our Crown Prince has allowed Christian tourism to the location I am taking you today. Despite our differences, we share a common value for the worth of humanity and a future we can inhabit together."

"That sounds so noble," Jack said. "And I'd love to believe it's true. But we all fought in Iraq and Afghanistan and know for certain there is no love lost between some sects of Islam and the Jewish people. The way I see it, hate exists everywhere."

"I agree. The human heart can contain good and evil," Hamid replied. "Often both at the same time. The question is, what do we choose to fill it with? I cannot solve the world's problems. But I can confront the things in my life and choose to grow. Perhaps I'm naive to think this, but if enough people did, the world would change."

Jack's jaw locked. Archer's eyes sank to the floor. Sykes rubbed the scar on his hand as if it could bleed out the doubt. They had each killed—dozens, maybe more—under the banner of duty, flag, and oath. They'd told themselves it was right. Necessary. But now the question pressed in, relentless: what if it wasn't? The air thickened, heavy with an answer none of them dared to speak.

The Rover rattled through scorched, sandy valleys littered with Acacia trees and towering mountain ranges. The hot oppression of the noonday sun was pressing down, baking everything. But suddenly, the introspection was interrupted by a sight none of them were prepared for. What they now saw pierced their imagination.

Ahead, a massive monolith protruded from a narrow ridgeline, standing tall in an arid wilderness like a lone sentry guarding a long-since-crumbled citadel.

"This is the split Rock at Horeb," Hamid said.

Captivated, the team watched the Rock become more prominent as the Rover drew closer. Around three hundred feet away, it reached into the sky nearly eight stories. The seventy-foot-wide natural stone formation stood for thousands of years on this same rocky outcropping. Much like the megaliths at Stonehenge, this rock was an impressive natural standing stone that would have drawn ancient peoples for millennia.

Archer once stood under Stonehenge's trilithons for a photo. But this loomed five times higher. His chest tightened in awe as he gazed

at that split down the middle as if some great power had cleaved it in
two.

"We can get out and explore around the Rock. As you do,
remember that this area gets less than an inch and a half of rain each
year," Hamid said.

The four men piled out of the Rover and gathered their things. Jack
reached the base before the others, scrambling hand over foot up the
steep incline. Ever the adventurer, he shimmied between the gaping
hole separating the rock's two halves and worked his way deep into
the split rock. Archer caught up and inspected a large groove at the
base of the rock.

"This is remarkable," he said to Sykes as the team lead scurried
toward him. "Hamid said this place gets less than an inch and a half
of rain each year. But this groove looks like it was blasted with a
high-volume explosion of water."

Sure enough, as Sykes looked around, the stone at the base of the
Rock was smoothed out. As if carved out of the sandstone with a
pressure washer. Nothing around it looked similar.

He was no geologist, but a clear impact of the material at the base
of the Rock presented itself to his imagination. Perhaps it was
because Hamid had planted this thought in his mind as they drove
in. Still, he could visualize the masses of Hebrews surrounding this
ancient Rock, drinking in the mythic water that had supposedly
poured from a miraculous source.

The site's geography was ideally suited for such an event. From
this ridge, Sykes could see for miles. They were in a broad and very
long valley that could have quickly become a reservoir had an
underground spring of water erupted from this location.

Ever the logistical thinker, Sykes was calculating how two million
people could drink from an aquatic event like this. The scale was
mind-boggling but plausible.

Was he going crazy? Standing here in the desert, imagining
something utterly impossible as if it were history. Religious claims

like this had always turned him off. But baking in the noonday heat, he knew that without a significant water source, travelers would not make it more than a few days in this terrain. He took a sip from his CamelBak and realized he was drinking the cool, refreshing water that had been drawn from Elam just a few hours earlier. He was already parched and had ridden in an air-conditioned luxury SUV. He could imagine millions of people panicking after three days of walking without water.

"Guys, come see this," yelled Jack.

Sykes turned and saw Jack's shoulder from deep within the Rock, waving them in. He and Archer made their way into the cool shade of the split.

"Check this," Jack said as he placed his hand on the massive stone slab between the two halves of the enormous Rock. "This looks to me like pressure flaking."

The small gap in the center of the Rock had numerous exposed erosional features as if water had penetrated the stone, breaking off sections of the slab over the years.

"The summer I spent hiking through Utah, I saw many rock formations created by thousands of years of water and wind erosion," Jack continued. "But Utah gets 8-10 inches of rain yearly, compared to the 1.5 inches here. All the erosional features I observed broke off the sandstone in a pattern that showed the water and wind coming in from the top and sides. This rock is broken off opposite, as if the water source came from below."

Sure enough, as the team inspected the unusual flaking in the protected center of the Rock, they could see erosional features that resembled a water source erupting from beneath the ancient standing stone.

"This formation makes very little sense to me," Jack said. "How was it split straight down the middle? No other rocks are around us to channel the little rainwater into the center. How did this lone rock even get here? Every arch I saw in Utah was carved from a larger section of sandstone. I've never seen anything free-standing like this, disconnected from a larger rock face and showing signs of significant water erosion."

"See, I told you it was magical," laughed Hamid, who had made his way up to the edge of the opening and was peering in at his engrossed guests. "You find the erosion patterns odd?"

"To say the least," Sykes replied. "What do you think caused this?"

"I think this is one more piece to the pattern of evidence leading us onward," he replied. "I can't prove this was the site of a miracle. But its location, scale, and physical features fit perfectly in the narrative tale of the Yahudi coming out of Egypt. Your Bible speaks many times of this Rock and the history of the Yahudi."

"There are other references to this Rock?" Archer's brows arched.

"There are," Hamid replied. "I do not know the specifics. But I led a small tour of shepherds from Korea to this place. They stood right here reading from their holy book. My Korean is terrible, and their English was not much better. But they kept saying 'split rock' as they read."

Sykes pulled out his phone and reopened his Bible app. He typed "split rock" into the search bar for the New King James Version, which returned three results.

"Here's one verse from Isaiah 48," he said, reading aloud. "*And they did not thirst when He led them through the deserts; He caused the waters to flow from the rock for them; He also split the rock, and the waters gushed out.*"

"Wow!" Standing in the split of the Rock, Jack looked up, seventy feet to the bright sky. "That's a pretty good description of where we're standing. What's the other one?"

"There are references in Psalms, too," Sykes replied. He read from Psalm 78, "*The daytime also He led them with the cloud, and all the night with a light of the fire. He split the rocks in the wilderness, and gave them drink in abundance like the depths.*"

Sykes reimagined the perfectly shaped valley around them, filled with enough water for two million people. "Abundance like the depths" was a spot-on description of how this area would have looked.

"These stories can't be true," Archer said to himself. It was more of a question than a statement, but the echo of the narrow space the three friends shared amplified it beyond his intent. Sykes looked up, understanding.

"I am wondering too," Sykes said. "Standing here imagining the plausibility of an unexplainable event and looking at these patterns of evidence messes with me. I know there is more to the natural world than I could imagine. I don't struggle with the idea that it's physically possible. But..."

"We've seen so much death and deception from those we should have been able to trust," interjected Jack. "How do we reconcile that with the idea that there is some higher power that is good and loving enough to do something like this?"

"Exactly," Sykes replied. "I don't have an answer to that question."

"Me neither," Jack said. "But it sure seems like there was a rich tradition of remembering whatever event occurred here."

Sykes and Archer stared at their snarky and cynical friend with quizzical looks.

"What?" Jack said. "I'm just doing what you asked, boss. I'm looking past my worldview to see what else is out there. You said there were three results. What is the last one?"

Sykes looked back at his phone and saw a reference to a verse in Matthew 27.

"This one doesn't talk about the Rock," he said. "It's some reference to what happened moments after Jesus was supposedly killed."

"What does it say?" questioned Jack. "Could be connected?"

"It says that the moment Jesus died, the curtain in the Temple was torn, an earthquake happened, and the rocks beneath him were split. Not connected," he said.

Jack was disappointed. He had never felt this sort of anticipation before. Standing in the shadow of the Rock, it was like he had tasted a hope greater than himself for the first time. He knew it was out of character, but he sincerely wanted all of these things to be connected and to make sense. Every other detail came together this morning, so why not this?

"Can I see your phone?" Jack asked his team leader.

Sykes handed it over, and Jack searched the open app for different words. The word "rock" yielded more than 135 results, which were too numerous to review at this time. He tried "rock + thirst," which produced three results pointing back to the same event. For some reason, he felt an urgency to find a connection between the split Rock and Jesus's crucifixion. He thought of how hot and thirsty he was in this barren land and what it would have been like to face death without any prospect of drinking water. He typed in "rock + drank" and suddenly found what he had been looking for.

"Guys, listen to this. It's in some document called 1 Corinthians," Jack said with an excitement that caught Sykes off guard. "What is that?"

"It's a book of the Bible, Jack. You're searching a Bible app," Archer said.

"I don't know anything about this," Jack hit back. "Cut me some slack."

"It's fine, Jack. But, more precisely, Corinthians was a letter an Apostle named Paul wrote to a coastal Greek town just west of Athens around 55 CE," Sykes said, the years of history his father had taught him were strangely fresh in his mind.

"Man, a 2000-year-old sentence never interested me so much," Jack said.

"Out with it," Archer urged.

"It's from that Paul guy's letter, 1 Corinthians 10: "*All ate the same spiritual food, and all drank the same spiritual drink. For they drank of that spiritual Rock that followed them, and that Rock was Christ.*" That is as explicit a connection as you can make! Whatever it means..."

Sykes was amazed and confused. Amazed that Jack had somehow been gripped with an interest in the history of the desert wilderness and religion after being such a jerk this morning. But also confused as to what it all meant. None of these places made sense.

But they all seemed woven into a tangled web...the meaning just out of his reach. Why did a two-thousand-year-old letter to a Greek city connect their so-called Messiah to a thirty-five-hundred—year-old event allegedly occurring at this exact spot? And did any of that matter to them today? Standing in the shadow of a great Rock in Saudi Arabia, he had more questions than answers. What else was out there that he knew nothing about?

But the team was immersed in an adventure that would change their lives. It was time to throw caution to the wind and wholeheartedly seek this thing that was presenting itself to them.

"Does it mean this Rock is Christ?" Jack asked.

Sykes looked at Archer, who just shrugged.

"Hamid, do you have any clue?" Sykes raised an eyebrow.

"I am not a follower of your Christ." Hamid leaned forward. "But I am amazed by the accuracy of your holy book. I have visited this Rock many times, but I never knew about this connection. Let us proceed to the mountain; maybe it will all make more sense there."

Sykes and Archer retreated from the shaded center of the Rock. Jack took one final look up from the center before leaving. This place made him feel alive for the first time in years. He realized he'd believed it was up to him to survive in a cold and cruel world for most of his life. He knew nobody was coming to his rescue. Nobody was looking out for his well-being. His family and friends were driven by self-interest, and he should be, too.

But if this Rock was a thing, it cracked the outer defense of his self-protection. Was there a God who was real and looking out for His people? If so, was Jack even one of His people?

He drew in one final breath in the cool of the Rock and said, "God, if you're real, help me know what's true. I've seen so much darkness and pain. But if you're good, please show me."

At that moment, Jack heard a voice. Not with his ears. But with his heart. And he knew he was not alone.

24

Sayyid had been forced to reduce speed about halfway to his destination to conserve fuel. The frustrating limitation had slowed his pace by nearly two hours, but it paid off as he rounded the jetty into the tiny Haql marina. It was connected to the regional Saudi Border Patrol office. He had his Saudi passport ready just in case, but he figured a noon arrival on Saturday would be uneventful.

He'd miss the orange and white water rocket. Steering it across 500 kilometers of the Red Sea was a pleasure, but he'd need a road vehicle of some kind to drive to the mountain's base, about 120 km away.

His mind drifting momentarily, he came in too fast and slammed into the small dock, which housed official Saudi border patrol vessels. However, the commotion seemed to go unnoticed in the oppressive noonday heat.

He grabbed his backpack, leaped off the boat, and scanned the rundown dock for a vehicle. Something that didn't draw attention. No more million-dollar racing boats. He needed to blend in.

He knew, without a shadow of a doubt, that Allah was with him and his righteous cause. There was only one vehicle in the desolate parking lot. A 2017 Toyota Land Cruiser with a large aftermarket front grill. Exactly what he needed for a trip to the desert enclave of Jabal al-Lawz.

Moses's exact mountain peak was disputed, but the various peaks of this famous range, Jabal al-Lawz, were now a tourist trap. A ski slope had just opened on the highest summit in the range, perched on the 38th parallel like D.C. and Everest. Sheer engineering audacity had turned the peak's arid snow scarcity into a three-month ski season.

His prey were tourists today, so he'd start there. You'd have to be a miserable guide to skip this site. They'd come, and he'd be ready. And so would his trap.

He walked calmly to the Toyota and pulled a slim Jim from his pack. He'd gained entry in a flash and went to work on the ignition. The electronics were not an issue; he fired the engine and put the vehicle in drive.

"Hey, you there! Out of my car!" bellowed a border patrol agent.

Sayyid's instinct was to race out of the parking lot. But he couldn't have a Saudi official calling in a stolen vehicle. He looked in the rearview mirror, and the agent was running after him, fumbling with his radio. Sayyid spun the SUV in a one-eighty, leaving an arch of molten rubber on the pavement. The eyes of the agent widened in fear. Sayyid gunned it, closing the gap before the man could react. Five thousand pounds of Japanese engineering slammed into him. The massive front grill crushed his chest, collapsing his shoulders and sending him flying across the pavement with a crunch.

Sayyid jumped out. A quick scan of the parking lot revealed no security cameras. A single bullet ensured that no further action was taken.

He was so close. He wouldn't lose hope that he'd intercept Ethan's team and achieve a victory for his Leader. Two hours of drive time were enough to formulate a plan to kill or capture four men and live to tell the tale.

He was finally on his way to the Mountain.

25

Ethan pulled a laptop from his bag and connected it to the in-flight WiFi. He needed a full debrief with his team, but now was not the time. So he fired off a quick text to Sykes.

"En route to London. Safe, but the situation is dynamic. Hold tight for 24 hrs. Will meet soon."

Ethan hoped they were resting. They would be needed in short order, but for what, he had no idea.

He could feel them all careening towards a massive conflict. With his father? Someone else? Who had come after them? Was the assault on them at Aten and the Red Sea connected to his father as well? So many questions, and his team had no idea what was happening in his world.

Come to think of it, neither did he.

Regus had been a chaotic bundle of contradictions. Over the past twenty-four hours, he'd gone from loathing her to realizing she was the closest thing he'd ever had to someone understanding him. Regus knew more about his life and past than Sykes. He told her things he'd never uttered out loud until last night.

He looked over and saw her sleeping peacefully. He smiled, remembering the fire she could breathe when her passions were ignited. He liked that—just maybe not so much fire in his direction. But his gut said she was indispensable for what was coming.

He remembered the first thing she ever hurled at him, questioning his succession theory and Hatshepsut's family line, which led down to the fourth generation and the murder of King Tut. She accused him of holding a theory that closely mirrored his personal story and claimed people had long-held concerns about how his family's business contributed to national destabilization and regime change. Yesterday, those statements had been utter nonsense. Today, they felt like a clue.

His mind swirled with the parallels between his father, Fortis, and the Pharaonic line of the 18th Dynasty. In Ancient Egypt, they ruled by way of awe, military might, and monumental building projects and technology that continue to mystify modern researchers, including himself. Fortis was a real-time representation of this archetype. While the Stones had never sought the spotlight like the Pharaohs, they had sought and gained power. They ruled in shadows with tech and weapons shaping nations. Three generations of Stone men had built a shadow empire without thrones or temples. Yet, their myth of the Angel of Mercy was power cloaked as divine purpose in the same way the Pharaohs held spiritual influence over their subjects.

His family saw themselves as spiritual guardians and suppliers of tools to liberate oppressed people from the tyranny of evil. Ethan had never been able to reconcile this belief with what they did. It was a little too ironic in the words of his favorite '90s alt-rock star.

He was surprised at the similarities he'd uncovered in this brief reflection. Dizziness swept over him as the question hit hard: how had he missed this connection?

But what about the accusation of regime change? His father's hand was in Iraq, Syria, Iran—successes and failures alike. How many more? The echo of dynasty was undeniable, and for the first time, Ethan felt the weight of his bloodline like a curse.

"Of course. This is why King Tut was murdered. He was the legitimate heir in an illegitimate line. Stop King Tut from inheriting the throne and expose his father as a fraud, and you could depose the whole dynasty," he said, continuing to talk out loud at 40,000 feet.

"This had to be why all hell broke loose in Egypt, leading to the collapse of the 18th Dynasty and the birth of the 19th with the Ramesses line. Regime change 101," he said. "Amazing. Is this what my family has been up to?"

"Of course," Regus said.

Her voice startled Ethan, and he glanced at her smiling face, nestled gently on the airline pillow.

"It took you long enough to see it." A thin smile played at her lips.

"How long have you been awake?" Ethan asked, slightly embarrassed.

"Long enough to enjoy your journey of self-discovery." She slowly transformed the bed back into a chair. "Glad you took my insights seriously."

"Well, I know how much women love to hear these words," he said. "You were right."

"Yes, I was," Regus beamed, now fully upright.

Turning towards Ethan, she leaned in and almost whispered in his ear, "Now, why are you involved?"

Regus had an uncanny ability to force him into very uncomfortable places in his mind. No, it wasn't his mind that protested. It was his heart. He'd kept the two separated for decades. But Regus had shattered the divide that held them apart. Hence, the internal havoc he'd experienced since meeting her.

He racked his brain to see what had to be right in front of him. But he accessed no information. A foolish thought blinked across his mental radar screen: the dream could help.

He would typically repress this crazy idea. But it was a new day, and he was way past preserving the old world. Did the dream have any insight he could use to understand the moment he was in?

He took a deep breath, closed his eyes, and recalled the dream. Instantly, he pictured the unidentified Pharaoh looking out over his devastated kingdom. Furious and frantic, Pharaoh spun from his balcony and raced into the bedroom of his only son, who was not to be found.

"Hold up," Ethan said out loud, suddenly having context.

"What is it?" Regus shifted in her seat, eyes narrowing.

"I've had a recurring dream, a nightmare really," he said. "It involves a Pharaoh I can't place in history watching his kingdom collapse."

"And why is that important?" Her brows arched.

"I know this will sound crazy, but this dream has been torturing me for months. It feels more like a memory than a nightmare. And, as ludicrous as that is, I'm almost in the place where I no longer care. My whole world is shaking beneath me, and I'm discovering I don't have access to huge parts of my subconscious. So, I'm entertaining new sources of insight."

"Sounds like a fruitful pursuit," Regus replied with a wry smile.

"You don't think it's crazy?"

"Of course not. At University, I studied all the major world religions. It didn't matter what era, continent, race, or language spawned the religious thought; every single one of them had a mystical, or should I say non-rational, experience at the heart of the ideas. The Western mind has been conditioned to trust only the empirical since the Enlightenment. But this recent myopic dependence on individual cognitive capacity is egregiously arrogant and profusely ignorant. Truth exists independent of our minds, so it stands to reason we could gain insights from outside the mental world of rationality."

It took Ethan a beat to understand what she'd said.

"It's not often I wish I had a dictionary when talking to someone from Columbia," Ethan quipped.

"It's not often I stump a world-famous Academic with a few big words," she fired back.

"Touché." Ethan grinned, eyes gleaming.

"Back to your dream. It sounded like it led you to a realization about your involvement in your father's business."

"Yeah, well," Ethan hesitated. It was one thing to entertain a crazy idea and another to say it out loud.

"Go on," she urged. "I won't think less of you than I already do."

Ethan appreciated the banter. It made him feel like he was talking to one of the guys, not a captivatingly beautiful woman whose emerald eyes were locked onto his gaze for the past few minutes.

"Well, in the dream, the Pharaoh was frantically looking for his son. I watch him race through the Palace in the middle of the night, where he finds that his son isn't in his bedroom. I hear the Pharaoh's thoughts, and he says, "Where is this ungrateful simp of an heir on a night my empire limps towards annihilation?""

"Whoa," Regus gasped. She'd caught the connection. "You think your subconscious is trying to say your father is looking for you?"

"I do. And I think it may be because his empire is under assault."

"From whom?" Regus asked.

"In the dream, Pharaoh says it's from a foreign power."

"What does that mean?" Her forehead creased.

"No idea." Ethan leaned back. "But my father would try to contact me if Fortis was in danger."

"How so?" Regus replied. "Are you part of the plan to save the company?"

"Maybe. A preposterous idea, to be sure. But it gives us the first inkling of a clue since we got shot at. The Stone men have always been intensely private and trusted no one. Fortis, and Stone Defense, before it, had never appointed another Executive. Not an SVP, VP, Director, or anyone with any influence on the company's direction. The company reins have passed to the son in every generation."

"How does that fact align with the Board they established in 2008?"

"An excellent question," Ethan said. "Why don't you tell me?"

"Well, they were in deep financial trouble during the global recession and accepted an infusion of cash from a group of Arab investors who took Fortis public. Part of their deal was the formation of a Board of Directors and a proper corporate structure."

"Correct, and that had to infuriate my father," Ethan added. "But I'm sure he figured out a way to continue answering to no one."

Ethan always felt conflicted when he thought about his Fortis shares. But he pressed it down and tried to make sense of another particularly nagging question: was his father trying to kill him or just bring him home?

"I still can't understand why my father is after me if I'm not being hunted," he said. "I don't care at all about his company and even less about the warmongering, profit-driven global cabal of regime change values that have guided Fortis for decades."

"Well said," Regus leaned forward and nodded briskly.

"I'm no AP messenger," he continued. "I'm its antithesis. I have given my life to seeking out artifacts because they ground culture in its shared story—successes and failures—so nations can hold on to what was life-giving and avoid repeating things that bring death and destruction. I don't want to play kingmaker with billion-dollar defense budgets. The story of evil never changes in human history— just the players, era, and the scale of misery humans can inflict on each other."

"Exactly," Regus's eyebrows shot up and held. She'd gotten the wrong impression of Ethan and decided then and there to discard that erroneous perspective permanently.

Ethan continued.

"In *The Communist Manifesto*, Karl Marx wrote, 'In [Capitalist] society, the past dominates the present; in Communist society, the present dominates the past.' This is a primary goal of the global powers. They seek to rewrite the past, topple, delete, and cancel the accurate historical record. Why? When the present is unburdened by what has been, it can build whatever future it sees fit—the 20th century testified that this glorious socialist utopia requires murdering hundreds of millions of expendables who love family and freedom more than state control. This was the crux of the fissure in my father's relationship. Too often, he made his bed with these ideologues, and I consider him complicit with the violent revolutionaries seeking to fundamentally transform the United States."

Ethan was getting worked up now.

Regus loved it.

"I am no pacifist, but I'm no war hawk either. I prefer the middle path trodden by men who dare to fight and bring to bear overwhelming violence of action, but who are also restrained enough to stand down when the time comes. I didn't relish the life-and-death decisions I had to make as a squadron commander. But if it wasn't me, it was someone worse. So, I accepted the role and spent a decade saving the lives of the men under my charge. Usually, by taking the lives of the enemy. That was war."

"This is all so interesting," Regus added. "It sounds like you're an excellent leader in an exceedingly high-stakes environment where every choice you make has cascading implications."

"You could say that," Ethan shrugged with a smirk.

"And you know the military inside and out?"

"From a boots-on-the-ground perspective, I suppose that's right."

"If my decade of research is correct, your father, grandfather, and great-grandfather each only ever had one son. Is that right?"

"It is."

"So, you're the fourth generation of Stone men," she pressed, trying to lead Ethan toward the brazenly obvious conclusion.

"I am. What are you getting at?" Ethan asked.

"In your lecture at the Met, you insisted that Hatshepsut could never have been Pharaoh because the throne was only ever passed to the firstborn son."

"Yeah, what's your point?"

Regus clasped the side of her head. She couldn't believe this savant professor was so blind about his father. She had to spell it out for him.

"Ethan, if your father is a modern-day Pharaoh, then maybe he wants to pass the Fortis empire to you, his firstborn son."

26

The condensation streaked across the window as Ethan stared out at 40,000 feet of blackness, his face expressionless but his mind racing.

Regus could see the storm brewing behind his eyes—a mix of confusion, rage, and resignation, all fighting for dominance. But when his gaze finally met hers, she knew which emotion had won. It was the cold, unyielding determination she had come to recognize— the kind of resolve that meant he would do whatever it took, no matter the cost.

"Me, leading Fortis," Ethan said out loud to no one in particular. "How interesting."

"Would you ever consider it?" asked Regus. Her mind was moving a million miles an hour. She could dismantle the empire from within much faster than attacking it from without.

"Lie down with the devil, wake up in hell," he said.

"What if you were different? You could change the company. Use the influence and wealth to do good in the world."

"It's not that simple. Things are the way they are for a reason, and change, in any arena, comes slowly and with a high cost. If at all. I couldn't just walk in there and reset a hundred years of company culture. Not to mention all the existing contracts and global networks of money, favors, and dirt that no doubt exist. It doesn't seem possible, even if I wanted to. Assuming a man I've hated my whole adult life wants to hand over the only thing he loves. It's an idea so outlandish it's hardly worth considering."

As his mouth said the words out loud, his gut told him he was wrong. He sensed the hidden motivations behind this chaotic day, and some irrational part of him knew this was indeed his father's plan. Moreover, his descents into the chaotic void, this one triggered by the recurring dream, were bellwethers for something massive on the horizon. Was this it?

He'd walked headlong into deadly firefights, but flying to London to confront his father was a different battle. He was going in, but was he prepared to engage? He needed to start gaming out what lay ahead.

"Let's assume we're on to something," he said. "And my father is not trying to kill me, but has set in motion a succession plan. If that is accurate, he has a detailed strategy we need to know."

"Why would he want to hand off the company now after all these years?" Regus asked.

"He would have to be at the end of his capability," Ethan rubbed the back of his neck, his eyes distant. "As a boy, he drilled into me that success is determined by a resilient team assembled to cover the limitations of its leader. Every great leader must know their weakness and build a team to support the gaps in their capabilities. I led this way in the Army. My greatest strength is taking fast and decisive action. Even if I'm unsure, I move swiftly before my adversary does. Action beats reaction every time, and I've won almost every fight. However, it also became my greatest weakness, leading me to miss some critical strategic implications of my actions. So, I surrounded myself with other leaders who think through every known scenario. My current team leader and former Air Cav, company commander Sykes, is that man for me."

"So what's the weakness your father's seeking to cover?" Regus cocked her head, eyes narrow, and fixed on him.

"That is the question." Ethan rubbed his chin. "He has never acknowledged weakness in his life. He pretends he's invincible, and his will goes for everything in his orbit. A man like that can't be trusted. So, when I lost trust, I left home. I would not be led into battle by a leader like him."

"Something must have changed. He's been working in the shadows to protect you for a while, maybe your whole life. If he's moving on things now, there must be an urgency. Given everything you've just said, he's not acting on impulse but disciplined strategy."

"You're right," Ethan said. "Again."

"When my father was dying, he opened up to me in a way I never saw as a child."

The abrupt change of topic took Ethan aback.

"It's okay," Regus said, reading his look of concern and compassion. "But I clearly remember the shift in our relationship when he knew his days were numbered. Hard men can soften when time is short."

"How did your father die?" Ethan asked.

"Cancer," Regus swallowed hard.

"I'm sorry." Ethan's tone dropped to a whisper.

"I brought this up because it could be relevant to us. Maybe your father has seen the end of his capacity, as you put it."

"You think he could be dying?" Ethan asked.

"That's one explanation for the sudden change in status between you two, the insight from your dream about the Pharaoh under assault, and your family history of passing the company to the first-born male sons," she said with a tilt of her head.

Ethan thought it was plausible. It would be an elegant solution to the confusion of the last day. But he wasn't ready to adopt the perspective. He'd just opened up to the idea of his father re-entering his life, and he wasn't prepared to cut him back out again.

"These are beneficial insights," Ethan replied. "You're a good analyst."

"My greatest strength is thinking through what's happening below the surface. Exploring what people conceal or is hidden from their minds," she said. "I've made a career of research and writing exposé pieces on what's lurking in the shadows."

That's why Ethan had never heard her name before! She wasn't an academic or historical critic for the Times. She was an investigative reporter. Ethan had been so focused on his crisis and her beauty that he completely ignored her life and story.

"I finally understand why you were stalking me at my Met lecture," Ethan said. "How far along on the Stone family exposé are you?"

Regus flashed a mischievous smile and said, "Almost finished. But my editor generally doesn't publish twenty-thousand-word essays. So, it may need to turn into a screenplay."

"Are you serious?"

She mentally revised some sections over the past 24 hours as she gained a better understanding of Ethan. Regus batted her eyelashes and said, "Yes. A few of the narrative arcs are in flux at the moment. But it's good."

"I don't know what that means."

Regus stayed silent and let her glistening eyes do the talking. Ethan kept the wordless conversation going for a few lingering moments.

"Well, if it turns into a movie, you must get Ryan Gosling to play my character."

"More like the dad from Family Ties," she said.

27

Hamid turned off the sandy track from the Split Rock onto north Highway 5.

"We have about thirty minutes till we reach our next destination. There are two main areas to explore ahead. One is the recently opened Trojena Ski Resort. It sits atop a peak in the Jabal al-Lawz range and has 36 kilometers of ski slopes, hundreds of outdoor activities, more than three thousand hotel rooms and apartments, and a massive man-made lake."

"An outdoor ski slope in the desert? No way," exclaimed Archer. "We have to see that."

"What is the other option?" asked Jack.

"There are ancient ruins a few kilometers to the south that will add data points to our discoveries this morning," Hamid replied.

"What are they?" asked Jack, eager to continue this journey.

"More rocks," smiled Hamid. "Lots of rocks. And some old art."

"Come on," begged Jack. "That's all you can say?"

"I am pleased to see you are coming around to the mystery of the Mountain, Mr. American Warrior."

Lights for a mandatory security checkpoint flashed ahead, and Hamid slowed the Rover. Across the brand-new highway, a military-style checkpoint diverted traffic off the main road.

"What is this?" asked a concerned Sykes. "Are we in some kind of restricted area?"

"Nothing of the sort," Hamid replied. "We are entering an important cultural heritage zone under active construction. We have tens of thousands of workers and new employees in the region, and we like to keep a visible security presence around the mountain."

They pulled up behind a Land Cruiser with a Saudi Arabia Border Patrol license plate, which had stopped at the guard shack. The driver was speaking loudly to the officer as he reviewed his passport. Sykes experienced a gnawing pit in his stomach, the same thing he'd felt at the Valley of Moses when seeing the racing boat.

"Do we need our passports for this?" he asked Hamid.

"It is a good idea to always carry identification in the Kingdom. But I'm sure it won't be an issue if you do not have them."

Sykes turned to the back seat and made eye contact with his team. They always carried at least two different passports with them. One was easily accessible in the zipper pocket of their CamelBaks, and the other was sewn into the stitching of their larger supply packs for emergencies. The decision to identify themselves to any law enforcement officer was not to be taken lightly.

"I don't know, guys. Did you grab your passports before leaving the room? We've got a security check and don't want to make these fellas sus we're guapless Americans," he said.

Hamid did not know what Sykes said, but Jack and Archer did. Sykes used their team code words to alert each other to danger and pass information through public communications. Sus, Gen Z slang for "suspect," meant a suspicious situation was ahead. Guap was slang for "loads of money." Sykes was giving the order to not share their passports. In their line of work, which involved traveling the world, few things were as valuable as an American passport.

"Sorry, man, I didn't think we'd be leaving the country today," Archer replied. "I don't have any ID."

"Me neither," Jack said.

"It's okay," Hamid replied. "Everyone knows me here. We will be fine."

Hamid had kept the windows rolled up to preserve the cabin's cool air, but they could hear shouting from the car ahead. It was in Arabic and largely unintelligible, even for Hamid.

"Does this sort of thing happen often?" Sykes asked.

"Oh yes," Hamid replied. "Most of the government workers are related in some way to the royal family. They often lose patience when low-level security people ask too many questions at such stops. It's nothing to be worried about."

After a few tense moments watching the escalating conflict with the Land Cruiser, Sykes started looking around the vehicle for an escape route. Something wasn't right. He'd learned to trust his gut. He knew this situation could get ugly fast.

Just as he began to chart a path on foot out of the Rover and into the desert, the guard returned the passport, and the Cruiser sped off. Sykes watched as it took a right at the road sign, "Trojena."

"See, nothing to worry about," Hamid said as he approached the guard. "As-salamu alaikum, Asim."

"Wa-alaikum as-salam, Hamid. Who are you taking to the mountain today?" the suddenly friendly guard asked.

"My American friends from Sindalah. They are already learning so much about our history and people."

"May I have their passports?" the guard replied.

"Sadly, Aisha did not remember to tell them of this requirement when she booked the tour with me this morning. Everything is good."

At the mention of Aisha's name, the young guard's face lit up like the Kaaba at night. "How is she?" he asked. "Have you told her about me? You will be our chaperone when she agrees to dinner, no?"

"Yes, yes, Asim, I have told her about you. She is barely twenty and still finding her way after the death of her father and brothers.

Give it some time, my boy."

Asim looked mildly dejected.

"She will come around, inshallah. Who was that man before us?"

Asim, clearly still thinking about Aisha, said, "Some border patrol agent who didn't have his government ID. He gave me his passport, and I asked for an ID to match the blue government auto plate. He started yelling at me about his family and why he'd driven his work vehicle without it. These men need to feel important, so I let him yell and moved him on."

"Ah, Okay," Hamid said. "Thank you, Asim. And be patient; you will find love."

Hamid put the Rover in gear and waved goodbye to the young security guard.

"How many security guards do you give dating advice to?" asked Jack.

"Just my nephew. He's a good kid, but lovesick for a woman out of his league. My sister has told me to stop encouraging him. But, if a boy can't long for the woman of his dreams, he will lose the motivation to work hard and elevate his station in life."

Jack pondered this statement. He'd never really gotten any advice from his father. His CIA career took precedence over the family. Though his parents were still together, he vowed never to become like them, lovelessly clinging to a bitter relationship to maintain D.C. optics. Like anyone cared these days about the family status of a retired spook.

So far, he'd never had a long-term relationship and had given up trying. Work was enough. At least it had been.

"We're approaching the turn-off to the Trojena Ski area. Should we go right or proceed straight to see more rocks?" Hamid asked his passengers.

"Trojena," Archer said.

"Straight," Jack said at precisely the same time.

Sykes did not pay any attention to this discussion but analyzed the man in the Land Cruiser. He was familiar. He didn't know from where, but he trusted his gut, which had warned him of grave danger twice today. That Cruiser in front of them was a problem, and he worried they would have to deal with it before too long.

"Boss? Where are we headed?"

Sykes came to and realized the situation.

"Straight," he said. "We'll go see the tourist traps later. For now, we have sites to explore."

28

"I am almost to the mountain resort," Sayyid told his Leader. "The moment is fast approaching."

"You're sure they'll be there?"

"I can't imagine I got here before them, but if I did, that would be a gift from Allah. It gives me a chance to set the perfect trap."

"But you are sure they will go to a resort? That doesn't seem like a place for these men."

Sayyid hated having to explain himself, but he could not afford to get cross with his Leader.

"They are being driven by a local tour guide who takes guests from Sindalah to the mountain. Trojena is listed as a "must-see" destination on the tour brochure I picked up from the hotel. He will bring them here. I am sure of it."

"You must finish the job, Sayyid. We can't put up with your continued incompetence much longer."

Sayyid's temper was at a boiling point. But he contained himself.

"I will succeed."

"See that you do. Today, I begin the final phase of the plan. There is no turning back now. We need to tie up this loose end. His team must be eliminated, and then Ethan must be captured and brought to

Doha."

"It will be done."

"I'm meeting with the Board in a few hours. We expect a result from you before then."

The line went dead, and Sayyid angrily threw his sat phone into the passenger seat floorboard.

"That cursed man! He only thinks about that stupid company and his obscene wealth. His love for the cause has grown cold."

Furious, he continued to drive silently, a plan forming in his head. When he succeeded today, he would return home and get his brothers to expose their Imam for what he was: an apostate, drunk on power and corrupted by Western money and values. But first, he needed to succeed in killing three well-trained U.S. Military men and perhaps their tour guide in the middle of a Saudi Arabian tourist destination. It would not be easy, especially if he had no plan in place. He needed to refocus.

As he drove up the winding road, jagged mountains rose before him, their sharp peaks throwing dark silhouettes against the sky. He pushed deeper; the temperature dropped, the wind a bitter stillness that made the hairs on his neck stand. He took the last turn, and there it was; he was speechless. There was nothing like this in Doha, not like this in terms of size and natural environment.

A man-made lake stretched before him, smooth as glass, held in place by an angular basin spanning the high mountain valleys that seemed to hang in defiance of gravity. The massive retaining wall structure jutted out over the cliffs, a geometric form starkly contrasting with the surrounding wild and untamed mountains.

He exited the vehicle, his gaze tracing the narrow bridge crossing the water at the edge of a cliff. The soft glow of lights along the path invited him forward, but he lingered, standing still as he let the scene wash over him.

In the distance behind him, clinging to the rugged cliffs, a futuristic city appeared—its structures glowing with a soft, otherworldly light.

It was as if he had entered a realm where time had blended, ancient earth and cutting-edge design existed in a perfect, dreamlike balance. The vibrant lights of the distant buildings pulsed gently, as if the city, cut from the rocks, breathed with life, hidden within the folds of the mountains.

There was no conflict here, at least, not yet—only a quiet harmony, where each element seemed to enhance the other. Standing there in the cool mountain air, he felt a sense of awe, knowing he was witnessing something extraordinary.

Sayyid began the long walk to the lake's precipice and looked over the valley beneath. Only a few tourists mingled along the walkway. The resort's grandeur had yet to capture international attention. To his left, a small cafe with an open-air chef's kitchen was set up for guests to enjoy the view. He approached the cafe and purchased a *qahwa*, a traditional Saudi coffee blend of lightly roasted Arabica beans infused with cardamom, saffron, and cloves, along with a small plate of dates and candies. He paid in cash and selected the umbrella table nearest the cliff edge as if to watch the coming sunset. Undoubtedly, the Americans would visit this place. And Allah would reward him for a lifetime of dedication to his righteous cause.

When his Leader had approached him more than twenty-five years ago, the U.S. forces had just invaded Baghdad. Part of the roughly 10% Shia minority in Qatar, Sayyid could still recall the hot rage that rose in him like an inferno. Fury at America's brazen assaults, he began attending his Leader's mosque. His fiery condemnations of the West and strict interpretation of Sharia had channeled Sayyid's anger, and the community had given him an outlet to express it. He formed a group of young men and made plans to join the insurgents in Iraq and help purge the invaders. However, his Leader had discovered his plan and approached him before they departed. He had laid out a vision for transforming Qatar by strengthening ties with Iran and Yemen without alerting the watchful eyes of the House of Al Thani and the United States government.

The tasks started small. He was put in charge of Mosque security and built a half dozen rotating three-man teams to keep watch during weekly prayers. But as the bombs continued to rain down on Baghdad and Western bullets tore apart the insurgency, outrage mounted that Doha was home to the United States Central Command forward base. Sayyid's backyard was the West's front door to Iraq.

He suggested to his Leader that they shift from defense to offense and attack soft targets in Qatar. His first offensive move was a car bomb in March of 2005, which succeeded in killing one British man and wounding at least twelve others at the local theater frequented by expats. This attack solidified Sayyid's place with his Leader, and three of his teams were sent to Yemen for more training.

Over the next decade, Sayyid hid in the shadows while the proxy war between Iran and Saudi Arabia raged, laying the infrastructure for the Shia resistance and strengthening Qatar's ties with the Persians. He found himself doing the bidding of Tehran and Sanaa as the architects of destabilization in Doha continued to pump their propaganda out through the meteoric rise of a news network. It was a remarkable time to be alive.

Then, as the global financial crisis gripped the West, his Leader organized a consortium of Arab and Persian money to bail out a struggling British defense company. They had calculated that if left unchecked, Western powers would continue to make and deploy devastating weapons against their people. They needed a seat at the table if they hoped to stem the tide of endless war against their interests. Flush with petrodollars, they succeeded in rescuing Fortis Defense from collapse and funded the completion of the Shard in London. This gave them a permanent seat in the inner circle of the military-industrial complex, and they never looked back.

Western culture was all about money, power, and debauchery; they had no principles. Sayyid was impressed with his Leader's ability to exploit those weaknesses. And a man who stands for nothing will fall for anything. They had the West right where they wanted it.

And then came the diplomatic crisis of 2017. Just one month after a rogue U.S. President visited Saudi Arabia, Israel, and the Vatican, Riyadh organized a severing of ties with Qatar, halting his plans and plunging Qatar into an international crisis. Influential players were now demanding that the news network be taken off the air, and Doha found itself isolated from its Gulf State allies. Moreover, the Saudi King stripped the Crown Prince of his title and passed the torch to the next generation of leaders. Under his youthful guidance, Western reforms took rapid shape in the Kingdom, and Qatar was further cut off from its rightful place in the halls of power.

Qatar struggled to regain its position within the Gulf Cooperation Council (GCC), and the economic blockade severely impacted its interests. A U.S.-led peace deal began to forge the hint of Arab unity. With the situation as dire as ever, Sayyid almost ended his own life in 2020. But the thought of losing everything he ever believed in stayed his hand. He emerged from jahannam with a resolve to do whatever possible to resist the Westernization of his people and homeland.

Then, in January 2021, Qatar was readmitted to the GCC—but Sayyid could not believe the terms the House of Al Thani agreed to. In his mind, Qatar was nearly lost.

But suddenly, a glimmer of hope emerged from the ashes. A new American President took power and reignited the Western lust for military dominance and regime change. America withdrew from Afghanistan and gifted the Freedom Fighters with more than seven billion dollars worth of military equipment. Over the next year, the Taliban became the largest supplier of black-market arms in the world. The U.S. then lifted sanctions on Iran, providing it with an estimated $90 billion. Then, on the 22nd anniversary of the glorious 9/11 attacks, the U.S. President approved the release of six billion dollars of frozen Iranian funds to be administered by his nation. Sayyid could not believe the transformation of fortunes.

The West was cannibalizing itself. But the policy reversals had saved Sayyid and his Leader. The final event in the miraculous salvation was the Russian invasion of Ukraine. The United States inexplicably sent hundreds of billions of dollars in military aid to Ukraine, with a single company, Fortis Defense, standing at the center of the mad cash grab. Sayyid thought this was the long-awaited moment of redemption and the beginning of the end for the United States.

That's when his Leader lost his way.

Sayyid had watched as twenty years of ideological commitment gave way to the temptations of unfathomable wealth and thirst for illicit pleasures. Perched atop his media empire, his leader lost his fire and passion. Instead, he traveled the globe in luxury, meeting with Heads of State and brokering arms deals from his Board seat at Fortis. One of Sayyid's brothers traveled on his Leader's personal security detail and sent him regular reports of early morning visits from the endless supply of trafficked minors on overseas trips. The wicked deeds being done by this holy man were the rule now, not the exception.

Sayyid had to do something.

"Another coffee, sir?"

The young waiter snapped Sayyid back to the present. He must regain focus, or he will die in the Kingdom of all places.

"Very well," he grumbled as the boy scurried away.

He stood from his chair and took two steps to the edge of the precipice. Could he push these men off and make it appear to be an accident? Would they even arrive at this place? If so, would they be armed? He'd killed many men, but only a few were trained fighters. And none had been in the U.S. Military. No, he needed something quiet. Something unexpected. He did not want to engage in a four-on-one shootout.

"Your coffee, sir," said the young boy.

Sayyid turned, and the waiter was departing from his table. He called out.

"Do you have any food?"

"We have a Kabsa, which is our most popular dish."

"Have your chef prepare that for me, and make sure it is Halal," he said.

"Sir, it is only me this afternoon. Our chef does not work on weekends. But I can prepare this for you."

"You? A boy."

"Yes, sir, I am training at the CATRION Culinary Academy. I promise you, it'll be the best you've ever tasted. And I would never prepare a dish that was not Halal."

Sayyid looked around for the other tourists, seeing none, a plan formed in his mind.

"Very well. I must get something from my vehicle, but I'll be back shortly and look forward to tasting your creation."

The boy smiled and walked back to the small cafe.

The trap was set. Now, he needed the bait.

29

Hamid put the Rover in park. "You said you wanted to see the sights the tourists never visit; well, now is your chance. We will be out of the car for about two hours. Please get all your necessary supplies."

The team double-checked their gear and suited up. Jack emptied the back of the Rover. Hamid had filled a 5-gallon bladder from Elam and shared the remaining water with the men.

As Jack filled his CamelBak, he thought of his life as an endless progression up the elitist ladder climbed by his father, reinforcing what he already knew. Today was a fresh start and a chance at something genuinely novel. Eager to see what else was buried in the desert, he trusted Hamid to show them. This man was more than a tour guide to Jack, now. He was his teacher, perhaps even his spiritual guide.

"We have three sites to see. The first is easily accessible, but the next two require special access. Please follow my lead as we engage with the locals," Hamid said as he turned and the team set off.

Jack drank in the view. Dust swirled in the occasional breeze, whispering across the valley floor that stretched before him. The dry, barren earth cracked where the heat had drawn every last drop of moisture. Scattered shrubs clung to life in small clusters under the relentless sun.

To his right, jagged, imposing mountains rose against the piercing, cloudless blue sky, where the distant cry of a harrier circling high above the peaks cut through the silence.

Upon the mountain, there was no sign of human life—only the raw, primal beauty of the desert, indifferent to time and human concerns.

They came up over a small ridge, and Hamid announced, "There it is."

A hundred meters in front of them lay an enormous pile of rocks surrounded by a twelve-foot-tall barbed-wire fence.

"They're guarding rocks?" Jack's brow furrowed. "Why do these get a security perimeter and the Split Rock doesn't?"

"In April of 1985, a team of two Americans, accompanied by a resident of Tabuk, surveyed this site. They were investigating claims that this area was home to the true Mount Sinai, also known as the Mountain of Moses. They photographed this location and did a molecular analysis of a nearby wadi. The Americans claimed their analysis revealed high quantities of gold particles. When they shared their findings with Saudi authorities, their data and images were immediately confiscated, and this fence was erected."

"Why did they come here specifically?"

"They claimed to be searching for the remnants of Egyptian jewelry, which your Bible says was used to create the Golden Calf."

"The what?" Archer asked.

"An idol crafted by the Yahudi that represented the Egyptian goddess Hathor," Hamid replied.

Jack's eyes widened, and he released a barely perceptible gasp. Goddess of love, of marriage, of motherhood. He'd seen countless carvings of Hathor in stone at Dendera, and etched into hieroglyphs, her worshippers forever frozen at her feet. When the Greeks conquered Egypt, they called her Aphrodite. Her myths still clung to Egypt's ruins, some twisted into excuses for wild drinking. But what was she doing here?

By the way Jack's brow tightened and he darted his gaze, Hamid could see he was puzzled. "Are you familiar with her? With Egyptology?"

Jack looked at Archer, who looked at Sykes. The three men said nothing, waiting for their team leader to respond.

"We've done some reading on the subject," Sykes replied.

"Very good. Then you should know that your Bible says the people were frustrated because Moses was gone, so they crafted a golden statue and worshipped it, just as they did back in Egypt. Your holy book says, "They rose up to play," an apparent reference to immoral actions of drunken debauchery. These, of course, were abhorrent practices for the Yahud. Your God became very angry with the people, and 3,000 lost their lives in this valley because of it."

"Here? Why do you think that?" Jack asked.

"Let us go find out." Hamid flashed a broad smile.

As the team approached, the scale of the site came into view. The twenty-foot-tall mound consisted of dozens of massive boulders arranged in a circular pattern. The summit at the center was a high, flat, rectangular stone thirty feet across.

"From 1986 until a few years ago, this site was off-limits," Hamid said as the team stopped outside the fence gate. "There used to be a sign here that warned trespassing was punishable by death under the orders of the King. But today, it is gone, and you may enter without fear."

"Ummm, not entirely without fear," Archer said. "I don't typically trust someone who says they're gonna kill me one moment, and the next they're like, 'Never mind, we're good now.' What changed?"

"As I've said, the Kingdom is undergoing a remarkable transformation. Our Crown Prince is helping the older generations understand that religious freedom, once considered so dangerous by our Wahhabist clerics, is an integral part of an open and free society. If we want to share our beloved nation with the world, we must respect the perspectives of other faiths. So, he opened these sites to religious tourism in the fall of 2019."

"What do these rocks have to do with religion?" Jack rested one hand on his hip.

"You should take a closer look at the rocks," Hamid smirked.

That was enough prodding for Jack. He wheeled about and entered through the gate to the fenced-off complex. As he approached the boulders, he saw what Hamid was referencing. He also understood why the Saudi Arabian government had fenced in this site.

Ancient carvings depicting a cow, etched into many of these massive rock faces, were scattered across the boulders. Jack scaled one and stood before a colossal carving of a bull with dappled markings on its body. He couldn't believe it. To his trained eye, these looked precisely like the carvings of Hathor he'd seen in Egypt.

He turned, and his gaze fell on another carving of a cow with tiny people standing underneath, both arms raised above their heads. This reminded him of a carving discovered at the Hathor Temple in the southern Sinai Peninsula. He'd be damned if he wasn't looking at an exact copy right now.

"Why are there carvings of early alphabetic characters on these rocks?" Jack asked. "And why are they connected to carvings of the Egyptian goddess Hathor?"

"What did you say about alphabetic characters?" asked Hamid, climbing up to Jack's location.

"This person here," Jack said. "It looks exactly like an ancient script from the southern part of the Sinai Peninsula at a place called Serabit el-Khadim. Researchers discovered a carving in the winter of 1905 that represented the first known step in language, moving from pictographs to phonetics—a monumental advance in written communication." He smiled at the thought of it. "Phonetics employs sounds generated by spoken symbols to create words that correspond to the objects or concepts they represent. An abstract idea that represents the material world through noises made by a human voice instead of simply drawing a picture."

"All this time, I thought you were just a military man," Hamid said admiringly. "You are teaching me something I never knew after dozens of trips to this site. Remarkable."

"Well, what's more, this carving looks like an early Proto-Sinaitic marking that means praise."

"Then that must be why it is stationed underneath the goddess Hathor. This is idol worship of an Egyptian cow goddess."

"It certainly looks like that to me," Jack replied.

Hamid breathed in the desert air and looked around the altar site, his deep brown eyes betraying the amazement that had overtaken him.

"I've come to believe this is the site of Yahudi idolatry. I grew up hearing the story in great detail in Surah Al-Baqarah, which means "The Heifer." However, I must research the remarkable idea that Proto-Sinaitic characters were inscribed on these rocks. It adds another precise data point to this pattern of evidence."

30

Archer drifted away from Jack and Hamid as they continued discussing the carvings. Their voices faded into the dry buzz of the desert air as he began exploring. Heat hammered his shoulders as he scanned the carvings, piecing together the story he'd dismissed since childhood. Catholic school lectures filed away with Santa Claus and the Easter Bunny rushed back, sharper now. He imagined hordes of revelers gathered around the idol, while Moses was on the mountain for forty days, speaking to God. And the recently appointed priests from the tribe of Levi were busy with a newly inaugurated altar site. So, the people did what was right in their own eyes.

If this truly was the place of idolatry, a second altar had to be here. Something other than these etched heaps of stones, heavy with the energy of selfish betrayal.

He scanned the horizon; the endless grey stone sea relinquished nothing. But the details of Mt. Sinai were stacking up too neatly to ignore. Hadn't Hamid mentioned there were two more sites to see today? If one held the remains of a compelling altar, he'd have to reevaluate his wholesale rejection of the myths his parents had ingrained in him.

He walked back to Hamid and Jack, still discussing the ancient characters etched in the rocks.

He heard Hamid ask, "You learned all this working for your boss?"

"Ethan is remarkable. He inspires everyone he meets to search for an ancient path so our future isn't so disconnected," Jack replied.

"I would love to meet him someday."

"You will, of that I am sure."

Archer broke in.

"Hamid, I was wondering if a site nearby could have been the approved place of worship for the Yahudi."

"Why yes. I can take you there."

Jack had his phone out, capturing the carvings, so Hamid stood and stepped up to Archer.

"You know of the other worship altar, do you?"

"I went to Catholic school growing up, so we learned some about the Bible. But I just had a memory of what supposedly happened here. If this is the Golden Calf location, which I can't even begin to believe I'm admitting is a remote possibility, then maybe there are nearby ruins of the other site mentioned in the stories?"

"I like the way you are thinking," Hamid replied. "Yes, the place is right over there."

Hamid pointed just behind them towards a narrow valley that disappeared up the mountainside. From his perch atop the engraved boulders, Archer could make out a dark outline cutting across what looked like a storm washout area. As his eyes adjusted to the flat desert shadows, he saw a line spanning more than three-quarters of a kilometer across the valley entrance.

"Is that another security fence?"

Hamid's eyes flicked toward the fence, voice even. "It is indeed."

"It has to be a few thousand meters long. We keep asking this, but why is that fenced off?"

"So people don't just walk in." He chuckled. "Come, let us venture across the valley."

Jack finished his digital archival, and the team jumped off the boulders and dashed out of the gate.

"For this location, I will need you all to stay silent until we get in," instructed Hamid as he guided them toward the perimeter and a small concrete shack on the valley's northern end.

"This site requires special permissions, and I did not have time to obtain them before our departure this morning. Please refrain from speaking when we reach the guards. They are not too fond of unannounced guests, especially Westerners."

They crossed a wide, flat section of the terrain separating the golden calf altar from the jagged mountains rising sharply ahead. Archer could feel they had crossed an invisible boundary, moving from the mundane into sacred spaces. His old religious senses rushed back to him against his will. He remembered this feeling from when his high school choir had toured Italy and Austria, singing in the grand cathedrals of those countries. This felt like a moment he'd experienced in the Duomo in Florence, its awe-inspiring domed basilica draped in the morning light, with a haze of sweet incense slowly circling from the silver censers to the heavens. He'd resisted the emotions back then, but they were present, nonetheless. Some places just felt holy. This was one of those places.

The concrete guardhouse door opened ahead, and three Bedouin men exited, standing resolute against the stark horizon of jagged mountains. These men each carried a Saudi-made AK-103, looking like men torn from another age, their layered dark robes stirring faintly in the stale breeze. Faces etched by sun and hardship gave them an air of silent authority, of strength that needed no words.

Archer tensed and slowed his stride. The other two Iraq vets immediately matched his pace and alert mode.

The guard's eyes narrowed as they scanned the strange collection of men approaching them. These Bedouins were the last line of defense, the protectors and enforcers of whatever secrets lay hidden in the remote mountain folds behind them. The quiet resolve in their stance hinted they were not strangers to violence, but men for whom the line between life and death had been tested—and blurred—time and again.

"As-salaam alaykum. My friends and I have come to visit the mountain," Hamid said. For some reason, he'd used English, not Arabic, to greet these men.

Silence.

The faint clatter of shifting pebbles caught Archer's attention. His eyes darted to see a scaly flash as an Egyptian spiny-tailed lizard scurried back to the safety of a nearby crevice. Swift, silent, and prepared to vanish at the slightest hint of danger, like Archer.

"I am Hamid, tour guide from Sindalah. May I have special permission to enter this area and show my guests Musa's altar?"

The first guard's leathery face twitched at the name Musa.

"Today closed," he said.

"That is most unfortunate. I bring guests of His Royal Highness here all the time. It has never been closed."

"Prince friends," he replied, his deceptively strong hand emerging from the flowing garment to raise his AK-103, which he waved in the direction of Archer and the team.

"No, no, these are my guests."

"Today, closed."

Archer saw Hamid's brow furrow at this second denial of entry. He was getting frustrated. Archer looked back at Jack and Sykes, his questioning eyes seeking guidance. Sykes nodded slightly toward Hamid, indicating they should wait and let this play out.

Archer shifted his weight, the gravel under his boots grinding into the dust in the quiet, tense afternoon heat. His gaze flicked from Hamid to the three Bedouin guards, each gripping an AK-103 with hands that looked as weathered as the rifles they held.

Suddenly, Hamid unleashed a torrent of sharp, biting Arabic words into the silent air, ripping through the silence and tearing into the guards. They jerked their heads up, their bodies rigid.

The oldest guard, whose face was set like stone, answered in a faint but steady tone. Hamid reached for his inside pocket and pulled out a thin wallet. He brandished it like a shield, and a faded, battered ID card flipped down, waving in front of the guards.

Silence hung heavy, creaking leather straps breaking it apart as the guards adjusted their grips on their rifles. Then, almost imperceptibly, the eldest guard's posture softened, and he waved them on. Whatever Hamid had said, whatever story his tattered ID whispered, had done its work.

Archer let out a breath he hadn't realized he was holding.

"Come, my friends, we should move quickly," Hamid said.

Archer, Jack, and Sykes kept their eyes on the guards as they walked past the shack, through the fence line, and out into the high desert expanse.

31

London, England

A mechanical whir triggered hundreds of triangular aluminum plates as the baggage carousel spun to life. A spotless black Tumi dropped from the conveyor, and Ethan snagged it in passing. His duffle descended shortly thereafter, and the couple headed out the arrivals gate to a waiting black car.

"The Ritz," Ethan instructed the driver, donning a traditional tweed Flat Cap in Loxley Green Herringbone weave.

"You fancy a kip before we track down ma dad," Ethan asked in an embarrassingly bad Cockney accent.

"We've been in London for all of thirty minutes, and you've gone native on me," Regus quipped. "No, I don't need a nap. And please, don't do that again."

"Just trying to rekindle my childhood," Ethan said, amused at her rebuke. "Believe it or not, I'm a bit uneasy about this idea."

"You'll be fine," she said, smiling as she placed her hand softly on his leg.

Ethan wasn't so sure. Since landing, his mind had been inundated with memories of the world he'd abandoned over twenty-five years ago, and two decades of moving on with his life had only produced a calloused heart. Yes, he could suppress the memories if he kept busy or had his fragments to occupy him. But the adrenaline of war and years of relic hunting had not prepared him to reenter this battlefield. And he felt a gnawing sense of growing danger.

"Well, I'd like to game out a plan before we take the hunt to Fortis HQ."

"Let's go see the house you grew up in," she said, her face pressed against the tinted windows as the motor wove in and out of slow-moving traffic. Ethan could see a childlike awe in her eyes, reflected in the glass. The kind of look one had when visiting a place for the first time. He was glad she was with him. A fresh perspective in a well-worn city produced new insights he imagined would serve them well.

"That'll give us time to lay out a plan and help you reconnect with your old life."

"Not a bad idea," Ethan replied. "I assume the investigative reporter already knows where that home would be."

"221B Baker Street," she said without skipping a beat, turning back to the window as the historic facade of the Ritz came into view, the bustling early afternoon St. James's district spinning about them.

The iconic establishment opened in 1906 and was as posh as Ethan remembered. He had accompanied his father on countless trips to this hotel. Royal dinners, meetings with heads of state, and late-night cocktail parties that became the stuff of legends were swirling in his head. He'd never understood why his father insisted on bringing his only son along on these decidedly adult outings. But the idea of him at the helm of Fortis produced a wildly new take on his father's strange behavior. He'd groomed Ethan to lead since he was a child.

The car pulled up to the front entrance, an ornate canopy stretching overhead. The Ritz crest gleamed atop the midnight blue awning. In a nod to subtle elegance, the doorman, standing tall in his uniform, tipped his hat in silent welcome. Ethan climbed out while the driver opened the door for Regus.

As Regus stepped from the sedan, Ethan felt like a bookseller from Notting Hill watching a Hollywood starlet greeting legions of her adoring fans. Her eyes twinkled with an optimism born deep within her, holding out hope for the future. He would need to be careful. Regus had gotten past his defenses, wreaking havoc on his usually sharp mind. But man, was she exceptional.

"Welcome to the Ritz," the doorman said with a timeless flair, "This way, please."

Ethan checked them into two rooms on the fifth floor.

Regus gasped at the opulence and rushed to the window to take in the view of Green Park and the tips of Buckingham Palace.

"Since you're not sleepy and you don't know where my old home is, meet me downstairs in thirty minutes. We'll go sleuthing," he said from the doorway just outside her room.

"Sleuthing? Why don't we take the Tube to Hampstead and walk a few blocks to Keats Grove? The neighborhood has many cute pubs and a great park I've been dying to see."

Ethan was genuinely shocked at her precision and ease in delivering the exact location of his old stomping grounds. How did she know all of this? And she was right; visiting the park together would be fun.

"So, you do know where I grew up?"

"Obviously," she teased, a sly smile playing on her lips. "I'll be downstairs in half an hour."

Ethan settled into his room, his mind occupied with thoughts of his old home and the possibility of encountering his father for the first time in his adult life.

Something kept telling him this whole adventure was just another archaeological exploration. He was digging in a new place; he didn't know what he was looking for or would find, but the hunt was on.

Or, as Regus would say, "The game was afoot."

32

Nobody spoke until they were well beyond earshot, the kind of distance only possible in a barren expanse where sound traveled endlessly, bouncing off jagged rocks and sinking into the shifting sands. The silence was heavy, weighted by the lingering tension of their encounter. At last, Hamid broke it.

"We are close to the next site," he said, his voice calm but purposeful. "Mr. Archer, I would greatly appreciate hearing your observations once we arrive."

Before Archer could respond, Sykes's agitation bubbled up to the surface. "Hold on a second, that's it? Those guards back there looked ready to light us up, and you switch to Arabic, flash some ragged badge, and suddenly we're strolling through like we own the place? What exactly did you tell them?"

Hamid offered a tight-lipped smile. "The truth."

Sykes scowled. "And what truth would that be?"

"That I was escorting my friends to see the ruins, and if they interfered, things would not end well for them."

"Well, that explains the vibes back there," Sykes muttered.

"What did you show them?" Archer asked, wondering what had gotten into his team lead.

"My tour guide ID," Hamid replied smoothly. "I bring guests here often."

Sykes wasn't buying it. "Tour guide ID, huh? Mind if we see it?"

Hamid chuckled, deflecting with ease. "Sight is simply directing your attention to the proper place. Your eyes don't lack information; it's your heart that is in need. We've arrived."

Sykes frowned but let it drop. The air between them cooled, but his suspicion lingered.

Archer trusted his friend with his life. If Sykes was asking questions, there was usually a reason.

Hamid wasn't exactly who he seemed; that much was clear from his interaction with the guards. Besides, Archer had picked up a decent amount of Arabic during his military days, enough to follow along with most conversations. But Hamid's dialect—thick with the cadence of the Hijaz—was a different beast. From his position a few paces behind, Archer had only caught fragments of Hamid's sharp, commanding tone. But he didn't need to understand every word to know Hamid had laid into those guards with the authority of a drill sergeant dressing down a row of green recruits.

They hadn't dared push back after the weathered badge came out. He tucked that detail away for later. For now, they had a ruin to explore, and he was grateful to be out of range of those AK-103s.

Hamid gestured ahead. "Mr. Archer, take a look. What do you see?"

Archer stepped forward, his eyes narrowing as they swept across the landscape. The high desert stretched out endlessly, but there, nestled into the earth like an ancient cipher, was something that didn't belong.

The formation jutted sharply, an L-shaped anomaly in a world of wind-sculpted curves. Too precise to be a quirk of nature, the double row of stacked stone, perfectly spaced in two parallel columns, starkly contrasted with the chaotic sprawl of rocks and debris around them. Each piece was deliberately placed, its surfaces worn by the years. It looked to Archer like what they used for cattle in his East Texas childhood home. What was it doing here?

And then there were the white stones arranged just outside the chutes. Scattered like breadcrumbs, they gleamed under the unforgiving sun. They weren't haphazard. No, these were markers, spaced with intent, clustered in small groups, while others stood alone. A few were large flat stones, others were cut like a column section pulled from an Egyptian temple. More ancient Egyptian artistry?

Archer's gaze lingered. These stones formed a pattern, a message, a story left behind by hands long gone, meant for those who could read its ancient language.

The wind howled around them. Fingers of dust brushed across the stones, rose on an updraft, like incense in an open-air cathedral. There it was again—holy ground.

Like the Duomo, this structure defied the ages and kept its secrets, but in a different way. And those white stones, brilliant against the dull earth, seemed to pulse with quiet energy, as if waiting for someone to uncover their meaning. Where did they come from?

"It's definitely not a random collection of stone," Archer said. "That L-shaped structure resembles a cattle chute, used to corral animals for slaughter. And the scattered white stones symbolize something. There's a purpose to this site."

"Very good," Hamid grinned, and his eyes sparkled.

"It feels sacred."

The words escaped Archer's mouth before his mind objected.

"Indeed."

Archer scampered down the ridgeline and walked through the left side of the L-shaped ruin. Rising to his waist, the wall of stacked stones didn't appear to have collapsed over the years. There was no rubble, which suggested the formation had always stood around this height. Perhaps some of the wall was buried beneath the ground?

He paced out the first section of the L to about 20 meters, at which point a 50-degree turn progressed another 15 meters. At the end of the line, both columns terminated in a rectangular pit outlined with more stacked stone. A blackened section caught his eye, and he squatted down, tracing his finger along the charred granite. There was no ash. Whatever caused this discoloration happened a long time ago.

"What is this place?" he asked.

"In the early 90s, the Saudi Arabian Department of Antiquities excavated this site. They concluded it was an abandoned mining home," Hamid replied.

"A home? These walls are less than three feet tall. How could this have been a home?" ·

"A fair question."

"Where is the rest of the structure?"

"Wouldn't there have been some remnant of the collapsed walls or roof?" asked Jack, now engrossed in the analysis alongside Archer.

"One would have thought," Hamid said. "But once the department issues a verdict, the conclusions are made."

Sykes paced the area, counting out nine distinctly circular columns, each with an approximately equal circumference but varying heights, none exceeding a few feet in height. But it wasn't their size that interested him.

"Where did these white stones come from?" he asked. "They look like rough-hewn marble. We haven't seen anything with this color or texture anywhere since we arrived."

"Another insightful question." Hamid arched a brow, inviting Sykes to chase the answer on his own. Catching a glimpse of white marble lightly covered by the sand, Sykes dusted off the surface, revealing a giant marble slab. He continued the impromptu excavation with his foot, uncovering a series of large, flat rectangular slabs arranged in a disheveled pattern.

Squatting down, he dug into the soil along the edge of one slab until he reached the base. Approximately six to eight inches deep,

these slabs were definitely cut and carried into place. Digging his
fingers into the earth, he gripped the back of one slab and tried to lift
it. Using all his might, he shifted the slab a few inches before
abandoning the endeavor.

Jack shimmied over the chute wall and joined Sykes in the
exploration. Both men were engrossed in analyzing the odd
placements.

"These slabs must weigh hundreds of pounds. How did these get
here..."

"And why," cut in Jack.

"Exactly. This stone must have come from somewhere nearby. They
couldn't have carried it with them from Egypt."

Sykes scanned the horizon, looking for clues to the stones' origins.

Jack pulled his phone out and began another digital archive while
Archer reviewed the rectangular pit at the chute's end.

Hamid watched the Americans pore over the ruins. He loved
seeing the Mountain's mysteries pull them in.

A few minutes later, he asked, "What conclusions can you draw
from this site?"

Archer stood up in the pit and offered his insights.

"Well, by themselves, these odd configurations don't mean much.
But when you place them in the context of all we've seen today, they
seem to beg the question: how are all these sites connected?"

"What do you mean?" asked Hamid.

Archer pointed back towards the Hathor rock carvings, "That site
is littered with Egyptian-style carvings of a cow goddess, and now
we have what appears to be an ancient cattle chute less than a mile
away. If I had to hazard a guess, this site is an altar for animal
sacrifice."

"Very good," exclaimed Hamid. "This was the conclusion drawn in
the 80s by the treasure hunters I told you about earlier. This was
where they detected a high level of gold molecules."

"Here in the pit," Archer asked.

"Not exactly. They focused their analysis on that."

He pointed past the outer wall of the L-shaped structure, and he and Jack shifted their attention to a feature they'd overlooked. The altar site was perched on the edge of a small valley that dropped twenty or more feet into a dry runoff area.

"During early spring rains, a river flows from mountain runoff. The men claimed this was where the Yahudi priests offered sacrifices, and Moses ground up the golden calf statue and threw the dust into the river."

"And you think this happened?" Jack's brows arched as his jaw dropped.

"Who can say? The treasure hunter's claims were never verified because the Saudi government seized their findings, including all the cameras and footage."

"That's a strange thing for an archaeological exploration if you ask me," Jack said. "Confiscating pictures of the desert and odd rock formations? What were they hiding?"

"His majesty's office does not permit foreign spies, nor does the information they collect and broker go unnoticed. Or unpunished."

Archer heard the same tone Hamid used with the guards: sharp, commanding, final. It betrayed a defensiveness with Jack that he hadn't heard today. Something about questioning the Saudi government on this point irked him. Based on the silence that ensued, he knew the team sensed it too. He looked towards the marble slab to gauge Sykes' response, and he wasn't there. He took a three-sixty scan of the area, but no Sykes.

Archer called out for his team lead, the name echoing through the stone valley. No response. He hopped the walls of the chute and peered into the dry runoff area, its vast smooth boulders hiding patches of greenery nestled in the shade of the rocks. Continuing right, he looked up the long, narrowing valley toward the summit. The valley was deceptively large, and he realized it must be a sight to behold during the seasonal spring rains. An olive-black Keffiyeh pattern darted between two rocks about 50 meters up. Sykes.

"Sykes," he tried again, in the right direction. "What are you doing?"

This time, his team lead heard him and turned.

"Found something. The marble!"

Sykes pointed up the valley toward the summit. He and Jack lifted their heads and looked. They saw a strange section in the mountain where the sides converged, touching the deep blue haze of the vast desert sky. The rocks in the valley around them were dusty brown and light-grey. But up there, a dark patch of the mountainside stuck out like a neon sign at night.

Archer glanced at the sun to ensure he wasn't seeing a shadow. The empty, cloudless sky beckoned him back to earth. He looked harder at the blackened section of the mountain. It almost looked burnt, as if some massive consuming fire descended upon it one day. He pushed that fanciful idea out of his mind; indeed, there must be a geological explanation for the rock formation. But, in the burnt distance, he saw a bright white vein of rock running through the blackened core.

"Is that what I think it is?" he asked.

"I hope you are ready for a challenge." Hamid's eyes narrowed on the horizon. "The journey to the marble quarry is no easy task."

33

Regus exited the lobby elevator in precisely thirty minutes.

From the hotel, the couple turned left down Piccadilly, passing through the Ritz's arch-covered retail walkway, and crossed the street into Green Park underground. They boarded the Victoria line to Euston, then transferred to the Northern line for four quick stops to Hampstead. Twenty-five minutes later, they emerged along charming brick-lined Heath Street. Then, Ethan led the brisk walk to Keats Grove.

"My father is a very cultured man," he explained to Regus as she kept stopping to peer into every pub they passed.

"So, when a property came on the market in the early 80s across the street from his favorite poet's house, he snatched it up and moved the family further into the city. In addition to Latin and Greek, I was required to learn from the great literary minds, including Homer, Virgil, Dante, Shakespeare, Byron, and Wordsworth. But above them all, he prized Keats's poetry, which is richly descriptive, filled with lush imagery that appeals to the senses. Keats championed the idea of "Negative Capability," the ability to accept uncertainty and doubt without seeking definite answers, emphasizing the experience of beauty as an end in itself."

"He sounds fascinating."

"He was most certainly that. But fascination with romantic ideals drove a deeply conflicted obsession with death. I never understood how a man so outwardly committed to the idea of liberty from tyrannical rule became a world leader in weapons of war."

"I suppose only strong men can dispose of tyrants."

"That is very true. One of his favorite lines from Keats was in an early sonnet, *On Peace*. It was never celebrated like his famous *Odes*, but it was quoted incessantly in the home."

Ethan slipped into a singsong voice as he recited the final few lines of the sonnet celebrating Napoleon's 1814 defeat.

"O Europe! Let not sceptred tyrants see / That thou must shelter in thy former state; / Keep thy chains burst, and boldly say thou art free; / Give thy king's law leave not uncurbed the great; / So with the horrors past thou'lt win thy happier fate!"

"That's beautiful," Regus said, her voice thoughtful. "And it aligns with the way you described his character earlier."

"How so?"

"You said he believed Fortis existed to shield people from the cruelty of evil men. It makes sense that he saw himself equipping nations with the tools to shatter the chains of oppression and break free from Napoleonic warlords. History shows us, after all, that liberty sometimes demands enduring the horrors of war."

"You're starting to sound like my father."

"Or Thomas Jefferson. He was the one who said, '*The tree of liberty must be refreshed from time to time with the blood of patriots and tyrants.*'"

"True. But where is the line drawn? Those who kill for freedom often give birth to systems that enslave future generations. War breeds war. Peace is but a stop along the long path of perpetual conflict."

"Yes, but the problem isn't the system. The human heart is deceitful above all things and desperately sick; who can know it?"

"Ah, you're quoting the Prophet Jeremiah to me?" Ethan replied with a slow, conceding nod.

"You recognized that? I didn't peg you as the religious type."

"I'm not. But how do you think I learned Greek? The Septuagint was mandatory reading."

"Fair enough. But because America stood against the world's tyrants in the twentieth century, peace was bought after a hundred years of bloodshed."

"Maybe," Ethan conceded. "But look at what followed. We don't live in peace today. The United States—fueled by my father's exceedingly profitable contributions—has been the chief architect of global instability for the past eighty years. They tasted blood; its metallic tang has intoxicated our leaders for two generations."

"My point stands. The heart is the root problem, not the system."

"But our system incentivizes profiting from destruction. It's the government that proliferates the war machine. Humans take the path of least resistance."

"It's true our system needs reforming. But John Adams said, '*Our Constitution was made only for a moral and religious people. It is wholly inadequate to the government of any other.*'"

"You're saying we should have a theocracy?" Ethan exclaimed, puzzle mingled with offense creasing the lines of his face.

"By no means," Regus countered. "I'm saying that war ends without when peace reigns within. No government will be just unless internal constraints on the human heart are in place. It's why America was born from the Judeo-Christian ideal that all men were created equal, because our Creator endowed us with certain unalienable rights. Without God, culture crumbles."

They turned the corner off Downshire Hill onto Keats Grove in silence. Ethan loved and loathed this discussion. He'd never been able to articulate these ideas out loud. But he had to admit, Regus made sense. Death reigned in the world because the human heart was evil. But he'd never been open to the possibility of internal reforms bringing about lasting peace. He believed Nietzsche was right; God was dead. We'd killed him.

"That's my house," Ethan said, pointing to a four-story structure that stood like a forgotten pearl, its white facade veiled in creeping ivy and its bow windows curving like watchful eyes over the sprawling circular drive. Half-shrouded in shadows, the dormer windows seemed to whisper secrets of the past—a place where time itself had grown hesitant to pass. Beneath its elegant Georgian charm lay a history as tangled as the vines, a story waiting to resurface with the arrival of its newest inhabitant, who seemed to have never come.

"I can't really see it over the fence, but it almost looks abandoned," Regus said. "The neighbor's house looks like it was just rebuilt, though. Someone must live here."

"Or come by on the regular," added Ethan. "I always wondered if my father would give up this place. He doesn't part carelessly with his possessions and rarely for financial reasons."

"We should find out who owns this," Regus replied; that same fire he'd seen yesterday at the Met burned in her eyes. "It may be a clue."

"You mean you don't already know something about my family?" Ethan retorted.

"I have been trying to find your exact residence for a decade," Regus replied, thrilled at the discovery. "I knew your father had been appointed President and CEO shortly before your grandfather's death and would probably move his family closer to the St. James's headquarters. For years, I have meticulously reviewed real estate transaction data in numerous affluent neighborhoods across the city. I narrowed it down to a dozen locations, but I was unable to find an address. What I dug up in Hampstead came from a local paper. Around the time your grandfather died, they reported that a prominent London businessman had purchased a home near the Keats house. I looked for answers, but nobody in your tax bracket puts their names on real estate."

"Then, back at the Ritz, how did you know this was the one?"

"You called me out and I sorta panicked. I blurted out the first district that came to mind," she said mischievously. "I was as surprised as you that I got it right."

"You are something else, Miss Britton."

"Would you like me to find the owner of this home?" she asked. "I've gotten quite good at following the convoluted and deceptive shell games you gilded rebels play to keep your names hidden and taxes low."

Gilded rebels. Nice. She may have some literary talent, after all.

"I'd love to know who owns this," Ethan replied. "How would you find out?"

"I have everything on my mobile. I'd need half an hour to research. But I highly doubt you'll know the entity I find. It's likely a shell company named as a nominee by a British Virgin Islands trust. Do you have anything I could use to get started?"

"Funny you should mention a BVI trust."

"Why?"

"I did business with a BVI wealth management firm back in 2017."

"What for?" Regus asked.

"I needed an infusion of cash to take my private contractor business to the next level. I have refused to profit from my father's wealth, even though he has transferred 13% of Fortis Defense stock into my portfolio. I'd never sell that blood money. But I did use 2% of it as collateral for a securities-based loan to get me started."

"A loan? How much did you take out?"

"Just a hundred."

"You've been able to maintain that Manhattan office and acquire all those artifacts with a hundred-thousand-dollar loan?"

"Um, not exactly," Ethan replied. "A hundred million."

He heard Regus swallow hard.

"I see. That would do it," she said. "And you don't think it's profiting from the blood money, as you call it?"

"I'm not using his funds," he replied, a defensive edge to his voice. "I'm spending the money of the BVI firm and have never cashed in a single stock. Besides, I signed away my voting rights via proxy as a condition of the loan. I own them still but have no claim to the company."

Regus didn't keep prying, and Ethan was glad. He'd never shared his financials with anyone and couldn't believe he'd let that detail slip.

"So, what do you need to start digging?" he said, eager to move on from this awkward topic.

"I suppose a quiet place to sit and work," she replied. "And the name of the firm."

"Let's keep walking. There's a park a block away with a great place to sit."

"And the name?"

"Azure Crescent Holdings."

Ethan headed down Keats Grove, his sneakers pounding the narrow street as he approached South End Road. He paused at the crossing, waiting for a break in traffic, his gaze flickering to two men in their late twenties slipping into a cafe just half a block ahead. Perhaps it was his unsettled state—his mind still tangled in the web of his past—or the lingering guilt of living off his father's wealth, but a knot of unease tightened in his chest as he watched them.

"Ready," he asked Regus, who was glancing at her mobile, searching for answers like an English Foxhound set loose in The Cotswolds.

She didn't reply or even look up, so he grabbed her free hand and walked briskly across traffic and into Hampstead Heath Park.

34

A boot thundered down, sending a Wadi Racer slithering from its sunny perch into the nearest crevasse, rocketing pebbles stinging its back. Sykes was stepping heavy, hustling up the valley. After nearly an hour of ascending, it had become more of a gully. The scale of the rocks he expertly leaped across grew as the journey dragged on, but Sykes loved it. No trail, just a destination and an iron will. He hadn't enjoyed himself so much in god knows how long. Mid-afternoon silence, oppressive heat, and his team's absence converged in a rare external reinforcement of his internal condition. Sykes was alone.

But Sykes was never alone. He was Mr. Responsible all his life—for his mom, his little brother, his men in Iraq, Ethan, and his team. He felt a twinge of guilt at leaving Jack, Archer, and Hamid in the dust as he ran up the rock face. If this had been his operation, abandoning his team would never have happened. But today, Hamid was the team lead, and he was a tourist. So, when Hamid confirmed the white speck he'd spotted was an old marble quarry, he made a flash decision to break off and do something for himself.

Sykes had always been called "an old soul." He hated that term. It was just a polite way to say he was a risk-averse kid and toxically committed to caring for people in his life who should have cared for him. But he flourished at his physical limits and was almost at the marble quarry as he drove up and over another ten-foot boulder. It was a weird way to carve out some "me time," but he was in heaven and didn't care.

As his body gave in to exhaustion, his mind grew sharper. He realized his frustration with Hamid surrounding the Bedouin guards was partly because his intuition had alerted him repeatedly today, and he hadn't been able to put the pieces together. Hamid was another data point in a wildly improbable scenario unfolding before him. He couldn't believe it all began early that morning in a hotel library.

He thought back to the moment he first felt something was off. It began with finding the *Gold Mines of Midian* book and the overwhelming sense that his life would change if he ventured to the mountain. And here he was.

Then, on the hotel ferry, he'd felt a darkness pass behind him. He'd disregarded that initially, chalking it up to exhaustion, having been awake all night, escaping Egypt. But he couldn't ignore his gut-wrenching feeling when the racing boat blew past the Valley of Moses, or again as they pulled up to the security checkpoint behind a border patrol car. He'd been sixty seconds from bursting out the door, the team in tow, and into the desert to fight off an invisible battery of enemy combatants.

Reflecting now, that sense still gave him pause. It seemed so unwarranted. He had no facts to back up his intuition, only twenty years of being right every time his instincts kicked in. But the confrontation with the Bedouin guards had definitely warranted an alert. What bothered him there was his lack of concern. His intuition told him Hamid had it under control, so he let it play out. What had come over him? It was the most irresponsible thing he'd ever done to cede trust and authority to another during an armed confrontation. Sykes had always defended himself and his team. Today, he allowed a civilian he had just met to assume the lead in a dangerous situation.

Who was Hamid? He appeared to be an overeager tour guide, but the way he'd handled their security situation with the Bedouin was beyond impressive. That badge he flashed must be some official ID. But why deflect his question with poetic babble about his eyes not lacking information but still unable to see?

Those unresolved questions were why he abandoned the team and pushed his body to the edge of exhaustion. It was the best way to clear his head of all the noise.

A stinging bead of sweat rolled into his eye, and he grabbed his keffiyeh to wipe it out. Jack's distinctive voice echoed faintly behind. He was intensely asking Hamid a question. Sykes smiled, realizing those two had become friends. Hamid may be hiding something, but he was a damn good tour guide and an even better person to win over Jack despite his well-known mistrust of the Saudis.

He slowed his pace to a walk and filled his aching lungs with deep, slow breaths. He'd been so immersed in thought he'd hardly recognized the blackened mountainside slowly coming into view. He was nearly into the darkened rockscape, standing on the edge of a distinct line of folded grey rocks butting up against the darkened matter.

As the relentless sun beat down on the burnt slope ahead, the black rocks began to take on a bluish hue. Heat waves distorted his vision, and he witnessed a shimmering surface of indigo and turquoise mingled with the darkened rock.

Not prone to exaggeration, Sykes was surprised at a growing sense of awe as he surveyed the glassy sea of stone. He looked to where the sea met the sky and saw a gleaming river of white marble fading over the ridgeline.

He was here.

He looked behind, spying the faint outline of his approaching team. He hoped he wouldn't have to wait long, as he didn't want to proceed without them. Whether it was the silence of the moment, his exhaustion, or the wonder that had overtaken him high up on this mountain, his mind suddenly found the missing piece: trust.

His intuition had been honed from years of mistrusting everyone and everything. He'd spent all his adult life, and most of his youth, protecting people and fixing what was broken. The constant belief that danger lurks in the recesses of unexplored places drove him to incessant analysis and calculation. That skill became second nature and developed into his intuition, which he trusted above all. No, he didn't trust it; he relied on it. Though he doubted it every time, he followed it because the other option felt like death.

That was what bothered him most about Hamid, the storm of doubt and second-guessing that had taken root since he'd held his tongue with the guards and left his team behind to race up the mountain.

Did he trust this man to lead them on today's adventure? A wave of relief swept over him. For some unexplained reason, he did. And at that moment, he knew—in a place that passed his understanding— that these discoveries at the mountain were critical. They were onto something that would revolutionize their understanding of Egyptology and help them succeed at Ethan's mission: finding the missing piece that unlocked the mystery of King Tut.

35

"The demonstration of Fortis AI was a smashing success," Ethan's father said, moby in hand. "With our system, we can remake the world order."

Pendleton eased the V12 gunmetal Ghost through Piccadilly Circus, turned right down Haymarket, and headed toward Pall Mall. Fortis Defense had been in the St. James's district for nearly a century. Its proximity to Whitehall, the Old War Office, Downing Street, and Buckingham Palace placed it at the heart of European power. Even in this exclusive part of London where the rich and powerful were a common commodity, his blacked-out Rolls-Royce drew gawkers of all types.

"Shall I begin shopping our intelligence to the highest bidder?" Celeste asked, compulsively straightening a folder next to the conference room speakerphone.

"Soon," Ethan's father said, not yet finished with his rumination. "Gone are the days of covert assassinations and embedded assets fomenting political unrest until the public overlooks preemptive strikes to calm the storm. In our new era of big data and surveillance state, leverage can be applied to anyone, anywhere, if you have the fulcrum." His booming voice crackling through the speakers.

Returning to the table—two glasses in hand—Celeste leaned closer to the phone. "Roosevelt often said, 'Speak softly and carry a big stick; you will go far.'"

"Precisely. I am now the only one who knows exactly where to place my stick…anywhere in the world," he replied, deeply satisfied with the realization.

"I'm here."

The eight-inch reinforced ballistic steel doors slid open as the Ghost slipped past the security perimeter into the underground garage beneath Fortis Defense HQ. Ethan's father exited the cab and headed for his office, flanked by a six-man security team.

"Good afternoon, Mr. Stone."

He kept walking past the new executive assistant, focused on one thing: saving his company.

Celeste Raines sat alone at the glass table across from his desk, a folder and two glasses of Pappy Van Winkle in front of her, with a single large rock placed in anticipation of the most significant meeting of her life.

"Tell me where we are," he said.

"The Board is set to arrive within the hour. The General Counsel's office is downstairs in the conference room, preparing. I have the documents for your review, and we will be ready to deal with anything they throw at us."

"I wouldn't be so cavalier. The Qataris are cutthroat, and this day has been coming for a long time."

"But our defense is airtight. Ethan is their only leverage. But they don't have him because he landed at Heathrow this morning."

"He's in London!"

Ethan's father could not conceal his shock. What was Ethan doing in London? Even after applying every resource at his disposal, he'd failed to get him here.

"You're telling me he flew here on his own?"

"Not exactly," Celeste said. "He's with an investigative reporter from the Times. One Regus Britton."

"The woman from the Met? Interesting. Where are they now?"

"They just checked into the Ritz less than a kilometer away. Do you want me to bring him in?"

"Negative. Too many years have passed for him to get on board in time. I needed him at The Hull this morning to convince him that Fortis was the future. Send a team to keep eyes on, and we can regroup after this ends."

"Very good."

Celeste relayed the assignment to the very timid girl outside their door.

"Shall we get started?"

Ethan's father sat at the table and sipped his Pappy's. He loved this bourbon, haters be damned. There was nothing overrated about the Family Reserve 23-year.

Celeste opened her folder.

"This is the poison pill we embedded in the corporate bylaws. We can review the strategy."

Celeste Raines was now his Chief Financial Officer. She came to him from HSBC in the year Fortis went public. She'd been a hotshot corporate banking attorney who blew the whistle on the London bank's loan practices. HSBC fired her before the financial crisis when they were forced to shutter their subprime finance unit.

He loved her moxie and knew a star when he saw one. He'd hired her after a ten-minute interview, and she'd immediately proved her worth.

Working in the Fortis General Counsel's office, she'd had the foresight to suggest the shareholders' rights clause to protect them against a future raid on the company. Her proposal almost didn't reach his desk, as the potential dilution of stock was a drastic move nobody wanted to take. But Ethan's father saw the brilliance immediately. If forced to cede control of his family empire with this public infusion of cash, he'd ensure that nothing remained if it was ever wrested from his hands. And that day was here.

"Walk me through it."

"The Board called this special meeting, so I'm sure they can pass a no-confidence motion. Your days at the helm of Fortis are in jeopardy. But even if they have the vote to initiate your ouster, we still have the shareholders."

She slid a spreadsheet across the desk, pointing to a flowchart of contingencies.

"We included a provision that triggers the issuance of new shares if any shareholder—or group acting in concert—acquires 15% of the company's stock. That's the threshold. If the Qataris hit fifteen, they're in for a nasty surprise."

"And what happens then?" Ethan's father asked, his eyes narrowing.

Celeste smiled grimly.

"The trigger activates the distribution of discounted shares to every other shareholder, except for the hostile party. That means their stake is diluted, and they lose the proportional influence they've been building. It's like flooding the market with fake currency—they can't hold enough power to complete their play."

Ethan's father's expression softened slightly, but his mind was racing through potential counters.

"And you're sure this won't spook the shareholders? Our stock has never been more valuable, given the world's perpetual state of war. If this backfires, they could turn against me like the Board when they see the company's value tank."

"That's the risk," Celeste admitted. "But the poison pill isn't meant to be used lightly. It's a deterrent. Suppose the Qataris are aware of the provision. In that case, they'll realize that triggering the pill will cost them hundreds of millions in additional shares, not to mention the ripple effects of a market adjustment. But without an additional 16% of the company, plus all the retail and insider stock, they don't have the power to take it over. Damned if they do, damned if they don't.

"This strategy buys us time to rally the loyal shareholders, propose a counterstrategy, and get you back in charge if you're voted out today," Celeste said with crisp assurance.

He stood, pacing to the window. The beautiful London day outside concealed the tempest within.

"What about the optics? They're already painting me as a tyrant clinging to power. Won't this add fuel to the fire?"

Celeste didn't flinch.

"This isn't about optics. It's about survival. Once the vote of no confidence is in place, they will make a play for the company. When that happens, we shift the narrative if the pill is swallowed. Release a statement highlighting the Qataris' predatory tactics—make it clear they're destabilizing Fortis for personal gain. Frame yourself as the protector of your family legacy and the shareholders' profits."

"That's when we get Ethan on board," he said, her strategy coming together in his mind. "I will make him see that everything we've worked for and all he's continued to benefit from is worth more than his wide-eyed ideals. The world suffers violence, and the violent take it by force; only dangerous men protect the people. It is our divine right."

Celeste took a shallow breath.

Ethan's father wondered how she had managed to stay in the CFO role for a decade with such apparent disdain for the Fortis mandate. It was a testament to her exceptional skill and the value she brought to the company. He hoped her allegiance would hold in this, their darkest hour.

"You know I am loyal to the end." She leaned forward, locking her eyes on him. "I don't have to share your spiritual vision of the world to know Fortis is the last defense against the rising darkness."

A chilly silence descended upon the office. She'd never given him a reason to mistrust her.

Swallowing the last of his Pappy's, the crystal tumbler precariously dangling between his thumb and middle finger, he said, "Semper Fidelis."

"Senatus Populusque Romanus," she replied.

36

"Thanks for waiting for us," Jack panted as he hauled himself up over the ledge Sykes was standing on. "You could've warned us before taking off."

"I know, I'm sorry," Sykes replied. "I had some personal matters to settle and needed a challenging climb."

"Well," Archer gasped, "mission accomplished."

The men took a few moments to catch their breath, drink some well water, and munch on protein bars. Jack was the first to survey the breathtaking view that had captivated Sykes for the past fifteen minutes.

"This hillside looks like a sapphire sea of stone!"

"Doesn't it?" Sykes replied, his awe at the sight still undiminished. "You see the marble quarry?"

Jack turned left and spotted the vein of white rock nestled into the blackened hill.

"Sure do."

Jack set off across the blackened rock face for the final 100 meters to the quarry, his mind still reeling from the hour-long conversation he'd just had with Hamid, discussing these sites' alleged connection to the Quran and the Bible. Jack had never believed the religious claims of any holy book. Still, his years with Ethan taught him that primary sources were the most valuable documents in archaeological research. And yet, he'd never considered the idea Hamid presented to him. Namely, the Bible was the most historically accurate source ever written, and these texts could be used as a written map of the region to trace the route of the Exodus out of Egypt.

The undulating slope descended into a slight depression, and they finally emerged at their destination. The gleaming white marble strained their eyes with brilliant, refracted sunbeams. The valley's massive grey boulders and the black stones of the burnt mountainside were gone. A smooth marble slab had risen to these heights eons ago due to the fracturing collision of tectonic plates. Jack estimated the marble vein was about fifty meters wide and an unknown length as it curved gently out of sight over the ridgeline.

The team traversed the surface to the summit and crested the final hill. An expansive horizon engulfed their senses.

The world unfolded like an ancient canvas—each stroke etched by wind, sun, and the passage of time. The rugged and raw ridge they stood on transformed into a mosaic of jagged peaks that cascaded parallel to the boundless desert below. The distant horizon quivered, and beyond the undulating peaks and barren plains, a thin ribbon of liquid gleamed: the Red Sea.

Jack recalled that they'd crossed it just twenty-four hours ago after he'd downed a multimillion-dollar helicopter.

He missed that drone.

Above him, the sky stretched vast and cloudless, a dome of brilliant cobalt so pure it felt eternal. The profound silence was loosely held by a whispering wind brushing against the stone—a melody of solitude and wonder. Jack stood mesmerized at the view of the mountains and desert.

"Remarkable," Sykes said. "You can see Egypt from here."

"Indeed," Hamid said. "Worth the price we paid in sweat."

After they all took a moment of silence to appreciate the lonely and divine view, Jack asked Hamid, "Why did you call this a quarry?"

"This way." Hamid led the team a few dozen paces along the ridgeline. "Down there," he said.

The scene below was not what Jack had anticipated. He'd imagined a sizeable modern quarry with slabs of marble cut from a bottomless pit. Instead, he surveyed an area no bigger than a residential swimming pool in the States, littered with broken stones and multiple small holes chiseled into the rock face.

"This doesn't look like a quarry," he said. "I assumed that since the L-shaped structure below was supposedly a miner's home, this quarry would be a bit more... industrial."

"That's modern Westerner reasoning," Hamid replied. "Remember what we discussed on the way up. Imagine this scene as if you were an ancient Easterner. Then, use the context of the grand story to look for clues."

Jack pondered this for a moment. Suppose the L-shaped site wasn't used for shelter but for animal sacrifice. That fits the bigger story of the Exodus from Egypt much better than industrial mining. If this were the case, there must be a logical reason that whoever made the altar had good cause to undertake an arduous trek up here to access the marble and bring it back down. Even without hundreds of pounds of stone on their back, that would have been an exceedingly challenging task. But they did it.

These hand-cut marble remnants resembled segments of Egyptian pillars. Their placement, less than a kilometer from ancient Hathor carvings and also done in the Egyptian style, led to an obvious conclusion: people at both these sites must have been exiled Egyptians or skilled Egyptian craftsmen.

"Of course!"

Jack's outburst startled Archer, who had also walked down to investigate. Jack leaped down from his perch, his virtual measuring app in hand, to survey the site.

Twelve holes, each roughly six inches wide and three inches deep, were carved into the face of the white slab. They were grouped into four different segments and evenly spaced around the slab. The segments consisted of a single hole positioned at each corner of an invisible equilateral triangle, making the area between the holes around eighteen to twenty inches apart.

"Archer, you remember the trip to Egypt last year with Ethan?"

"When we tried to join the Aten dig site?"

"Yeah, where did we go after that?"

"To Aswan, and then that famous rock quarry, home to the giant unfinished obelisk they chiseled from the... Oh..."

Archer had figured it out now.

"The water pegs."

"Exactly."

The ancient Egyptian method of quarrying stone involved chiseling strategic holes into a slab, placing long wooden pegs, and soaking them in water. When the wood expanded, it fractured the stone along weak points, dislodging the material. The holes before them now were placed to quarry stone roughly the width of the marble segments found below. The dozen shallow holes carved into the slab must have been remnants of the bottom few inches of the peg placements.

The pair looked about the area with renewed interest. Lying just off the marble slab on a level section of the ridgeline, they found a stone remarkably similar to the pillar segments at the altar site.

"The craftsmen probably discarded this," Jack said. "It's been quarried and chiseled into a column, but see this large fracture? It must have developed while they were working, so it was useless."

"This has to be the location for the stones down at the altar site."

"One hundred percent. But why? What would have possessed someone to make this climb, cut stone from the top of a ridge, and carry thousands of pounds of it back down?"

"Service to God," Sykes said.

Archer and Jack looked up and saw their team lead standing atop a jutting boulder; the early afternoon sun silhouetted his frame.

"Doing what?" asked Jack.

"Service to God."

"That's what I thought you said. Even the second time, it makes no sense."

"Sure it does. You don't have to believe in a god to recognize that people worldwide build remarkable structures to represent their devotion to the Divine. Architecture has always been the primary means by which cultures and religions enshrine and elevate their deities. We've visited Karnak and Luxor, as well as the Temple of Hatshepsut. The Romans built countless temples. The Pantheon to honor all the gods, the Temple of Jupiter on Capitoline Hill just above the Forum, and scores of smaller sites to Aphrodite, Zeus, Jupiter, Mars, and on and on. The Greeks built the Parthenon to honor Athena and the Temple of Apollo in Delphi, home of the world-famous Oracle. Catholics have St. Peter's Basilica, the Sistine Chapel, the Church of the Holy Sepulchre in Jerusalem, Israel, and thousands more. Muslims built the sprawling complex in Mecca and Medina, the Dome of the Rock in Jerusalem, and the Hagia Sophia in Istanbul, though it originally started as a Byzantine church. Cambodia's Angkor Wat is the largest religious complex in the world, built originally for the Hindu god Vishnu in the 12th century, but was later turned into a Buddhist temple."

"You suggesting there is a temple somewhere around here?" asked Jack.

"Maybe. But, more likely, if we examine the source of the stone column segments at the L-shaped altar site, the most reasonable motivation for carving and transporting these stones down the mountain is service to God. These stones represented something meaningful to the builders that displayed their devotion and obedience."

"And what would that be?" Archer asked, engrossed in what Sykes was suggesting.

"I have no idea. I'm not an expert in Hebrew scriptures or their culture. But I know we are standing on a mountaintop, looking out over a vast expanse of desert and sea, contemplating the historical probability that the Jewish exodus from Egypt occurred. And if this is true, which I'm not quite ready to believe, then these stones—dug from a gleaming white vein of exposed marble amid an expanse of burnt rock—must have religious symbolic meaning."

"Hamid, what do you think?" asked Jack.

"I agree with Mr. Sykes. I have only been here a few times with guests. Most are unable or unwilling to venture up here for such an insignificant site. But today is the first time I've thought about this site or these stones carrying symbolic meaning."

"Nobody else you've been with has discussed this?"

"None. Perhaps your boss, this Ethan, would know?"

"Ethan is an expert in Egyptology and their symbolism. He doesn't pay much attention to anything related to the Bible or ancient Israel."

"A shame. Without that understanding, much is hidden from view in this part of the world."

Hamid's words pierced Sykes. Is this why Ethan had never unraveled the mystery of King Tut's murder? Did he need to look at the epic collapse of the 18th Dynasty from a biblical perspective? How on earth would that make any sense, much less any difference? But his gut told him today would change his understanding of Egypt and the team's mission. After all, less than twenty-four hours ago, they'd undertaken an illegal midnight LiDAR scan looking for what Ethan hoped would be an undiscovered temple to the controversial god Aten. How was this all connected?

"Do you know anyone who could help us answer these questions?" he asked Hamid.

"Perhaps. I have a friend at Hebrew University in Jerusalem who is a Professor of Islamic and Middle Eastern Studies."

"The university to which Einstein willed the copyrights to all his public writings?"

"That is the one. Not many know of the Einstein connection."

"I am a bit of a fan," Sykes replied, smiling at Jack.

"Well, my friend," continued Hamid, "is a world-renowned Arabic and Hebrew scholar who has studied ancient texts her whole life. If anyone would know, it would be her. Perhaps I can introduce you all someday."

"That would be great."

"Should we depart for our final stop? The evening is fast approaching, and if you want to see Trojena, there is a remarkable cafe where we can have a coffee and watch the famous Saudi sunsets."

Sykes did not yet want to leave the mountaintop. His jumbled mind was crisp up here, and he was on the verge of a discovery.

"Is there anything else to see on the mountain summit?"

"Summit," Hamid replied. "Mr. Sykes, this is a small ridgeline along the Jebel al Lawz range. The summit is more than a thousand feet higher than this. If you want to experience the true grandeur of the mountain of Moses, we must go to Trojena."

37

Sayyid was always overprepared. But never more so than today. The weapon he'd dangerously carried since his Leader assigned him this task was a gift from Allah. He'd been suspicious when instructed to arrive at the Russian Embassy in Doha at precisely one minute past midnight. However, he'd appreciated that his Leader did not command working during Isha prayer. The Ten Practices of the Religion for Shia Muslims was a command that he adhered to throughout his adult life. At least the corrupt Imam still respected prayer.

Nonetheless, he'd never been in contact with the Russians and was deeply skeptical of the assignment. Surely, his connections to the man brokering billions in Western weapons to arm Ukraine would infuriate the Russians.

Years of war had torn both nations apart while unfathomable wealth accumulated in the hands of a few powerful men. It was the nature of the war machine.

But the Russians either did not know his connections or did not care, as they had given him something only they could have possessed: the most potent assassin weapon ever to pass into the hands of men.

He placed the nondescript vile, no bigger than a cologne sample, in his pocket. Tonight, it would fulfill its purpose and solidify Sayyid as one of the greatest freedom fighters Qatar had ever produced.

After repositioning his vehicle, he raced back to the cafe, desperate to arrive before the young waiter chef finished preparing his meal. Everything depended on his next move, and then, it was up to fate.

"Marhaba," he said to the young man, waving as he approached.

"I'm glad you returned. I have your dish prepared."

Sayyid took his seat at the empty cafe table closest to the ledge, and the boy brought him a steaming hot plate of aromatic chicken served over long-grain basmati rice and vegetables. The spice mixture of cardamom, saffron, cinnamon, black lime, bay leaves, and nutmeg reminded him of home. He savored a mouthful, transported back to his childhood, growing up under the roof of an angry, absent father and a selfless mother. He missed his Omra.

"This is delicious," he said to the upcoming chef, who had tarried by the table to gauge his reaction. The boy was gifted. It was a shame this would be the last thing he ever prepared.

A gratuitous smile formed on the boy's face, and he spun around, returning to the open-air kitchen. Sayyid finished his meal as he mapped out the next few steps. Setting the trap would not be hard, but he had no way to lure his prey. A wave of anxiety washed over him. How could he have been so reckless as to put all his hopes in the Americans stumbling into this exact location? If they did not come, what then? Would he ever have another chance?

His Leader was probably already in London, laying the final preparations for a takeover that would secure an unlimited supply of weapons. Success rested on the next few hours and his ability to complete the assignment. Events that shape history must be recognized by those positioned to seize the moment. This was his time.

The boy was cleaning up in the kitchen. Sayyid surveyed the surroundings. The vast expanse of the man-made lake, suspended in place by the dramatic, angular dam, was still empty. Now was the time.

He stood from his chair and walked up to the counter.

"What else can I get for you?" the boy asked.

"Nothing. The Kabsa was remarkable. You have a talent."

"Jazak Allah khayran! Thank you very much, and may God reward you with goodness. My Omra will be so proud to hear a man of your stature enjoyed my dish."

His Omra…

The cost of war always weighed heavily on Sayyid. His enemies had shown no mercy; neither should he. But this boy was no enemy. He was a devout young man who had shown kindness, hospitality, and respect for the cause. Sayyid was a fighter, not a monster.

"You are most welcome. On second thought, could I have another coffee before I depart?"

"Certainly."

The boy turned to retrieve the water kettle from the kitchen. That's when Sayyid struck. He leapt over the low counter, sliding briefly on the surface, and pulled his suppressed Beretta 92FS from its holster. The boy didn't know what hit him. He collapsed in a quiet crumple and was pulled deeper into the kitchen.

Sayyid removed a pair of flex cuffs from his pocket and tied the boy's hands behind his back. Dragging him into the nearby closet, Sayyid tore the sleeves from his chef's coat into segments. He stuffed a dish towel into his mouth and tied it in place with the cotton strips. He'd probably regret this, but he wouldn't become what he hated, an indiscriminate killer.

Moving with practiced swiftness, he donned another chef's jacket from the closet holding the unconscious boy and unpacked his supplies. He carefully placed the vial and a small syringe on the deck of the espresso machine, familiarizing himself with the setup. He'd need to make a decent cup if he planned to be successful—unless they ordered *gahwa*, which he could make in his sleep.

He grabbed the nylon sack from his duffel and peered out the back door. Still alone. Removing the 100-meter dynamic climbing rope, he walked a few meters to a section where an Almond tree rose from an embedded planter box. He looped an end around the eight-inch steel railing that ran dramatically across the top of the solid concrete half-wall, which capped the massive, angular retaining basin. He tied the loose ends together with a quick hitch and tossed the two coils over the ledge. Leaning over, his head turned slightly to hear the faint thud of the rope's ends hitting the ground nearly fifteen stories below.

He slid the exposed rope under a low-hanging branch and returned to the kitchen. Finally, he buttoned up the chef's jacket, realizing it impeded access to his Beretta. Allah willing, he would not need it. But he placed the weapon on the top shelf underneath the service counter to ensure nothing could go wrong. Nothing, that is, under his control.

His trap was set. He was in position to succeed at his most daunting assignment yet. All that was left to do was wait.

Standing in the stillness of the coming sunset, he took a deep breath as the early evening breeze wafted through the open-air cafe. He despised the Saudis, but they had outdone themselves at Trojena. It was nothing short of breathtaking. Perhaps after today, the resort would be stained with the blood of the infidels, and the world would forever shun its decadence.

38

"This place is unreal," exclaimed Sykes as the team exited the Rover.

It had taken them nearly an hour to drive the 30 kilometers up a winding road leading to the Trojena parking area just below the summit of Jabal al-Lawz. The staleness of the valley floor had transformed into crisp, cool mountain air, and his lungs thanked him for the refreshing drink. The team walked along the edge of the freshwater lake in quiet awe. None of them had ever seen anything like it. This place didn't belong in the rugged expanse of craggy peaks and plunging valleys. But somehow, here it was—an oasis of heaven on earth.

"There is nothing like it in all the world," beamed Hamid. "His Royal Highness had the vision to remake the Kingdom, and this is the jewel adorning his crowning accomplishment."

"I'd usually scoff at such flowery language," remarked Sykes, "But this, this deserves all the praise the tongue could bestow."

Golden hour was nearly upon them, bathing the mountain in warm, otherworldly light. The sun's journey had burnished each ray, as if the sky itself were a master artisan weaving a ballad of longing and homecoming.

"True beauty always catches one by surprise," Hamid said.

They continued silently, taking in the ever-changing colors at sunset with each new step. As they neared the lake's edge, the glassy waters disappeared into the amber sky, merging the two realms into one impossible vista.

"Here is the cafe I told you about," Hamid said. "We can finish the day with a coffee, should you desire, a debrief on all you've experienced today. It is a shame we do not have more time; there are still a few mysteries of the mountain yet to be uncovered."

"What else is there?" Sykes asked.

Enraptured by the scene, he wrestled with a mix of wonder, longing, and doubt. His worldview was being reshaped in real time, and he was beyond the point of no return.

"We did not visit a cave hidden in the slope above the cattle altar, nor a high plateau above. Along the road, we also passed an extensive field of standing stones. That area is off limits, even to my guests, but the legend is that the field is littered with graves." Hamid said as he entered an open-air cafe that blended ancient style with modern flair.

"Whose graves?" Archer asked as he glanced around at twelve concrete tables spaced across a patio punctuated by planter boxes that contained young flowering Almond trees and native shrubbery.

"That is the legend," smirked Hamid. "We are here."

Jack set his pack on a table along the patio's edge and walked over to the half-wall between him and certain death hundreds of feet below. Leaning on an eight-inch steel railing, he glanced out and over at the receding basin stretching down to the valley floor.

"This is remarkable engineering. Normally, dams are built along a river. But I can see no signs of that here. Where did all this water come from?"

"An expansive pipeline system was constructed to bring in water from the Red Sea," Hamid said as he pointed across the lake to a ridge in the distance. "On the other side of that hill is an enormous pump house and state-of-the-art desalination plant. Not only have we filled this lake, we've supplied hundreds of thousands of annual workers, residents, and guests with an unlimited source of fresh water in a dry land."

"Constructing a body of water this high up in a desert landscape is unheard of."

"The marine life and water sports here are world-class. There is also a Ritz-Carlton Reserve, should you ever want to extend your stay to explore the mountain further."

"Sykes, we should bring Ethan here and show him this place."

Sykes did not hear Jack. The mention of a graveyard had captured him. More than any other find, human remains were the linchpin of any historic dating scheme. You find human DNA, and you've unlocked the secrets of a site. Now, who was supposedly buried there, were remains even present, and what, if any, was their relationship to the other locations visited today?

"I will get us coffees," Hamid said.

Archer walked with him, peppering him with questions about the unexplained legend.

"Sykes," Jack prodded. "You with me, buddy?"

He came to and glanced at Hamid and Archer as they headed to the cafe counter.

"We should come back with Ethan," Jack repeated now that he had Sykes's attention.

But once again, Sykes didn't hear him. His internal alarm sounded at a level he'd never experienced. Stepping out from the patio area, he scanned his surroundings. The cafe was empty, except for their team and a lone worker behind the counter. No other tourists were out on the lake edge. They must all be at the other end, where an evening concert was underway at the outdoor amphitheater. He looked up, seeing the distant lights dancing across the waters and the steady, muffled beat echoing through the valley.

Where was the threat? He knew this was not a moment to let his guard down. Ceding his responsibility to Hamid had worked in the valley, but here, he must lead.

"Something is wrong," he whispered to Jack, who had followed him. "Very wrong. Stay alert."

He looked back at the cafe counter, where Hamid and Archer had already placed an order and were returning to their table. For a moment, his gaze lingered on the worker. He was a fair-skinned Arab with a wiry frame, standing just under six feet tall. But the way he stood betrayed a confidence unmatched by his nondescript appearance. Like a Geiger counter, Sykes's intuitive warning system was spiking off the charts.

That's when the attendant looked over and caught his eye, sending shivers down his spine.

39

"Marhaba. Four gahwa, please, and some dates and chocolates."

"Very good," Sayyid replied. "I will bring it to your table."

"Thank you kindly," replied the tour guide, who was deep in conversation with one of the American team members.

Sayyid watched as they returned to their table, marveling at his good fortune. He glanced over at the other two team members who had left the patio area for the walkway at the end of the lake. The largest of the Americans looked like a formidable foe; his broad shoulders and commanding frame stood facing the opposite side of the lake. Next to him was a man of equal height, leaner but intimidating. Sayyid was glad he didn't have to engage these men in a fight. Instead, they'd die slowly over the next 48 hours.

The largest man suddenly turned and looked right into his eyes. In an instant, Sayyid's soul erupted in rage for the years of brutality and oppression heaped upon his people by America. These men were servants and workers of iniquity sent from the Great Satan to spread evil into the world. His mission was to repel the invaders and cleanse the earth of their presence. Soon, the Hidden Imam would reveal himself and lead his people in the final battle.

But his eyes must have betrayed contempt, and he knew

immediately this American had sensed his rage. He spun away into the kitchen to fetch the kettle. A good cup of traditional Arabic coffee took around thirty minutes to prepare, so he would need to speed up the process. They only needed to take one sip.

He placed whole beans and cardamom in boiling water and then arranged dates and chocolate on a serving dish. When that was completed, he checked the coffee and was satisfied that the aroma was nearly complete. He picked up the tiny vial from the espresso machine deck and cracked the yellow seal with a black icon, its protective sheath falling unnoticed to the floor. He took four ceramic Finjan crafted to resemble the husks of the date palm, inserted his syringe through the vial's remaining plastic covering, and placed two minuscule droplets into each traditional coffee cup.

He found a Dallah, poured the steaming hot coffee through a sieve into the golden serving thermos, and set it on a tray alongside the tiny, nearly empty cups. He considered pouring the coffee in the kitchen to guarantee the colorless and odorless poison would not be spotted in the cups, but that would be an unforgivable breach of tradition for the tour guide. He would know something was wrong.

If he were to complete the mission, he had to hide the hate that raged within him. That American would not likely drink if he left the look they'd exchanged unaddressed. So, he said a prayer, picked up the silver coffee tray with one hand and the plate of dates and chocolates with the other, and walked out to confront his enemy face-to-face.

40

"There is something off about the cafe worker," Sykes said.

"What?" asked Jack, unaware of his team leader's concerns.

"This is the fourth time I've had a horrible feeling we're in great danger."

"Seriously?" Jack crossed his arms. "And this is the first time I've heard about it!"

"I kept it quiet because today has been unlike anything I've ever experienced. With all we've seen since getting on that ferry, I couldn't be sure my intuition was working."

"Yeah, it's been a day for sure. What were they?"

"The first was when the racing boat passed us, and then we pulled up at the guard station behind a border patrol car for number two. Neither made any sense to me; I had no evidence of danger—just a feeling. The third was when Hamid and that tattered badge got us through the guarded fence line. That one made complete sense. However, something is off right now. And I think it has to do with that cafe attendant. His eyes hold a darkness that chilled me to the bone."

Jack looked deeper into the open kitchen, where the man was busy gathering dates and arranging a plate for them. Jack watched as he brought four small ceramic cups to a sleek two-group commercial espresso machine, where he lingered for a moment, his hands and body obscured by the stainless-steel work of art. But he wasn't making lattes, as he didn't touch the machine.

"You're right; something does feel off," Jack said. "We should alert Archer."

Jack and Sykes returned to the table where Archer and Hamid were discussing the legend of the graveyard. Jack hastily sat and leaned in to warn the men, but Hamid kept going.

"The Bedouin locals claim the area is full of jinn," Hamid said. "Or, as you may say, ghosts or demons. They are required to guard the area but are terrified of it."

"Ghosts of who?" Archer asked.

"Well, the legend says it is a Yahudi graveyard."

"Jews? Why would they be buried there?"

"Because of the Golden Calf Altar. Both the Bible and the Quran say many people were killed when they engraved Hathor into the rock and fashioned a golden image. They had to be buried somewhere. Your Bible is most explicit here, saying three thousand were taken away from the people and buried outside the camp."

"And no one has searched the area to confirm or dispel the legends?" Sykes asked jumping into the mesmerizing discussion.

"Not so far."

"What would it take to get a permit to excavate the area?"

"This is not possible. We have just opened Trojena to the international community. His Royal Highness is not interested in stirring up controversy. For now, the graveyard must remain a whisper amongst friends."

Jack was drawn to the allure of a forbidden site.

"Oh, there are always ways," he said. He might organize another late-night LiDAR scan later this week.

"Your gahwa."

Jack looked up, startled to see the cafe worker addressing Sykes.

They'd forgotten all about him!

Neither had warned Archer or Hamid.

"My apologies for the intense look I gave you earlier," he said in perfect English. "I got caught up in my head as I realized we had run out of native Arabic coffee beans for you. We usually have a special reserve single-origin coffee from the southern coastal region of Jizan, but it seems we're out. I'm most disappointed. I have prepared an import for you that is a very close second."

The attendant smiled broadly at Sykes as he laid the small cups on the table. Placing the dates and chocolate in the center, he quickly poured half a cup into each finjan. Picking up the first cup, he handed it to Hamid, turned the dallah handle towards him, bowed slightly, and departed.

Sykes looked at Jack, and both men couldn't tell if the danger had passed.

"In the Kingdom, we have rich traditions at this moment," Hamid said, raising his cup.

"Please join me and remember all we have experienced this day. The coffee is hot, so please swirl it gently, right to left to cool; do not blow."

Hamid continued speaking as the four men sat swirling their coffee.

"The sun is about to set, and we are most blessed to have been divinely aligned for a day together. The mountain is a sacred place. Any who wish to see beyond the tyranny of the urgent are invited to slow down, look up, and gaze into an ancient story much bigger than ourselves."

Jack smiled, thinking about the moment he stood in the shade of the Split Rock.

"I have come to enjoy you men very much. Mr. American Warrior, you changed today. I bear witness to your transformation. Whatever you have come through to bring you here was necessary, so you were prepared for what lies ahead."

"Mr. Sykes, I can see you are the leader because these men respect you. Very few powerful men also command the loyalty of their team. Do not waste that."

"And Archer, you have a thirst for knowledge that drives your exploration. If you seek, you will find, if you seek wholeheartedly."

With that, Hamid raised his cup and took three sips of the aromatic, ebony liquid. He closed his eyes and breathed deeply, savoring the rich flavors and the company of his friends.

Jack raised the cup to his lips and glanced over Hamid's shoulder. His gaze landed on the cafe attendant peering at them from behind the espresso machine. Darkness hung about the man like a solar eclipse, and Jack felt a penetrating evil reverberate through his soul. His malevolent countenance radiated hate, and in an instant, Jack knew his friend was in mortal danger.

"Don't drink," he yelled at the others, throwing his half-full ceramic cup, shattering it onto the patio.

He leaped from the table. Yanked the tan Sig Sauer P320 M17 from the waistband holster he'd illegally carried all day.

"Stop, or I'll shoot," he barked at the cafe worker.

In one swift motion, Sayyid reached below the counter. Beretta in hand, he spun towards the team. Muzzle flash. A storm of 9mm gunfire rained down.

Jack hit the floor. Concrete chips from the planter sprayed.

Sayyid swiveled to the other men. Spent his final dozen rounds ripping the table apart.

Grabbing his backpack, Sayyid bolted through the kitchen, disappearing out the back. He gripped the rope he'd slung over the steel railing, fixing his gaze on the sandy deck below. With the wind howling around him, he yanked the ropes between his legs, looping them around his back, then swung them in front of his right hip, his movements fluid despite the chaos unfolding around him.

Arms crossed over his chest and shoulders, he swiftly formed a loop at the nape of his neck, the coarse fibers digging into his skin.

His adrenaline surged. Tightening his grip with his right hand, he took a leap of faith. Hurtling off the 150-foot retaining wall, the unyielding rope his only lifeline.

Jack's bullets ricocheted off the rocks in a cacophony of danger.

Sayyid plummeted too quickly. His agonizing scream sliced through the air. The rope melted the flesh on his braking hand.

Above, Jack leaned over the retaining wall, firing down at him. He hit the valley floor hard enough to break a leg, but the surging adrenaline masked any pain. He swiftly untied the quick hitch knot to separate the rope halves and frantically pulled one side to release the rope from its anchor. So, nobody above could follow.

He leaped into his nearby Cruiser, fired up the powerful engines, and left a cloud of dust, confusion, and death behind him.

41

Sprawling across North London like an untamed oasis, Hampstead Heath's wild beauty starkly contrasts with the city's polished edges. These ancient woodlands, rolling meadows, and tranquil ponds were Ethan's second home. He'd spent countless summers lost in the forests that litter the 790 acres of green space, swimming in the ponds or playing rugby and cricket on the open green.

He walked an engrossed Regus past the car park and the water-lined residential neighborhood, across the bridge separating the mixed bathing pond, and deeper into the heath.

She didn't look up once until they hit a bit of an incline leading to the summit of Parliament Hill.

"Where are we?" she asked, puffing slightly.

"Welcome back," teased Ethan. "You are quite good at not looking where you're going."

"I'm getting close already," she exclaimed, ignoring his comment and forgetting her question. She was immediately pulled back to the phone, apparently on the scent.

Ethan decided not to be offended. She wasn't mean, just focused.

A few minutes later, he crested his favorite view in all of London, which unfurled like a painter's masterpiece. Below, London's skyline glimmered in the hazy distance, a canvas of iconic shapes—the shard of glass piercing the heavens, the dome of St. Paul's resting solemnly against the horizon. The tall summer grasses danced in the breeze, surrounding a dozen public benches where thousands of dreamers sat before him, contemplating the mysteries of being.

Ethan was once one of those dreamers—vibrant, youthful, and alive—but his spark flamed out years ago, leaving a void of meaning.

Into the void descended despair, and from despair rose reckless abandon. That abandonment fueled a decade of adventure, danger, and attainment of academic prestige and growing wealth. It had also worn him thin.

He sat on a bench, and Regus followed, still oblivious to her surroundings. From two feet away, he could study her face without reproach. It betrayed a passion and zest for life he didn't possess. She wasn't just interested in what she was doing; she was on a mission. Something inspired her to aim up, to set her sights on a higher-order good and move through the world with everything she had in its pursuit. He spent years crawling out of holes; she seemed to be soaring toward an ideal.

It's not that she hadn't suffered. He saw pain in her eyes when she spoke of her father and fury when she spoke of his. But somehow, she transformed that sorrow into an energetic power source while he had collapsed into a vacuum. He wanted what she had.

He thought about the last time he had sat on this bench with his father. In his early teens, they'd visited it many times. His father had been unusually active in his education, constantly grilling him on his Latin pronunciation, arithmetic, world history, and especially the poets. Always the poets.

"Plato wanted to kick the poets out of the Republic for a reason," he'd say. "Because they were dangerous, my boy. Dangerous men will never be allowed to live in a society ruled by philosopher-kings. That's why we Stones are men of the people. Never forget this."

Ethan had long internalized this message, making it a creed he lived by. Although it felt like a lifetime ago, just yesterday, he took a moment to ground himself before delivering his lecture to a packed hall. He reminded himself that he was a man of the people, a teacher, before being a scholar.

A strange emotion overtook him, rising slowly as a preceding wave but crashing like a tsunami upon the shores of his disconnected heart. A cataclysmic earthquake had happened in his soul's deep, unexplored waters. And he was experiencing the onrushing emotion bursting all boundaries of his walled-off subconsciousness.

He respected his dad. No, he loved him. And needed to see him again.

Sitting on the Parliament Hill high place overlooking his childhood, a refrain from his favorite poet began singing in his mind:

"Grave men, near death, who see with blinding sight
Blind eyes could blaze like meteors and be gay,
Rage, rage against the dying of the light.
And you, my father, there on the sad height,
Curse, bless, me now with your fierce tears, I pray.
Do not go gentle into that good night.
Rage, rage against the dying of the light."

A tear broke from his eye and cascaded down his cheek. Years of animosity and endless flight had brought him back to this bench, looking out on the horizon, wondering about his dying light. No, he would not go quietly.

It was decided. Ethan had come home. If his father wanted him, he'd enlist.

"I got it," cried Regus, abruptly throwing her arms in the air as if Arsenal had just scored a winner.

Her raucous shout drew the attention of the other bench sitters scattered across the hill. Ethan glanced around to assess the size of the spectacle she'd created and noticed two men sitting together a few meters back. His throat tightened. It was the ones he'd seen duck into the cafe as they crossed South End.

"Ethan, I found it! The owners. And it's not some random shell company. Well, not the one at the bottom of the pile. I had to work through ten entities spanning two continents. But, I found it."

"That's great, Regus. We need to go."

"What, go where? And where are we?"

She looked around for the first time in almost an hour.

"Oh," she gasped, "This is Parliament Hill! I've always wanted to come here. I fell in love with Notting Hill in high school, and Julia Roberts was my favorite actress…"

Ethan stood up, casually grabbed her hand, and, for the second time in as many days, urged her to move away from impending mortal danger.

"We've got company. Again," he said. "Don't look around; just stand up and walk with me."

Her triumphant demeanor shifted immediately into calm resolve. Ethan threaded her hand around his right arm, and they walked arm-in-arm down towards the swimming area. The two young men waited for a beat and got up to follow.

"We've got a tail," Ethan explained. "I noticed them as we left my neighborhood and crossed into the park."

"You think it's your father again?"

"Possibly. There's only one way to find out. Keep going."

Ethan released her arm and spun around, walking back up the hill directly into the path of their tail. Regus played her part perfectly, continuing uninterrupted.

"Oye," Ethan said as he approached the men. "My girlfriend left her moby on the bench. Did either of you gents see it?"

The momentary hesitation at being addressed by their mark bought Ethan all the time he needed. He closed the gap on the first man before he realized the fight was on. Ethan spotted the concealed carry holster, so he stepped inside his right shoulder, executed a lightning-fast spin, and buried his elbow in the man's diaphragm. He snatched his Glock from its holster as he keeled over, raising it on the second man before he had time to react.

"Why are you following me?" Ethan barked. "Who are you?"

Wisely, the second young man stood still, not moving for his weapon. Ethan backed up to keep the winded partner in view. He lowered the Glock to waist level to avoid the inevitable attention that came from brandishing a public firearm. This wasn't New York; the Brits were still squeamish about guns. Nobody said a word.

"My dad sent you?"

The upright one nodded, "We was told to keep eyes on. That's it. Wasn't gonna touch you this time."

"This time? You one of the fools in black that tried to kill me in New York," he shot back.

"Kill you? No, we was told to bring you to London. Shouldn't have fired at ya. We got in awful trouble for that we did."

Regus rejoined Ethan as he lowered the Glock and tucked it into his waistband.

"Mystery solved," Regus said.

"You got a car around here?" Ethan asked, no longer concerned for their safety, his new objective crystal clear.

"Yes, sir," said the one who had lost his gun. Apparently, he was the driver.

"Why don't you boys complete your task from yesterday... and bring me in?"

"Ethan, are you sure you're ready to do this?" Regus whispered.

"Trust me," he said, "It's time I came home."

"Oh," Regus squealed again, remembering her discovery so rudely interrupted by these stalkers. "Ethan, I didn't get a chance to tell you what I found in my search. Your childhood home..."

"Who owns it?" he cut in with curiosity and mild foreboding.

"You do."

42

"What do you mean they are alive?" the Leader screamed into his phone.

"Everything was set perfectly, but the insignificant tour guide was the only one who consumed the poison," Sayyid replied. "The Americans were about to drink, then one of them figured it out and started shooting."

Sayyid was roaring down the mountainside, headed to nowhere in particular, just away from the scene. He felt unbearable guilt that his carelessness had corrupted the mission. One glance, that was the difference between glory and abject failure.

"You said it would be done."

"It will."

"Do not return until it is. Otherwise, I will be forced to visit these failures upon your mother and daughters. Ethan's team must die, and he must be captured." The Imam thought for a second and added, "And then killed."

He ended the call, placing the phone back beneath his robes. This was most unfortunate. It raised the stakes of the special meeting dramatically. The threat of Ethan returning for his shares increased a thousandfold if his team was still active and he was still alive. He needed a victory today at all costs. Everything depended on the next few hours.

His black stretch limousine glided silently to a halt outside Fortis HQ, the building's historic stone facade reflecting in the tinted windows. A liveried chauffeur stepped briskly to the rear door, opening it with a practiced flourish. Imam Khalid Al-Nasir, having composed himself from this most distressing phone call, emerged from within, his presence as imposing as the heat rolling off the hot Yorkstone paving slabs of the private guest entrance.

He was draped in a bespoke black bisht embroidered with fine gold thread, the luxurious fabric catching the light in sharp glints as he moved. Beneath it, his immaculate white thobe was pressed to perfection, and an aura of wealth and authority hung about him like a garment. A turban of cream silk, adorned with an intricate gold pin bearing his family's crest —an azure crescent moon —crowned his head, framing his hawkish features and piercing dark eyes that scanned the small, welcoming party with measured indifference.

The rhythmic click of his polished leather sandals seemed to mark time itself as every onlooker froze in silence, transfixed. Beside him, an aide carried a leather briefcase emblazoned with the same embossed crest on his turban—its contents were said to contain documents that could move markets. His hands were clasped lightly behind his back. A ring adorned his finger, set with a massive, uncut Lapis lazuli bearing its distinctive gold-colored flecks, rumored to have been blessed centuries ago in a secretive desert rite.

The Fortis executives, flanked by their entourage, awaited him at the building's entrance. Khalid paused for the briefest moment, allowing the whole spectacle of his arrival to settle in their minds before offering a faint, knowing smile. With a subtle nod, he ascended the steps, a figure who seemed less a man and more an omen of power incarnate.

Celeste Raines greeted the Imam.

"Good afternoon, Sheikh Khalid. Welcome to London."

"Many thanks, Miss Raines. It is my pleasure to be in your vaunted city."

"The Board is assembled and awaiting you just down the hall."

Ethan's father had insisted on using the boardroom on the first floor, a sign that this delegation was not welcome deeper inside his fiercely private headquarters. If they were to wrest control of his family legacy from his capable hands, it would be done in the room where vendors ironed out contracts, not in the corner boardroom on the fifth floor with a perch overlooking nearby Buckingham Palace.

She turned and led his delegation past the armed guards, down the concrete and glass hallway, into the secondary boardroom where two dozen people were already gathered. The boardroom, nonetheless, was a fortress of authority, with its dark walnut table stretching like a command center under the glow of precision lighting. Twelve high-backed leather chairs circled it. Behind tinted windows, the tree-lined St. James Park loomed, a reminder of the global stakes tied to every word spoken within these soundproof walls.

"Where is Mr. Stone?" the Imam asked, clearly annoyed that he was not the last one in the room.

"He will be down shortly. Please, take your seats."

The Imam ignored her. His morning began as he liked it, with an Eastern European girl brought to his hotel room for breakfast. He wouldn't let some bossy Western hussy ruin his good mood. He made small talk with other members of the Board, but all remained standing, taking their cues from him.

Celeste also stood, positioned at the head of the table, waiting for Mr. Stone as instructed. The Imam knew that every detail of this tense corporate dance was highly choreographed. Each action and reaction was calculated to signal defiance and control. Someone would walk out of here today a winner. It had better be him.

"Good afternoon, everyone," bellowed Ethan's father, who entered the boardroom through a hidden door none of the other board members had access to.

"Come, come, please sit."

The eight board members were seated in leather chairs, and staff members were positioned along the wall behind them. As Chairman of the Board, Ethan's father always sat at the head with Celest to his right, being the only non-board executive allowed at the table. To his left was Fortis General Counsel. Across from him, at the other end, sat the Imam with his General Counsel. The pieces set in this high-stakes chess match were nine board members, two lawyers, and a CFO.

"Let us begin," Ethan's father said.

The Imam glared down the fifteen-foot table at the insufferable CEO and his arrogant little lapdog finance officer. He knew she'd been the one to embed the poison pill in the bylaws during his negotiations to take them public. Inexplicably, his teams had missed it during due diligence, and once the Securities and Exchange Commission had approved their listing, they couldn't unwind the document. That little deviant had added a decade of work and billions to his costs.

But they had received a Level III bank-sponsored American Depositary Receipt, the most prestigious ADR available. With the Bank of New York Mellon (BNY) as their sponsor, the British company could be listed in America. The fact that BlackRock owned BNY, was the icing on the cake. Their ideological alignment had been a boon for Fortis and its ultimate goal of owning the defense giant.

Beneath his immaculate robes, the Imam trembled as adrenaline coursed through his veins. He'd spent two decades working towards this moment. And he was going to enjoy every second.

"As you know," began the Imam, "your continued leadership of Fortis no longer meets the shareholder objectives of a safe, sustainable, and profitable company. We have called this special meeting to relieve you from your duties."

His opening move was as direct as it was aggressive. He'd advanced the king's pawn two squares forward and staked his claim to the center of the board.

He expected the mirror from his adversary, and then the fun could begin.

43

Ethan's father was roiling beneath the surface.

"I'm sorry you feel that way, and I look forward to the productive discussion I'm sure will ensue on this topic. But before we get there, I have prepared a dossier for the board's review on a strange collection of activities in Latin America." He'd beaten better players than this degenerate seated across from him. So, he came out harder with his own fierce counter.

Celeste Raines stood, placing a folder containing the Fortis AI findings from earlier that morning in front of every member.

"As you can see," continued Ethan's father, "this is an intelligence report detailing the activities of several Colombian drug lords and their financial web of influence."

As he spoke, Celeste pulled up a map overlay on the screen behind him.

"These are cartel homes and trafficking routes into America via the U.S. Southern border. The pins indicate a different caravan of people headed to the border over the past four years. Red pins are drugs - primarily fentanyl; blue pins are children."

"What has this got to do with our meeting?" the Imam asked with a twinge of anxiety.

"An excellent question." He paused, fingers steepled, the picture of a man already savoring the winning move. "As you are all aware, Fortis has been collaborating with the United States Department of Defense to provide drone surveillance equipment globally. It came to my attention some time ago that as these surveillance deals were being brokered, our most illustrious Imam was traveling to the same locations and engaging in, how shall we say it, unsavory behavior unbecoming of a Fortis representative."

"How dare you accuse me?" the Imam roared, lurching forward in his seat.

"Of what exactly?"

"Of whatever you were going to say."

"So, you deny you followed the Fortis team across Europe, using your board seat to curry favor with our clients as we closed the deals?"

"To accuse me of impropriety is to impugn my honor. I have done nothing unsavory." Sweat glistened at the Imam's temple despite the cool air.

"Nothing? So, you are entitled to your morning breakfasts, and no one should notice or care?"

"Get to the point, Mr. Stone," the Imam's General Counsel interjected.

Trembling with rage, the Imam fell silent.

The bit about breakfast had landed. Ethan's father held a stone-still, unreadable expression, but within, he sneered with sly mischief. He'd touched a fulcrum.

"I noticed a pattern emerging in places we sold our surveillance equipment." he continued. "In every location, there came an increase in disbursements to digital wallets owned by Eastern European organized crime rings. Those disbursements coincided with an increase in the flow of trafficked minors, which we have monitored for years."

"How could you possibly know this?" spat the Imam, the venom still dripping from his tongue.

"My good sir, you forget with whom you're speaking," Ethan's father calmly replied with a razor-edge.

The two Alpha males waged a silent battle through their unyielding glares—neither man willing to blink, let alone concede.

"As I was saying, this pattern of evidence indicated an anomaly too coincidental to ignore. In the interest of protecting our company, I explored the connections by overlaying the patterns of crypto disbursements with the geographic regions Fortis operates in. Which brings us to this Colombian dossier."

Ethan's father leaned back in his leather throne. Fortis AI was deadly. The Imam's face—stricken with foreboding of what was unfolding—sat motionless, drenched in sweat.

"As you can see," he continued. "In 2021, Fortis partnered with Gustavo Petro, a former M-19 guerrilla and the controversial mayor of Bogotá. Our equipment helped him secure the Presidency in 2022 and strengthened our ties with Caracas. Interestingly enough, just after the victory, a similar pattern of crypto disbursements began for Colombian cartel members who subsequently flooded the American market with drugs and trafficked minors, like Eastern Europe."

Celeste changed the screen.

"Here is the relational web connecting all the individual cartel members, their organizational structure, and the complex digital financing matrix funding it all."

He paused for effect, expecting a furious interjection from the opposite end of the table. None came. He had their attention.

"Notice the name at the center of it all: Azure Crescent Holdings, a registered BVI wealth management firm."

He looked up at the red-faced Imam, whose massive Lapis lazuli ring trembled on his neatly folded hands.

"We all know the utility of the BVI secrecy laws, so I cannot tell you who is behind this organization. However, that name reminds me of a certain family crest I often see at these board meetings. Care to enlighten us, Sheikh Khalid?"

"I care to do no such thing," the Imam replied, working overtime to control his rage. "This is the precise reason we are gathered here today. Your insane lust for power, which supersedes all reason."

"So, you have no idea who is behind the company funding child trafficking across Eastern Europe and Latin America?"

"You speak as if this dossier has any credibility or accuracy. We have no information about the reliability or origins of your information. It all appears to be fiction written by a madman clinging to power. Where did you get this data?"

"From Fortis AI."

My little demonstration made a bigger splash than anticipated.

"What is Fortis AI?" replied the indignant Imam.

"My secret black site project built to carry Fortis into the brave new world."

His acknowledgment to the Board of a secret black site sent murmurings rippling through the conference table.

"I have achieved what most of you said was impossible," he continued. "The future of Fortis is digital."

"Madness," shouted the Imam. "You claim to have a hidden project none of us are aware of, and yet you cannot see what is unconcealed. Your days at Fortis are over. These sorts of bold proclamations, conjecture, and circumvention of corporate governance are why we have decided to remove you from your seat."

"I'd like to see you try." Ethan's father stood. He was tilting towards violence with every syllable slung his way. He saw the Imam as a soft man, a weasel who paid others to do his dirty deeds.

I'll make quick work of this fool right here in front of everyone.

"Sit down," snapped Celeste, her whispered voice hot in his ear as she reined him in. "We knew this was coming. Stay the course." Ethan's father retreated to his chair.

The Imam's General Counsel stood, "Fortis requires a two-thirds supermajority vote to remove the CEO."

He handed everyone a copy of the relevant bylaws governing the removal of executives. "All ballots are verbal yea or nay, and since all Board members are present, we have the quorum."

The General Counsel looked towards the Imam.

"I propose a motion to remove the Chairman of the Board, President & CEO," he said.

"I second," came a thin voice from the third seat.

"All in favor of removing Sir Ethan Stone the Third from his positions at Fortis, say yea."

As expected, six yeas sounded off.

"All those opposed."

"Nay," Ethan's father said, expecting two more from his longtime friends and Board allies. But none came.

"Six in favor, one opposed, and two abstentions, the motion carries. Sir Stone, you are immediately relieved from your duties as Chairman of the Board, President, and Chief Executive Officer of Fortis Defense."

44

Jack's eyes narrowed as the mysterious worker disappeared down the winding valley, a shadow swallowed by the dust. Gone.

A muffled commotion snapped him back to the moment—raucous shouting outside the cafe. Heart pounding, he bolted around the building into a scene spiraling out of control.

Sykes stood toe-to-toe with half a dozen armed guards, their MP5s glinting in the early sunset. The tension crackled like static in the air, teetering on the edge of violence.

Archer lay crumpled on the ground, a keffiyeh cinched tightly around his shoulder, dark blood soaking through the fabric. Pale and unsteady, Hamid clung to the back of a chair with one hand, the other fumbling inside his jacket pocket.

Jack sprinted to him. "Hamid! Can I help? Are you okay?"

Hamid's voice was thin, strained. "Please... get my badge. Show them."

Jack reached into Hamid's jacket, pulling free a battered leather wallet. An ID card in Arabic script, worn but unmistakably official, slid into view. Jack's hands shot up, his steps deliberate as he moved toward the guards.

"Sir!" Jack shouted, locking eyes with the closest one. "My men are injured. We're here on official business."

He thrust the ID forward, the wallet flipping open like a lifeline. A beat passed—a long, charged silence—before the guards lowered their weapons. One stepped forward, his English clipped but clear. "What do you need?"

"A doctor," Jack said, his voice urgent. "One of my men's been shot. Our guide—he's fading fast. We think he's been poisoned."

Orders barked into radios sent the guards into motion. Two crouched beside Archer, pressing gauze against his wound, while others hauled Hamid into a chair, his breath shallow, sweat pooling at his brow. Sykes rushed to Archer.

"Are you alive?" Sykes asked, crouching beside him.

Archer grimaced, teeth bared. "It's but a flesh wound," he muttered with a smirk, mimicking a British drawl. "Seen worse shaving."

Hamid was slumped forward, his face ashen, his breath wheezing. Kneeling by him, Jack gripped his shoulder. "Hamid, how are you feeling?"

"Like fire... inside," Hamid rasped. "Can't... breathe. Can't..." His voice trailed off, eyes fluttering.

"Stay with me!" Jack yelled as he shot to his feet. "Sykes! He's going under fast. We need to know what he ingested. Stay with him. Don't let him close his eyes."

Sykes nodded, barking orders at a guard who relayed another frantic transmission.

Jack tore into the kitchen like a man possessed, pulling open cabinets, ripping through shelves, boxes, bottles, anything—think, think—what poison moves like this? Tasteless. Odorless. Fast-acting. A killer's favorite signature.

The kitchen was a wreck by the time Jack stopped to breathe, his brain firing off possibilities. His eyes darted to Hamid, slumped at the table, Sykes practically hovering over him while guards swept the perimeter. Jack clenched his fists. Think!

Then it hit him. The worker. The lingering glance. The coffee. The espresso machine.

Jack turned and lunged for the espresso bar, tearing it apart. Stainless steel tools—frothers, tampers, cups—crashed to the floor—clatter, smash, chaos. Nothing.

A cold sweat broke on Jack's back as he crouched low, pulling out his tactical Maglite. He flicked it on, the beam sweeping under the cabinets. The light froze. There, framed in the glowing beam like an accusation, lay a small plastic sheath—a broken seal.

Jack's gut dropped. He reached for it with trembling hands, mind spinning. This wasn't just poison—this was precision. Whoever that worker was, what he'd slipped into Hamid's cup wasn't random. It was a planned assault from a trained assassin.

He picked up the cap, where an iconic design—a bold, black trefoil—spun like a silent warning, set against a stark yellow circle. Three sharp blades radiated outward, resembling the quiet spread of something invisible, something deadly. The dark center held Jack's gaze, a void where secrets and danger converged, harbinger of a catastrophe.

The radiation symbol didn't scream; it didn't need to. Its silence is the language of death, whispered across a world of shadows and secrets. This symbol wasn't just a warning—it was a promise.

Jack sprinted back to Sykes and Hamid, seal in hand.

"The poison was radioactive."

Sykes took the tiny plastic cap, spinning it in his massive fingers.

"Polonium-210," he said. "The most deadly and stable radioactive poison."

"Has to be."

"This is very bad, Jack. Hamid is not likely to make it. Nobody survives this stuff."

A roar filled the blood-red evening sky, and both men looked up just in time to be blinded by rotor wash. A gleaming white and green Sikorsky S-92A Helibus dropped from the heavens, its sliding double door ripped open, and a team of paramedics exited, encircling Hamid. He was on a stretcher and loaded into the helo in no time. A paramedic team had also led Archer to the flying trauma unit, and he was climbing in unaided.

"We need you in now," shouted one of the flight crew.

Jack and Sykes were standing somewhat dazed by the paramedics' unexpected appearance and their speed and professionalism. Was this the standard response for guests at Trojena?

"Get in now," the crewman shouted again and returned to the helo.

Sykes and Jack followed, taking their seats in the first two rows of the plush passenger accommodations. The bird took flight as paramedics hooked Hamid to IVs and drew blood. The crewmen handed Jack and Sykes flight helmets in the front seat.

"Repeat, what did he consume?" asked a paramedic in their ear.

Jack knew the answer.

"We think it was Polonium-210."

On cue, six heads swiveled as every paramedic stopped their work and looked at Jack.

"Say again," came a voice over the comms.

"We think it was Polonium-210. I found a radioactive seal under the espresso maker where the worker had paused just before bringing out our coffee. Hamid's symptoms and rapid decay fit the profile."

"Show me," came the voice. A hand from the front appeared. Jack produced the seal and handed it over.

"Change course," the crewman said over the comms. "Sheba Medical Center, Ramat Gan, Israel. Administer the ARS agent."

The paramedics jumped into action.

"Israel? That's three hundred kilometers away," Sykes said. "And I didn't know Saudi flew into the country at all. And what is ARS?"

"Israel has the best radiation treatment," the crewman replied. "They've developed a new drug for hematopoietic acute radiation syndrome or H-ARS. The American National Institute of Health funded $5 million in research, and the U.S. Department of Defense purchased the FDA-approved orphan drug for their troops in Ukraine. If he has radiation poisoning, the ARS agent will slow the ionizing effects on his bone marrow and critical organs. We must stop the internal hemorrhaging and prevent infections and anemia. The Israelis know what to do better than anyone."

Jack was speechless. He knew the Israelis lived in a tough neighborhood, but the weight of the Iranian nuclear threat never really hit home for him. But as the Saudis flew his new friend to Israel to try and save his life with an experimental drug, the NIH and FDA funded and approved, he realized the Middle East was more complex than he'd imagined. And he had the wrong view of the Kingdom.

"All this for a tour guide," he said quietly to himself.

"A tour guide," came the voice over the headset. "Hamid is not just a tour guide. He is a private intelligence agent for the King and is married to His Royal Highness's eldest daughter. Nothing is to be spared for Hamid; the King commands it."

45

"Now that we have that unsavory action out of the way," the Imam said. "Any motions before we conclude our business?"

"I move to appoint Sheikh Khalid as Interim CEO," came the mousey voice three chairs over.

"I am honored," he replied. "I second."

"Sir," his General Counsel said, "Shall we remove the non-board members from the room?"

"By no means. They need to see what comes next."

"Very well. All in favor, say yea."

Six voices rose in consent.

"All opposed?"

Silence.

"Motion carries. Welcome, Imam Khalid Al-Nasir, Interim CEO of Fortis Defense."

"Thank you. As my first action as CEO, I formally accept the acquisition bid from Azure Crescent Holdings."

His aide flipped the crescent moon latch, opened up the briefcase, and passed around his company's Letter of Intent to purchase Fortis Defense.

"So, you admit it's your company running drugs and kids across the world," Ethan Sr. exclaimed.

"Baseless accusations," he replied with a dismissive drawl. "As you can see, the offer from my prestigious company is generous, granting all shareholders a two percent premium. Moreover, I intend to take the company private to prevent such burdensome incidents from happening."

Ethan Sr. laughed out loud.

"This is utter nonsense," he said. "You don't even have a majority stake in Fortis. What makes you think you can get 90-95% control to take it private? I'll never sell you my shares."

"You forget, good sir, with whom you are speaking," dripped Khalid in mockery of his defeated foe.

On cue, his General Counsel produced another document outlining the Azure Crescent Holdings position.

"As you can see, our early morning moves today have secured us the remaining 14% stake in Fortis."

Ethan Sr.'s eyes widened, and he glanced at Celeste.

"What? Did you expect us to swallow your poison pill? Only a fool would walk into that obvious trap."

"Congratulations, you read the bylaws," Ethan Sr. said. "But you'll never get the retail shareholders to go along with you."

"You'd be surprised what creative marketing, patience, and access to unlimited capital can do. Turn the page."

Ethan Sr. flipped the spreadsheet and saw a tacky, full-page ad for an Arabic-language sweepstakes to win a lifetime premium subscription to an online platform.

"What is this?"

"Your retail shares."

"Excuse me? I don't understand."

The Imam had two devastating revelations to deliver. But because of that nasty little poison pill, this first one had taken him nearly twenty years and almost ten billion dollars to secure. And today, it all came into the open. He knew Fortis would fight it, but he'd concocted the plan in 2009 with the U.S. Secretary of the Treasury and the head of the Securities and Exchange Commission. He was one hundred percent confident it would hold up in court.

"For nearly twenty years, my company has been running the sweepstakes you see here. Hundreds of thousands of my Arab brothers and sisters have won a lifetime membership to the online service. To maintain that coveted account, they must do two things: keep a current phone number and email address, and re-up their sweepstakes win every year with a simple digital signature."

Ethan Sr. slammed his fist against the table, his voice a thunderclap. "Who cares about this?"

Khalid leaned back, the corner of his mouth curling into a predatory grin. "You will," he said coldly, "if you stay quiet long enough to see your empire burn."

"You don't have my empire!" Ethan Sr.'s voice cracked with fury, his face reddening. "And you never will!"

Khalid's eyes gleamed with a dangerous calm. "Oh, but I can already hear it—the dying gasps of a kingdom crumbling under the weight of its failed leader."

The room fell silent, the air between them thick with tension, like the moment before a detonation.

"Well, for each of the numerous winners to claim their prize," he continued, "they had to register for a free account at the Azure Crescent Holdings customer portal. There, they could maintain their compliance and sign all necessary legal documents. Once initial registration was completed, we offered them a special addition: for just ten dollars, they could purchase one hundred shares of an American defense company stock to be owned by them but held in a trust until the company was sold. At this point, they would be paid the share's retail value via their customer account."

Ethan Sr. was at a loss for words. He could see where this was going.

"I can tell you understand the predicament this simple

sweepstakes has placed you in. I shall continue."

This was a dream come true for Khalid.

"Not one person ever turned down the stock purchase. And because every individual purchased the stock in their name and kept it in their wealth management trading account, which I manage, I have never violated your shareholders' rights clause. I subsidized the stock purchase, but that is a small perk for winning such a prestigious sweepstakes."

Celeste had pulled away from the table and was having a heated discussion with the Fortis General Counsel.

"I'm sure you know what the annual signature requirement is all about," said Khalid, working towards the pinnacle of revelation number one.

"Yearly assignment of proxy rights," replied a dejected Ethan Sr.

"Bob's your uncle," he said in a sardonic cackle that morphed into a guttural roar.

"And do you know how many retail proxy votes have now been assigned to me?" he shouted, slamming his hand down on the walnut table. "Twenty-six percent," each syllable a staccato burst like live ammunition hurtling across the table.

That figure tore into Ethan Sr., the dangerous rounds knocking the air from his lungs like a sudden punch. His brain was gasping for answers, panicked and frantic. He looked at Celeste for help as he started coughing uncontrollably.

"That cannot be legal," she interjected. "We are already preparing a suit to challenge this vile and immoral tactic."

"Do your worst," he bellowed. "You will waste your time and resources, only delaying the inevitable by a few months."

"Even if it holds up, that only gives you forty percent of the company. You'll never get a majority stake."

"Ah, you forgot about the insider shares," a vicious grin spread across his pointy face. "Care to run some quick calculations on the number of shares represented in this room?"

Celeste didn't need a spreadsheet. She knew what the Imam's allies' six board seats represented.

"That's six percent. Still not enough," she nearly shouted back to this wicked man. The confidence she radiated an hour ago unraveled like a free-fall stock market.

Khalid's malevolent grin gave way to a deep and menacing laugh.

Celeste glared at the ashen, downcast faces of the two Fortis board allies who abstained from the vote.

"Marcus! Lila," she shouted, "How could you!"

"It's time for a change, Celeste."

Celeste couldn't believe this. Her closest friends had betrayed her.

Ethan Sr. managed to calm the coughing fit, streaks of crimson staining his French cuffs.

"You've still only got forty-nine percent," he sneered.

"And this brings us to your son, Ethan Stone the Fourth."

That cursed briefcase creaked open again, and Khalid slid forward a contract dated September 22, 2017, with Ethan Jr.'s signature scrawled boldly at the bottom. It was time for the final revelation.

"What's this?" he growled, the spasms in his lungs returning.

"The masterstroke of my plan. Your precious only son, who loathes you more than I, has betrayed you."

"Ethan has never sold a single share of Fortis! I've watched every portfolio transaction he's made."

Blood was now gushing from Ethan Sr.'s nose and mouth as he lost all control of his coughing.

"You are correct. He didn't sell them; he used two percent as collateral on a hundred-million-dollar loan." Khalid let that final line linger like the last leaf in autumn.

Time to deliver the death blow.

"And, he signed away his voting rights... to me."

Ethan Sr. convulsed again, his eyes black and glossy, fluttering swiftly from side to side.

In a sudden and violent rage, Ethan Sr. leapt from the table, closing on Khalid.

"Where is that ungrateful simp of an heir," he roared, "on the day my empire limps towards annihilation?"

But Khalid, undeterred by this feeble assault, watched in gleeful fascination as the once intimidating man, now defeated and helpless, collapsed at his feet in a pool of blood and fury.

Celeste rushed to her boss, shouting for a medic. Chaos in the boardroom erupted as security teams burst into the room and cleared a space around the fallen ex-CEO.

Board members and staff scattered while the two General Counsels argued furiously over the revelations.

Khalid moved with the poise of a newly crowned monarch, not one of those regional kings like his Saudi and Emirati neighbors. No, he had attained real power, his throne secured at the helm of an actual kingdom. He commanded a war machine before which the world would soon tremble. He was the master and commander of an Empire, a King like one of the Pharaohs of old.

"Check," he whispered, standing over Ethan Sr. as paramedics ripped open his shirt. He watched as one of them found the space between the fifth and sixth rib just below his nipples and cut a three-centimeter incision deep through the subcutaneous tissue and muscle layers, opening up the chest cavity.

All his plans had converged in a single moment with glorious success—all, that is, except for Sayyid's failures and the miserable son, who was impossible to locate. He may have the shares to secure the company takeover, but Fortis would never be his until Ethan was dead and his loan defaulted.

He looked down at Ethan Sr., lying motionless on the floor; the inserted chest tube gushed foamy, coagulating crimson as the emergency thoracostomy sought to empty the fluid from his lungs.

He hadn't known about this apparent sickness concealed by Ethan Sr. These were probably the final moments of his life.

But he felt no pity for this man. He had chosen his path, and fate had come for him. It was the curse of the kings.

46

The satin grey Bentley Flying Spur Mulliner, with twenty-two-inch self-leveling wheels, whizzed past security into a chaotic scene.

Ethan saw a stretch limousine parked behind two hospital ambulances. Their bright yellow checkered Battenburg markings and blue lights cast an ominous flicker on the guest entrance to Fortis HQ.

"What's going on?" Ethan asked.

"We don't know," the young man in the front left passenger seat replied. "Nobody would answer their phone."

They parked in the last VIP guest spot, exited the surprisingly exotic sedan for a private security team, and headed up the stone steps.

A rush of bodies surged past them and out into the car park, dispersing into a bevy of waiting vehicles idling behind them.

"Who are these people?" asked Regus, knowing Ethan had no answers.

That's when Ethan saw him. The thin banker, who had closed on his loan a decade ago, was dressed in the traditional garb of a traveling Arab holy man, flanked by two security personnel and two aides. Ethan almost didn't recognize him in the cream turban and black robe.

"Mr. Khalid," he shouted over the klaxons' wail.

The Imam froze in place.

Ethan continued approaching the man who'd made everything he'd done in the past decade possible. "It's so good to see you again. What are you doing here?"

The Imam managed a thin smile and said, "Ethan. I might ask you the same thing?"

"I've come to see my father. Have you seen him? What's going on?"

"Your father has had... a difficult day," he replied. "I must keep my schedule. I look forward to reconnecting soon."

He, too, rushed past Ethan and into the waiting limousine, which sped out onto The Mall behind an official escort vehicle.

The security team that brought them kept moving deeper into Fortis HQ, their pace quickening with every tense step.

"Celeste," one of them called out.

The thin, forty-year-old redhead dressed in a sharply cut navy blazer with subtle pinstripes and a coordinated pencil skirt spun at the sound of her name. Her terrified face morphed into amazement when she saw the guests her security team had brought.

"Ethan!"

"Do I know you?" he replied, the welcome back to Fortis unlike anything he'd imagined.

"Your father, he's," she faltered. "He's in here."

She led them down the hall and into the boardroom, where scores of medical personnel were furiously working on the man now lying on a stretcher.

A raspy whisper escaped Ethan's constricting throat, "Dad."

Ethan tried to get close but was pushed out of the way by an emergency worker carrying a high-flow oxygen bag-valve mask. Ethan watched as the BVM was carefully placed over his dad's face, with pulse oximeter sensors clipped to his fingers, and ECG electrodes attached across his chest to monitor his heart activity. A flexible, medical-grade silicone tube rose from an incision in his ribcage below his chest, attached to a drainage system reservoir.

He felt a hand slip into his, its fingers interlocking with a gentle squeeze.

His mind spun as he watched the powerful man he'd remembered from his youth cling to life. Celeste spoke.

"Your father is sick, Ethan. He has been battling Adenosquamous Carcinoma, a rare cancer that causes heavy bleeding in the lungs."

Regus couldn't believe she was hearing this. That was what her father died from—the burn pits.

"I'm so glad you're here," Celeste continued. "Your father was removed as President and CEO of Fortis by that despicable Imam who just left. We are in real trouble, Ethan, and your father needs you. The company needs you."

"Needs me for what?" Ethan managed to ask, his mind hazy, but the smoke was clearing.

"To lead."

So it was true, and Regus was right; his dad wanted him back at Fortis because he was dying. The refrain from Dylan emerged again amid the chaos of his heart: *Do not go gentle into that good night.*

"Who is the Imam?" Ethan asked.

"That man in the black robes."

"Mr. Khalid," Ethan asked. "He's my banker."

"We just found that out," Celeste replied, pushing down her rage that the broken relationship between Ethan and his father had cost them the company. "He's also a Shia Imam who has been coming after Fortis for decades. We will need to discuss everything."

Stabilized, the teams from London's largest private hospital whisked Ethan Sr. from the conference room; Ethan followed in silent shock, Regus still holding on.

They moved him down the hall, into the lead ambulance, and out of the Fortis compound in a flurry of piercing alerts that faded into the late afternoon hum of central London.

Ethan stood on the steps of his dad's empire, the onslaught of competing emotions from surging oxytocin and norepinephrine flying across his neurotransmitters.

But he wasn't simply having a neurochemical response. Biology didn't explain what had gripped him. He was watching his dream unfold before his eyes. His father's empire was on fire, assaulted by a foreign power, and he had been absent.

"Come on, Dad," he whispered, "Rage, rage against the dying of the light. It can't end like this. We were just getting started."

47

Tel Aviv, Israel

Jack peered through the glass at Sheba Medical Center, watching scores of doctors and nurses swarm around Hamid. All engaged in a desperate attack on the relentless radioactive invader. Tubes snaked his arms as the IV pump clicked in a relentless rhythm, chelation drugs dripping into Hamid's veins, forcing the radioactive poison toward his kidneys to flush it out.

On the flight in, the Saudis pumped Hamid's stomach, dragging many of the radioactive isotopes out before they could seep deeper into his muscle and blood cells. Then they pumped in a jet-black liquid—activated charcoal—coating his insides, trapping and absorbing the poison that lingered.

He received critical care within an hour, and the rest was up to the Israelis.

Sheba Medical Center was truly a hospital without borders, treating Palestinians, Lebanese, and Syrians. This ethos of care was woven into the fabric of Israeli society and their Torah.

That a Saudi aircraft had pierced Israeli airspace at all was miracle enough. No treaties. No ties. Approval could only have come from the very top—a silent signal of shifting ground in the Middle East.

Archer was treated for his gunshot wound in the transport on the way to Israel. The bullet had torn straight through his outer shoulder and hurt like hell, but he'd be fine in no time.

Sykes' phone rang.

"Ethan!"

The team gathered around as Sykes put it on speaker.

"Where are you?" he asked.

A calm but tense voice rang out in the waiting room. "I'm in London at Fortis HQ. I got here right as..."

"You went to Fortis to see your father," Sykes nearly shouted in shock.

"I did, but he collapsed just before I arrived there from a rare cancer that filled his lungs with blood."

"What," continued Sykes.

"Is he okay?" asked Jack.

"We don't know."

"Who's we?" Archer asked.

"I'm with my dad's CFO and Regus."

"Who is Regus?"

Ethan paused, not knowing how to answer the question—the last twenty-four hours had been a lifetime. He decided on the snark that had kept him and his team alive in life-or-death situations like these.

"An amateur detective who's been stalking me for a decade."

Regus glanced at him, mildly scandalized, having heard the conversation from Ethan's speakerphone.

Ethan forced a smile and said, "You'll love her. Where are you?"

"Also, a hospital. But in Israel," Sykes replied.

"What are you doing there?"

"That is a long story," Sykes said, "But the spark note version is our tour guide was poisoned with Polonium-210 by an assassin chasing us as we discovered Mt. Sinai, and after Archer got shot, the King of Saudi Arabia called in a favor and flew us to Israel from a resort city nested high in the desert mountains."

"Ummm, that's a lot to unpack. Archer, you okay?"

"Just a flesh wound," he said, repeating his British accent from earlier, trying to milk it for a laugh that never came.

"Sounds like we need to meet up. Can you all make it to London today?"

"Negative," Jack replied, cutting in. "We have some items to take care of here, and I'm not entirely sure about our immigration status. We arrived in a Saudi Royal transport without going through customs. Can you come to us?"

"You can use the Gulfstream," chimed in Celeste.

"Are you serious?" Ethan asked.

"Absolutely. We're only four hours from Tel Aviv. We have a few items to discuss first, but I'm sure Ethan will allow it—if he's conscious," she said with another wave of sorrow glancing across her face. "Regardless, I'll have it ready to go."

"Okay, we'll come to you," Ethan said. "We can firm up the details shortly."

The line went dead.

The team looked at each other. No one knew what to say. Ethan going back to London was as likely an occurrence as Sykes playing ice hockey in Hades. But his venturing back into Fortis HQ, seeing his father, and getting cozy with company executives who would loan him a multi-million dollar jet to fly to Israel was incomprehensible.

"Who did we just speak to?" Archer asked. "You sure that was Ethan?"

"I know," Sykes replied. "You hear how he harassed that Regus girl? He only does that for close friends. Something's changed in him."

"Sounds like he had a day like we did," added Jack, who walked back to the observation window to check on Hamid.

The flurry of activity had died down. A single nurse stood by his bedside, scribbling notes on his chart. A physician entered the waiting room and approached the team.

"Hello, Dr. Liora Halevy, Head of our Nuclear and Radiological Medicine Unit. Your friend is very sick, and his chances of survival are not good; we have seen this before."

"You've treated a patient poisoned by an assassin with rare nuclear material," asked an emotional Jack, clearly shaken by the news. His biting tongue activated in moments of distress.

"Yes," Dr. Halevy replied matter-of-factly. "This is Israel. But, the good news is that because emergency responders removed some of the radioactive material before it entered his cells, we estimate the dosage to be less than one microgram."

"And that means what?"

"One microgram is the threshold for statistically assured fatality."

"So he's going to be okay!"

"I did not say that," Dr. Halevy replied gravely. "But there is a minimal chance he could survive. It will take a few days before we can further determine his prognosis. But we will give him the world's best care and alert you if any changes happen."

"Thank you, Doctor," Sykes said as she turned and went down the hallway. "Who's hungry? There is no use in staying here. We should find some dinner and debrief."

"Agreed," added Archer. "I hear Tel Aviv has great food. Jack?"

Jack wasn't ready to go but knew staying was pointless. Hamid had become like a father to him, and, as foolish as that sounded, he didn't want to lose the one thing he'd never really had.

48

Sana'a, Yemen

Seventy-five hundred feet above the sea, a wiry teenager in a tattered Nike shirt and stained Levi's, cranked his bicycle on two shriveled sticks, snarling in frustration, jostling against four and a half million souls while weaving through the chaotic street.

Old men lounged in plastic chairs, along the ochre curbs, chewing khat, and watching a streak of Jordan red on a bike kicking up shards of rock and glass from the littered curb.

He blazed through the old city wall, up chipped concrete steps, down a narrow alley, and across the ancient square, on a mission not even Allah himself could stop.

Ditching the bike, he bolted into Souq Al-Milh, a bustling UNESCO World Heritage Site. Despite its name, there was more to the market than salt.

He found the weathered wooden door, knocking in a deliberate rhythm: Long, Short... Pause... Short, Long, Long... Pause... Short, Long, Short.

A brief silence followed, broken only by the metallic clanking of deadbolts and security chains unfastening. They had accepted the sacred code: Noor—the Light.

"Come, come," urged the hooded servant, "you must get inside."

He suddenly found himself standing among the great ones of Yemen—the inner circle of the Houthi rebel leadership that had taken over Sana'a in 2014: the Supreme Political Council.

"What is the message, child?" asked the elder.

"The Imam says, 'I have it. You will never again want for weapons. Deploy the reserves immediately; replacements are on their way.'"

49

Khalid hated entrusting his most precious secrets to a child, but operational security was necessary to protect their interests. The time had come to move all his pieces onto the board, and he prayed his hidden knights in southern Arabia would respond quickly to the call.

"Get me the MODAFL immediately," he told his aide with the briefcase.

A direct line to the Iranian Ministry of Defense and Armed Forces Logistics (MODAFL) was established within moments, and his headset started ringing. He'd waited too long to make this call.

"Khalid," said the voice on the other end.

"It is done. We can finish the deal," he said. "You have my word as the new Fortis CEO; nothing stands in our way. I will deliver the UAVs, ballistic missiles, small arms, and munitions as negotiated."

"This is most welcome news. It's been years since this deal was corrupted."

"The time of fulfillment is now upon us. You can release the final reserves to Lebanon, Gaza, and Yemen. I will replenish."

"See that you do," said Lieutenant General Kian Rostami-Bahrami, "I'd hate to have another strained relationship with one of our neighbors."

The line went dead.

That was it then. The Iranian arms deal was back on.

Like a fine Persian rug, his billion-dollar plan to acquire Fortis was woven from patience, cunning, and sacrifice. With Yemen in motion and Iran resuming shipments, one frayed end dangling on the edges of his masterful creation remained.

"Get me, Sayyid."

He could not allow Ethan to keep slipping through his grasp, unraveling his life's work. No, he must trim every tattered edge and finish the job.

"Where are the Americans?" he said to Sayyid without greeting him.

"I do not know."

"Can you get to Turkey?"

"Yes."

"I'm sending you a contact at the Embassy in Ankara. He has your next assignment. We must regroup. Ethan is in London. I ran into him today."

"London," said a shocked Sayyid. "I will come to you."

"I need you in Turkey," he said with a decided air of finality. Hopefully, Sayyid could take a hint.

"Very well," he replied. "I will be there tonight. But I did not know the Americans would..."

Khalid had already hung up. He was done with the whimpering failure's excuses. He'd need a new operator to get Ethan's loan into default. Lucky for him, England hadn't had a border in decades; finding a group of young men in London who shared his ideals wouldn't be a problem.

His issue: Where is Ethan?

50

Celeste led Ethan and Regus upstairs into his father's office.

"Care for a bourbon?" she asked, unsure of his tastes or how to treat him. For ten years, she'd stood at his father's side, memorizing every preference, tic, and pressure point. What she hadn't expected was ending this day in his sprawling office, facing the spitting image of her boss, only twenty-five years younger and a good deal hotter.

"Yes, please," Ethan replied. "Big Rock Bourbon style if you can."

"Of course," Celeste smiled as she opened the wall freezer. "Same as your father." She popped a block of ice from its mold and dropped it into the barrel-shaped press as she glanced at Regus. "Miss?"

"Oh no, I'm fine," Regus said. "You two go ahead."

Leaning gently on the press, melting the ice into a perfect sphere, Celeste turned her attention to Ethan. "We need to discuss your father's succession plan.

"For the past few years, your father has prepared for you to come home," she said, grasping the perfectly translucent ice ball with stainless steel tongs and placing it in a weighted crystal glass.

"While not the scenario we'd imagined, today is the day we need you, Ethan Stone the Fourth, to lead Fortis."

She shimmied off the Pappy's stopper, poured him two full fingers, and handed him the glass.

"What do you say?"

Sipping the amber nectar, Ethan replied without hesitation, "I'm ready."

"You are," stammered a dumbfounded Celeste. Ethan Sr. had convinced her this would be the most challenging negotiation of her life. She'd been authorized to grant him anything requested to close the deal, with a heavy emphasis on anything.

"I am. I've had quite the day," glancing over at Regus, who had sat in a high-back leather chair. "And I'm ready to be the CEO of Fortis."

"That is great news," she said, genuinely enthralled at this response, but her eyes betrayed the fury simmering beneath.

"Why do I sense you're unhappy with this outcome?" asked Regus. "I'm quite familiar with that seething rage in your eyes."

Celeste looked over at the girl in the chair, wondering who she was and what she was about. But she wasn't wrong.

"Yes, well, had this decision been made a few hours ago, we may all be in a different place."

"You hold me responsible for my father's illness and the board vote," Ethan asked.

"No, no. I just..." Words escaped Celeste as another crushing wave of grief gripped her. Ethan had no idea what he'd done.

"You just what?" asked Regus. "Trust me, we've been through a lot today, and whatever you're holding on to, it's not gonna phase us."

Celeste had finished making her drink and raised it towards Ethan. "Here's to whatever is next." She clinked glasses and downed the expensive bourbon with one tilt of her head.

"Ethan Sr. knew he was dying," she continued. "And he prepared detailed instructions for me to carry out. I will not allow today's events to thwart his wishes and my duty."

She set the tumbler on the glass conference table and paced to the expansive view overlooking St James' Park.

"We also knew the Board ouster was coming. Our next move was to rally the shareholders, remove the Imam from the board, and reinstate Ethan Sr. But…" she trailed off, another wave.

"We did not expect they would already have the votes for a majority share. This was not in our game plan. And it presents a serious obstacle."

"You're telling me that Khalid can take over Fortis?" Ethan asked; his burning fire to protect what he'd committed to had been lit. "How did they get enough shares?"

Celeste looked at him, softening as she thought about what a hard man his father was. She could not blame him for the division.

"You, Ethan. The deciding shares were your 2% proxies assigned to Azure Crescent Holdings."

Ethan staggered. Had he caused this? He had a hundred million reasons why he didn't give a damn about Fortis and should never feel regret. But the only thing he could think about was his dad on a stretcher, fighting for his life.

He'd just opened his heart to his dad, only to be reunited with an unconscious cancer patient. Then he'd opened his mind to leading Fortis and taking them in a new direction, only to discover he'd never get the chance because a selfish loan of a few million shares had cost his dad his company.

"As unexpected as this is, your father will have a plan," Celeste said.

"He always has a plan," Ethan agreed.

Celeste's phone rang.

"This is Celeste," she said.

"Madame, Sir Stone has regained consciousness and demands that you and his son come here immediately."

"Give me the bloody moby, you plonker," Ethan Sr.'s voice rang out in the background.

"You just hold your peace, Sir Stone," the feisty nurse fired back.

"As I was saying, Sir Stone is back to his old, insufferable self and requests the pleasure of your presence at the Platinum Medical

Centre as soon as humanly possible."

"We're on our way," Celeste firmly replied.

51

The polished marble floors, warm lighting, and spacious waiting room exuded a serene commitment to wellness, reminiscent of a luxury spa. But London's most sought-after private hospital was more than hot stones and body wraps. Besides the advanced oncology department, robotic-assisted surgical systems, bespoke rehabilitation services, an on-site chef, and a personal concierge, the most valuable feature was the VIP care suites and discretion afforded to the rich and famous.

John Spencer, 8th Earl Spencer and father of Diana, Princess of Wales, received care here in the final month of his life, as did the drummer from Foo Fighters after a wild heroin bender during their European tour.

The American-owned hospital had cared for three generations of Stone men and secretly held the passing of two. Margaret Witcombe wasn't going to let a third go just yet.

"Good evening, Miss Raines," she beamed as the trio of guests entered the hallway leading to the private suite, but her haggard brow betrayed the stark reality of the moment.

"Hi, Maggie. How is he?"

"Angry, sick, and waffling between crazy and scary focused. One moment, he was jabbering on like the clappers about some holy man and his fifty-one percent, the next he sits there snickering, whispering on repeat, 'Thou wast not born for death, immortal Bird!'"

"That's Keats," Ethan said. "Ode to a Nightingale, one of his favorites."

"You must be his son," Maggie replied. "He'll be mighty glad to see you."

Ethan shook her outstretched hand, the words sinking deep—he was about to meet his dad.

"Before you go in, you ought to know..." Maggie trailed off. "He is not long for the world. He's rejected our last attempts at treatment and wants to be transferred home for his final days."

"Thank you, Maggie," said Celeste. "We are ready."

Maggie gently opened the door to the suite and allowed them into the living area. The space felt like an upscale Manhattan apartment, with comfortable seating, a small table, and a flat-screen TV. To the rear of the space was the bedroom, lit with beeping lights and the cyclically rhythmic whoosh of the ventilator.

Ethan Sr. lay semi-upright in the center of the room, eyes closed. A custom all-in-one turntable played a haunting tune of swelling crescendos, evoking the burning of empires and drastic loss as the silent in-between spaces, carved out by raw string dissonance, climbed to heights and crashed into emptiness. Samuel Barber's *Adagio for Strings* is a devastating and transcendent composition played at Franklin D. Roosevelt's funeral and after the John F. Kennedy assassination and the 9/11 attacks.

Ethan had heard it every Friday as his father decompressed from the week.

"Dad."

Ethan Sr. opened his eyes and looked at his son for the first time in twenty-five years.

"My boy. Thank you for coming home."

The Stone men stood rigid as the Tower of London, two vaunted pillars of strength and resolve riddled with secrets, lies, and betrayal. The greeting conveyed more than words, dedicated to the proposition that Ethan had returned to his father's house.

"Sir," Celeste cut into the silence. "How are you feeling?"

"I'm nearly dead and haven't time for niceties," Ethan's dad replied. "You have come because it's time to set the transfer in motion. Have you secured the commitment?"

"We have. Your son is ready and willing."

At that, Ethan's dad let out an ear-splitting laugh—more a release than a response to the news.

"That's my boy," he said. "So, let's get to it."

Celeste pulled the end table closer to the bed, sat down, and opened her satchel.

"Here are the documents."

Reaching out, Ethan Sr. grabbed them in handfuls like a wad of Christmas tissue paper.

"These are all worthless now," he spat, throwing the crumbled papers across the room. "The Imam has broken Fortis in two; we are finished. No. There is a new plan. And you, Ethan, have made it all possible. Celeste, sell my remaining shares of Fortis to that wretched fool according to the tendered 2% premium offer."

"You're giving up," she nearly shouted back. "How can you after all we've been through?"

"I recommend you sell your shares as well," he said, ignoring her outrage. "Get out now and get out fast."

He looked at Ethan, piercing eyes conveying authority, conviction, and devious intent.

"I need you to sell as well, my boy. You know your shares, having used a small percentage as collateral."

"I'm so sorry, Dad. I had no idea it would lead to this," Ethan stammered.

"It's okay; you did what you thought was best for you. But today, please help me do what's best for you. Sell everything. Cash out and let the monster have his playground. I am defeated, and it's time to take the money and run."

Celeste could not believe what she was hearing. Had Ethan's dad lost his mind? He'd never spoken like this in all her years of working for him. Something was up, and it wasn't just facing mortality. "You're not making any sense."

"Do you trust me?"

"Always. I've never wavered before. But this, this is ludicrous. Are you sure you're not impaired?"

Ethan's dad laughed. "Asking a crazy man if he's crazy? Come on, Celeste. I know what I'm doing. Ethan, my boy, will you sell?"

"And give away the thing I just agreed to lead? I don't know, Dad. It doesn't make sense."

"And it shouldn't," Ethan Sr. replied. "I'm playing a game here that few can see, much less understand. 4-D Chess is not a game for mortals."

Ethan Sr. took a labored breath. The chest drainage system kicked on. Trickles of crimson fluid slipped through a tube running from beneath his gown, falling into the graduated collection chamber on the floor like rain droplets on a tin roof.

"No, only AP messengers can survive now. Sell all Fortis shares under our command. This will crush him and everything he's stolen from me. Forever."

More wheezing and streaks of red, this one signaling a growing storm.

"Will you sell?"

"I will," Celeste replied. "But what is next? How does this solve anything?"

"Ethan?"

"Okay, Dad. I'm with you."

"Bravo, my boy."

A fierce coughing fit brought Maggie into the room, only to be waved off with a snarl.

"I'm not dead yet, you harpy."

Maggie smiled and backed away, concern and affection for this complex man written across her battle-worn face.

"So, here's what's next," he said. "Celeste tells me you need the Gulfstream. Need to see your team in Tel Aviv?"

"How did you know I had a team?" Ethan replied in mild shock. "And that they were in Israel?"

"Your boys cost me a fifteen-million-pound heli last night," he said. "I presume it was Jack who took it down?"

"That was you," Ethan replied, the shock turning to awe. "Why were you following them, and how do you know all of this?"

"All will be made plain in due course, my boy. For now, you need to know I was only trying to get you and your men to London."

"How long have you been watching me?"

"Your whole life. There isn't a move you've made that I didn't see. I'm proud and impressed by what you've become."

The battered shores of Ethan's heart were pulsating with further waves of emotion. This news changed everything but healed nothing.

"All I have is now yours. Use it wisely, or it will drag you to Sheol like it did me."

Ethan stood in stunned silence, gasping for sanity in the onrushing tides.

"Who is this exquisite creature behind you?"

The reminder that Regus was watching the unfolding scene brought reprieve.

"I'm Regus," she said, stepping boldly forward to address the man she'd pursued with every ounce of determination she could muster. Ethan saw fierceness in her eyes, but they carried empathy, not hate. How did she do it?

"Apologies for my team. They should not have fired on you in New York. They have paid dearly for that."

"Strangely, it has brought us here," she replied. "Precisely where we all should have ended up."

"Ah, yes, you see the bigger story unfolding in the pages of history. Well done, Miss Britton. Your father would have been proud."

It was her turn to be overtaken by the enormity of the moment. Her eyes swelled and spilled onto her cheek.

"You remember him," she said almost imperceptibly.

"He was a good man. You, too, will know the truth one day. For everything, there is a season and a time for every matter under heaven."

Alarm bells pierced the melodic silence mediated by the final refrain of the Adagio, fading into nothingness. Maggie rushed to the bed with three other nurses to tend to the broken man, now fiercely coughing up fluids.

"I'm fine, I'm fine. Quit mithering me, you moaners, and take me home," he said, regaining his breath. "I've got a few more weeks to go, and it's not going to be spent excreting in this hellhole."

The nurses continued to work around him. Ignoring his acidic tone, they released 10mg of morphine into his IV.

"Ethan, go and get your men."

His ghostly face was framed by hollow, glassy black eyes, which fluttered in visible agony.

"Bring them to London and meet me at the Keats Grove house when you return. I need you to save my empire. You need them to save yours."

52

Mid-summer eve in Tel Aviv crescendoed towards jubilation. Shabbat was over, and the weekend's final hours would be spent outdoors. The team had ventured into the heart of Tel Aviv and its historic market, Shuk HaCarmel. Scores of people, young and old, were spilling into the streets, vendors in full swing. Vibrant piles of fresh produce lined the crowded walkway, rows of green cucumbers, blazing red tomatoes, and purple eggplants stacked in an elegantly disheveled coordination. A smoky drift of sizzling lamb spinning slowly on the vertical broiler filled their senses, mingling with the fresh spices from a neighboring shop. Saturday night in the shuk was a time for joyful camaraderie, mediating a savory flavor explosion.

The sights and smells of the Middle Eastern market were all too familiar to the team. Still, they felt especially at home when they saw three uniformed IDF service members, each with a standard-issue Israeli Weapons Industry Tavor X95 bullpup rifle slung about their shoulder as they devoured shakshuka and rustic sourdough.

"This looks like a good place to land," Sykes said, stopping at the open table next to them.

They agreed and sat down, drawing a young server over to get water, bread, and a menu. A nearby street musician began to play an oud, its rich, melodic tune drifting through the crowds.

"I haven't had anything to eat since this morning," Jack said. "Save protein bars and a single candied date before Hamid was poisoned."

The men fell into an unplanned moment of silence as they reflected on the past twenty-four hours. It was hard to understand how they'd ended up in Israel after escaping Egypt and Saudi Arabia.

Three armed Israel Defense Force soldiers, split between two men and a woman, sat next to them. A sight none of the team had seen in their years of service. The U.S. DoD lifted its direct combat role restriction for females in 2013, just as they were getting out.

"Could you imagine serving in the trenches with a female?" asked Jack, who wanted to think about something different and was genuinely curious about his team's thoughts.

"Would have been much better than your ugly face staring back at me every day," Archer said.

"Fair enough," laughed Jack.

"I've watched clips of female IDF soldiers handling their business on Temple Mount in Jerusalem," shouted Archer over the swelling music now carrying the booming cadence of a Darbuka hand drum. "They are as tough as anything I've seen."

"You have to be over here," Sykes replied. "Eighty-five hundred square miles surrounded by a sea of nations and terror groups openly calling for your annihilation."

"That'll put anyone on edge," Jack said. "Who else is shocked Israel let us land on a Saudi Arabian royal helicopter?"

The music stopped midsentence, and Jack's question rocketed beyond his table in the sudden silence. He saw the female IDF soldier glance up in his direction.

"I am," Sykes replied. "Something must be shifting behind the scenes."

"They've never had diplomatic ties with the Saudis," Archer added. "So why now?"

"You think it has anything to do with the NEOM project?" Jack leaned in and lowered his voice, keenly aware that the IDF table was listening to them.

"With everything we just saw, I think that's a possibility," Sykes replied. "If the Saudis want billions in global tourism dollars to flow into the region, perhaps they've realized it's time to recognize Israel as a legitimate sovereign nation?"

"That would be a very good thing," came a strong, accented voice behind Sykes. Jack had seen them get up and walk over. Sykes and Archer turned to address the IDF soldier standing over them.

"Good evening," Sykes said to the fierce-looking woman, her dark hair fashioned in a long, loose braid.

"You said the Saudis flew you into Tel Aviv. This is not possible."

Her no-nonsense, deadpan demeanor demanded respect and a tremor of fear.

"That's what we're discussing," Sykes said. "But I can assure you, it just happened."

"I do not believe it. How did you get into Israel?" the soldier demanded.

Sykes stood when he saw the three silver pips on her shoulder.

"Excuse me, Captain. Might I know your name?" Sykes asked, now face-to-face with the woman.

"Captain Talia Raviv, Sayeret Matkal, elite reconnaissance unit. And you are?"

"Captain Sykes Adler, Pegasus, 82nd Combat Aviation Brigade, Retired."

The two captains, separated by an ocean, a decade, and a world of military ethos, stared each other down, the roaring of the shuk swirling around them.

At last, Captain Raviv relented.

"Welcome to Israel," she said, extending her hand. "You arrived most unusually. Do you care to share more with my team?"

Sykes looked over at the table and back at Jack and Archer. Both nodded.

"We'd be glad to."

"Very good. Please come."

The team stood, pulled their chairs, and sat at the IDF table.

"So, how did you arrive here in a Saudi Royal chopper?" asked Captain Raviv.

"We were exploring Mt. Sinai in Saudi Arabia, and our tour guide was poisoned. The Saudis flew us to Ramat Gan for care," summarized Sykes.

The three IDF members sat silently, their faces filled with quizzical looks. Nobody spoke.

"I'm sorry," Sykes broke in. "Is there something I said that offends you?"

"No, no. It's that..." Captain Raviv paused. "I was just explaining to my team Mt. Sinai's monumental role in our people's history and heritage. So few of the younger soldiers are aware of our spiritual roots. I've heard of the Sinai theory in Arabia. And you just came from there?"

"We did," Jack said. "It was quite the experience."

The three Americans nodded in agreement.

"You should go sometime," Archer said.

"We cannot travel to Saudi Arabia," the captain said. "Only for religious or business purposes, and even then, it is highly restricted by the Saudi Foreign Ministry."

"Shame," Archer said. "Standing high on a desert hill, a rock is split down the middle with water erosion all around. There are also areas littered with Egyptian cow goddess carvings and an L-shaped altar site at the mountain's base."

"That site could be the first place animal sacrifices were offered to God," cut in Sykes.

"That sounds very intriguing," replied Captain Raviv. "Have you been to the last place Israel offered a legitimate animal sacrifice to Adonai?"

"Where is that?"

"Temple Mount in Jerusalem."

"The Dome of the Rock," Archer asked.

"Sort of," replied Captain Raviv. "That Mosque was built around six hundred years after the Romans destroyed the 2nd Temple in 70 CE"

"So the area lay empty for centuries?" Jack arched one brow.

"Not exactly," Captain Raviv replied. "LiDAR evidence suggests the Dome was built on the foundation of an earlier octagonal temple structure. In 135 CE, Roman Emperor Hadrian outlawed our people from living in Jerusalem and further destroyed the city. He renamed the whole province of Judea, Syria Palaestina or Palestine, as an insult to the Jews, deriving the name from our mortal enemy, the Philistines.

"He then rebuilt the ruins of Jerusalem and called it Aelia Capitolina. Finally, to obliterate all Jewish memory from the holy city and Temple Mount, they erected an octagonal temple on top dedicated to the god Jupiter. Its shape is identical to that of the largest temple ruin in Lebanon, Baalbeck."

"Fascinating." Jack's voice softened with awe.

"If you want to understand Israel and the Exodus, you must visit Temple Mount. It is empirical proof that the Jews have a historical right to our ancestral homeland. Adonai gave us the land after He called us out of Egypt and brought us to Himself. He established us as a nation at the mountain, gave us the Law, and even instructed Moses to build a structure of twelve stone pillars at the base to symbolize the new nation he created from amongst the tribes."

"What did you just say?" interjected Sykes. "The part about stone pillars?"

"Yes, Exodus 24:4 tells us that Moses wrote down all the words of Adonai and built a structure of twelve pillars. It was a way to represent the new government and signify devotion to Adonai."

Sykes couldn't believe his ears.

"This is what the marble was doing at the altar site," he shouted above the humming nightlife to his team. "The pillars!"

"And the quarry," yelled Jack, the shuk now exceedingly noisy.

Just then, a siren's wail tore through the uproar, and the IDF table leaped to its feet.

"Come immediately," commanded Captain Raviv. "We must get to a bomb shelter."

All around the shuk, people moved briskly but orderly to the safety of shelters as if this were an everyday occurrence, which, unfortunately, was far too often the case.

Sykes stepped off the curb with Captain Raviv and suddenly understood the low-frequency noise he had heard for the past few moments.

He glanced up in time to see the distinctive V-shaped tail fin of a long-range fixed-wing reconnaissance drone slice into the market behind him. The drone struck the earth and erupted with a fiery vengeance. Moments later, the payload detonated, sending Sykes, Captain Raviv, and their teams hurling through the air.

53

Sykes came to, covered in rubble; chaos and carnage engulfed him. Plumes of acrid black smoke rose from the furnace at the blast's epicenter. Women and children ran screaming past where both teams had just sat, the shop windows blown out, and tables all overturned.

He picked himself up off the ground and made a personal assessment: nothing but light blood from ruptured eardrums. He quickly scanned for secondary threats. Because he saw the UAV, he reasoned it was improbable that any enemy combatants were on the ground. They send drones in when they can't or won't send in men.

His men...

Jack was a few steps behind him when the bomb went off, and he was driven into the restaurant. He lay motionless underneath a table, covered in glass and bleeding from multiple abrasions along his arms.

Sykes got to him and checked the carotid artery, feeling a strong and steady pulse. He was just knocked out. Thank God.

"Jack," he said, giving a light shake to return him to a state of readiness.

Jack's eyes rolled open, and he shot upright.

"Where's Archer?"

"I'm here," his voice rang out from behind. "Unhurt."

Sykes raised Jack's hands out in front of him to inspect the cuts, pulling a few shards of glass from his forearm.

"Nothing here to worry about. Are you able to move?"

Jack stood to his feet, wiped his bloody arms on his pants, and asked, "What about the IDF team?"

The men spun about in time to see the three-person team race toward the blast site, weapons hot and radios squawking.

"Follow them," commanded Sykes.

The Americans fell into a run a few meters behind the Israelis and into the heart of the destruction. It was worse than Sykes imagined.

The drone struck the market center; Sykes estimated a fifty-foot blast radius, consistent with a 5 kg RDX payload. A dozen or more bodies, men, women, and children, lay scattered about the burning wreckage. Sykes came upon an Arab teenager slumped against an overturned stainless steel food service counter. She was in shock, staring blankly ahead while blood poured from her forearm where the hand used to be. Sykes pulled his keffiyeh from his pack and triaged the hemorrhaging stump.

Jack and Archer continued searching for others impacted by this senseless and cowardly assault. They found more wounded and maimed civilians and tended to their injuries.

An armed security perimeter had formed around the site, as dozens of Israeli civilians with semi-automatic weapons took up a defensive position. Within minutes, the wailing sirens of Magen David Adom were upon them, and scores of medical personnel flooded the zone, the distinctive red Star of David emblazoned on their backs.

After thirty minutes, which seemed like hours, all the injured had been triaged and were being taken to various nearby hospitals. Sykes rallied his men.

"We should get out of here," he said. "Our presence is no longer needed and will probably raise more questions than we care to answer."

They turned to depart as Captain Raviv came upon them. She was covered in the blood of the fallen and wore a fierce expression of rage and authority.

"Thank you for your help," she said. "I saw what you did for our people. We have no better friends than you, Americans."

"It was nothing," Sykes replied. "Anything else we can do?"

"No. I suggest you get moving. It would be better if you were not here when the Mossad arrived. You should consider leaving Tel Aviv altogether. Jerusalem is much safer."

"This drone," asked Jack. "It looks Iranian. How'd it get past your air defenses?"

"You are correct; it is Iranian. Probably sent from Yemen. They fly them up the Red Sea, out low over the Mediterranean, and into soft targets along the coast, effectively avoiding our early warning system and missile defense batteries. This is the second such attack this year."

"That is outrageous," Archer said. "How do we end this?"

"It would help if your government stopped funding Iran's genocidal ambitions with easing oil sanctions, pallets of cash dumped from American planes, and backroom arms deals," she replied, obviously not one to sugarcoat the reality of the escalating geopolitical quagmire in the region.

"You should go see Temple Mount," Captain Raviv continued. "If you want to know more about Adonai's purposes for Israel, you must understand the covenants. They are why He rescued us out of Egypt and brought us to Himself."

Sykes remembered the twelve pillars and what Captain Raviv said they meant. The same unexplainable yearning he'd felt in Sindalah to visit the mountain returned.

"Thank you, Captain Raviv; I would like to do that," he said.

"My abba is a Rabbi in Jerusalem. I can have him meet you there tomorrow morning if you'd like a guide."

"Thank you," he said, remembering fondly his last mountain tour guide. "Here's my number. I look forward to hearing from your father."

54

Sayyid was grinning ear-to-ear as Royal Jordanian Air flight 0722 began its initial descent into Ankara, Turkey. Plastered across every screen on the Airbus A320 was Al Jazeera's in-flight coverage of a drone attack on Tel Aviv. Sayyid watched in gleeful awe at the devastation unfolding on the twenty-four-hour global news cycle. The Houthis had already taken credit.

He'd personally developed the Imam's network in Sana'a and knew of this tactic. The Supreme Political Council (SPC) had obtained a half dozen Iranian-supplied drones for this purpose years ago. Still, they had used them sparingly since 2018 when the U.S.-brokered Iranian deal collapsed. Something must have changed if the Houthis' leadership was willing to send a multimillion-dollar drone 1,300 miles to its destruction. He hoped his new orders in Ankara had something to do with this. Indeed, this was the Imam's doing. Had he achieved the goal? Was Fortis theirs?

The plane touched down with the setting sun and taxied to the terminal. He exited, backpack slung across his shoulder, one vial of Polonium 210 lighter. He abandoned the substance in the Saudi desert before crossing into Jordan. It was no longer worth the risk to carry across borders, especially when flying commercially, as most international airports had screening sensors that would easily detect gamma rays hidden in his bag.

He hailed a taxi and paid the fare to the outskirts of Ankara in cash. The Qatari embassy was situated on a high plateau dotted with official government buildings, upscale homes, and new shopping complexes. Qatar's large facility sat below a ridge; its cream and white structures terraced along the undulating property line.

All was quiet at security as he exited the cab. The guard scanned his maroon passport and moved him through the narrow chute for visitors arriving on foot. Once inside the compound, he approached the main entrance to find his contact.

"Brother," a booming voice rang out as Sayyid stepped into the ornate marble embassy hallway. He could not believe his eyes.

"Brother!"

He and the embassy guard embraced.

"What are you doing here? I thought you were traveling with the Imam," Sayyid whispered.

"I was. But we stopped here on the way to London, and he told me to stay. He said I had an important job and that he'd be back. What are you doing here?"

"He called me from London yesterday and ordered me to go to Turkey. Told me to meet a contact for my new assignment."

His brother's bearded, weather-worn face registered a look of foreboding bewilderment.

"You're my assignment," he said.

"I am," Sayyid replied.

"Yes, I'm supposed to guard a private meeting with my life. No one is to enter or exit the room while Sokolov is there."

"That name is familiar. Who is Sokolov?"

"Your contact. From the Russian Embassy in Doha."

"Ah, yes," Sayyid cried. "He was the one who..."

He caught himself just in time. Even though he'd met his brother decades ago at the Imam's Mosque and trusted him with his life, one doesn't simply announce the Russians gave you nuclear material.

"The one who what?"

"Who… received me last time I was at the Embassy. This must be a crucial meeting."

"Agreed. I am proud of you, brother. You are making a difference for our cause."

"And so are you. Where is Sokolov?"

"Waiting downstairs."

The two long-time friends walked through the embassy and down to secure meeting rooms below. Exiting the stairwell, they stepped into a windowless basement hallway that terminated at a large steel door, which gaped open.

"He is there. I'll be outside, brother."

A draft of redolent air caught his nose as the door swung open, revealing an expansive, brightly lit room with upscale, eclectic furnishings. The room's far end boasted a large mahogany work desk offset by two brown leather club chairs and a Chesterfield couch in crushed red velvet. Opposite lay an electric fireplace, framed by a rough-hewn stone mantel, and a flat-screen television.

A bear of a man stood in the center by a fully stocked bar shelf suspended above a matte gold cabinet. He opened the cabinet's frosted crystal doors and retrieved two tumblers.

"Sayyid," Sokolov greeted him without turning around. "You made perfect time from Saudi Arabia. I did not expect to see you so soon."

"It was important to complete my mission and fulfill our Leader's wishes."

"Always such an eager little soldier," Sokolov's thick Russian drawl dripped with disdain. "And he's my business partner, not my leader."

He turned and placed the tumblers on the black marble countertop, pulling a bottle of Beluga Gold Line vodka from the suspended shelf.

"The Imam told me you had some trouble with the Americans. Care to explain?"

"It was an impossible task," Sayyid began. He didn't like where this was going.

"A putrid excuse from a failed henchman," scoffed Sokolov. "Why are they still alive?"

Sayyid's vision of an essential new assignment vanished like Soviet glory after the Cold War. He watched Sokalov open a bottle of Essentuki alkaline sparkling water, his Damascus steel paring knife slicing through a lemon with finely honed ease.

"Had I been allowed a team," he continued, "the outcome would have been different. I almost had them. Their tour guide drank, and the Americans were seconds from death."

"Yes, but all of them are still alive," shouted Sokolov, his pockmarked face red with fury. "And you know the worst thing about your vast incompetence?"

Sayyid remained motionless, his mind assessing the situation, grasping for a way out of what surely was coming.

"You used my weapon on the King's son-in-law. Now I have the whole Saudi government searching for the man who poisoned a royal family member with radioactive material."

"The tour guide was royalty?"

"More than that, he was the King's private intelligence officer stationed in the north."

Regaining his composure, Sokolov poured vodka and water into the glasses, garnishing them with a lemon twist. With this news about the tour guide, Sayyid knew he was in mortal danger.

"And now," Sokolov continued, "I have more heat in Doha than a July camel race. What, shall I do, dear brother?"

Silence.

"You can imagine why I have come. Your leader sent me to retrieve what the Saudis want. The dead body of the man who tried to murder the King's son-in-law."

The air was thick with the scent of aged vodka and freshly cut citrus. The electric fireplace hummed around them, casting an orange light against the stark, windowless walls of the basement room.

Sayyid's lean, sinewy frame was built for speed—his only advantage against Sokolov, who looked like he was carved from Russian granite—that, and surprise.

Sayyid struck first.

He feinted left. A low kick to the knee. Then an explosive uppercut to Sokolov's jaw.

The Russian barely flinched. Instead, he swung a wrecking-ball fist.

Sayyid ducked, sidestepping just in time.

The massive hand smashed into the mahogany desk. Wood splintered. Shards flew.

Sayyid moved like a whisper. Slipped behind. And rammed his elbow into Sokolov's kidney.

The Russian grunted. Spun on his heel and sent a vicious knee shot toward Sayyid's ribs.

Sayyid twisted, barely in time. Took the brunt on his side. Pain exploding through his torso.

Sokolov seized the moment—a bear-trap grip clamping onto Sayyid's throat.

The world tilted as Sokolov lifted him clean off the ground and hurled him across the room.

Sayyid crashed into the couch, momentum sending him tumbling to the floor.

Sokolov charged at him like a bull.

Sayyid rolled, grabbed the half-full vodka bottle from the bar, and hurled it.

The glass shattered against Sokolov's temple and drenched him with the premium liquid.

Staggering the big Russian for half a second. Just long enough.

Sayyid was already moving. He shot forward, low, fast, precise—

sweeping Sokolov's leg out from under him.

The Russian slammed onto the floor hard.

The entire room rattled with a thunderous tremor.

The door handle rattled. "What's going on?" the man he called brother shouted from the hallway and began pounding since the room was locked from inside.

Sayyid wasted no time.

He straddled the brute, raining fists, elbows, and hammer strikes into his face.

Blood sprayed. Bones crunched.

Sokolov roared in rage and threw Sayyid off him like a rag doll.

Sayyid landed, rolled, and sprang to his feet. His ribs burned. His knuckles throbbed.

Sokolov was getting up, bleeding, furious, and still dangerous.

Sayyid's eyes flicked to the bar—a Damascus steel knife.

He moved. One step. Two. A blur of motion. His fingers wrapped around the blade just as Sokolov lunged.

Sayyid twisted, pivoted, and threw.

The steel cut through the air with a deadly whisper as the blade sunk deep into Sokolov's throat.

The Russian staggered, eyes wide in disbelief. Blood gushed onto his chest, soaking his ruined suit. He clutched at the hilt, trying to speak, but only a wet, gurgling rasp came out.

He swayed, dropped to his knees, toppled to his side...and lay as still as stone.

Sayyid exhaled, wiping his bloody knuckles on his sleeve. He walked to the bar, grabbed the remaining cocktail, and took a drink.

Again, his childhood friend shouted, "Let me in."

Sayyid walked over to the door and opened it just as his friend released a coiled front kick.

He came barreling into the gruesome scene, off balance and full of fear. "Brother, what have you done?" he shouted, scanning the shattered table, overturned couch, and the Russian official bleeding out on the carpet.

"Him or me," replied a breathless Sayyid, still sipping from the tumbler. "Help me get out. Our Leader sent him here to kill me."

"Are you sure?"

"The West has corrupted him. He no longer lives to advance our cause. He just pads his bank accounts and satisfies his desires."

Sayyid's brother surveyed the carnage, processing the betrayal of two decades of ideological commitment to the Imam.

"Help me escape," he pleaded.

Sayyid's brother took one final look at the dead Russian and said, "Okay. I'll help. But where are you going?"

"To London. To finish this."

55

"Here, you can use the jet," Celeste said as the sun settled onto the horizon, casting a vermilion glow across a sleek $78 million masterpiece redefining the pinnacle of private aviation. The Fortis matte black Gulfstream G700 was idling on the executive tarmac of the Royal Air Force Northolt jet center.

"I've instructed the pilots to take you wherever you need, for as long as you need," Celeste said as she finished her walk-through. "The plane is well equipped."

"That is an understatement," Ethan replied, stepping out of the main cabin configured for thirteen passengers with four living areas, a master suite with a full-size bed, and an en-suite lavatory with a shower.

"I'll keep you abreast of your father's condition," handing Ethan a satellite phone. "Call if you need anything."

"Thank you, Celeste," Ethan replied. "We'll be in touch."

She watched as Ethan helped Regus grab her Tumi from the boot and board the craft. She ducked back into the sedan, and Pendleton sped off. She had a lot of paperwork to complete.

Between her shares and those of Ethan and Sir Stone, she had to file Form 4 with the SEC for each insider selling shares and then execute the Private sale to Azure Crescent Holdings.

"Good evening, Victor," she said to her General Counsel as he picked up her call. "I need you to prepare the acceptance of the Sheikh's buyout offer at a 2% premium."

All she heard was the noise of children playing football in the background. She waited. Victor said nothing.

"I know," she said. "I had the same reaction. I can assure you this is not a sadistic prank. Sir Stone has instructed me to sell everything, along with Ethan's shares. I have his portfolio information at the office."

"This can't be real," he finally managed to say.

"It is. And we need it completed tonight before the New York markets open in the morning."

More silence.

"I will meet you at HQ in an hour. Please give my sincerest apologies to Samantha and the kids," she said in a steady tone, soft with empathy.

"I'm on it," he replied, and hung up.

Celeste was now shaking uncontrollably. She couldn't process what was unfolding at a blinding pace. Sir Stone was dying, Ethan was home, and everything she had helped build in the last ten years was getting sold off.

She grabbed sparkling water from the chill box in the back of the Ghost, struggling to open the cap.

"It's all going to be okay," she told herself. "I've been preparing for this day. Sir Stone knows what he's doing."

She didn't believe her lies but steeled herself to call that hypocritical monster Sheikh Khalid. Child trafficking was a ubiquitous part of her childhood growing up in Whitechapel on the East End. But her exposure to its evils hadn't seared her to its destructive force. The Fortis AI Dossier on the Sheikh made her want to launch a career in vigilante justice. He was the one getting everything.

"It's going to be okay," she lied again.

Pulling out the offer sheet, she found the Sheikh's number.

"Hello," he answered.

"Sheikh Khalid, this is Celeste Raines. Fortis has accepted your buyout offer."

Her conversation partner had nothing to say for the second time in five minutes. She would be damned if this call took a second longer than necessary.

"If you want the company, be back at Fortis HQ in an hour." She hung up by throwing the phone across the backseat onto the floorboard.

Suddenly, dozens of inbound messages lit up her handset. She unbuckled and crawled over to snag it, still cursing under her breath.

She opened her encrypted messaging app. Two dozen threads awaited her attention. The first was from Fortis' contact for all weapons sales to the United States government, the Under Secretary of Defense for Acquisition & Sustainment.

"Did you see images from Israel?" it read with a link to a news article: "Drone attack kills 18 and injures dozens in Tel Aviv Market."

Celeste opened the article and skimmed the contents. The news was horrible, but she'd seen many war images and had grown calloused to the destruction. Besides, she had enough trauma for the moment with her world on fire.

Next in the thread was an HD video on X from @TelAvivTaster. She had been filming a street vendor review and captured the drone flying low overhead moments before impact.

The message read, "UAV tail profile look familiar?"

This one caught Celeste's attention. There was no question that the UAV was a Fortis design. Its distinctive Inverted-V tail was an advancement Fortis pioneered in the early days of autonomous vehicle flight. The tail was inspired by the Beechcraft Model 35 Bonanza, introduced in 1947. It reduces radar signature, lowers weight, and increases aerodynamic efficiency.

"Not sure what you mean," she replied, knowing fully what the DoD man was implying. "We don't sell to Iran or proxies."

"Ever?" Came back the instant reply.

Celeste knew better than to answer that question. No secure, encrypted app could keep the NSA away should they ever come looking. That's why they'd built Fortis AI. She couldn't believe it was now all gone.

"My condolences to our allies in Israel," she replied.

Israel! How could she have forgotten?

She grabbed the satellite phone and dialed Ethan.

"Turn on the TV in the mid-cabin. There's been an attack in Tel Aviv."

"What happened?" Ethan asked, the roar of the business jet loud in her ear.

"A UAV crashed into a crowded market; its payload killed 18 and injured dozens."

"Anyone claiming responsibility?"

"The Houthis. Have you heard from your team?"

"No," Ethan replied. "I'll call them now."

"Ethan, the drone was a Fortis design."

"You sell weapons to Iranian proxies?"

"We do not. But," Celeste paused. "Sometimes what we sell gets— reallocated."

"Are you talking about the Russian delivery of a hundred million in arms to Tehran a few years back?"

"Maybe."

Celeste didn't want to think about how many weapons her company had loosely distributed to war theaters worldwide. This must be why Ethan resisted getting involved in the family business.

"Check on your team. And bring them back," she said. Not wanting to clog the line, she hung up and resumed checking her messages.

The more she read, the worse things got. This was a terrible assault on Israel, and Fortis was going to be pulled into the middle of it. It was always a PR nightmare when your weapons fell into the hands of terrorists. The Americans went through that when Hamas fighters used U.S. weapons left behind in Afghanistan to kill U.S. citizens in Israel.

She needed to focus. Everything was falling apart, but she had her orders. She would sell off all of Fortis as quickly as possible.

"We're here, Mum," said Pendleton as he pulled back into the scene of the tragedy earlier in the day.

Victor's car was already in the underground lot, and Celeste took the elevator to the top floor to meet him in Sir Stone's office. He had his four attorneys with him, who were quickly working on the requested documents.

"Evening, Victor."

"Celeste. What are we doing here?"

"I know," she said, holding up her hands. "But this is Sir Stone's order. He has appointed me as his executor, and this is his wish. How close are we?"

"We are nearly done. We can execute the Private sale tonight and file the SEC paperwork tomorrow. It will depend on my getting Sir Stone's notarized signature, but we are ready to go when the Sheikh arrives."

No sooner did he say that than front gate security called to inform them the Sheikh was here.

"Let him in and bring him to the 5th floor," Celeste replied.

The team cleared out the executive boardroom just before the Sheikh entered with two Fortis guards, his assistants, and the General Counsel.

"I am so glad you've seen what is best for the shareholders," he said to Celeste as she nodded in his direction from a seated position at the table. "I'm glad we don't have to get into a protracted fight over this."

Celeste couldn't speak. Not yet. Her fury was not abated.

He continued.

"How is Mr. Stone doing? He did not look well last time I saw him."

At this jab, Celeste erupted.

"Listen to me, you sniveling pile of demented filth. Not only do I know the kind of man you are, but I also know where all your secrets lie buried and what lengths you go to keep them hidden."

The Imam just laughed. "Your threats do not scare me, little girl. Do you agree to my terms, or will this takeover become more complex?"

Celeste remembered Sir Stone's wish and swallowed her pride.

"We agree."

Her General Counsel slid a document across the table.

"Here is your counter-signed offer to acquire Fortis," she said. "Additionally, we have prepared a simple agreement for you to purchase our remainder 49% of Fortis stock at a 2% market premium, along with all legal Fortis-owned divisions and assets. With one exception: we wish to retain this HQ building, which has been in the Stone family for generations."

The Imam was staggered. They were selling everything? Today's events would be retold for centuries to come.

"I am feeling magnanimous," smiled the Sheikh, concealing his jubilation. "You can keep your toy house in the corrupted heart of London. I have much bigger plans for Fortis than this wasteland."

"Good, it's settled then. The 2% premium brings us to £54.20 per share for 1.78 billion shares—a total deal of £96.48 billion in shares and an estimated £1.5 billion in assets. This agreement purchases you the shares immediately and begins 90-day due diligence to evaluate the assets."

Victor slid the agreement across the table, and the Sheik's attorney began to review it.

"Any questions?"

"Yes. I was so happy to see Ethan Jr. earlier today, but we didn't have much chance to visit. I see you included his shares in this sale. I suppose he will pay back his loan now. Where is he? I'd love to congratulate him."

Celeste wouldn't give this man anything else today.

"Yeah, we got his shares. He returned to tell his dad to go to hell and gave them all back after discovering what you had done. I have no idea where he is now."

"A shame. He would have been such an asset to lead my company."

"This document looks in order," the Sheikh's attorney said.

"Excellent," he said, grabbing a pen from inside his robes.

With practiced flourish, he signed the agreement and stood to leave.

"Wonderful doing business with you, little girl. Thank you for the company."

"I know how much you like little girls, Imam, but I am not one of them. So you better keep your mouth shut as you walk out of my building."

The Sheikh reached a breaking point. Maybe it was because he just got everything he wanted, but his Western facade came tumbling down as he showed Celeste his true self.

"Listen to me, you little tramp. No woman speaks to me this way. I ought to have you arrested for blasphemy and hung in the city center for your insubordination. All you Western hussies think you can do and say whatever you want. But you wouldn't be standing right now if you were one of my women. You'd be coiled in a corner learning to guard your tongue."

"Yes, well, sadly, I'm not for sale, so you cannot make me one of 'your women.' Guards, please see these guests from the building."

The two armed security personnel strode towards the Sheikh as if they dared him to do something. He received the message and departed the office as quickly as he had arrived.

56

Sykes led his team out of the shuk to a park bench overlooking the sea, where they sat in stunned silence. White-tipped waves of the emerald sea crashed against Aviv Beach's sandy shores. Blue hour was nearly over, and darkness descended on the city, which felt like a normal Mediterranean metropolis. Only five blocks from the destruction that had occurred an hour ago, Sykes was amazed at the Israeli resilience. The men were used to carnage, but the dramatic transition from missing limbs and burning rubble to pristine waters and palm trees was hard to comprehend.

Sykes saw the blocked number on his phone and decided to answer, realizing they had not checked in with Ethan.

"Sykes," came Ethan's steady voice. "Tell me you're all safe."

"We are."

"Were you near the attack?"

Sykes looked down at his blood-soaked pants and realized his keffiyeh was probably still tied around the young Arab girl's arm. Jack looked on with full eyes and bleeding arms while Archer, numb from the devastation, sat listening in, his clothing blanketed with dried crimson and a gunshot wound to the shoulder.

"We were."

"Where are you now?"

"The beach."

"I am en route to Tel Aviv, but there's a full ground stop on incoming planes for the next few hours. We will circle and land at Herzliya Airport, just north of Tel Aviv, when possible. Probably the morning."

"Okay."

"You can get aboard and come back to London."

"No," Sykes said, his clipped responses surprising even himself. "We're not ready to leave. We must get to Jerusalem."

"Why?" Ethan asked, worried for his team lead.

"You'll see," Sykes replied. "I'm glad you'll be here. You need to come with us. We're on to something and must see it through."

"Okay. If you say it's important, Regus and I will join you."

"The reporter? She's with you?"

"She is, and believe me, she's worth having around."

"If you say so," Sykes said, not having the energy to fight Ethan on this.

"Can you get a hotel and be ready in a few hours when the ground stop lifts?"

"I suppose. We've not slept in more than thirty-six hours."

"Everything is changing around me, Sykes. The world is not what it was yesterday."

"You can say that again. We've experienced the same thing. What's going on for you?"

"I met my dad. He was as crusty as I remember. But he's ordered everything to be sold off."

"What? Everything?"

"The whole company, all the stock, all the buildings except the HQ in St James'. Everything."

"What about your shares?" Sykes asked, remembering the day he and Ethan had closed on the hundred-million-dollar loan in the British Virgin Isles.

"I sold them all, along with my dad's."

Sykes could not believe his ears. He'd pushed Ethan to use his stock to fund their fledgling operations. Three years into their venture, they desperately needed to expand budgets to fight back against the scourge of ISIS. Ethan relented, but he accused him of forcing a compromise on more than one occasion. While he was not privy to the details of Ethan's portfolio, he figured that much money must have nearly depleted Ethan's accounts.

"Since you sold out your collateral," Sykes asked with trepidation. "Will you have to repay your loan?"

"Yeah."

"Will the proceeds from the sale cover the loan and keep us running?"

Sykes knew he was pushing the boundaries of their operational relationship, but as Ethan's best friend, he wanted to ensure the safety of both himself and their venture.

"Ummm," Ethan hesitated. "The current global demand for weapons has skyrocketed Fortis' stock. We'll be fine."

"That's good to hear," Sykes said, stretching his legs out from the bench. "And do you feel okay about using the funds directly now?"

"That's one of the things that has changed. I never thought I'd say this, but yes. And Sykes," Ethan paused. "We now have a new problem."

"What's that?"

"We must find a way to use twelve billion pounds for good."

"Come again," Sykes said, sure Ethan had misspoken.

"My stock was worth twelve billion pounds. I'll need your help to ensure we don't get corrupted."

Sykes was flabbergasted. And he was exceedingly glad he hadn't put this call on speakerphone for the team. Jack and Archer gazed at him with intense curiosity.

"Okay. We can figure that one out. I'm here for you."

"Thank you. What is going on for you guys?"

"It's hard to explain over the phone," Sykes relayed, scratching his temple. "But I think we have some new insight into the murder of King Tut."

"What? How?"

"I'm not sure exactly." Brushing a few shards of glass from his pant leg, Sykes stood to pace along the boardwalk. "But we spent the day exploring a range in Saudi Arabia that may be the biblical Mount Sinai. My gut tells me there is a connection between that mountain in Arabia, the Temple Mount in Jerusalem, and your theory on who murdered King Tut."

"How is that possible? That sounds too far-fetched even to entertain."

"I agree," Sykes replied. "But I'm telling you, everything is changing underneath me. The same thing that's happening to you. Yesterday, I never believed you'd fly to London, meet your father, and start using his 'blood money.'"

"Fair enough."

"That's why we must go to Jerusalem. I think we'll find the missing piece that unlocks this mystery."

"And you know this how?"

"Instinct," Sykes said.

They'd spent countless hours in the field together and knew Ethan respected his instincts as much, if not more than he did. That's why he was the team lead.

"Well, it's a new day. I look forward to finding out what your instincts are telling you," Ethan rolled his shoulders in a loose shrug, settling into his seat. "One more thing, you know that dream I've been having?"

"The one about the unknown Pharaoh?"

"Yeah. That dream explains everything I experienced today."

Sykes abruptly stopped pacing, turning to his men in shock and awe.

"It does," his whispered voice barely audible to Ethan at 50,000 feet.

"Yeah… It was about my dad… and me. I was the missing son the Pharaoh was looking for while his empire was burning."

"Did you discover who the Pharaoh was in history?" Sykes asked, himself shaken by the convergence of puzzle pieces locking in place.

"No," Ethan replied. "I don't think it's a historical person; it's just my subconscious revealing that my dad was looking for me and needed my help."

"I'm sure that's right."

"You don't sound convinced?"

"Well…didn't you always feel like a historical truth was hidden there?" Sykes replied, pacing back to his team.

"Yeah, but that's an utter impossibility. At least now I can put it to rest and move on," Ethan said with an air of finality. "Speaking of rest, let's try to get some and start fresh in the morning."

"Sounds good," Sykes replied, letting it drop. "There's a hotel right behind us, so we'll check in and be ready at 0700. You gonna be able to sleep on the plane?"

"We'll be fine," Ethan said, easing back the leather captain's chair as Regus handed him a glass of champagne she'd scavenged from the galley. The engines purred beneath them, smooth and steady— private jet smooth. He raised his glass, eyes glinting. "You'll see tomorrow."

"What'd he say?" asked Jack the moment Sykes pulled the phone from his ear.

"Ethan will be here in a few hours, and we can discuss everything in the morning."

57

The ground stop lifted at 3 a.m. Israeli time, but the pilot circled for a few more hours, allowing his passengers to sleep. Ethan gave Regus the master suite at the back of the plane, complete with a full-size bed and shower. His fold-out twin up front was remarkably comfortable, and he'd been out the moment he lay down.

Regus nudged him awake.

"Good morning," her damp, freshly washed hair hung about her shoulders. Her gentle smile and glowing skin were softly illuminated by the morning sun streaming through the oval windows at 50,000 feet. "We're starting our initial descent and must prepare the cabin."

Ethan sat up, instinctively reaching for his mushroom fragments. He quickly realized he wasn't home. More than that, he didn't even want them. He couldn't remember facing a new day with such peace or being surrounded by such beauty.

"You look confused," Regus beamed. "I felt the same way when I woke up. Took me a bit to grasp that I was circling the Med in a private jet."

She tussled her auburn hair with her fingers. "Time to get going," she said.

Ethan watched her walk to the back of the plane, then swung his feet out of bed. He padded lightly across the plush carpet; he missed Ellie. He covered the ten steps to the forward galley, marveling at the Gulfstream's amenities. It was about the size of his apartment back in Manhattan, only it flew. He made an espresso, the gourmet pods pulling a rich aroma into the cabin as his 4-oz double-walled glass cup filled with fuel.

He texted Sykes his ETA, confirming a 0700 arrival. Sykes replied that he'd arranged private transport to take them to Jerusalem. They had an 0830 rendezvous with a tour guide at the Jaffa Gate and a day of exploring the Old City of Jerusalem ahead of them.

Ethan had never been to Israel because he'd never wanted to. But something new stirred in his soul. Maybe it was the past few days' events, the billions headed into his account, or the beauty at the back of the jet. But he knew it was something more than material. Today was going to be a good day. He could feel it.

Ethan and Regus exited the elite craft. Sykes, Jack, and Archer had grins the size of the Great Pyramid plastered across their faces.

"Your daddy's got fancy toys," Jack said as the men embraced. Ethan looked at Sykes with a questioning look.

"It's your news," Sykes said. "I've only told them you'd be here. We've got an hour's drive to Jerusalem. Plenty of time to catch us up on all that's taken place."

"Fellas, this is Regus," Ethan said.

"Great to finally meet you," Jack said. "Ethan told us so little about you."

"Well, he's had his hands full doing something important," Regus fired back, familiar with how military men showed affection. "Maybe one day you'll make the list of people worth keeping in the loop."

Archer laughed out loud as Ethan smiled. The team hugged her before piling into the Sprinter van and heading for the Holy City.

"So, you're telling me your dad gave you everything?" an

incredulous Jack said when Ethan wrapped the dramatic retelling of the past forty-eight hours.

"That's what he said," Ethan replied. "I still don't know exactly what it means, but as I understand it, Fortis has been completely sold off, and we're sitting on my proceeds."

"What's the Imam going to do with the company?" Archer asked. "He doesn't sound like the person I'd want controlling a vast arsenal of weapons and billions in defense contracts."

"I don't know," Ethan replied. "My dad said he had a plan and that selling all the stock would crush him. But I can't see that happening. He owns everything."

"You said the UAV that hit the market was a Fortis design," Sykes said. "That's got to be an issue for the Imam."

"It's his problem now, I suppose," Ethan replied. "But I think we need to game out our strategy on him once we talk with my dad."

"Agreed," Sykes said.

The final climb into Jerusalem, a bright city on a hill, was in front of them. The driver moved into the left two lanes to exit Route 1 onto Ben Gurion. He had been silent the whole trip, but the lull in his passenger's conversation allowed space to do what Israeli drivers love best: to talk about their beloved country.

"We just exited Route 1, a critical lifeline in the city for over twenty-five hundred years. During the 1948 Israeli War of Independence, the Arab forces choked off the supply lines coming in from Tel Aviv. In April of 1948, a convoy of doctors and nurses headed up this route to Hadassah Hospital was ambushed by Arab forces. Seventy-eight men and women were massacred.

"But this valley was in use long before the rebirth of the State of Israel. A Jewish King named Hezekiah withstood one of the greatest military forces the ancient world ever marshaled. In 701 BCE, the Assyrian warlord King Sennacherib and his army traveled up this valley to lay siege to Jerusalem. Recorded in three books of the Bible, this siege ended with a miraculous intervention: overnight, 185,000

Assyrian soldiers were struck down by an invisible power as they camped in the valley surrounding the Old City. This event caused the armies' withdrawal and the city's salvation."

Ethan was familiar with the Assyrian king, one of the most famous in history, but he had never studied his connection to biblical history. In fact, he'd never investigated anything about Israel on all of his tours around the Middle East. But his mind lit up when the driver got to the Assyrian king's withdrawal from Jerusalem. This story mapped onto an artifact he used to examine as a kid during educational trips with his dad.

"Wait a minute," he said. "This story is corroborated by a clay document housed at the British Museum. It's called the Taylor Prism. Found in 1830 in the Iraqi city of Nineveh by Colonel Robert Taylor, it's written in Akkadian cuneiform and is an official account of Sennacherib's conquests in Judah."

Jack leaned in from the backseat to catch Ethan's revelations.

"The document records that he came upon Jerusalem after laying waste to forty-six fortified cities. He shut the Judean king you mentioned 'up like a caged bird' and forced him to pay tribute. But then, surprisingly, the armies withdrew and retreated to Nineveh. It's amazing that he claimed to have destroyed all the other cities and never made that statement about Jerusalem."

"Does that mean the Bible stories are true?" Jack asked, eyes wide, his experience standing in the Split Rock fresh in his mind.

"I don't know about that," hedged Ethan. "But it is an interesting historical validation."

"You will find many such instances in Jerusalem," the driver said. "It is the most fascinating city, with four and a half billion followers of the three Abrahamic religions claiming it as holy. It's home to three of the world's most significant religious sites: the Western Wall, the Church of the Holy Sepulcher, and the Dome of the Rock. There is no other place in the world like Jerusalem.".

Ethan felt a growing sense of awe as they rounded the hill and entered the heart of Jerusalem. Ahead was a soaring, harp-like structure spanning the road they were on. The suspension bridge, which supported a rail line and glass pedestrian walkway, looked like art.

The van fell quiet as they took in the hustle and bustle of the modern sections of Jerusalem. The driver exited the main road and began to weave through crowded pedestrian areas, passing an open-air market where scores of Israelis were headed to work or sitting at cafes on the streets for breakfast.

The driver turned right onto HaNevi'im Street and then took another right onto Route 60, where the old city wall appeared; its famous Jerusalem Limestone provided a backdrop for soaring date palms and centuries of historical drama. They drove along the outskirts of the wall for a few blocks before entering a tunnel, emerging on the other side to a breathtaking view of the ancient Jaffa Gate, the Citadel of David behind it, and an expansive vista of the Judean hillside to their right.

"We are here," said the driver, who made an abrupt U-turn and stopped the vehicle in the morning sun, looking up at the 43-foot-tall gate.

"This is Jaffa Gate. Built in 1538 by Sultan Suleiman the Magnificent, its strategic location in the old city and the Jewish Quarter made it a scene of many fierce battles through the years. As you can see, Thompson SMGs, Bren guns, and heavier 20mm rounds left visible scars on the stone."

The team piled out, imagining the battle scenes and thanked their driver.

"Who are we meeting?" Ethan asked.

"A Rabbi," Sykes said as he checked his phone. "He is the father of an IDF Captain we met while triaging the wounded. He's inside the gate at a cafe."

The team entered the Old City, walking through the soaring entrance along the path that General Edmund Allenby walked on

December 11, 1917. It was a historic moment at the close of the First World War, marking the end of 400 years of Ottoman rule in Jerusalem.

Ahead, a red and white umbrella cast unnecessary shade on a wire table where a handsome silver-haired man sat reading a paper. He wore loose-fitting trekking gear favored by American tourists, along with a small cloth kippah. He looked up as the group of five approached.

"Shalom, shalom," he said, extending his hand to Sykes as he stood. "I am Rabbi Uriel Raviv. It is an honor to meet you."

"Thank you for taking the time today," Sykes replied. "My team, Jack and Archer, met your daughter in Tel Aviv."

"A pleasure. Talia told me what you men did to care for our wounded yesterday. We do not have the words to thank you."

"We were honored to have been able to help," Archer replied.

"And this is Dr. Ethan Stone and Regus..." Sykes trailed off, realizing he didn't know her last name.

"Britton," Uriel said. "A pleasure to meet you both. I enjoyed reading up on you when Talia told me of this visit last night."

The look of shock on the five Americans' faces made Uriel laugh.

"You seem surprised I know something about you," he said with a chuckle. "Don't be worried. This is Israel; we always research our allies. Besides, as commander of a combat recon unit, my daughter was obligated to verify the claim that you flew to Israel on a Saudi Royal Chopper. You don't think she'd send her little old abba into a meeting with four U.S. Military vets unprepared, do you? Especially since you seem to have Saudi royal connections, and one is the son of the infamous Ethan Stone the Third."

Ethan thought about his dad clinging to the final days of his life. He hoped to make it back in time to see him again. "Don't hold it against me," he said.

"It's not our family or relationships that define us," Uriel said. "But actions which forge our character."

"Your daughter had a rich understanding of Israel and its roots, which go back thousands of years," Sykes said. "We are very interested in understanding more of the history."

"Very good. You will have your fill by the end of our time together. What would you like to see first?"

"Talia mentioned Mount Sinai and Temple Mount are connected," Sykes replied. "I would like to know how."

"Ah, yes, one of her favorite topics. She is somewhat of an expert on the Exodus from Egypt. That event is the Rosetta Stone of the Bible. It isn't easy to understand the Text without understanding the Exodus. With it, you can see Adonai's presence in Egypt, Canaan, Israel, Persia, Rome, and the larger Middle East. The foundation laid in the Exodus built Judeo-Christian ideals that spread worldwide."

Ethan was taken aback at this statement. The Rosetta Stone was perhaps the most significant linguistic breakthrough in human history. It was written in three scripts but in two languages: Ancient Greek was the language of the ruling Ptolemaic dynasty in Egypt. Demotic was the standard script used for daily Egyptian writing, and Hieroglyphs were the formal script used for religious and official inscriptions in ancient Egypt. Only about 3% of the ancient Egyptian population, and nobody in the modern era, could read or write Hieroglyphics before Jean-François Champollion unlocked its secrets in 1822. However, the presence of a map connecting a known language—ancient Greek—to the Egyptian symbols opened a treasure trove of knowledge. The story of the Exodus, and how it could reveal the history of the Bible, the land of Israel, and Egypt, was of sudden intense interest to him.

"Ethan, I understand you are one of the very few people who can read Hieroglyphics," Uriel said.

"You have done your homework," a flicker of pleasure crossed Ethan's face. "I am something of an expert in ancient Egypt."

"America's most notorious academic," Regus smirked.

"I am well aware of your background, Dr. Stone," replied Uriel. "I am honored to have time with you. Shall we go?"

"Please lead the way."

58

"To understand the connection between the Exodus, Mt. Sinai, and the Temple Mount, we must begin with the City of David."

Uriel led the team toward the Jaffa Gate and a gift shop carved from inside the wall, where he purchased six tickets and passed them out.

The team followed him up a narrow, winding stone staircase to a floor-to-ceiling metal turnstile.

"We will traverse the old city wall along the Rampart's Walk to the Western Wall and exit to the City of David."

The team shimmied through the metal barriers, winding their way to the top of the stone walkway, which opened onto a panoramic view of Jerusalem. The team stood gazing east over the Old City and the massive structure dominating the view.

"What you see on the horizon is the Temple Mount or Har HaBayit - The Mountain of the House," Uriel said. "Also known in Arabic as Al-Haram al-Sharif, the Noble Sanctuary. Perhaps the most hotly contested real estate in the whole world, holding the history of thousands of years of conflict, religious observance, and mystery."

Prayers murmured in Hebrew, Arabic, and Latin echoed through the labyrinthine streets below as Ethan stood by Regus. High up on the wall, adrenaline rushing through him, drinking in the Old City of Jerusalem, he could see clearly, maybe for the first time.

"Here in front of us is the Citadel of David," Uriel said. "But David didn't build it or live in it. He died 900 years before King Herod finished the construction. But centuries of misidentification with what was considered David's home made the name stick."

Uriel's voice carried over the wind as they followed him along the ramparts. "The Ottomans built these walls around 1550 CE," he said, tapping the stone with his palm. "They took the city from the Mamluks—who took it from the Ayyubids, who took it from the Crusaders, who took it from the Seljuk Turks." He smiled faintly. "And so it goes, three thousand years back to the Jebusites and King David. We'll get to him soon enough."

Regus ran her fingers along the weathered stone. "So many empires... all for the same hill."

"Exactly," Uriel said. "Nearly two centuries of war between Christian and Muslim armies ended here in 1260, when the Mamluk Sultanate crushed the last Crusaders. They ruled Jerusalem from Egypt for the next two and a half centuries—rebuilt the walls of the Temple Mount, raised new mosques and minarets, restored the gates. But they never built walls for the city itself." He turned toward them, eyes glinting beneath his glasses. "Jerusalem wasn't a strategic military position. Not then."

Ethan looked out across the city, the sunlight burning gold on the domes. "And yet," he murmured, "it's still standing."

He understood the preference for Egypt over Israel. His training had drilled it into him—Israel wasn't strategically important. Not in the preservation of history, not in the defense of culture. But as he walked the walls of Jerusalem, the thought began to splinter. Every stone beneath him whispered of endurance, of a people who'd outlasted empires. Strategy, he realized, had nothing to do with it.

"Then an upstart Islamic power rose," Uriel continued, leading them along the rampart. "The Ottomans crushed the Mamluks in

Cairo on December 9, 1517. In a single stroke, Jerusalem, Mecca, and Medina were folded into their empire. That victory made them guardians of Islam's holiest sites—the Kaaba in Mecca and the Prophet's Mosque in Medina." He paused, letting the words hang over the city. "And with those secured, their sultan claimed the mantle of Caliph—the ruler of the Islamic world."

The group followed as he walked, his voice steady against the wind. "The Sunni Ottomans clashed with the Shi'a Safavids of Persia for the next hundred years. By the sixteen-fifties, the Ottomans ruled the Islamic world—but the Safavids refused to yield. The rift hardened, carving the battle lines between Shi'a and Sunni that still shape the Middle East today."

They stopped at a lookout on the southern wall. Below them, the Valley of Jehoshaphat stretched toward the Mount of Olives; the City of David glimmered ahead, and Mount Zion rose to their right.

Uriel rested a hand on the stone. "The point is this," he said quietly. "For thousands of years, the victors of war have claimed new lands, while the defeated—if they were lucky—lived to see what might have been. Jerusalem stands as the record of it all. A living archive of conquest... and a testament to the State of Israel's promise of religious freedom in the heart of the Middle East."

No one spoke. Only the wind answered, whispering through the cracks between ancient stones.

Ethan's thoughts whirred as he looked out over Jerusalem. His family's shadow stretched across a century of conflict. His great-grandfather had watched the Ottoman Empire fall in 1917, and seven years later, the Caliphate itself dissolve into dust. The founder of Stone Defense had been there too—at the table of the 1916 Sykes-Picot Agreement—where men with pens carved borders through deserts they'd never seen. Lines that split tribes, scattered the Kurds across Turkey, Iraq, Syria, and Iran... and forced enemies to share the same flag. Few of them did so peacefully.

"You may be asking yourself, how can so many different groups peacefully coexist here, and why have millennia of conflict been focused on this tiny strip of land?" Uriel spread his hands, prompting them to think about that.

"Exactly my question." Ethan's brow furrowed. "What is the fascination with Jerusalem?"

"To answer that," Uriel said, "We must venture across the street and deep underground to witness the remarkable recent excavations of the City of David."

Ethan, Regus, and the rest of the team followed Uriel down to the Dung Gate and out the exits. They emerged along a Ma'ale HaShalom, a busy street lined with tour buses emblazoned with names written in a dozen languages. They darted across a break in the traffic and through a chaotic neighborhood where a smattering of residential and commercial structures mixed with wooden barriers obstructed views of active dig sites.

They arrived at the City of David, walking through the modern entrance to one of Jerusalem's most important historical sites.

Jack gasped in awe at the beauty of the Davidic Harp, displayed amid three limestone arches. Uriel lead the team over a glass floor through which they peered, glimpsing the three-thousand-year-old structures below.

They continued down a long flight of stairs, stopping at an open-air gallery covered in sunshades, which looked up at a terraced wall excavated from the rubble of thousands of years of conquered and resettled cities.

"You're looking at the outer palace wall built by Israel's great King David," Uriel said. "Dating back to the 10th century BCE, this is believed to be where King David established his presence in the newly conquered city."

"Who lived in the city when David got here?" Archer leaned in slightly; his gaze fixed on Uriel.

"Great question. A group known as the Jebusites occupied the city for hundreds of years—the books of 2 Samuel 5:6-10 and 1 Chronicles

11:4-9 record David's conquest."

"Why did he choose this location?" Jack tilted his head as his eyes gleamed with curiosity.

"There are a variety of speculations. As you've seen, the city sits on a hill with plunging valleys, making it strategically defensible. Its placement near the center of the land allotments of the twelve tribes of Israel made it an ideal location for uniting the divided tribes, who were warring among themselves. And, perhaps most importantly, it contains a natural spring in a very arid region. Without water, nothing lives."

"Where is this spring?" Sykes asked with a faint quickening to his tone. "I haven't seen any evidence of water all day."

"Ah, yes, let us answer that question with a journey underground. I hope none of you are claustrophobic."

Regus grabbed Ethan's hand and gave a little squeeze.

"I hate tight spaces," she whispered, looking unnerved.

"You'll be okay," Ethan said softly, squeezing back. "I'll be right there."

Uriel led the group up a small flight of metal steps, the clang of their boots and shoes echoing in the confined space. Reaching the top of the stairs, they entered the cool, dark interior of a massive underground excavation.

The group journeyed deeper into the earth, winding down steel staircases built into the ancient openings. The subterranean uplights cast an eerie glow as they bounced off the hewn bedrock.

Uriel stopped on a landing, and the team gazed down a narrow opening that plunged into darkness.

"This is what's known as 'Warren's Shaft.' A natural forty-three-foot vertical fissure in the rock connected to the Spring of Gihon below."

Jack leaned over into the void, and a rush of cool air brushed his face, tingling his skin.

"2 Samuel 5:8 says that David instructed his men to take the impenetrable stronghold through a 'water conduit or shaft,' a *ṣinnôr* in Hebrew." Uriel gestured to the opening. "Most archaeologists believe this is the access point King David's men used to conquer the Jebusite city."

Ethan didn't know what to make of this. He'd spent twenty years in these sorts of holes, looking for lost treasures of the Levant or in Egyptian tombs. Why hadn't he learned about these connections to the Bible and other ancient texts? It seemed that his vast academic knowledge had obscured truth, hiding a critical piece of the puzzle.

Uriel continued down the staircase, which took a sharp left, exposing the group to the unmistakable sound of running water.

"We have arrived," he said. "Before you is the entrance to Hezekiah's Tunnel."

"Hezekiah," Ethan exclaimed, still wondering what else he'd missed due to his biblical illiteracy. "We were just talking about this king on the way into Jerusalem. Why is this tunnel named after him?"

The group gathered on the final steel landing, which ended at a hole carved from the bedrock no bigger than a man. Beneath their feet, a stream of water flowed down and into the opening, quickly disappearing into blackness.

"In 701 BCE, Jerusalem was put under siege," Uriel said, shifting his weight.

"By the Assyrian army," Ethan cut in, "and the warlord Sennacherib. That episode is recorded in a cuneiform tablet housed at the British Museum."

"Precisely."

"What does this tunnel have to do with that invasion?" Jack asked.

"You may know from the tablet, which I'm assuming you've read, Dr. Stone, that the Assyrian armies had laid waste to cities for months. King Hezekiah was concerned with protecting the capital during a siege. What is the most important resource to guard during a siege?"

"Water," Sykes piped up, his tactical mind already piecing it together. "You can live without food for months. But you'll be dead in a week without water."

"That's right," Uriel smiled. "And so Hezekiah had a problem. Jerusalem's only source of water was outside the city walls. They didn't have time to build a sufficiently fortified extension to protect the water. The solution stands before you and is one of the greatest engineering feats in the ancient world.

"Sennacherib left Nineveh in the spring or summer of 701 BCE, which puts him in the Northern Kingdom of Israel in early fall. The Kingdom of Israel had already been destroyed in 722 BCE by his predecessor, King Sargon II. So, Sennacherib headed south and laid waste to forty-six cities, which, as you mentioned, is recorded in the Taylor Prism."

Jack's face was stricken with perpetual amazement at these connections.

"The last to fall was Lachish," Uriel continued. "A heavily fortified city perched atop a hill along the critical military and trade routes between Egypt and Mesopotamia, it was Jerusalem's last line of defense."

Ethan knew the name Lachish. His eyes were burning with a fire only kindled when unraveling ancient mysteries.

"The siege of Lachish is documented dramatically on massive stone reliefs found in Sennacherib's palace in Nineveh," Ethan said, his face brightening with scholarly discovery.

"They depicted the unfolding scene in great detail," Ethan continued. "They show Assyrian soldiers storming the city, and captives impaled on pikes while the King looks on from his throne."

"And if you visit the ruins today, you can walk up the Assyrian siege ramp they built to deliver troops to the city walls," Uriel replied. "A truly gruesome and dark moment in Israel's history."

"So, how long did Hezekiah have before the armies got to Jerusalem?" Regus asked.

"The best guess is somewhere between six and nine months," Uriel replied. "Which is what makes this tunnel so remarkable.

"To protect the water source, they frantically chiseled through 1,750 feet of bedrock with bronze and iron hand tools. Modern construction estimates have this task taking up to five years to complete."

"How on earth was it accomplished?" Regus' jaw went slack as if she could hardly believe what she was hearing.

"Evidence suggests that two teams worked around the clock from both sides of the tunnel, meeting in the middle."

"How is that possible?" Sykes asked. "They had no modern surveying instruments. It is unimaginably complex to cut a tunnel deep underground from both ends and retain the downhill slope required for a gravity-fed aqueduct."

"They likely used measuring ropes marked in cubits, around 18 inches, and weighted plumb lines to hold the slope," Uriel replied. "From the angle of the chisel marks inside the tunnel, you can see they made constant calculations and adjustments as they dug. And probably used some type of echolocation, perhaps striking heavy wooden poles above ground against the rock to guide the workers below."

"Amazing." Ethan shook his head slowly; wonder etched across his face.

"The tunnel path meanders through the underground, a sign they followed some naturally occurring water flow. A series of sharp turns near the tunnel's center indicates where the two teams broke through to connect the project, last-minute course corrections that ensured success."

"And they managed to complete it in time?" Ethan wondered.

"It appears so. Jerusalem did not fall, and the Assyrian army retreated."

The group was so engrossed by the story that they almost didn't see the Rabbi step off the steel platform and into the chilly water.

Regus was the first to notice he was ankle-deep in the spring.

"You're not going in, are you?" she asked, fear evident in her voice.

"If you truly want to comprehend the connection between the Exodus and the Temple, you must leave the old world behind, and pass through these waters."

And he turned, disappearing into the darkness.

59

The Imam's jet touched down at Dulles International Airport, just outside Washington, D.C.—news of his overnight purchase and intent to take the defense giant private shocked the market. Stocks shot up on the news, despite the brewing controversy over the Fortis drone used in the Houthi attack. The Imam was now one of the most talked-about people on the morning shows.

After leaving Fortis HQ, he sent an urgent message to the Office of the Under Secretary of Defense for Acquisition and Sustainment (OUSD A&S) within the U.S. Department of Defense. He knew Fortis had a Change of Control (CoC) clause that required all contracts to be renegotiated when the entity changed hands. His priority was retaining his new company's most significant contract. Though he'd never spoken with the DoD office directly, he'd been party to numerous negotiations with the Under Secretary of Defense (USD). He seemed to have a great relationship with the ex-CEO, and the Imam hoped that it would transfer to him.

His driver approached the Pentagon's VIP River entrance, which looked out over the Potomac and offered sweeping early morning views into the heart of Washington, D.C.. The city was even more than the capital of the United States; it was the nerve center of global dominion—the most powerful city in the world. He needed to secure his seat in this city to succeed in the next phase of his plans.

He and his general counsel passed through Security and approached the grand, neoclassical colonnade lining the northeastern side of the Pentagon. The expansive set of stone steps led to heavy glass doors, and behind them, the Pentagon Force Protection Agency stood guard. His credentials granted them access to the windowless hallways in the E ring; they surrendered their phones at the storage facility.

"Welcome, Shiekh," a member of the OUSD A&S staff said. "The USD is awaiting you." He turned and walked them through the polished granite hallway, past massive framed pictures of the President of the United States and top Pentagon leadership, and into an elevator, where he punched the third floor.

In moments, the doors slid open and led to the Pentagon's E-Ring on the River Entrance side, the most exclusive section. Home to the Office of the Secretary of Defense, the Chairman of the Joint Chiefs of Staff, Undersecretaries, and Service Secretaries of the Army, Navy, Air Force, and Space Force, the third-floor outer ring represented the pinnacle of global power to the Imam. He belonged here. He'd made it.

"Good morning, Shiekh," greeted the receptionist. Her civilian dress was modest and appropriate, except for the glaring lack of decency she exuded with her uncovered head. He could not correct her in this setting and refused to acknowledge the greeting.

He was escorted into a windowless conference room, whose thick, soundproof walls were lined with metallic material that blocked radio frequencies. The broad conference table had a single secure, hardline phone on top but was otherwise empty, save for the lone man sitting at the head of the table.

"Good morning, Shiekh." The USD stood and extended his hand. "You made quite the stir in Washington this morning."

"Well, it was a small acquisition in the grand scheme," replied the

Imam, the glee in his voice evident in the sardonic tone oozing from brittle lips. "We still have much to accomplish for global peace and shared security."

"Cut the BS," the USD curtly replied. "I took this meeting because Sir Stone has been my friend for decades. I don't know what kind of game you're playing with his legacy, or who was piloting your drone when it exploded in Tel Aviv. The United States will not do business with a defense company that's been compromised. Are you compromised, Shiekh?"

The USD's steely grey eyes glared at him, looking for the answer beneath the Imam's reply.

"I can assure you, Mr. Stone, his board, and even his son were pleased to sell me their shares. And that drone was before my time."

To his credit, the Imam knew how to maintain calm in negotiations. But his relaxed demeanor and leisurely pace masked a seething rage. He needed this relationship as much as he needed control of Fortis. Without both, he had nothing.

"I suppose you're here because of the CoC," the USD said.

"I am. As you know, the relationship between Fortis and the DoD is long-standing and mutually beneficial. With my new ownership, the company's structure will not change, except for a few top executives taking a generous buyout. I suggest we continue all existing contracts as is, without renegotiating."

"You're right that America depends on the weapon systems supplied by Fortis. And I have no wish to upset this arrangement."

A smile crept onto the Imam's face despite his efforts to suppress the elation.

"I can see this pleases you," said the USD. "I assume you have also secured the Fortis IP?"

The Imam's eyes grew wide; a tremor of panic threatened to crack his calm exterior. He looked to his General Counsel.

"I am sure we have everything in order," he replied. "The sale included all Fortis-owned assets, including the Intellectual

Properties."

"Well, that is the sticking point," the USD said. "Have you secured the nominee trust held in the Cook Islands? Before I could finalize our arrangement with Fortis, I verified that every piece of IP in the Fortis portfolio was indeed assigned to this secretive trust."

The Imam glared at his General Counsel, whose terror-stricken eyes betrayed a growing cataclysmic concern.

"I'm sure you're familiar with the workings of such trusts," the USD continued. "So, you'll know that even the United States government could not determine its ultimate owner. But our requirements were satisfied when the law firm holding the notarized Power of Attorney for a sealed Letter of Wishes outlining a succession clause confirmed the current assignee was Sir Ethan Stone III."

"I have never seen such a letter," the General Counsel exclaimed. "Even if it does exist, it was not disclosed as a Fortis asset, and they are in breach of our agreement. We will win a lawsuit and retain our rightful property."

"Of course, you never saw this letter. It is not a Fortis asset. It is the Stone family legacy's private estate protection and succession plan."

The Imam's shattered confidence broke through to his countenance.

"This is outrageous. There is no such letter," he nearly shouted across the secure conference table.

"I have seen it," the USD said, enjoying himself immensely. "While I don't know the letter's contents, I can assure you the Stone family has held this company for three generations and only ever passed it to their firstborn sons. I would guess that all Fortis IP will privately transfer to Ethan Stone IV in the event of Sir Stone's passing."

"Impossible," the Imam roared.

"Maybe so," said the USD with a grin.

"I just spent a hundred billion pounds on this company!"

"You can understand our position. To continue our valuable relationship, you must verify to me that you own the IP. Otherwise, all you bought was a hundred-billion-pound shell."

The Imam sat stunned. His General Counsel sweated profusely.

The USD stood. "Thank you for coming. Please get back to me when you can confirm ownership. In the meantime, I am suspending all DoD payments for orders placed pending verification. Good day."

He turned his back and walked out of the room.

60

"I can't go in," Regus confided, trembling now with anxiety. "I can't."

Sykes, Jack, and Archer had already plunged into the shallow waters after the Rabbi, leaving the couple alone on the landing.

"I'm sure it's perfectly safe," Ethan replied gently. "It's been here for thousands of years. I doubt there is any chance the walls will collapse on us."

Regus shuddered visibly at the new thought of being buried under tons of mountainous stones.

'That was probably not helpful," Ethan said regretfully.

"No. It was not. Not at all."

"What are you worried about?"

"I don't want to get trapped."

"Trapped, how?" Ethan asked.

"Stuck in a dangerous place with nowhere to go," she replied, getting worked up. "Forced to endure relentless pursuit without self-determination to escape. Held against my will in a situation I have not chosen or consented to but find myself in nonetheless. Trapped!"

Ethan was no expert on the female heart, but even he could see this was not about tight spaces. They needed to get moving, as their group was already out of earshot.

"I understand. That all sounds terrible."

"It is," she retorted, emotions capturing her momentarily.

"Remember when you told me I needed to speak to my dad? Not just call him, but go to him? That was, for me, an unthinkable idea. But when I chose to confront the fear voluntarily, everything changed."

"The thing you need the most will be found where you least want to look," she said, the memory pulling her out of her myopic trap.

"Exactly. So, if you choose to walk into this tunnel, you are no longer trapped—you're courageously moving forward. It won't change the reality of the unknown ahead. But it does transform your experience along the way."

Ethan stepped into the water and held out his hand. Regus looked down at him, her fear transforming into resolve.

"If I take your hand, it'll be the second time you ruin a pair of my shoes."

"Like I said before, you should probably take them off."

Regus smiled and did just that. She tied her laces, stuffed her socks in the shoes, and slung them over her shoulder. Taking Ethan's hand, she placed her feet into the cool spring-fed pathway, toes gripping ancient stone as she stepped into history.

The tunnel was beyond dark.

It immediately got too narrow to walk side-by-side with Ethan, so she let go and placed her hand on his shoulder, with him leading the way. Two minutes in, she couldn't see his back a foot in front of her.

The water was cool but not cold, and the air didn't feel musty or contaminated. Everything, except for the terrifying darkness and compressed space, was relatively comfortable.

"You doing alright back there?" Ethan asked.

"It's okay," she said, the slight ripple of the running water mingling with their sloshing footsteps. "Feels nice on my feet."

They continued in silence, Ethan leading the way with one hand tracing the wall and the other lightly extending above his waist, irrationally ensuring they didn't run into anything.

Then, the waters began to rise.

At first, Regus didn't notice. But alarm bells fired when her foot didn't clear the surface as she stepped.

"Be brave," she told herself. "This is your choice."

But a familiar, relentless, impenetrable darkness crept into her soul when the water hit her waist. Suddenly, the horrors of her teenage years mashed into one gruesome and vivid scene, casting themselves on the screen of her mind.

She could see her father lying in a hospital bed, emaciated from chemo and the ravages of cancerous invaders in his lungs. Her older brother sat slumped in the corner of the room, bleeding from a self-inflicted gunshot wound to the head, scores of blood-splattered bills and rejection letters from the VA strewn about his feet. Mom was nowhere to be found; a crippling anxiety had beaten her into medicated retreat long ago.

Regus stood amid the hospital room, alert and alone, surrounded by those who'd loved her well but left before their time. None of them was able to comfort her desperate heart. She didn't blame them for leaving. She knew they'd fought until the end. She was just the last one standing, the final Britton who managed to hold on to her sanity in a world gone mad. But plodding through an underground deathtrap headlong into rising waters with no vision, her sanity was slipping.

She was trapped.

The tremor began in her throat, but it consumed her entire being. A wail erupted from the deep within her, somewhere beneath her memory and her will. It pierced the blanketed emptiness of the tunnel, simultaneously a cry for help and a curse for the devastation of life and all that was forever lost. The reverberating waves carried a hopeless hunger for comfort she'd given up ever receiving, but it hadn't stopped the need.

Ethan spun at the shattered silence and enveloped Regus in his arms, pulling her close. Her wailing turned to sobs as fear, grief, rage, and loneliness spilled forth. She buried her face in his chest, and Ethan held tight while she purged the pain.

Regus wept in the darkness.

But then, she became aware of the rhythmic beat racing against her cheek. Her tears dried up, and stillness descended once more. But this time, her face pressed against Ethan, she heard a sound in the silence. It wasn't just a heartbeat; it was a promise. She knew it wasn't from Ethan, but his closeness in her suffocating fear helped the truth ring out: though her heart and flesh may fail, she had a strength and sustainer who would walk her through anything. She was not trapped; she was on a journey out. She, too, was going home.

Brilliant light flooded the tunnel, washing over them as they stood locked in an embrace.

"Ethan," Jack shouted, his trusty tactical Maglite out, racing back toward them.

"Here," he replied, the light's diffused reflection getting stronger. "Round the corner."

Jack came upon them and lowered the beam. Regus hadn't moved, and Ethan didn't dare let go. Jack knew better than to harass his boss at this moment.

"We just reached the center of the tunnel," he said. "Right around this bend, the tunnel starts to zigzag like crazy until the two ends meet in the middle. The rabbi told us about an inscription found at this spot from the 8th century BCE when we heard the cry. We'll wait for you."

Jack slid the still-on Maglite into Ethan's back pocket and retreated, its beam casting a haloed canopy of illumination around them.

"Are you going to be okay?" he asked her.

Regus looked up; she thought her puffy, tear-stained face must be a sight.

"Thank you. I needed this."

She slid her arms, which had been swallowed by Ethan's embrace, out from in front of her. Reaching around him, she snagged the light from his back pocket.

"Can I have this?" she asked.

"Please. Why don't you lead the way?"

She smiled and pressed past him in the narrow tunnel, their bodies disengaging from the desperate moment in the darkness.

"I won't forget this," she said, beginning anew on the journey out.

61

The group emerged from the thirty-minute walk beneath the city to a cut-stone basin, divided by a tall wall. The day school next door was on break, and the sound of playing schoolchildren filled the ruin, cascading down from above like a joyful rain.

Regus hardly noticed when they exited the cramped tunnel. She'd drifted into a place in her heart that had lost all sense of confinement. She was free from a prison she hadn't known existed. But her release defined the captivity, and each new step out was a step away from her old life. And with that, shoes still in hand, she stepped closer to Uriel, so she would not miss a word about the Pool of Siloam.

"Pilgrims would come here to cleanse themselves in ritual baths from the First Temple period under King Hezekiah, to the Second Temple period, and during Roman occupation in the first century." Uriel extended his hand toward the water as if inviting them to imagine the scene. "Priests of the Holy Temple also came each fall to fill a Golden vessel."

"Why did they do that?" Regus asked, her gaze darting from Uriel to the rippling water as though searching for the answer herself.

"Tradition. Each year, during a Feast, called Sukkot, the priests came early in the morning to scoop up spring water, what they called

'Living Water,' and carry it along 'The Pilgrimage Road' up to the Water Gate and onto the platform of the Temple Mount. There in a solemn procession, they poured the water on the altar of sacrifice, praying for rain to fall from the heavens to nourish the crops for the coming year."

"So they believed water carried life straight from the divine...like a blessing poured into the soil to create the crops they needed to live," Regus said.

"Very much so. Even today, tens of thousands gather at the Western Wall during this feast to sing, dance, and celebrate the joyous occasion of Adonai leading us in the wilderness for forty years after we left Egypt. The faithful do not forget."

"Is this a connection to the Exodus?" Sykes asked, eager to find out why they had walked through a watery tunnel beneath the city.

"It's a major touch point. The Exodus was a pivotal event in our nation's founding. Before we had a land, the Jewish people were bound by the Law, not by conquest, but by covenant. It was cut with Abram, renewed with Moses, and reaffirmed with King David. We were tiny tribes with no home, but Adonai's promise to us was long before we had a land of our own. The nations of the earth do not need to recognize this as true for it to be so. And this twenty-seven-hundred-year-old pool is physical evidence of its endurance through the ages."

Ethan stood in his soaking-wet sneakers, thinking about this. He'd spent his adult years preserving ancient artifacts he believed would ground a rudderless culture in history the West should never forget. While postmodern culture had denied the existence and importance of such history, Ethan knew it was the key to preserving American ideals. And, with all her flaws, America was still a great light amongst the nations. But he'd never even considered that the Biblical stories had a place in this grand narrative.

"To come out of bondage in Egypt, my people first passed through the waters," Uriel's eyes carried a weighty knowing that settled on the team. "But this alone is not enough. We have one final road to walk. Come, let us ascend to the Mountain of the House of the Lord."

Uriel led them into a newly opened pathway outside the pool's entrance.

"This is the gateway to an ancient Roman road used during the first century: 'The Pilgrimage Road.' After a decade of painstaking excavations, it has recently opened to the public."

The group walked up a small series of metal steps leading into a wide underground roadway supported by countless steel beams and support structures.

"The Israeli government funded this excavation, ensuring the Arab homes above remain undisturbed as we unearth our ancient history."

The group entered the vast, well-lit Roman street, which had a gentle ascent back towards the Temple Mount.

This tunnel felt like a modern superhighway after the pitch-black walk through the bedrock.

Ethan heard Regus sigh.

"Is this tunnel a little more to your liking?" he asked her.

"This one is great," she exclaimed. "It's huge."

"This road was the main artery from the Temple down to the pool and out into the valley below," Uriel said. "It was lined with shops, homes, and beneath it, something rather mundane but exceedingly important: a drainage ditch."

Uriel turned right and descended a narrow ladder to a hidden chamber ten feet below the ancient road. Ethan, Sykes, Jack, and Archer followed and soon stood in a narrow channel that followed the same path as the road above.

Regus stood over the opening, looking down at the men huddled together in another tight space.

"Well," she said, looking around at the broad road, they were not taking. "I enjoyed it while it lasted. Back into a tiny tunnel." With a shrug she followed them down.

"We are now passing through the main drainage channel for

Jerusalem. Waste and rainwater were collected here and sent down the hill and into the valley. Discovered in 2011, it contained a treasure trove of 1st-century artifacts.

"During the Roman siege of Jerusalem in 70 CE, Josephus describes how terrified inhabitants took refuge below the streets, hiding from the bloodbath of Roman destruction above. However, this was but a respite, as Roman soldiers soon found us, dug our people out, and slaughtered us where we stood."

Ethan was surprised to hear the Rabbi's language. "Why do you use the term 'us' when you recount this?"

"For you, this is history. For Jews, it is memory," he said. "We do not forget what has been done to our people over the years by nations seeking our destruction. When madmen say they want to wipe Israel off the face of the map, we believe them."

That statement hit differently for Ethan. The current situation in the Middle East took on a new hue as he walked these ancient paths through thousands of years of Jewish history, architectural accomplishments, and deep suffering. The black-and-white gloss media outlets cast upon the modern conflict was shifting from monochromatic to living color.

"We are almost at the end," Uriel said. "But this channel produced several invaluable artifacts, including Jewish coins minted during the 66 CE revolt, cooking pots and oil lamps, providing evidence this was inhabited, and even a 24-inch iron sword, remarkably preserved within its Roman leather scabbard."

They came to a spiral staircase and a massive, immaculately cut stone wall. It looked like the corner of an ancient building. Its enormous stone blocks were smooth and perfectly straight, with an inch margin chiseled around the edges.

"What is this?" Ethan walked over to place his hand on the blocks.

"Good eye," Uriel said. "They're beautiful examples of Herodian stone here in the southwest corner of the Temple Mount. Beginning in 20 BCE, King Herod expanded the Temple Mount structure, and this distinctive stone design was named after him. Look around the walls above, you'll see these blocks everywhere."

They all followed Uriel up and out of the tunnel. Once Ethan's eyes adjusted to the bright noonday sun, he was shocked to see where they'd ended up. More than six stories above them soared the remarkably intact Western Wall.

The modern excavation teams had left the area precisely as it was after the Temple's 70 CE destruction. Sections of the enormous slabs of stone used to construct the Roman roads were shattered and upended by the force of the collapsing wall above. The distinctive Herodian stone design was evident on many of them.

Ethan began to fully comprehend the tragedy that was the siege of Jerusalem, envisioning the bloodshed that had filled this two-thousand-year-old street.

"I had no idea there was such detailed evidence of Jewish presence in Jerusalem and the price of butting up against Roman might," he said.

"Sadly, it is distinctive of my people's experience for thousands of years," Uriel said in a heavy tone. "It is why we are committed to never letting this sort of thing happen again."

Sykes, Jack, and Archer stood silent in the rubble of the assault. Ethan could tell that his team lead was in deep thought.

"What's going through your head?" Ethan offered a warm, supportive smile to draw him out.

"It was just yesterday I was standing in the ruins of the drone attack on Tel Aviv," Sykes said, his voice trembling. "I saw shattered bodies, flames swallowing the shops, teenagers missing limbs. This street must have looked the same. How is this still going on after all these years?"

"Evil," Uriel replied matter-of-factly. "It is a simple answer to a complex question. But three thousand years of historical assaults on Israel happened because evil grips the human heart and doesn't let go until it breaks everything in its path."

The group lingered for a few moments, the hum of the Western Wall Plaza above serving as a backdrop as they contemplated his response.

"This brings us to the first strongman who enslaved my people. And the Exodus connection."

62

Sir Ethan Stone III lay motionless in his bed, awaiting private transport to his favorite home. He'd moved out of the Keats Grove house the week after his son left for good. The memories of the four-story Hampstead structure were too painfully entwined with his son and ex-wife to be left behind. But he'd held on to the Georgian mansion for when Ethan returned to the family empire, and that day had come. It was cruel serendipity that he would transition into the next life as Ethan transitioned back into the fold.

"Sir," broke in Margaret, "You have a phone call from America. Will you take it?"

"Of course, I'll bloody take it. My mind isn't broken, just my body. Give me the moby."

She handed him his cell, which he'd consented to relinquish, given his off-and-on status this go around at the Wellington.

"Stone here."

"Ethan," replied the Under Secretary of Defense. "Good to hear your voice."

"General. Thank you for getting back to me."

"Your buyer just left my office. He had no idea about the trust."

"Bravo, ol' boy!"

"I think they will be paying you a visit in short order."

"Of that, I am sure," replied Sir Stone.

"What games are you up to, Ethan?"

"The fun kind."

"Danger is your only fun."

"In all the decades our families have known each other, have we ever played a game we didn't win?"

"Never. But these Qatari are no joke. Reports from the office next door show they funded last night's Tel Aviv drone attack."

"They fund everything in the region, contrary to Saudi or Israel," scoffed Ethan.

"I cannot do business with a Qatari-run company, Ethan."

"You don't need to worry about that. He will never have a company. It's just a name, no IP, no contracts, and a mountain of ill will. I'll be back in no time with the next iteration of Fortis."

"I heard you're dying."

"My son has come home."

"What then?"

"He will lead the next chapter of Fortis, or whatever we call it. Every new Stone changes the company name when ascending to the throne. It's a rite of passage."

"Your family has strange rituals."

"Well, they've brought us this far. Mark my words; the next generation will be greater than the last."

"I hope that is true. America needs your systems, and we can ill afford to lose them."

"The development of Fortis AI is complete. Forget active measures; psyops from the Cold War era are dinosaurs compared to this. We can get 'em by the short and curlies, anyone, anywhere, without a human asset. It's beyond anything you've ever imagined."

"Sounds intriguing. I look forward to the demo."

"My son will be contacting you shortly. Thank you for the coverage."

"My pleasure. It's been good knowing you, Ethan."

"Oh, do me a favor—none of that soppy farewell bollocks, yeah?"

"Alright then. Goodbye. See you on the other side."

Sir Stone hung up and released the coughing fit he'd managed to hold back for the last few minutes. He hoped Ethan was on his way home.

He didn't have the will to hold on much longer.

63

The team moved silently through the Western Wall Plaza. With yesterday's attack in Tel Aviv and today being a workday before lunch, only a few tourist groups were present.

"The 43,000-square-foot public space and its overflow areas accommodate up to 100,000 people during festivals," Uriel said. The stillness made the site feel even more profound.

"This exposed segment of the western side of Herod's expanded complex is about 180 feet long. The rest of the 1,500-foot Herodian wall is covered by the Muslim Quarter and centuries of earth," Uriel beamed with pride. "It is one of the closest sites to the historic First and Second Temples, where my people can pray."

Jack looked about in awe.

"In 1967, Israel was reunited with our capital Jerusalem for the first time in nearly 2,000 years," Uriel continued. "Immediately, we opened up the space surrounding the wall, creating this modern plaza and the world-renowned pilgrimage site."

Archer was engrossed in the scene. His summer spent touring the grand cathedrals in Europe rushed back to mind. There it was again, holy ground.

"Compared to the 370,000-square-foot Kaaba site in Mecca, this place is tiny," Uriel said. "But we Israelis always celebrate whatever access we can reclaim, even if prayer is still prohibited on the Temple Mount." A not-so-subtle tinge of disdain evident in his voice. "If you wish to visit the wall, now is a good time. Regus, there is an entrance point to the right if the gentlemen want to follow me."

The group split up, and Uriel walked the men over to the left side and handed each American a disposable kippah.

"These are a simple sign of respect for religious culture," he said, "and an external symbol of submission before God."

"Do we have to wear this?" Jack asked.

"These are not obligatory for non-Jews," Uriel said. "You may do as you please without reproach."

"I'm impressed they let non-Jews even visit this site," Sykes offered. "Remember what Hamid said about that Burton character? Non-Muslims can't even get into the city of Mecca, much less visit their prayer site."

Jack placed the paper cap in his back pocket, and they walked into the prayer area. Scores of plastic chairs were stacked off to the side of the vast plaza, while men in long black garments stood facing the stone, gently rocking back and forth, their heads and shoulders covered by white prayer shawls. A few tourists mingled about, but the atmosphere was one of quiet reverence.

Ethan found an open section along the wall where thousands of tiny, folded slips of paper were tucked, overflowing in the cracks between the massive limestone blocks. He placed his hand on the stones, worn smooth by countless touches, and thought about his dad.

He'd always represented an unbridled lust for power and wealth fueled by weapons of war. Ethan was dead set against this image of his father, which was still present in his consciousness. However, another form had emerged, less precise but, in some ways, more convincing than the two-dimensional one from his youth.

Hard things were demanded of strong leaders in impossible

situations. Life and death hung in the balance for someone, somewhere, every moment of every day. Some leaders stepped into the biggest arenas to lead these people, while others hid away. He knew his life was on the verge of shifting irrevocably in one direction, depending on his following choices. He wasn't worried anymore about distancing himself from his dad. He was concerned about becoming him.

How would he respond to the immense wealth and power he'd just been handed? Was he even the kind of man able to bear up under that? He'd trained his whole life to be a fighter. But he knew you couldn't defeat your enemy by simply being against them. You needed a strategy and vision to lead toward a goal worth throwing yourself into wholeheartedly. And then you needed the time, talent, and dedication to work toward that end. No excuses. No turning back.

He saw Israel as a nation of leaders who'd borne the endless weight of wars, regime change, and civil division, always standing on the brink of annihilation. And yet, here they were—a nation again, thriving in their ancient, historic homeland. Where were the Pharaohs, the Romans, the Visigoths, the Huns, and the Assyrians? They'd all come and gone, but Israel was still here.

Why was a two-thousand-year-old broken-down wall a place of prayer to an entity he didn't believe existed? What motivated the Jews to keep going in the face of relentless opposition? Who but the Jews had survived so many historical attempts at systematic extermination? And most disturbingly, how would he reconcile all the pieces of an ancient puzzle now coming together with his academic pedigree that denied what he'd seen firsthand?

Of all the things discovered today, this final realization at the Western Wall was perhaps the most important: he was not as smart as he thought.

Sykes tapped him on the shoulder. "Ethan, you up for one last stop?"

"Where to?"

"Not sure, but we're ready to go."

The two long-time friends departed the wall and rejoined the group.

"You sure spent a long time with your hand on the stone," Regus said, cozying up beside Ethan. "What were you thinking about?"

"I'll tell you mine if you tell me yours," Ethan replied.

Regus grinned, "Maybe someday."

"Come on, we have one more place to visit," Uriel said as he led them up the plaza.

He stopped at a large glass door resembling a shopping mall entrance.

"What's this?" Jack shifted his weight from one foot to the other.

"The Western Wall Plaza is the closest most visitors to Israel get to the ancient Temple. But you are not most people."   '

The door to the Western Wall Tunnels slid open, and Uriel led them inside.

The air was immediately cooler after the few short steps leading into a long hallway. Inground lights cast a muted glow across low arches, turning the rough ceilings into a tapestry of age and endurance. Glass panels etched with Hebrew letters glimmered with emerald LEDs, pointing the way forward.

Uriel led them deeper down the secret passage beneath the streets. Their footsteps echoed off the walls until the path opened onto massive, chisel-marked blocks of Herodian stone, highlighting their timeless splendor.

"This is the Western Wall," Uriel said. "And these stones were visible at street level during the days of the New Testament."

Again, Ethan couldn't help but feel awe, mixed with a growing resentment at his academic tradition, which had utterly ignored the Biblical sources. He'd stood at the base of the Great Pyramid in Giza and even ventured inside on more than one occasion. He remembered standing in the King's Chamber and the Grand Gallery, deep inside, marveling at the largest stones ever cut for a pyramid, enormous granite beams as heavy as 70-80 tons that spanned the central support structure for Khufu's tomb—a remarkable feat in any era. But the stone in front of him put those megaliths to shame.

"This stone," he asked, touching the perfectly carved face of the limestone behemoth, "How big is it?"

"That is the largest stone in the wall. It's over forty feet long, twelve feet high, and fourteen feet deep. At over 600 tons, it weighs more than two fully loaded 747 aircraft. Herod probably put it there to impress the people at street level. He was a bit of a showman."

"And a murderer," added Archer.

"That too," Uriel nodded.

This rivaled anything ever found in Egypt for scale and beauty. Ethan had only seen two finished Egyptian carvings that were larger than this one. Both were granite Colossi depicting the pharaohs, but neither had been cut for construction purposes.

"This architecture is remarkable," he said.

"I couldn't agree more. Men build monuments of stone to secure their grip on power. This was Herod's work. But Adonai built something far greater."

Uriel continued down the narrow walkway along the Western Wall until he reached a distinctive opening filled with stone rubble.

"This is known as Warren's Gate. Warren was a prolific explorer in the mid-1800s," Uriel said, pointing toward the ancient arch along the tunnel wall.

The team examined the small, arched niche illuminated by a strip of commercial LED lights.

"Just two hundred feet away, directly through there was the holy of holies. This is the closest a Jewish person can get to the Holy Temple." Uriel said softly, his chest rising with a deep, steady breath.

"Why is this Temple so important?" Ethan tilted his head slightly, confusion clouding his features.

"Because it was here that Adonai rested among his people. This is where the Exodus story falls into place."

Finally, Ethan thought, some answers.

"The purpose of the Exodus is summed up by the words Moses was commanded to speak as he stood before the Pharaoh.

"Adonai said, 'Tell Pharaoh to let my people go so they may serve me in the wilderness.'

"Adonai didn't deliver us from Egypt's chains just to set us free. We passed through the waters so we could worship Him, unbound, at the mountain.

"Adonai commanded that worship at Sinai be through the building of a Tabernacle, set in the midst of His people at the mountain's base. That Tabernacle, later transformed into this very Temple, became the innermost dwelling place of His Holy Presence— what we call the Most Holy Place."

"Does the Bible say who this Pharaoh was?" Ethan asked in a tone of urgency, starved for any clue that would piece the puzzle together about Egypt.

"It does not," Uriel replied. "I was hoping the world-famous Egyptologist could tell me this."

"Unfortunately, I'd need a time frame before I could analyze anything."

"I can give you a date." Uriel held his gaze, unflinching. "Because the biblical text is a primary source in antiquity, which also happens to be the most historically accurate and archaeologically verifiable document ever written, we use its detailed internal records to date the Exodus."

"That's reasonable," Ethan said.

"Good." Uriel took a deep breath. "We begin the analysis in Kings 6:1, four years into the reign of Solomon, where it's recorded that King David's son began building the first Temple. This passage also ties the Temple construction to the Exodus, saying work began 480 years after the Exodus event took place."

"Why tie this to the Exodus event?" Jack's eyes narrowed as his forehead creased.

"Because of what I said earlier, Adonai set the people free *from* Egypt to be free *for* worship. Solomon's temple stood until 586 BCE when King Nebuchadnezzar besieged Jerusalem, destroying the Temple and taking my people into exile."

"I don't remember that detail." Ethan ran a hand through his hair, his face tight with the effort of trying to make sense of it.

"Nebuchadnezzar's siege, you're referring to, happened in 597 BCE. We know because it is recorded on a cuneiform tablet known as the Babylonian Chronicles. It records how Nebuchadnezzar took the Judean king captive and put in a king of his choosing. It doesn't say anything about destroying the Temple."

"Correct. However, that tablet confirms precisely what is written in the Bible: King Jehoiachin was taken captive to Babylon, and the last king of Judah, installed exactly as the tablet states, was a puppet of Babylon. His name was Zedekiah."

"And this is all in the ancient biblical texts?" Ethan leaned back slightly, his gaze fixed on Uriel, as he tried to piece the facts together.

"It is. Especially in the books of the Kings, fragments of which were found in the Dead Sea Scrolls. This specific information is written in 2 Kings 24 and 25."

Ethan was undoubtedly going to revisit these sources.

"In these internal records," Uriel continued, "the reign for each King of Israel and Judah was recorded, beginning with Saul and ending with Zedekiah. Compiling these years, we discover the length of time between the start of Temple construction and its destruction. That period is 380 years.

"Now, if you add up the three numbers, Solomon began construction 380 years before the Temple was destroyed in 586 BCE, which was 480 years after the Exodus. Thus, for the dramatic event recorded in the Torah, you arrive at 1446 BCE."

Ethan couldn't believe his ears. This placed the Exodus precisely in line with his theory of the Thutmosid Succession.

The wheels in his mind spun faster than ever. Fragments of Egyptian history that had felt scattered and misaligned began to click into place. For the first time, the biblical story was mapping itself onto the Egyptian timeline.

Uriel caught the look on his face. "What is it?"

"I think I know who the Pharaoh was," Ethan whispered, his voice trembling with awe.

"If I'm right... it changes everything."

64

"I need to know everything you discovered about the Exodus," Ethan told his team. "We've not even had time to debrief about your experiences."

"We can do that," Sykes said. "But it'll take a while."

"Come," Uriel said, "We can't stay in the hallway. But a beautiful synagogue near here is open for study and prayer."

"Perfect," Ethan replied. "I will also need to know what the manuscripts say happened to the Hebrews in Egypt."

Uriel led them further along the hall, past Byzantine, Crusader, and Ottoman structures that weighed down on them from above. Heading deeper into the sprawling underground complex, the group felt an electric spark of anticipation.

They came upon a spectacular two-hundred-seat room hollowed out with low, arched ceilings. The polished stone floor, illuminated from beneath, warmed the space with an even glow, creating a canvas for the wooden benches, each inlaid with golden carvings of the Seven Species of plants mentioned in the Torah.

The center of the room was a golden globe housing the Torah scrolls, with Hebrew characters engraved on its surface. A large golden menorah behind it added to the chamber's beauty and mystique. Surprisingly, the room was empty, so the group sat down. Sykes began filling Ethan in on everything, from the discovery of the book at Sindalah to the team retracing their steps along the Valley of Moses, to the 12 wells of Elam.

This was followed by the rousing discussion in Jethro's house before heading to the Moses well, and then to the mysterious rock split down the middle.

Jack chimed in about his experiences along the way, handing off the discussion to Archer, who chronicled the Golden Calf altar, the encounter with the guards, and the analysis of the L-shaped altar site. Sykes could hardly contain himself as he relayed the information about the white marble quarry and the connection to the foundation stones that Captain Raviv revealed just before the drone strike. It was here that Uriel spoke up for the first time.

"I have heard of this Sinai in Arabia theory but have never given it much thought," he admitted. "Your tale sheds much light on its plausibility."

"I'm glad to hear that," Jack said.

"Another section of the text that comes to mind references these artifacts. It is from the Prophet Isaiah, who was calling a wayward nation back to Adonai. He warned Israel not to trust Egypt for protection, for on the day of trouble, their help would fail. This warning was given a few years before the history we discussed in Hezekiah's Tunnel. The prophecy explicitly calls out a future Assyrian siege of Jerusalem, stating that Adonai, not Egypt, would turn it back. He says in Isaiah 31:8,

> *'And the Assyrian shall fall by a sword, not of man;*
> *and a sword, not of man, shall devour him;*
> *and he shall flee from the sword,*
> *and his young men shall be put to forced labor.'*

"Wow," Ethan replied. "This is exactly what our driver talked about on the way into Jerusalem. A miraculous force intervening."

"He then goes on," Uriel continued, "To say in Isaiah 32:1-2

> *Behold, a king will reign in righteousness,*
> *and princes will rule in justice.*
> *Each will be like a hiding place from the wind,*
> *a shelter from the storm,*
> *like streams of water in a dry place,*
> *like the shade of a great rock in a weary land.'*

Jack's face lit up with these final lines.

"Isaiah calls out the Split Rock," he exclaimed. "That's unbelievable. I stood in the shadow of that great rock, thinking about the streams of water that could have miraculously erupted. Does this sort of thing happen a lot in the Bible? The referencing of its history."

"All the time. It is the most self-referenced document ever written. Remember, this is memory for us. The accounts are embedded in the hearts and minds of our people and the physical land that continues to bear witness."

Ethan still counted himself among those who thought religion was a bunch of fantastical myths created by humans. But, since he was not as smart as he thought, it may be time for a reasonable reevaluation.

"What else did you discover? Or was that it?" he asked.

"Then we went to Trojena, a high mountain resort near the summit of Jabal al-Lawz," Jack said in a rush, trying to cram everything in. "Our tour guide, Hamid, was going to show us the summit, but we were attacked. Then he was poisoned, and a medevac transport took us to Israel."

"In a Saudi Royal helicopter," Uriel added. "I am still waiting for someone to tell me how that happened."

"Our tour guide was—is married to the King's daughter and works as an intelligence officer for the Royal family," Jack replied.

Ethan wanted to know a lot more about this, but he needed to stay on track. He was very close to unraveling a mystery—he could feel it.

"We must speak more about this," he said. "But I need information about what happened in Egypt before, during, and after the Hebrews left."

"Where would you like to begin?" Uriel asked. "There is much detail in the Text."

"According to established theories, your 1446 BCE date places the Exodus during the early years of the Thutmosid Dynasty," Ethan replied. "Also called the 18th Dynasty, it is probably the most complex and difficult-to-understand period in Egypt. In my view, the established consensus on who was Pharaoh in the 18th Dynasty and when misses the mark by about 130 years."

"Why is that?" Uriel asked.

"A variety of reasons. Dating anything in antiquity is difficult. There are thousands of artifacts to sift through to reconstruct the timeline, including 3rd-century CE manuscripts listing Egyptian rulers and monumental inscriptions on many stone artifacts mentioning the number of years a Pharaoh reigned.

"But one of the most important for timeline reconstruction was a star we call Sirius. It was a cosmic timekeeper for the Egyptians, playing a significant role in both the civil and religious calendars. Every year, the star makes its first visible appearance on the horizon, rising in the dark morning sky just before the sun. The heliacal rising of Sirius marked the Egyptian new year, the start of the Nile's flood season—the lifeblood of Egyptian culture—and set the dates for calculating how long a Pharaoh ruled."

Jack shifted in his seat, the weight of the revelation pulling him deeper.

"Because of the Earth's rotation, the rising shifts a few days earlier each year. Every 1,460 years, the Egyptian calendar resets. That drift could move dynasties forward or back by decades."

Jack leaned in, elbows resting on his knees, trying to catch the math mid-air.

"Location mattered too. Memphis in the north, Thebes four hundred miles south. Different horizons meant different dates. Another swing by decades."

Archer let out a slow breath. "So, the whole system was unstable."

"Then the gaps. Records broken, lost, or deliberately erased. Take Hatshepsut. She ruled as Pharaoh, one of the most famous women in Egyptian history. Yet her statues were smashed, her name carved out. Why? Likely a scandal. Which means her rise—and the key dates tied to it—are gone."

Sykes rubbed the scar on his hand, as if the missing history itched at him. "Erased queens. Shifting stars. Perfect way to bury the truth."

"One thing remains certain. Pharaohs overlapped. Co-regents. Shared power. The Thutmosid Dynasty depended on it. Many of the so-called kings were the same ruler, renamed as he moved from co-regent to Pharaoh."

Jack's jaw tightened. "And the establishment refuses to see it."

"Exactly. Without co-regency, their timeline is broken, shifted by nearly 130 years."

The room held still, the weight of centuries pressing down on the present.

"How does anyone ever make sense of this?" Uriel asked.

"With much uncertainty," Ethan replied.

"Why, then, are the dates presented as facts by so many?" Archer asked.

"I think it comes down to funding and world views. Excavations are unbelievably expensive. Money always comes with strings. Funders expect results that fit their objectives. To maintain their support, you must deliver what they want. That pressure doesn't exactly encourage unbiased research."

Jack frowned, the line between science and politics suddenly clearer than he liked.

"In Egypt, it's even stricter. The government doesn't recognize the Exodus as legitimate history. So they block digs that might uncover Biblical artifacts or evidence of a Jewish presence.

"The Supreme Council of Antiquities controls every site. If they don't approve the question, you'll never touch the ground to ask it."

Archer shook his head, bitter. "So the silence isn't absence. It's enforced."

"My own time in academia shaped me the same way. I learned to dismiss the Biblical manuscripts as irrelevant. That's why I searched everywhere but Israel."

Sykes shifted, jaw flexing. "And all this time, the real trail was buried in plain sight."

Ethan's voice dropped. "Exactly. Which is why today has been such an eye-opener."

The room went quiet, tension coiling like a wire.

"What can we do?" asked Jack.

"Well," Ethan said, hesitating before the words found their shape. "The puzzle pieces matter because truth hides in the story itself. All through history, meaning hasn't rested on raw facts. People grasp meaning through narrative.

"In Egypt, since dates are slippery, dig sites are restricted, and funding's biased, I started piecing together the bigger picture—how the story of that entire period fits.

"If the fragments—inscriptions, ruins, manuscripts—line up into a coherent story, that carries more weight than gambling on a timeline we can't pin down.

"That's why I need to know what the biblical manuscripts actually say about the Hebrews in Egypt. I'm close to pulling a thread that unravels the whole thing."

Ethan paused, eyes distant, caught inside the riddle of a puzzle almost solved.

"But I need more data."

Uriel stood and walked to the golden globe. He opened the ornate doors, carved with Hebrew characters, and retrieved a Torah scroll. Bringing it back to where the group was sitting, he unrolled it.

"This is the book of Shemot, Hebrew for 'Names.' We title the books based on the first few words; this reads, '*And these are the names of the sons of Israel.*' What do you want to know from the Exodus scroll?"

65

The group settled into the wooden pews of the small synagogue. Uriel remained standing near the front, hands clasped as though the story itself were a kind of prayer.

Finally, after pondering the next step, Ethan broke the silence in the synagogue.

"Let's start with Moses," Ethan rubbed his chin. "What does the scroll tell us about him?"

"He was born when the new Pharaoh had forgotten the blessings my people once brought to Egypt," Uriel began, his voice echoing softly off the stone walls. "Our ancestor Joseph rose to become second in command. During the famine, he made Egypt rich—his wisdom filled the storehouses while nations starved. The scrolls say he married the daughter of the Priest of On and lived in comfort with his family—seventy souls in all. They were fruitful, and they multiplied."

He moved slowly between the pews, gaze distant. "But memory fades. A new Pharaoh arose—one who knew nothing of Joseph, nor of the God who saved his empire. He saw our numbers as a threat, our strength as rebellion. So he decreed that every Hebrew boy be slain before he could rise against him."

Uriel paused before the ark, where the Torah scrolls were kept. His voice lowered. "Moses was born into that terror. His mother hid him as long as she could, but Pharaoh's reach was absolute. So they placed him in a reed basket and set him in the bathing pool of Pharaoh's daughter."

Ethan leaned forward, brow furrowed. "Wait," he said. "The Greek Old Testament says he was placed among the reeds of the Nile. Why are you saying it was a bathing pool?"

"The Hebrew word is *sûp*," came the reply. "Its meaning is difficult to pin down. Rabbi Rashi, in the 11th century CE, translated it as '*reeds*,' and that interpretation stuck. But it isn't entirely accurate.

"The word is also translated as '*red*,' as in the '*Red Sea*,' in many older texts. But in dozens of other places, *sûp* refers to a boundary or a termination point. For example, Jonah—when swallowed by the whale—sank until the *sûp̄* restrained him. It marked the border, the sea floor itself.

"So the image is clear: *sûp̄* isn't reeds. It's a boundary. A limit that cannot be crossed."

"Interesting," Ethan said. "Keep going."

"The scroll says he was placed in the *sûp̄* along the river's edge. This Hebrew word '*edge*' means '*bank*' or sometimes '*language*' or '*lips*.' It carries the idea that it was the edge of a container, as in a body of water, or a body of words like language that flows from the container of the lips."

"Remarkable."

"So he was placed at the boundary of a container in the Nile. It makes sense that Moses' sister put him in a royal bathing pool—one cut from the Nile's banks where Pharaoh's daughter could easily find him. Hence, a '*bathing pool*.'"

"It makes perfect sense," Ethan said. "Those sorts of pools were widespread for the wealthy class. Continue."

"Pharaoh's daughter came out one day to find Moses in the pool, and she took compassion on him; seeing it was a Hebrew baby, she took him in as her own."

"The scroll says that? She knew it was a Hebrew baby?"

"It does."

"How did she know that?"

"Well," Uriel hesitated. "We Jews have a custom for boys that is quite different from many other cultures."

"Oh, of course," exclaimed Ethan. "He was circumcised."

"That's correct," Uriel said, his tone thoughtful. "I've often wondered why the daughter of the very man who ordered the death of Hebrew infants would bring one into his home. If Pharaoh feared the Hebrews might grow too strong, why take one in at all? And the scroll tells us that Moses was raised in Pharaoh's house, as one of his own. It has never quite made sense to me."

Ethan was trembling. This was too much.

"I know why," he said. "There was a Pharaoh in this period with a single daughter and no male heir. Adopting a Hebrew boy would have been the perfect insurance. It secured a successor to carry on his rule, and at the same time, gave him someone who could keep the Hebrews under control.

"If he could convince the child to embrace Egypt, the dynasty lived on—and the threat of rebellion stayed buried."

"Do you know who this Pharaoh and his daughter could be?" Archer asked.

"This was the famous Hatshepsut, daughter of Ahmose, the founder of the 18th Dynasty. Supposedly, she was one of the only female pharaohs of Egypt," Ethan replied.

"Hatshepsut was Moses' mom," groaned Jack, head swiveling to Sykes and Archer, eyes wide with wonder, not disdain.

"Maybe," Ethan replied. "But conjecture alone isn't enough. I need more. Keep going."

"Well," Uriel continued, his hands clasped behind his back as he paced slowly before the ark, "Moses was raised for forty years in Pharaoh's household. One day, he saw a Hebrew slave being beaten.

The sight enraged him, and he struck down the Egyptian who was doing the beating. Word spread quickly. Pharaoh, humiliated, sought to kill his adopted son. So Moses fled—into the land of Midian—where he lived another forty years."

Jack straightened in his seat, eyes alight. "Midian! That's where we found the evidence—those traditions about Moses in northern Saudi Arabia."

Uriel nodded, but his brow furrowed. "Yes. And yet this part of the story has always troubled me," he said quietly. "Why would Pharaoh turn so fiercely against him? A single dead worker meant nothing to a king with thousands. Why cast aside your adopted son for something so… trivial?"

The question hung in the silence, echoing off the ancient stone.

Ethan leaned forward, his voice low but certain. "It only makes sense if Moses chose blood over power," he said. "Pharaoh counted on him to keep the Hebrews in check. But if Moses turned and sided with them, everything Pharaoh built was in jeopardy. The only thing worse than having no heir would be watching your own son ignite the uprising that destroys you."

He paused, the weight of the idea settling over the room. "Moses had to die. That's what Pharaohs do when power slips—they kill to keep it."

Uriel stared at him, astonished. For a moment, the Rabbi's certainty gave way to wonder. Interpreting the sacred text through the lens of geopolitics revealed something both ancient and alarmingly modern. He exhaled softly. "Indeed," he murmured. "There is nothing new under the sun."

"What happens next?" Ethan asked.

Uriel unrolled the scroll a little further.

"After forty years in exile, Moses encounters Adonai at a bush on fire but not consumed. He is told to return to Egypt and demand that the new Pharaoh let all Hebrews go."

"Forty years," Ethan said. "That is interesting. Long enough for a ruler or two to come and go. If his mother were Hatshepsut, she would have been dead, and Moses' replacement would also have died."

"So, Moses returns with a message from Adonai," continued Uriel. "And a series of dramatic signs occur in Egypt."

"Are these the plagues?" Ethan asked.

"They are. Each of the plagues confronts a specific Egyptian god. And each time a miraculous event happens, Pharaoh's heart gets harder and harder, and he refuses to let my people go."

"Describe some of these plagues," Ethan asked.

"The first is the most famous, the Nile turning to blood. The second is a plague of frogs."

"That's Heket," Ethan cut in.

"What?"

"You said each plague dealt with a specific god of Egypt. The frog goddess was Heket, the goddess of fertility and childbirth. What else?"

"There were plagues of flies and boils and diseased cattle."

"That's Apis and Hathor," Ethan said again. "The sacred cattle god and goddess."

"We found Egyptian carvings of Hathor at the base of Mt. Sinai," Archer said. "The Golden Calf."

"There were also plagues of hail and locust, leading up to the deep darkness that descended on Egypt for the ninth plague."

"That would have been Ra," Ethan said. "He was the highest god in the Egyptian Pantheon, and Pharaoh was considered his firstborn son. I can only imagine what the Pharaoh must have thought if some foreign power showed up and darkened the skies over all the land."

"Didn't your dream have something to do with a foreign power?" Regus asked, stopping Ethan in his tracks.

He looked at her, dumbfounded.

"What dream?" Uriel asked.

Sykes looked at Ethan, surprised that he'd divulged this private part of his life to her. Nobody who knew anything spoke. This was Ethan's to share.

"I've had a recurring dream for over a year," he admitted at last. "In it, a Pharaoh is attacked by what he calls a 'foreign power.' He wakes around midnight to cries echoing through his land. His empire burns with looting after a storm tears his city apart and plunges everything into chaos. Women weep in the streets, carrying the bodies of children through the shadows, raging against an unseen enemy."

Uriel leaned forward, his voice measured.

"That sounds like a fusion of the seventh and tenth plagues. The seventh was the hailstorm—devastation like Egypt had never seen. The tenth was the death of the children, the final strike against all the gods of Egypt."

"Why do you say that plague touched every god?" Ethan asked.

Uriel unrolled the scroll a few inches further and began to read. "This is Shemot 12:12, where Adonai says, '*For I will pass through the land of Egypt this night, and will smite all the firstborn in the land of Egypt, both man and beast; and against all the gods of Egypt I will execute judgment: I am the LORD.*'"

Ethan struggled to process this information. Had he been dreaming about the Exodus for a year? Why didn't he see that? Could it be this simple? Finally, he understood his dream.

"The firstborn! This is unbelievable," he said. "It wasn't just a plague; it targeted the Egyptian system built on the firstborn male requirement. From the priests to the sacrificial animals, to Pharaoh himself as the firstborn of Ra, every Egyptian god was a firstborn. If God wanted to deal a death blow to the power structures of Egypt, this would be the way."

"There is one more piece," Uriel said, "that fits into your dream."

He found the place on the scroll and read the Hebrew words first, then translated them into English.

" '*At midnight, the LORD struck down all the firstborn in the land of*

Egypt, from the firstborn of Pharaoh who sat on his throne to the firstborn of the captive who was in the dungeon, and all the firstborn of the livestock. And Pharaoh rose up in the night, he and all his servants and all the Egyptians. And there was a great cry in Egypt, for there was not a house where someone was not dead.' Exodus 12:29-30.

"Do you see it?" Uriel asked, his voice low but charged with urgency. "The connection between this final, most devastating plague and your dream?"

"It's exactly what I've been seeing for a year," Ethan murmured, his eyes distant. "Pharaoh waking up, looking over the ruin of his nation."

"There's more," Uriel pressed, leaning in. "Something else you need to see."

Ethan fell silent, his mind racing, unraveling the threads of revelation. The synagogue was still—until, in a sudden, electric burst, he bolted upright, his voice shaking the stone walls.

"He's not dead!"

"Who," Regus asked, stirred by Ethan's excitement but unaware of the connection.

"He's not dead! This is the answer. He's not dead!"

"Precisely," Uriel said.

"Who," asked Regus again.

"Pharaoh," Ethan panted excitedly. "He should have been dead."

Ethan rose from the bench and paced the chamber. His understanding cracked open like a code finally broken, one that seemed cryptic and was now unmistakably clear. He'd found what he'd desperately sought. Indeed, the Exodus was a Rosetta Stone.

"Will someone please explain this?" Regus begged.

"The Pharaoh in the Exodus was supposed to be the firstborn son," Ethan said. "But in this story, all the firstborns in Egypt are killed, and then Pharaoh wakes up. He's not dead. Either he was the one person who escaped the plague. Or…"

"He's not a firstborn," Regus finished.

"Exactly. And in that moment of death and destruction, he was exposed as an illegitimate ruler. A madman clinging to power, hiding his history from the nation, like his grandmother. But this night, a foreign power comes to claim his heir and the future generations of leaders. All the firstborns of Egypt."

"And do you know who this person could be?" she asked. "Who was the Pharaoh at the Exodus?"

Ethan looked around at his team, Regus, and the Rabbi, all leaning in, waiting for an explanation.

"Who was he?" they said in unison.

"Thutmose IV. The one who placed the Dream Stela between the Sphinx's paws. He knew he didn't have a right to the royal throne, so he created propaganda to seed the narrative as a co-regent before ascending as Pharaoh Amenhotep III."

"So, your dream was about a historical person," Sykes said. "I knew it!"

"It must be," Ethan replied, shocked that the tormenting nightmare driving him across the globe was, in fact, true.

"This discovery explains why the propaganda was needed," he went on. "Hatshepsut couldn't be Pharaoh outright. So she adopted a Hebrew child from the Nile and placed him forward as the figurehead. A firstborn male to satisfy cultural demands. Meanwhile, she ruled from behind the curtain.

"That's why we see so many carvings of her in full royal regalia. But if the Exodus scroll is right, when Moses fled Egypt, the fragile balance she had built collapsed overnight.

"His disappearance forced a scramble for power. And if the truth leaked—that she had used a Hebrew child as her mask—it would explain the rage that led to her statues being smashed. She was suddenly exposed as illegitimate, yet untouchable. The only way to remove her was to erase her memory."

He leaned back, voice low. "My succession timeline fits. Moses vanishes for forty years, then returns to confront Hatshepsut's grandson, Amenhotep III—the dying gasp of a corrupted dynasty."

The group sat frozen, the weight of it pressing down on them. Could this be the reason it remained illegal to even search for archaeological evidence of the Jewish presence in Egypt?

"And we all know who the son of Amenhotep III is," concluded Ethan. "The one who dies in the plague."

"King Tut," Regus said, remembering his lecture at the Met.

"That is the one," Ethan replied. "Amenhotep III's firstborn son. The boy king died in mysterious circumstances, yet his tomb was untouched for thousands of years. The visual symbol in our modern age of Egypt's power is, in reality, a casualty of a corrupt structure holding its nation in bondage, imprisoning millions of Hebrews as they ruled with a terrifying iron fist."

"Until the system collapsed under its lies, exposing all the false gods of Egypt," Uriel added. "And demonstrating the power of the One True God."

At these words, Ethan's countenance fell in the hallowed lights beneath Temple Mount.

Was God real?

His mental clarity vanished. In its place, a rising terror so familiar beckoned him back into the old world. This convergence of his personal and professional life and the whole new realm of possibilities Fortis presented was overwhelming. But more than that, he found what he most desperately sought, and it shattered all of his conceptual boxes. It seemed to be the inevitable answer... but he didn't believe it.

What do I believe?

"For my whole academic career, I've been trying to discover who killed King Tut. According to this evidence," he hesitated, blinking slowly as if controlling the urge to lash out, "God killed him. And I don't know how to believe in that."

"If I may," Uriel said, "You do not have to believe in Adonai to see he is not the one who killed King Tut."

"Explain," Ethan asked, forcing a tight smile that didn't make it to his eyes.

"This story is the archetype of refusing to grow when confronted with deception," Uriel said. "Pharaoh spent his life inside a lie. Three generations had carried it forward, but he expanded it, amplified it, built walls of propaganda to conceal it.

"Then a voice rose from the wilderness. A sage who had lived the lie and knew what Pharaoh had hidden. He came back with something greater than Egypt itself, ready to tear down an empire of corruption, slavery, sacrifice, and the murder of children. For the first time, Pharaoh was confronted with Truth."

A spark of knowing glinted in Ethan's eyes.

"At every step," Uriel continued, "he had a choice: release the captives or sink deeper into the shadows. Each time, he chose the old order—the prison of lies. And with each exposure, he hardened further. Until the entire nation was plunged into darkness, and he stood revealed as the fraud he had always feared he was. That refusal to grow cost him everything—his son, and the future of Egypt's throne."

Regus's eyes glistened as she looked at Ethan. "It was his father's corrupt empire that killed Tut. A regime that repudiated truth, even when their lies were laid bare." She, too, had discovered what she'd sought for a decade.

It was clear to everyone in the synagogue that Ethan understood.

"I have to admit it again," Ethan said with a grimace. "You were right, Regus. My personal life mirrors this story. In ways we probably can't even comprehend."

"I had no idea how deep this went," she said, eyes moist with empathy. "For you and me. I confronted my pain in the tunnel's darkness, and I'm sorry for my aggressive confrontation with you in front of the Met audience. That was more about my pain than your theory."

"No need to apologize," Ethan smiled. "But I understand. And I can promise you this: I will not suffer the same fate."

Ethan stood, breathing slowly as he paced to the ark housing the Torah scrolls. This was his Rubicon—a point of no return. The old life was no more. A new future awaited.

Spinning, he whispered into the stillness a commitment bearing the weight of his whole being. "Fortis will change. We will see it come to pass."

66

London, England

Maggie dried her eyes before entering Sir Stone's room for the last time.

"We're all set, Sir. The Keats Grove house is prepared, and private transport awaits outside."

"About bloody time," he said. "I was worried you wanted me to rot in this room to indulge your cruel fear of being alone."

"My fear is I'll never be rid of your miserable carcass. I'm glad to have something to look forward to finally."

Sir Stone smiled and nodded. "Then it is settled. We both get what we want."

Maggie supervised while the transport teams wheeled the bed out into the hallway.

"You can leave my phonograph," he barked. "I want the next poor soul to enjoy something profound in this despondent place."

"I will make sure of it, Sir," replied Maggie.

"Thank you," he said, reaching out his frail hand for hers. "You've always been good to me."

Maggie took it as she turned away. He hated it when she cried.

The transport team loaded Sir Stone into an unmarked ambulance and pulled away from the Emergency Room circle. A late-model black SUV, crammed with seven oversized men, pulled out behind them as they all turned left onto Wellington Road and around the circle to Prince Albert.

The convoy moved in silence for three kilometers, no lights, no sirens. The ambulance slowed to turn left onto Keats Grove and gently pulled right into the Stone House after a driver got out to open the metal security gate.

The SUV kept barreling down the one-way, turning into the heart of downtown Hampstead before pulling over in front of a pub. The front passenger dialed his boss.

"I got them," he said. "House on Keats Grove in Hampstead."

"Excellent work," the Imam said, already en route to his plane at Dulles. "Make sure nobody leaves. I'll be there soon."

The disastrous meeting at the OUSD had shaken him to the core. But he'd come this far and would finish the job.

The tramp, Celeste, had already agreed to meet next week after his General Counsel demanded a full accounting of the Intellectual Property. But he would not be waiting for the set time at Fortis HQ. Now that he knew where they were, he would come to them.

Sayyid was in the air, headed to London, before the Imam's jet filed a flight plan out of Dulles.

"I got you," he said out loud, closing his mobile.

He'd arrive a few hours earlier, giving him a short window of time to prepare. His brother's network was working on a vehicle for him and the necessary tools of the trade. This would be his final action, not for the Imam, but against him.

The gruesome scene in the basement of the Qatari embassy had shocked his brother awake. Fighting enemies was one thing. Fighting your allies shattered the thin veil of ideological unity, exposing the

Imam's true bond with them—greed. Together, they fled the compound and rushed to the airport. He departed for London while his brother returned to Doha to rally the faithful.

Sayyid had cleared his head and sharpened his focus. He couldn't cleanse the world of unbelievers while doing the bidding of one. He thought back to the early days of Ad-Deen. Hadn't the faithful assassinated Caliph Uthman ibn Affan for his corruption and growing family influence? This would end the same way. The Imam must die.

Ethan had just passed through the security exit at the Western Wall when his sat phone rang.

"Celeste," he said. "How is he?"

"Not well. We need you." Her tone was tight, pressed with urgency.

"Also, there's been a development with Fortis," she said. "Your father had a hidden move."

"What?"

"I don't fully know. But the Imam's General Counsel just called me, enraged. They're demanding an immediate accounting of all Fortis Intellectual Property, claiming we must turn over some undisclosed letter that outlines Sir Stone's succession plan."

"A secret document outlining a succession plan? That sounds like him."

"Doesn't it?" she acknowledged. "Just when you think he couldn't get any shrewder."

"His life's been shrouded in deceit. Why not his death?"

Ethan's words rang out before he grasped them, striking an unspoken nerve and halting the conversation.

They both knew it was upon them. His dad was about to die.

Celeste forged ahead. "We are meeting with the Imam next week to address his concerns, but I am headed to the Keats Grove house. Meet us there as soon as you can."

"I am on my way, wheels up in about an hour and home before dark."

Ethan stuffed the phone into his bag and addressed the group.

"Uriel, your hospitality and insights have been transformative. Thank you for today. I won't forget it."

"You are most welcome. You have also opened a new layer of meaning for me. I will spend time pondering its implications. Please let me know when you return to Israel. We'd love to have you all for Shabbat."

"Will Captain Raviv be there?" Sykes asked.

"If you time it right," replied Uriel. "She is often deployed, but I'm sure she'd return home if you were coming."

The private transport pulled into a circular drive behind them. The group hugged the Rabbi and climbed into the Sprinter van—everyone but Jack. He lingered, gazing back at the Temple Mount, paper kippah in hand.

"Something troubling you?" Uriel asked.

"I am sorry I could not wear this," Jack said. "I meant no dishonor."

"This is nothing to be sorry for. Your presence here and exploration of our history are an honor enough."

"I just don't know how Jews, Christians, and Muslims all live together in this city."

"It is complicated." Uriel cocked his head. "But we recognize that Adonai made all people in His image, regardless of their beliefs. So, each person is valuable, worthy of respect, and free to choose their path."

"I've followed my father's example of how to live." Jack exhaled sharply. "Seeking power from position, denying religious claims, and hating the Saudis. However, in the past few days, I've walked through the tangible remains of biblical sites alongside a Muslim Saudi royal family member and a Jewish Rabbi. Both of you have convinced me that my worldview doesn't align with what I've seen with my own eyes. I don't claim to believe your truths. But I can't deny them any longer."

"It is enough." Uriel embraced the American.

"My friend Hamid is at the hospital in Ramat Gan, fighting for his life. Would you check in on him for me?"

"I will."

"Thank you," Jack said as he turned towards the Temple Mount.

He placed the kippah on his head, took one final look, and joined his team in the van.

67

Night had fully descended on Hampstead before Ethan and the team arrived. The Fortis convoy, two Bentley Bentaygas, braked at the security gate, and the lead driver jumped out to open it. Then, they parked along the large drive, which was hidden on all sides by a reinforced brick and steel security fence, as well as a hundred-year-old London plane tree, along with oaks and sycamores. Beyond the wall stood the four-story white Georgian mansion Ethan remembered from his youth, though it was clear his dad had made significant upgrades.

The property next door had been purchased, torn down to the dirt, and rebuilt into a beautiful glass, steel, and concrete addition. Connecting elegantly to the family home, the main entrance to the compound stood like a bridge between two worlds—two centuries colliding in stone and steel. To the right was the 18th-century Georgian mansion, its white façade whispering of old money and older sins. To the left, the new steel-and-glass structure was cold, modern, and sharp as a blade.

And in between them? A door. A monolithic slab of rich wood, set between towering stone sentinels. A deliberate path of stepping stones over gravel created a walkway that forced hesitation. And above, glass windows stretched like silent eyes reflecting recessed lighting beneath the overhang.

There stood Celeste.

"Good evening," she said. "Your father is in the study."

Sykes, Jack, and Archer exited the rear vehicle as Ethan and Regus approached Celeste.

"It isn't exactly like I remember." Ethan's gaze swept across the compound, brow furrowed.

"Your father's been preparing for your return for a long time," she replied. "He's in good spirits tonight."

"Team, this is Celeste, Fortis CFO and confidant of my dad."

Sykes, Jack, and Archer shook her hand as Regus flashed a radiant smile.

Celeste led them through the modern entrance into the older part of the compound, where an immense chamber carved from another era emerged. The weight of history settled in the air with the scent of aged leather, pipe smoke, old parchment, and a trace of cedar from the firewood crackling the massive stone fireplace—a behemoth built to cast warmth and shadow. Its inferno guarded by an iron grate, darkened by decades of use, the marble hearth worn smooth where restless hands had once braced against it, contemplating the weight of decisions that shaped empires.

Ethan's dad sat in a vintage leather chair before the fire, clothed in an elegant 20th-century smoking jacket that mostly concealed his emaciated frame. A genuine smile softened his handsome yet fatigued face, revealing that tonight was the culmination of decades of cunning and foresight.

Gone were the sights and sounds of the hospital that had weakened the giant of a man in Ethan's mind. Tonight, Sir Ethan Stone III was the vision of power and authority that had guided an empire for four decades. A final look at the legend who forged the status quo, now in its fourth turning.

"Welcome home, my boy. Please sit."

Ethan and the team took their seats, arranged for each in a semicircle facing the glowing hearth.

"Which one of you is Jack?" Ethan's dad asked.

"I am," Jack replied, surprised that he'd asked.

"Bravo, young man," Ethan's dad replied. "I have retrieved my men from the Red Sea, and they regaled me with your exploits. Never had they seen a racing drone retrofitted with a mini electromagnetic pulse (EMP) device. I must have the design. Would prove exceedingly useful in our line of work."

Jack didn't know what to say, so he nodded and managed, "Yeah, sorry about that."

"And you must be Sykes," he said, looking at Ethan's team lead. "I've followed you for some time. You made good use of the night vision scope I provided to your unit in Afghanistan. Thank you for saving my son's life."

Sykes, too, didn't know what to say. How did this stranger know so much about them?

"And Archer," Ethan's dad finished. "I want to see the footage you captured with your LiDAR at Aten. That modification to our drone design was a stroke of genius."

Ethan's memory flickered to life as their original mission had been lost in the weekend chaos.

"I agree," Ethan said. "We do need to see that footage. Was there a Temple under the sands?"

"Maybe," Archer replied, hedging. "There *was* a structure exactly where you said it would be. But it's unclear what it could be." He too was amazed at Ethan's dad's knowledge of their business.

"Well, it sounds like you all have much to discuss," Ethan's dad said. "Tonight, we must settle the issue of Fortis Defense. You are all aware that the company has been sold. What you may not know is that it's worthless."

Celeste handed Ethan a folder embossed with the Fortis logo. Inside was a notarized letter signed by Ethan Stone III and Ethan

Stone II, dated September 22, 1981.

"What is this?" he asked.

"The assignment to me of all Fortis IP from our family nominee trust. Ever since my grandfather's designs for the 420-mm artillery shell gun were stolen, the Stone men have never entrusted our IP to anyone, even the company. The true value of what we do is hidden in these designs. And tonight, they all pass to you."   '

"So, the company you sold to the Imam, what was it?"

"Nothing. A name and illusion. We have a change of control clause in all our contracts that requires any new owner of Fortis, including yourself, to renegotiate all existing deals. Those contracts also require proof of IP ownership. The Imam wasted billions on a company that will implode like the Hindenburg."

Ethan looked over at Celeste, her hands folded comfortably, a thin smirk ghosting her lips. She must have been briefed while he flew in.

"And since you have agreed to run Fortis," continued his dad, "Our first order of business is to rename the company. Do you have any ideas?"

The room thrummed with anticipation. Ethan's ragtag team felt the weight of the moment, though they barely grasped the implications of what the next few minutes would bring.

Flying home from Israel, Ethan had reflected on the parallels between the Stones and the Thutmosid dynasty. He'd spent his entire adult life studying ancient families while running from his own. The Exodus Scroll had laid bare the secret of King Tut's murder and the disastrous consequences of living a lie. A drastic course correction was required if he was to escape looming disaster. No, he would not become another son buried beneath his father's throne.

But Ethan now knew he could not run from his destiny. He was Dr. Ethan Stone IV, the new leader of an empire rising from the ashes. Every deal his family had made was up for restructuring, and he would chart a very different course through the world.

"For twenty-five years, I have run from you," he told his dad. "But

I've come to see I was really running from myself. Tonight, that ends and I take my place in this family—as Dr. Ethan Stone the Fourth."

"So, what shall you rename Fortis?" Ethan's dad asked again.

"ESF Defense," he said. "Ethan Stone, the Fourth Defense."

"Bravo, my boy," exclaimed his dad. *"Est Salus Fortis!"*

Ethan's face registered shock at how perfectly the accidental Latin acronym fit the Stone family legacy.

"Thank you for keeping the tradition alive," his dad said, pride radiating from his hollow face. *'Salvation is Strong.'* This is a remarkable statement for the future of the family empire!"

Ethan didn't need another confirmation that this was his path, but he had it, nonetheless.

"Second order of business: implementing Fortis—or ESF AI. For the past fifteen years, I have perfected an Artificial intelligence system that will revolutionize the defense industry. I have trained it by tracking every digital move you and your team have made. The system's full capabilities remain unknown, but at the very least, it can identify and compile digital signatures for any individual or entity in the West. You can use the information for many purposes. Or, as the case may be for you, and your men, you can erase it."

The team looked around at each other, a glance expressing realization of why Ethan's father knew so much about them.

"I see you grasp the power," he said. "I have been tracking—and then erasing—all of your activity from the internet since 2016. Many bad actors have tried to harm you over the years. And they were all thwarted, thanks to my AI. All of them, save your financial entanglement with the Imam."

Ethan's guilt over the collapse of Fortis had eased somewhat with the news of the IP structure, but shame lingered. He was sickened he'd been party to such deception.

"I am sorry for that, Dad." He said quietly. "I had no idea."

"Understood," his dad replied. "But that man is worse than you realize. After you took down my heli, I ran more prompts on your operation in Aten and discovered the Imam had sent a man after you, someone tasked with bringing you in. He tracked your team across Egypt and into Saudi Arabia and carried out the assault at Trojena."

Jack's eyes darkened, hatred rising as he recalled Hamid gasping for breath, the assassin vanishing into the dust beneath the mountain.

"The Imam sent the assassin," he said.

"Indeed. And I fear we must once again face his true threat to the Empire. My contact at the DoD spoke with the Imam earlier today and informed him that his purchase was worthless. It would be in our best interest to use your team's skills to strengthen the defenses around our home immediately."

Sykes, Jack, and Archer looked at one another in disbelief.

"I suspect the Imam will send his assassin to try to stop what we are about to set in motion. We would be wise to prepare."

68

The Imam's jet touched down at RAF Northolt and taxied to the hangar. He stepped from the plane into his waiting sedan, which then left the airport and headed onto W End Road. Sayyid turned in behind him, keeping a safe distance, and merged onto the A40 headed towards Hampstead.

Like a Persian leopard stalking its prey, Sayyid knew any misstep could cost him his life... and his prize. He planned to finish this before the Imam discovered Sokolov's fate and unleashed his wrath against Sayyid's wife and daughters.

Celeste led Ethan and the team from the study back towards the entrance and into the compound's new section, where the stone and stucco of the 18th-century Georgian transformed into concrete and steel.

Celeste came to a broad, barren hallway on the first floor, stopping midway at a seam in the slab. She placed her hand along the wall, and a hidden biometric sensor pad beneath a concrete veneer lit up, scanning her handprint. A hiss of compressed air broke the press of silence, and the entire wall swung inward, opening a secret chamber.

The team found themselves in the most impressive armory they had ever seen. The stark concrete walls were lined with various hanging shelves and weapon racks.

Jack's eyes went wide, like he'd just stumbled into Fort Knox on open house day.

"Damn, Ethan—your old man's armory makes Bezos' rocket hangar look like a used car lot."

Ethan ran his hand along the matte-black receiver of an M134 Minigun mounted in the corner, the six barrels cold and menacing under his touch. The kind of gun that spat out 6,000 rounds a minute and chewed through vehicles like tissue. He couldn't help the grin. "Welcome to the new normal, Jack. Better start practicing your billionaire laugh."

Jack hefted a rifle, chuckling low.

"Roger that. Normal never looked so expensive."

"Please take what you need," Celeste said, walking over to a bank of monitors illuminated with dozens of security camera feeds inside and outside the compound.

"You can plan out your perimeter from here. We have secured an overwatch position on the neighboring home's roof, providing views of all rear access points. However, none of the alarms, approach sensors, or front gate security are active, as we did not anticipate needing a complete system yet. You can put the final touches on compound security, Ethan."

"Jack, Archer, load out for close combat," Ethan said, regretting they didn't have a place for the minigun. "You're on breach for the perimeter lockdown. Sykes, take overwatch. I will game out our mission plan."

Sykes selected the MK14 EBR, a semi-automatic 7.62x51mm NATO rifle with a modified 16-inch barrel, suited for urban sniper engagements. It was fitted with a Trijicon ACOG 6x48 and a clip-on FLIR PTS536 for rapid thermal switching. He paired that with a Glock 19 Gen 5 MOS 9mm sidearm, fitted with a threaded suppressor and a laser sight.

Jack snagged an HK416 short-barreled rifle with a suppressor, Wilcox RAID XE laser sight, and an angled grip for close-quarters combat, paired with a semi-automatic Benelli M4 Tactical Shotgun loaded with breacher rounds for door-busting and buckshot for close kills.

Archer grabbed the MP7 PDW, an armor-piercing compact, SMG if they got into tight hallway gunfights, and a SIG P320 XCarry Legion 9mm with a red-dot sight for quick-draw engagement.

"Explain to me the property entrances and overwatch," Ethan asked Celeste.

Sayyid weaved stealthily along the Hampstead side roads until the Imam pulled left onto Keats Grove. He paused, watching the sedan stop at a tall brick and steel wall outside a sprawling four-story Georgian mansion compound.

Sayyid wondered what this place was and why the Imam had come. The compound had an air of power surrounding it, whereas the neighborhood felt affluent. Thinking this was the final destination, he gambled and left his tail to prepare for the assault. If the Imam were going in, it'd be much better to finish him there than outside, under the watchful eye of London's million-plus CCTV cameras.

He drove for a few blocks, finding a large car park nearby. He pulled into a space under a low-hanging tree. The dim glow of a single overhead light cast long shadows as he grabbed his pack. His brothers had done an admirable job sourcing weapons for him, but guns were scarce in London.

He slid a single SIG P226 9mm, fitted with a suppressor, and four extra mags into his leg-drop holster. Sayyid moved with practiced precision, donning his tactical vest and tightening the straps until it felt like a second skin. Each blade had its place—an inverted karambit on his chest for quick, instinctive draws, and a tanto blade sheathed at his side for deeper, deliberate work. He flicked a throwing knife between his fingers, checked the familiar balance, then slipped it back into place.

The vest hugged his frame as he rolled his shoulders, the silent weight of steel pressing against him like old instincts awakening. He reached for the shoulder-mounted dagger, adjusting it with a slow, deliberate touch—this was for when the job got close, when breath and blood mingled in the dark. One last check—mag pouches were low-profile, multi-tool secured, and nothing was out of place.

He exhaled. The hunt had begun.

"We have the main front entrance you came through, a rear entrance into the garden, and a servants' quarters entrance along the Georgian side," Celeste said. "The new side has a private entrance to the VIP guest quarters, a rear opening into the shared ground-floor garden, and an expansive wrap-around second-floor balcony off the master suite overlooking Hampstead Heath."

"That's five ground-floor entrances and one balcony. What about the overwatch?" Ethan asked.

"It's a narrow five-story home on an adjacent lot we own. It's never been occupied and is connected to this compound by an underground tunnel. The covered roof perch provides concealed views of rear entrances and balconies and a clear line of sight for all approaches."

"Sounds perfect. What about the front entrance and the two sides?"

"From overwatch, you can see the servants' entrance to the west, but not the VIP residence to the east or the main entrance. We'll rely on the cameras for those."

Celeste handed Ethan a tablet with active feeds to the security cams. "Keep this with you."

Ethan rallied his team.

"We're dealing with an unknown threat, but probably a single tango. Sykes, here's the underground route to your perch. You're our eyes; alert us to all incoming traffic, regardless of their threat status. We're in an urban environment at night, so it will mainly be civvies. But I want to know everything that moves."

"Roger."

"Archer, how's your shoulder?"

"It's fine. Just…"

"A flesh wound, I know," Ethan said with a smirk. "Good. You're in the rear garden. Find a concealed position with views of the three ground-floor entrances and the balcony. If someone does make a play, it'll most likely be back there where you and Sykes can engage from the shadows.

"Jack, take the front entrance. Stand guard in the circle with a view of the gates and the VIP entrance. Sykes can't see you, so keep the comms updated with anything you spot."

"Copy that, boss."

"I'll be with Regus, Celeste, and my dad in the study, finishing some business. We need to make it through tonight, then reassess in the morning. Hopefully, this will be a boring shift."

Sykes, Jack, and Archer outfitted themselves with flashbangs and graphene-lined black tactical suits. Ethan grabbed an HK G38 fitted with a SOCOM556-RC2 suppressor and a pair of Glock 19s, then tested his active noise-canceling communication earpieces.

"Alright, boys, we do this clean. No wasted movement, no wasted shots. Eyes on your sectors. Watch your six.

Let's move."

69

The Imam knew this was reckless. Confronting them alone, uninvited, and most certainly unwelcome? Madness. Not a fool's madness, but a man's whose patience had run dry and whose fury burned hotter than reason.

He grabbed his leather briefcase and stepped out of the vehicle, smoothing the crease in his overcoat as the cool London night air settled around him. Without looking back, he instructed his driver to pull down the street and wait with his General Counsel, ensuring their presence wouldn't draw undue attention to what was about to unfold.

He had orchestrated and financed some of the most devastating terror attacks of the twenty-first century, watching from afar as chaos spread like wildfire. But Fortis—that had always been the prize. The final weapon. Owning it meant wielding power like gripping the Dhulfiqar, the very sword Allah had gifted to Ali ibn Abi Talib—the Prophet's rightful heir. And like that sacred blade, Fortis was meant to be his.

Ten minutes after he was inside, his men would breach the estate —just enough to distract Ethan Stone III and his CFO. He would retrieve the cursed letter, severing the last thread that held the succession plan together. Without it, the transition could not begin, buying him time to figure out a counter.

He knew there was a chance Ethan Stone IV was inside. If he were, he would die tonight. The Stone dynasty would crumble, and with it, every obstacle standing between him and total control. He had paid for this victory in blood and fortune. It was his.

He waited for his vehicle to disappear down the darkened street, then stepped forward through the still-open security gate. Inside the compound walls, the grand entrance loomed before him, flanked by two black Bentley SUVs, their chrome catching the soft glow of the perimeter lights.

They were likely his vehicles, purchased with his money—another insult he would rectify tonight. With measured, confident strides, he walked toward the imposing wooden door, his pulse steady and his rage under control.

It was time. Fortis would be his. Or he would burn this house and everyone inside it to the ground.

Just then, the door swung open, and an armed guard emerged dressed in black tactical gear, holding a rifle and a shotgun slung across his back.

"Stop," he shouted, raising the weapon to his face. "Identify yourself?"

The Imam kept a cool head. He figured there would be at least one armed guard, hoping that was all.

"I am a guest and business associate of Sir Stone," he said, raising his thin hands before him. "We have a meeting tonight. He's expecting me."

The guard lowered the weapon. "I have a male, mid-sixties, dark suit, overcoat, leather briefcase with a turquoise crescent moon," he spoke into his earpiece.

"It's Azure," the Imam muttered.

The guard blinked, surprised, then stepped aside.

"This way," he said. "Mr. Stone is expecting you."

The Imam entered, the guard keeping watch a few paces behind. He heard voices to the right, a flickering firelight dancing on the walls ahead. He turned the corner and saw his defeated foe, hollow yet proud, sitting in a large chair. Firelight flickered across the portrait above—a 1900s gelatin silver print photo of a young man standing beside a massive WWI-era Howitzer gun.

To his right was Ethan Stone IV.

"I thought you'd be stopping by," came a weak voice from the leather throne. "Looking for this?"

The Imam saw a single sheet of paper clutched between his trembling fingers. Ethan Stone III was clearly in agony and working hard to sit upright of his own volition. It was a bittersweet consolation as that paper represented the Imam's defeat and humiliation. He must have it.

"A cunning maneuver, I must say," replied the Imam. "But one that will ultimately fail. My lawyers are the best in the world, and I have great favor in the American court system. You sold us the company. I own those rights."

"You'd never have come if you believed that," spat Ethan Stone III. "You own a vapor, a haze vanishing into the night."

"I own Fortis Defense," he bellowed, his composure collapsing in the ignominy of the insults he knew were true.

Ethan Stone III was laughing now, slipping into a dreamlike state, his thin voice growing stronger with every sing-song, Keatsian syllable drawn from the deep recesses of his tortured soul.

"Fade far away, dissolve, and quite forget
   What thou among the leaves hast never known,"

"Give me that paper," shouted the Imam over the lyrical taunting.

"The weariness, the fever, and the fret
   Here, where men sit and hear each other groan."

The Imam lost all control and lunged at the tormenting provocateur. Decades of death and indulgence had hardened his heart and driven him forward. Frantic to possess what he most desperately sought, he was blind to everything else.

A blur of high-strength polymer flashed through the air and slammed into his skull. He stumbled to his left, crashing into a lamp and spinning out of control to the floor. A river of blood filled his vision before the room went black.

Ethan stood over the wicked man, his HK G38 in hand, just as the compound erupted into a war zone.

70

Sykes caught the movement first—a flicker in the tree line where there had been nothing seconds before. No approach, no sound, just motion breaking the stillness.

Then the assault came.

The strike on the Keats Grove house hit like a shallow breath—sudden, sharp, gone before you could react. A seven-man unit swept in as one, a storm of disciplined violence. They moved with practiced precision, years of bloodshed abroad distilled into brutal efficiency.

A suppressed rifle barked from below. The round slammed into the wooden railing inches from Sykes's face, splintering it apart.

He didn't panic; he acted.

"Contact," he said into his comms. "One tango, garden level. Engaging."

Pivoting fifteen degrees, he captured the heat signature in his thermal, slowly exhaled, and squeezed. A single round spat from his MK14 EBR, the counter-sniper's head snapped back, and his body crumpled to the grass. One shot, one kill.

"Tango down."

A wave of assailants poured into the garden below, moving from the shadows in a disciplined fashion. Archer had just finished settling into the servant's entrance on the compound's western side when the first three invaders reached the fountain. The crack of Sykes' shot held their attention for an instant.

Long enough.

Archer snapped the MP7 to his shoulder, sights aligning in a heartbeat before the controlled chaos of a three-round burst hit center mass. He heard the metallic resonance of his armor-piercing rounds shredding the enemy's chest plate.

"Tango two, down," he said. "We have at least two more out back. Jack, you copy?"

The first shot rang through the night—Jack was already in motion, bolting for the entrance, his pulse hammering, driving him back to his post before the second crack. He heard Ethan three steps behind, pounding down the concrete and into the connecting hallway. The practiced pair split the doorway, moving from the threshold into the circle drive in tandem.

A barrage of molten lead rushed towards them from both sides, shattering the concrete around them as they slid for cover between the two Bentleys. Jack saw an assailant tucked behind a planter to his left.

"Contact, one tango in the circle," he said, just as Ethan's suppressed HK G38 erupted in the opposite direction, drawing return fire that tore through the Bentayga windshields and front quarter panel, the 6.0L W12 engine finally stopped the spray.

"Contact, two flanking right, heading towards the VIP entrance," Ethan said.

"That makes seven," Sykes said. "Two down, five to go."

"Sykes, you got a read on VIP?" Ethan asked.

"Negative."

Another round of suppressing fire began from behind the planter as Ethan saw two men race for the cover of the VIP entrance. He flattened out and unleashed his barrage on the men, splitting the pair as one retreated to the massive oak they'd camped out behind.

"Jack," Ethan whispered in the momentary lull of the firefight. "CCTV showed a large drainpipe along the eastern wall. It runs right past the master suite window and balcony. I think they're climbing. Get upstairs and hold the position."

"Copy."

"Suppressing," Ethan said as he swapped mags at lightning speed, spun, and engaged the tango at the planter.

Jack darted from cover, low and fast, back into the entrance, shards of white stucco and two-hundred-year-old English brick raining down on top of him.

He flew down the concrete hallway, past the armory door, which Celeste had wisely shut, and into the VIP living quarters. He'd not had time to familiarize himself with the expansive layout, and his ignorance cost him precious seconds while he did a lap in the kitchen before finding the staircase.

He raised his weapon, the green target acquisition beam slicing through the dark. He crept silently, resisting the urge to move fast now that he owned the route to the study where Ethan's father, Regus, and Celeste had hunkered down.

He'd cleared half the steps when the master door creaked open, the distinctive barrel of a Russian-made AN-94 coming into view. Jack fired a burst into the opening, painting the walls as he went. The door slammed shut, and he heard the slide of a large deadbolt locking into place.

"Sykes," he said into the comms. "Can you see inside the balcony windows? I'm outside the master door."

"Negative. I do see a faint heat signature on the railing along the eastern wall. You trap a rat?"

"Affirmative. Keep watch on the doorway; don't let it out."

Jack slung the HK, pulled the Benelli, slammed the muzzle against the door handle, and fired. The breaching slug blew the lock.

The door exploded inward behind the force of Jack's shoulder. Before the dust had settled, he'd shifted back to his rifle, flicking the safety off as his combat rounds pierced the darkness with the flash of his muzzle and sweeping laser.

Breaching blind and alone was reckless, but he made it into the en-suite alive. Ear-splitting return fire erupted from the tango on the other side of the wall. Jack hit the floor hard, expecting the posh accommodations to be shredded from the AN-94's hyperburst 5.45×39mm rounds. Instead, he heard the rhythmic tang of two rounds being buried in quarter-inch ballistic steel inside the walls. A deep resonating hum formed in the en-suite while the steel vibrations carried the shockwaves outward.

The man in the next room got the hint and stopped wasting rounds. They were at a standoff. Jack was untouchable in the en-suite and had a clear line of sight to the only downstairs exit. But he refused to sit still while his team was engaged.

"Sykes, switch off thermal and watch for the rat. It's gonna get bright."

Jack pulled a flash-bang from his vest, yanked the pin, and cooked the two-second fuse for one Mississippi before reaching around the door and tossing it into the master bedroom.

The near-instant detonation drove his adversary knee-jerk out onto the balcony. Sykes picked him up in the optics and drilled a single round into the back of his head, sending his limp body sideways over the railing and into the bushes below.

"Whoo-whee," Sykes said. "Helluva move, Jack. That boy was lit up like a rook who left his IR laser on during a stealth op. Easiest shot of my career."

"Tango three, down," Jack replied.

"I could use some help over here," Archer said. "If y'all ain't too busy."

"Me too," Ethan said. "Holding off two tangos alone in the driveway isn't as glamorous as it sounds."

Sykes picked up the two shooters who pinned Archer down, engaging them from above.

Jack rushed to the east edge of the balcony, swung his leg over the railing, and clamped his hands around the six-inch steel drainpipe, throwing himself down in a friction descent.

"Ethan, I'm heading to your position along the path from VIP."

"Come slow, I'll push your way."

Ethan was still pinned between the two Bentleys, which had been torn to shreds by the live fire on either side of the circle. He shouldered his SBR from a crouch and pulled a Glock 19 from underneath each arm. He steadied his breathing and broke from cover, moving away from the house, his arms crossed in front for stabilization as he pumped two full magazines of 9mm in opposite directions. His bold move drew the two tangos into each other's direct line of fire, which slowed their response time.

Ethan's Glocks ran dry, the slides locking back in unison. There was no time to reload. He let them fall, his hands shifting, grabbing the G38 slung tight to his chest, snapping it into position as he broke east. The moment the stock hit his shoulder, his finger squeezed the trigger.

The rifle erupted.

A ferocious burst of 5.56 tore through the night, rounds slamming into the tree just inches from the target, who had raised his weapon to return fire. Bark exploded outward, splinters whipping through the air like shrapnel, the force sending the enemy stumbling sideways, exposed, vulnerable.

Jack had just cleared the side of the house when he took the profile shot, burying two rounds in the enemy's exposed temple. Ethan spun and reengaged the target behind the planter. Jack joined in, offset just behind and to Ethan's left—his HK tight against his shoulder. They advanced in a tactical V formation on the entrenched position. He didn't stand a chance.

"Tango's four and five, down," Ethan said.

They heard a half-dozen rounds from Sykes' EBR, followed by Archer's muffled shouts in their earpieces, chaos, and static before a single 9mm shot rang out.

The gunfire had begun before Sayyid slipped into the compound property. This wasn't his fight—not yet. So, he bided his time, preferring the path of least resistance. The Imam was inside. That much was certain. Sayid wanted him dead almost as much as he wanted to be the one to do it.

Two shooters had pinned down a single guard in the stairwell of the servants' entrance. But when the balcony exploded in brilliant white, he made his move. The falling body distracted the two shooters long enough for an overwatch sniper to find and engage them.

That's when Sayyid struck, moving on the lone guard.

His quiet approach did not work. The struggle started with a scuffle and ended with a bullet to the chest.

"Breach, breach," shouted Sykes. "Two tangos are inside, and Archer is down. I repeat, Archer is down."

Jack and Ethan raced inside and made it to the study just as the first man emerged through the garden hallway. Regus and Celeste had moved Ethan's father into the corner, away from the garden, but they couldn't take him much further in his condition.

"Get them to safety," shouted Ethan as he closed on the man, turning the corner before he could be detected.

"We're going to the VIP en-suite," Jack told Regus and Celeste. "Second floor, top of the stairs."

Regus bolted immediately, but Celeste hesitated.

"Get going, you obstinate woman," growled Ethan Sr., "You've known my fate for years. ESF needs you; serve my son how you've served me."

Celeste was a mess. Regus had come back and grabbed her hand, pulling her from her boss.

Jack removed the Benelli, racked four rounds of buckshot, and handed it to Ethan's father. "Hold this, I'll be right back." And he escorted the women upstairs.

Ethan had his back against the wall as the intruder entered the study, pistol in hand. He snatched the attacker's wrist, twisting hard —bone and tendons straining under the torque. The gun jerked upward, firing a wild shot into the ceiling.

Ethan spun into the open, confronting the man, who fought back viciously, slamming an elbow into Ethan's ribs. It landed solidly, knocking the breath from him, but he didn't break his grip.

"Control the weapon. Control the fight," thought Ethan.

Ethan drove his forearm down, breaking the attacker's grip and sending the pistol skittering across the floor. The intruder reacted fast, going for a blade—a gleam of steel flicking from his belt.

Ethan anticipated.

He moved inside the wild swipe, slamming his elbow into the man's face—once, twice—bone to bone, brutal but not fatal.

The intruder staggered, his knife clattering loose, but he wasn't done. He snarled, lunged forward, and locked his hands around Ethan's throat.

They hit the ground hard.

The back of Ethan's skull smacked against the stone floor, stars bursting in his vision. The intruder was on top now, weight pressing down, hands tightening around his windpipe. Ethan choked against the pressure, his vision tunneling, fingers clawing for a grip— anything to break free.

Then he heard it—the deep, familiar clack-chk of a shotgun being racked.

The intruder must have heard it, too, because he froze for half a second, long enough.

Ethan grabbed the attacker's shoulders, brought his feet inside the man's hips, and with the last of his strength, released his coiled legs while he rolled, arms extending upward, launching the man over his head.

A thunderous blast explosion through the room.

The shotgun blast caught the intruder midair, buckshot tearing through his torso. The force threw him back, slamming him into the kitchen, where he collapsed in a twitching heap.

Ethan coughed, dragging in burning, stinging air as he twisted onto his knees, looking up at the smoking barrel of his father's shotgun.

Ethan Sr. lowered the weapon from his throne before the fire, exhaling sharply.

"You alright?"

Ethan wiped the blood from his lip and stared at what was left of the man on the floor.

"That was so AP, Dad."

71

Sayyid crept through the servant's quarters, blood dripping from the barrel of the gun he'd fired point-blank into the body outside. An intense struggle in the next room, a sudden blast, and he dove for cover.

He lingered in the shadows, watching the man he'd hunted for months gather himself. He'd found Ethan at last, but he no longer wanted him. The Imam was his prize. Nonetheless, Ethan would be a formidable foe.

A scream erupted on the far side of the house.

"Regus!" Ethan yelled, panic cutting through his voice. He snatched the shotgun from a shadow by the hearth and sprinted towards the noise.

He was alone.

Sayyid drifted from the dark, stepping into the flame's glow, emerging like a specter from the void. Ethan Stone III sat motionless by the fire. Sayyid crossed the room, stepping over blood pooled on the floor where some poor fool had been torn in two by a close-range shotgun blast.

No doubt lured by the Imam's promises of glory.

The flickering firelight cast jagged shadows against the walls, revealing Ethan's frail father.

But where was the Imam?

"Here to kill, are you?" Ethan Sr.'s voice was steady, but his eyes searched the room.

Sayyid smiled. "You? No, of course not. I'm here to help. Where's the Imam?"

Ethan Sr. hesitated, his gaze flickering toward the space beside him, realization settling like a weight.

"You're missing something," Sayyid murmured.

Ethan Sr. stiffened. "Where is he?"

Sayyid's lips curled. "Probably in Jahannam. Unless..."

"Unless what?"

"Unless you let him go."

Ethan Sr. didn't answer. But his eyes did. They flashed wide, not with fear, but with the awful realization of something terrible lurking in the dark.

Sayyid's reflexes snapped into motion—but not fast enough.

A hand like iron wrenched the dagger from his shoulder rig.

Sayyid twisted, instinct overriding thought, his forearm shooting up to block.

The Imam was already inside his guard, blade flashing in the dim firelight.

Sayyid barely evaded the first strike. The steel hissed past his throat, missing by a breath. A second slash came, aimed for his gut— he pivoted just in time.

The Imam's movements were unnatural, too fast for a man his age, too fluid for a zealot who spent more time behind words than weapons.

Sayyid had underestimated him. This was no frail preacher. This was a man who had lived and breathed death longer than Sayyid had been alive.

Sayyid backpedaled, but the Imam advanced like a phantom. The crimson river flowing from a wound to his forehead meant nothing to the knife in his grip, which wasn't wild or desperate—it was surgical.

Sayyid launched a counterattack, his hand darting for his karambit. Too slow.

The Imam was already inside his reach. A sharp elbow struck Sayyid's ribs—then a palm to his jaw sent him stumbling back. His fingers closed around his knife, but the Imam didn't wait.

The blade came low. Sayyid twisted—not enough.

Steel bit into his side, tearing through muscle. The pain was a cold fire spreading through his ribs. He gasped, but there was no time to recover.

The Imam didn't stop.

Sayyid barely parried the next strike, redirecting the blade past his throat. He swung his knife in a short, precise arc for the Imam's neck.

Blocked.

The Imam moved like water, stepping into Sayyid's guard and trapping his wrist. Then, with a single brutal twist—

CRACK.

Sayyid's wrist snapped.

His blade clattered to the floor.

Pain exploded through his arm, but the Imam didn't let him fall.

A knee drove into Sayyid's stomach, folding him forward—just in time for the Imam's elbow to hammer into the base of his skull.

Sayyid collapsed, coughing, blood dripping from his lips. His vision blurred. He fought to rise, but his body wouldn't obey.

The Imam crouched beside him, knife still steady, not a single drop of sweat on his brow—just blood.

Sayyid's breath was ragged. He had never lost a fight like this. He had never faced an opponent who moved with such calculated certainty.

This wasn't just a warrior. This was a man who had never been beaten.

The Imam tilted his head, studying him. Then he leaned in close, voice barely a whisper:

"Did you think you were the first to try?"

Sayyid's heart pounded. Then, steel sank into his chest. The pain didn't register at first—just the overwhelming cold. The Imam twisted the blade slowly and deliberately.

Sayyid exhaled sharply, and a final, broken sound was ushered forth. The last thing he saw was the firelight reflected in the Imam's glassy, evil eyes.

And then—darkness.

72

"Well, that was messy," Ethan Sr. said, still seated.

The fire crackled. Leaving the dagger where it lay embedded in Sayyid's ruptured heart, the Imam slid the tanto blade from his side sheath. He rose, turned to Ethan Sr., and stepped forward, his presence a towering weight.

"Now, where were we?"

Ethan Sr. swallowed hard. Now, he understood.

This was no media mogul. No mere holy man cloaked in religious zeal.

This was a god of war—a Pharaoh reborn, the kind he had crossed paths with before. The kind who never ran, never bowed. And this, he realized, was likely the last.

The Imam didn't hesitate.

In one smooth, deliberate motion, the rock-hard CPM 3V steel sank deep into his abdomen. No sudden thrust—just a slow, merciless push, the blade carving its way inward, ensuring an agonizing, drawn-out death.

Ethan Sr. didn't let a single gasp slip through his lips. The Imam would not get the pleasure. In reality, he had longed for this moment for years—freedom and peace, at last. His surviving generation was home, ready to go further than he ever could.

The Imam stood over him, hand on the hilt buried in his belly, his eyes searching for terror. Instead, he only found resolve.

A whisper now. Labored but strong. A refrain from Keats.

"Thou wast not born for death, immortal Bird! No hungry generations tread thee down; The voice I hear this passing night was heard In ancient days by emperor..."

Pause... then he spat, splattering blood across the Imam's face.

"...and clown."

The Imam shifted his weight, twisting the knife once before stepping back.

"Your son will pay for that," the Imam said, his forearm wiping deliberately across his cheek. "And it starts with this."

Ethan Sr. watched helplessly as the Imam plucked the letter from the side table, folded it neatly, grabbed his bloody briefcase off the floor, and slipped through the carnage and out the back entrance into the night.

In agony, he reached for the CCTV tablet next to him, checking for the Imam on the servant's quarters camera. He only saw Archer lying motionless in the stairwell.

Upstairs, Jack was sitting upright against the wall inside the master, Celeste tending to a bleeding wound in his leg.

He watched as his son fought hand-to-hand with yet another attacker in the hallway outside the VIP bedroom, the shotgun lay useless at the bottom of the stairs.

Motion inside the master.

That vision of a woman, Regus, snatched the attacker's pistol from the entryway and turned down the hallway. Feet set shoulder-width apart. Weight forward, balanced on the balls of her feet. The web of her right hand was on the pistol's backstrap. Her left hand was wrapped in, thumbs stacked along the frame. Arms locked out, a triangle of steel and bone, her torso square to the target.

"Bravo, Alistair," Ethan Sr. muttered. "You taught your girl to shoot."

Regus' index finger slipped from outside the trigger guard onto the firing lever when Ethan knocked his attacker backward.

Ethan dropped.

Regus fired.

And all was still once again.

Ethan Sr. couldn't be happier. His son was home with a crack team of loyal men and a beautiful woman whose family pedigree nearly matched his own. Celeste would ensure the transition to ESF Defense went off without a hitch. Fortis's General Counsel had come and gone, leaving with his notarized signature for the sale.

He just needed to hold on a few more minutes; Celeste had a final job to complete.

73

Ethan rushed toward Regus and they collided, not in battle but in something just as raw, just as seismic. It had been a weekend of war, shattered assumptions and beliefs, reforged souls, and all that tension released in this moment.

He clutched her tightly, arms locked with a fervor he'd never known, a fusion of gratitude, respect, and sheer relief. They were still standing. They were still breathing.

Jack heard the shot and whipped around the corner, a makeshift tourniquet, just a pillowcase, cinched tight around his leg, the CFO turned field medic right on his heels.

"Tango down," Jack chirped into comms. "That's all of them."

"Roger," Sykes responded, his breath steady despite the chaos. "I'm almost out of the tunnel from Overwatch. Archer, you copy?"

A labored silence.

The adrenaline-soaked team stood frozen, the hallway pressing in around them.

"Archer!" Sykes barked, urgency lacing his voice. "Talk to me!"

Nothing.

Ethan's pulse kicked harder as he saw Sykes emerge from the basement, boots hammering against concrete. He blew past Ethan's second-floor position, heading for the source of the silence.

Ethan and Regus followed down the stairs at a dead sprint, Jack and Celeste hobbling behind.

Then, static crackled through the comms.

"I'm fine," Archer's voice finally came through, strained but alive. "Lost my damn earpiece wrestling."

Sykes let out a slow, exhaled prayer. "Thank God. Thought we lost you."

Archer huffed. "Somebody tell me they got the assassin."

Jack frowned. "What assassin?"

"The dude from Trojena."

"He's here," Jack said. "Where?"

"I don't know. But right after you boys lit up the master, he pounced from the bushes."

A beat.

Then, Archer's dry, pained laugh.

"And shot me in my other damn shoulder."

A cacophony of relieved chuckles fired across the secure comms.

"Well, you're safe now," Sykes replied. "All out of shoulders."

"Stay alert," Ethan replied, raising the shotgun he had picked off the floor. "Until we've got eyes on."

That didn't take long.

Sykes was the first to experience the carnage of the study, immediately spotting the assassin in front of the fire, a protrusion in his lifeless chest glinting in the dying embers.

Sykes, stepping over a mangled body missing most of his pelvis, passed shattered walls and broken tiles on his way through the servants' quarters. Archer needed help.

Celeste saw her boss crumpled on the chair and rushed to his aid.

"Sir," she pleaded, shocked to discover the hilt of a blade in his abdomen. "Who did this?"

"Celeste," came the dying rasp of a proud father. "The Imam. He took the bait. Get to the safe."

Celeste sprang into action.

She ran to the fireplace mantel and pushed in on the bottom left corner of the portrait frame. A click, release, and the picture hinged open. Her palm unlocked the high-tech safe, where she retrieved a matte black folder, a recording ledger, and a small wooden box.

"Ethan, come here," she ordered.

Celeste pulled a single sheet from the folder and filled in the day's date, September 22.

"Sign this and take it to your father. I have to notarize before he…" she trailed off.

Ethan scrawled his signature and took the folder to his father.

"Dad, what's this?" Ethan's heart was racing.

"Your appointment, my boy, in the Nominee Trust. The wealth of the Stone men is now yours."

Ethan laid the folder across his forearms for stability before placing the pen in his father's trembling hands. His father scraped the ink-stained bearing loosely across the signature line.

Celeste snapped the paper away, affixed her unique Notary Public embossed seal, and recorded the date and time in the ledger.

They had done it. All Fortis IP was now officially Ethan's.

"You did well, my boy," he murmured, barely above a breath. "You still got it."

His chest heaved, shallow and weak, the effort to breathe becoming a battle he was losing second by second.

"You can take a different path from me. But you can't stray from the truth: you've been chosen as a protector. The Stone men have always been chosen."

His vision blurred—shapes smearing together as his body began its final surrender.

"I spilled blood to save lives. But I took more than I rescued. I guess you can't set people free using the tools that enslave them."

His hands stopped trembling, his grip loosened, the pen tumbling to the floor.

"Forge your future."
One last exhale.
"I'll see you when you get there."
His head lolled back.
And then—stillness.

EPILOGUE

Trojena, Three Months Later

Regus stood on the balcony, gazing down at the high mountain lake. Like the brisk wind that sent tremors of snow dancing across the thinly frozen surface, her thoughts drifted to her father. He'd been gone for more than a decade, but she still felt his absence more deeply than anyone else in her family. Her brother's suicide and her mother's addiction had hurt her, but losing her dad left her truly alone. At thirty, she was too old to be pitied but too young to have no family, friends, or prospects.

After watching Ethan reconnect and then bury his father in the same week, she knew the days of her youth had been a blessing beyond measure. The subterranean encounter in Jerusalem had changed her, and so had the gunfight in Hampstead. Life was too short to be frozen in regret or consumed by rage. Somewhere between callousness and collapse lay a forward path.

After returning to NYC from her impulsive trip to Israel and London, she'd tried to find the path, discovering only that all her willpower to walk alone had vanished. Or maybe it was spent, used up, from the last season of her life. Whatever the reason, she was done obsessively hunting for ways to topple Fortis Defense. Strangely, that had already been done; now, she was wondering how to rebuild.

She looked out over the stunning valley, skiers dotted the foreground, weaving down the gentle hill, from where pine trees flanked the lodge. A soft snow flurry caught the low winter sunlight, and she watched a glistening cloud descend to earth.

Ethan stood at the edge of the slope, looking up, his skis slung over one shoulder, breath curling into the icy air. The lodge loomed before him like a cathedral carved from nature's breath—its bespoke alloy curves forged overseas, rising and falling like a song etched in architecture. Above, on the second-level balcony, Regus leaned on the railing, silhouetted against the gold-glass glow of the interior.

She hadn't seen him yet.

The snow whispered as he climbed the side steps, careful, quiet. As he reached the balcony, he paused. For a moment, he just watched her.

Regus was still in her ski jacket, a wool beanie tucked over her ears, strands of auburn hair lashing gently in the breeze. Below them, the slope stretched wide and alive—families, couples, laughter in motion. But up here? Just them.

"You always did like the view from the high ground," Ethan said gently.

Regus turned, smiling without surprise. "And you always show up right before I convince myself I prefer solitude."

He stepped beside her, leaning on the railing, but his eyes were on her, not Mt. Sinai. "Lunch was good?"

"I had soup that tried to convince me it was born in Provence," she said, chuckling. "Almost succeeded."

Ethan tapped the railing softly. "I was thinking… don't let the day end just yet. Grab your gear. Let's take one last run before sunset. You and me."

She tilted her head, considering. "You think you can keep up?"

"No," he said, grinning. "But I'm smart enough to fall behind you on purpose. There's no better view."

Her laugh broke gently, like snow from a tree branch. She studied his face for a moment—eyes that held mountains of their own, and a promise of warmth even in this high desert wonderland.

"Give me five minutes," she said, the words a soft challenge, a truce, maybe something more.

As she turned to go, Ethan stayed at the rail a beat longer, heart thudding, not from altitude, but from the quiet avalanche that was her.

And when she came back, gloves and hat in hand, hair blown wild by the wind, he knew: the day wasn't ending.

It was just hitting its stride.

The door creaked open against the hush of falling snow. Ethan and Regus stepped inside, boots dusted white, cheeks lit with windburn and something more intimate, an energy that lingered even after the slope had fallen silent behind them.

Ellie rushed to the door, spinning in excitement as Ethan dropped his gear to greet her. The warmth of the lodge hit like an embrace: wood walls glowing with golden light, the scent of clove and cedar in the air, and the unmistakable crackle of the hearth fire where three old friends sat in the kind of relaxed intensity that only comes after years of shared danger.

Sykes had his woolen feet on the hearth, five cards loose in one hand, a glass of bourbon in the other. Jack leaned forward, shuffling chips, sharp eyes hidden behind unnecessary sunglasses, face worn with thought. And Archer—always the watcher—sat back, arms crossed over his chest, a glint in his eye as he tracked the room like it might break into combat at any moment.

"Well, look what the snow dragged in," Sykes drawled, placing his cards face down on the green felt table.

Regus smirked and shed her coat, hanging it near the carved doorway. "You boys finally decide the fate of the free world, or just burn the rest of the bourbon trying?"

Archer raised a brow. "Both. We multitask."

Jack leaned back and raised his shades. "Boss, Celeste called. Fortis Defense litigation's dead. Clean sweep. The IP is officially ours."

Ethan stilled mid-step. He turned, gaze sharp now. "Adjudicated? All the way up?"

Jack nodded. "Final ruling came through this morning. Dismissed with prejudice. No more challenges. We own all weapon designs, the AI platform, and the London HQ. The filthy Imam has the name and company assets, which he's leveraged to go on an acquisition spree. It appears he's desperately trying to cobble together a defense company from the ruins."

"Did Celeste say if he showed up at any of the hearings?" Ethan asked.

"Not a one. He's totally dark. Word is he's holed up with the clerics in Iran."

Regus came to stand behind Ethan, resting a hand lightly on his back. "Then it begins."

Sykes leaned forward, cards forgotten. "Yeah, and that's the question. We've got an AI platform that can upend an entire theater without boots ever hitting sand. Billions in liquid capital and no leash."

Jack added, "And no oversight yet. The question's not whether we can deploy it. It's where do we start? Who do we trust? And how do we make sure we don't become the very thing we were fighting?"

There was a long silence. Only the fire spoke.

Then Ethan said, quietly but firmly, "We take it to where it started. No contracts, no boards. No favors to the old guard. Just mission clarity and moral weight. This was built to keep the world from being ruled by shadows. Let's not cast any of our own."

Sykes finally moved, pulling a leather-bound folder from the table. "I've drafted scenarios. Three initial deployments. Strategic deterrence only, eyes on. I'll brief you after dinner."

Regus gave a half-smile. "Christmas Eve, and we're planning international defense grids. Romantic."

Ethan turned to her. "We can build peace on a night like this. Isn't that the point?"

She leaned in and kissed him, just a breath, soft and sure. For a moment, the room was quiet.

Then Sykes grinned. "God bless us, everyone. Now, somebody tell me why Jack's still bluffing with a busted straight."

Outside, snow blanketed Saudi Arabia's strange, stunning mountains.

And inside, in a fortress of friendship and firelight, a new chapter was being written, one that began not with a war cry but with a card game, a kiss, and the slow uncoiling of hope.

PHARAOH: DEEPER DIVE

Not every secret in these pages is fiction. Every shadow cast across this story rests on real ground. The archaeological sites are authentic. The scriptures are recorded. The artifacts endure. The deserts of Arabia still whisper their truths—if you know where to stand and listen.

If you're ready to go further, the trail doesn't end here. Step beyond the book and into the world itself:

• Download the Google Maps files at PharaohChronicles.com/qr and follow the routes Ethan's team uncovered across Saudi Arabia.

• Sign up for the Pharaoh newsletter to stay close to the fire when new discoveries, insights, and artifacts surface.

• Watch for the Pharaoh Study Guide, a companion that will pull back the curtain on the history, relics, and scriptures beneath the story.

This tale is built on facts, each one carefully unearthed. The shadows still reach into our present.

And know this—the story is not finished. Ahead lies the collapse of Egypt's golden age in the Amarna period… and the rise of a modern evil, lurking in Iran, that threatens to reshape the world.

You, dear reader, must seek the Truth.

AFTERWORD

We tell stories to remember.

To remember who we are.

What we've lost.

And what we might still become.

Pharaoh: Curse of the Kings began as a question that haunted me: **What if the truths buried in the past could still alter the fate of the present?** Not as a metaphor, but as blood and stone. As a revelation.

This novel is not just a thriller. It's a warning. A key. A curse.

Ethan Stone is the man we send into the labyrinth when everyone else is afraid to look in the mirror. He's imperfect. Haunted. But he's moving toward truth in a world that rewards illusion.

If you've come this far, thank you for walking the line between reason and madness with me. I hope the journey thrilled you, disturbed you, and maybe—just maybe—changed the way you look at the dark.

There's more coming.

This is the first of a three-part series exploring the Egyptian, Arabic, and Hebrew histories within the Exodus. For millennia, empires have risen and fallen as leaders build, cling to power, and sacrifice the next generation to preserve their legacies.

Book Two will pick up with the fall of the house of Pharaoh (Fortis) and what emerges in its place (ESF Defense). A new kind of order that tries to right the wrongs of the past but falls prey to the unexplored recesses that lurk in the human heart.

Fortis is reimagined as a new company—ESF Defense—dedicated to utilizing AI for the greater good. The first attempts have a significant effect, but the "Benevolent Dictator" soon falls into the same temptations of regime change that plague Fortis Defense. Only when the commitment is made to lay down the allure of global domination can the long-term structures be established.

Overlaid on the Egyptian history known as the Amarna Period,

Book Two presents another minority view of the timeline established in **Book One** and shows the rise of an apostate Pharaoh, who built the city of Aten. This short-lived structure is built on the ruins of the collapse. Yet in this ultimately failed attempt at building structure after a collapse, old foes, undefeated in **Book One**, are confronted before the new world can begin.

Book Three chronicles ancient history as the people who emerged from Egypt establish themselves as their nation, driven by a single, unifying purpose. Order is complete, and great prosperity is unleashed. But the lack of unity amongst the people threatens their existence.

Stay connected for more.

https://PharaohChronicles.com
https://AdamSchindler.com

Adam W. Schindler
September 22, 2025
Washington, D.C.

AKNOWLEDGEMENTS

To my wife—thank you for giving me the space to vanish into the firelight, tapping away long after midnight while the rest of the house slept. You not only endured the clatter of keys but also read the raw, early drafts when they barely held together. Your laughter in the right places and your raised eyebrow in the wrong ones kept me honest. This book is as much yours as it is mine.

To my editor—you didn't just polish sentences, you sharpened the blade. You challenged me to cut deeper, to strip away the fat, and to remember that a thriller slows for no one. Whenever I thought I'd nailed it, you reminded me there was one more gear to find. For that push, I'm grateful.

To my ARC community—you were the first into the breach. You sent me notes that were funny, fierce, and sometimes brutal (in the best way). You caught the stumbles I missed, flagged the twists you didn't see coming, and reminded me that readers bring their own heartbeat to every page. You made this book faster, sharper, and stronger.

This series also explores the intersection of faith, religious themes, and geopolitics—topics that many refuse to engage with, yet ones that our culture desperately needs to confront. Stories, when told honestly, can help us see beyond what we already know. They can open doors to conversations that politics, pulpits, or news cycles often leave closed. If even one reader walks away from these pages with sharper vision and more profound questions, then the work has done its job.

And finally, to you, the reader—whether this is your first time stepping into Ethan's world or you've been here since the beginning —thank you. Stories don't live on hard drives; they live when someone turns the page. Thanks for joining me on this chase into the shadows, where faith, history, and power collide—and where the truth is always just one step ahead.

This is only the beginning. The following two books in the *Pharaoh* series are already stirring, but they can only be birthed if you walk with me—by reading, sharing, and following along. Every voice, every recommendation, every reader who presses this story into another's hands is part of bringing the next chapters into the light.

AUTHOR BIO

Adam W. Schindler works in Washington, D.C. and is a strategist, theologian, and storyteller, uniquely positioned at the crossroads of history, faith, and global power structures. With a background spanning pastoral leadership, executive strategy, and digital engagement at the highest levels of government and business, Adam brings a rare depth of insight into the interplay of faith, geopolitics, and cutting-edge technology.

His career has taken him from leading churches and mentoring CEOs to working alongside former White House officials, policymakers, and business leaders, shaping narratives that influence culture and leadership worldwide. He has been a trusted advisor to faith-driven executives, a Biblical Scholar for a major motion picture, a key architect of digital mobilization strategies, and a thought leader on the intersection of history, power, and belief.

With a degree in Philosophy of Eastern Religion, a Certificate in Biblical Studies, and ordination in Christian ministry, Adam has spent years studying ancient texts, biblical archaeology, and the real-world implications of faith-based narratives. As an organizer for the Jerusalem Prayer Breakfast and a founding member of various prayer networks, he has worked extensively on faith-based diplomacy and global Christian engagement with Israel.

This unique fusion of historical expertise, geopolitical experience, and profound theological insight makes Adam uniquely gifted to write this novel at a time when the world is grappling with the role of faith in global politics, the rise of AI-driven warfare, and the enduring mysteries of history.